Charles Herbert Levermore

The Republic of New Haven

A History of Municipal Evolution

Charles Herbert Levermore

The Republic of New Haven
A History of Municipal Evolution

ISBN/EAN: 9783337338862

Printed in Europe, USA, Canada, Australia, Japan

Cover: Foto ©Andreas Hilbeck / pixelio.de

More available books at **www.hansebooks.com**

THE

REPUBLIC OF NEW HAVEN

A History of Municipal Evolution

By CHARLES H. LEVERMORE, Ph. D.

Fellow in History, 1884-5, Johns Hopkins University

———

BALTIMORE
N. MURRAY, PUBLICATION AGENT, JOHNS HOPKINS UNIVERSITY
1886

ISAAC FRIEDENWALD, PRINTER,
BALTIMORE.

TO

Dr. HERBERT B. ADAMS

AT WHOSE SUGGESTION THIS WORK WAS UNDERTAKEN, AND WHOSE KINDLY
INTEREST IN ITS PROGRESS HAS NEVER FAILED

THIS VOLUME

IS RESPECTFULLY DEDICATED

PREFACE.

This volume is designed to contribute toward a constitutional history of the New England township. The purpose has been to depict the steady evolution of various forms of local government from the assembly of freemen, to detect the far-reaching influence of the Church organization at the centre of social activity, to describe the gradual differentiation that took place within the official structure, to observe the operation of political and social agencies, whether external or internal, and to discern, throughout the vicissitudes of two hundred and fifty years, the permanent characteristics which make up New Haven's strong individuality.

Since Tocqueville's day, the New England Town-Meeting, as an institution, has not pleaded in vain for recognition. But the scientific study of the evolution of the Town-Meeting and of the inner workings of our local government has only just begun to receive due attention. In 1881, Dr. H. B. Adams's monographs upon "The Village Communities of Cape Ann and Salem" and upon "The Germanic Origin of New England Towns" led the way for a host of similar essays. During the last five years, trained specialists have been associated together in the work of observing and describing various forms and institutions of local government in every part of the land. Out of these researches there will arise, for the first time, a comprehensive classification of our local usages, and eventually also an accurate conception of the part which different local institutions have taken, and still take, in the development of the nation.

The republic of New Haven presents to the student of local institutional growth a field abounding in materials of historic interest. Its founders cherished high ideals, and their community has always retained something of the early impress. The lineaments of the ancient type have been repeated in a long line of younger townships. The fathers of the town preserved copious accounts of their public actions, as though conscious that future generations would be interested in every word and deed. It follows that the work of investigation is now both easy and difficult: easy, because the whole story is manifest; difficult, because so much of it must be omitted.

It is from these records of town, colony, and city, most of which are in manuscript, that the present volume is mainly derived. They have been carefully epitomized, and copies have been compared with originals. Records of the neighboring colonies and colonial literature in general have been laid under contribution. Publications of the New York Colonial Documents and of the Massachusetts Historical Society have been especially serviceable. They are quarries where no workman can fail to find some stone for his structure. By the aid of the former, the pathetic story of New Haven's conflict on the Delaware can be perfectly known; in the latter, Davenport, Eaton, and their friends draw their own portraits for us. The files of New Haven newspapers date from about the middle of the eighteenth century, and they have afforded much assistance.

In the beginning of the work the two Puritans who were the nucleus of the company receive consideration. The opinions which they entertained, the laws which they established, the usages which they followed, pass in review. Sir Thomas More did not sit down to write his "Utopia" with a clearer idea of his model State than Davenport and Eaton had when they framed their model of a State "whose design is Religion." The little village, stranded on the shore between an ocean and a wilderness, quietly assumed independence of earthly potentates. Nevertheless, like an ancient Grecian colony, it patterned itself after the example of the mother-city, and, in turn, began to send forth new settlements on either hand. A complete system of public instruction, crowned by a college such as grew up long after, was planned.

The division of the newly-acquired lands is followed step by step. The little settlement unconsciously reverted to the forms of village community-life, and the Germania of Tacitus was more than suggested in the town at Quinnipiac. In legislation, Mosaic decrees and the Common Law of England were curiously intermingled. In 1643, New Haven yielded to the forces that were even then beginning to make for American Union, and, from that time on, the progress of evolution is slow, continuous, and direct. Out of all this movement, after one hundred and fifty years, amid many warring political and social elements, a city emerges, and thus another germ-idea of the Quinnipiac fathers is finally realized. The narrative closes with a review of all the departments of the existing government in school-district, city, and town, and with a critical analysis of some salient features of the local organization and administration. So long a time and so much action cannot be fully treated in small space. The book is not so much a history as an historical essay; it is a study rather than a completed work.

It is safe to say that a constitutional history of the United States is yet to be written. Dr. Von Holst has not fulfilled the promise of his title. His work is a valuable criticism, from the standpoint of a foreigner, of the political history of our country, but no satisfactory constitutional or political history of the United States can appear until the constitutional and political development of the various national subdivisions has been exhaustively studied. Some one must, for instance, describe adequately the vast influence of New York State politics upon national affairs from the days of Burr and the Clintons to the times of Tweed and Tilden. Some one must do full justice to the connection between the growth of a State-banking system west of the Alleghanies and sundry prevalent financial opinions and doctrines about the powers of Congress.

But the constitutional and political history of the separate States will present so numerous and complicated tasks to the inquirer that no one historian can hope to bear the burden. That work is to be done at home, within the States themselves. Thus the fundamental character of the local historian's labor becomes apparent, for the evolution of our States is the story of the assimilation of localities. So far as the older States are concerned, this statement is obvious, and the newer States spring from the loins of Virginia and New England. Bancroft has written, "He that will understand the political character of New England must study the constitution of its towns, its schools, and its militia." Since the happy termination of the Civil War we have, not two civilizations, but one. In the ultimate analysis, therefore, the future authoritative history of the nation is seen to depend largely upon the history of the Town-Meeting.

Connecticut is a small State, but it is old enough and large enough to have had crises of its own. Our knowledge of the more prominent political controversies of its colonial age is, perhaps, not small, yet the story of the Pequot War and of Uncas, which every one hears, is less important than the story of the Saybrook Platform, of which most people are ignorant. The management of the public lands has interested our political philosophers since 1777. The care of the States for the undivided lands within their own borders has attracted comparatively little attention. Histories speak of the conflicts between Connecticut and Pennsylvania in the Wyoming Valley, but the domestic influences that shaped Connecticut's course in that contest have not yet been brought entirely into the light. Moreover, the principles that influenced the various localities in dividing their own common lands, or in allotting new townships, have scarcely received the attention which is their due, for they lie at the foundation of our land laws. The " Toleration " controversy of 1814–18, in Connecticut, has been hitherto handled gingerly, if handled at all, by historians—always excepting the admirable work of Schouler—yet the triumph of the Tolerationists completed the triumph of the French Revolution in New England.

For whatever interest the constitutional history of the State of Connecticut may possess, New Haven and the region which it controls are, to no small extent, responsible. It will afford pleasure to the author if his pages may be found to reveal and explain some of those minor activities which New Haven, as one town among thousands, has added to the great sum of national well-doing.

C. H. L.

University of California,
Berkeley, September 1, 1886.

CONTENTS.

Contents. vii

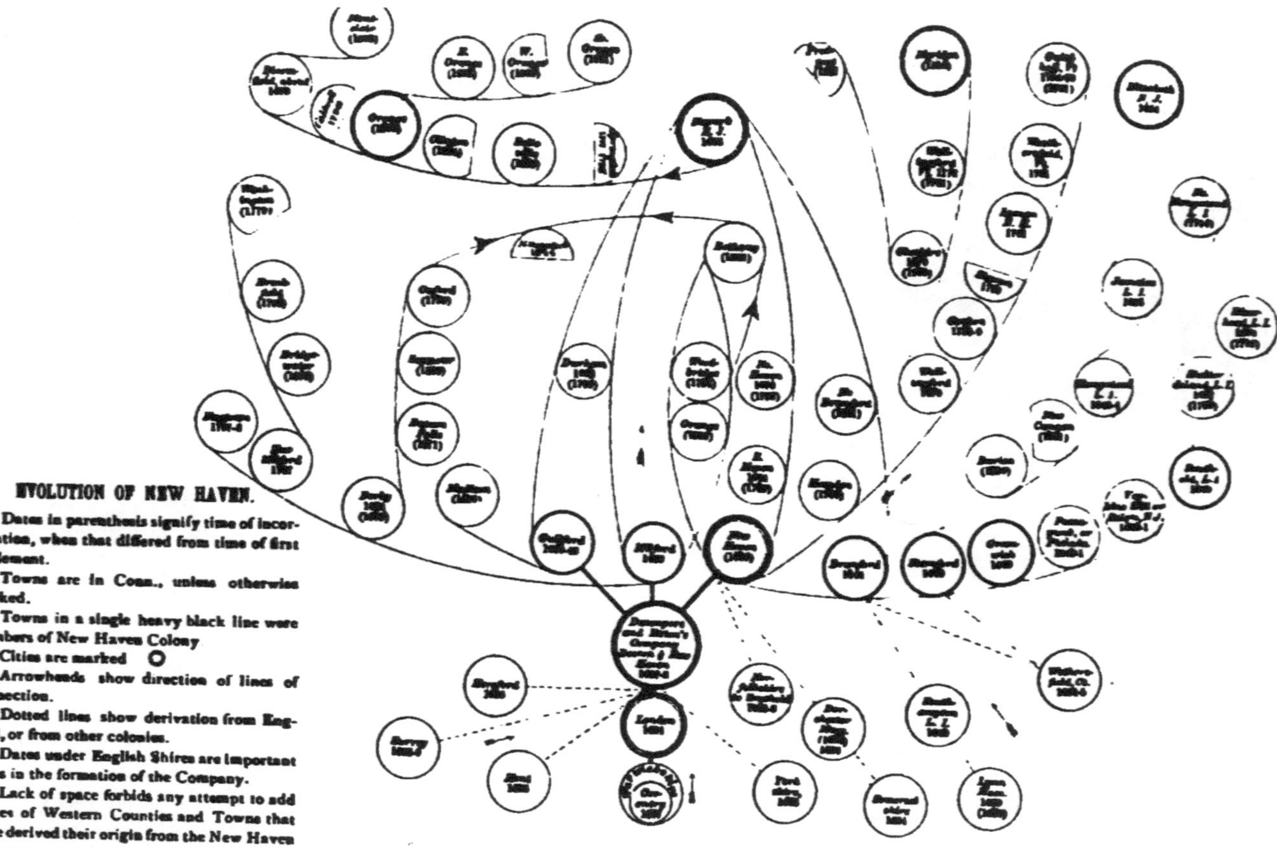

EVOLUTION OF NEW HAVEN.

Dates in parenthesis signify time of incorporation, when that differed from time of first settlement.

Towns are in Conn., unless otherwise marked.

Towns in a single heavy black line were members of New Haven Colony

Cities are marked O

Arrowheads show direction of lines of connection.

Dotted lines show derivation from England, or from other colonies.

Dates under English Shires are important dates in the formation of the Company.

Lack of space forbids any attempt to add names of Western Counties and Towns that have derived their origin from the New Haven region.

THE REPUBLIC OF NEW HAVEN.

CHAPTER I.

THE GENESIS OF NEW HAVEN.

DAVENPORT AND EATON.

As the modern English vestry or parish-meeting is the nearest lineal representative of the ancient tun-gemót, so the municipality of New Haven traces its descent from the Parish of St. Stephen, Coleman street, London. That parish was once the channel for those elements of individual thought and personal influence that have given life and strength to the miniature republic of to-day. In the assemblage of St. Stephen's Parish, on the 6th of October, 1624, New Haven's town-meeting was a nascent possibility. The parishioners of that church possessed the valuable privilege of choosing their own vicar by popular election. The congregation was large, and composed of that middle class wherein lay the vigor and the hope of the Puritan cause. Many of them were traders or wealthy merchants, enemies alike to Spaniards and to Prelatists. On that memorable October day such men met together in parochial conclave, and, of their own free will, by an almost unanimous vote, elected the Rev. John Davenport to be the incumbent at St. Stephen's. From that time onward, for forty years, the figure of this clergyman was the central point around which clustered the forces that finally shaped the colonial destiny of New Haven.

The newly-elected rector of St. Stephen's was twenty-seven years of age, the son of a family of distinction at Coventry, in Warwickshire, a graduate of Oxford, and already for eight years a preacher. That he was a ready and diligent student may be inferred from his admission into Oxford at the age of fourteen years, and from his entrance into the Anglican ministry only five years afterward. His fine presence and his thoughtful, ingenuous countenance bespoke the well-cultured, well-nurtured man. The curve of his lip and the poise of the head betrayed the sensitive spirit, quickly attracting, readily responding. We are told that he "preached with an energy and an agreeableness of which few of his brethren were capable."[1]

It was conference with the Rev. John Cotton especially that led the young vicar of St. Stephen's to espouse gradually the Nonconformist cause. When the Rev. Messrs. Cotton, Hooker, and Stone were about to sail for America, Mr. Davenport and several other London ministers attempted to reclaim them to conformity. The conference proved to be a boomerang. The Puritan malcontents were not converted, but Mr. Davenport was. Moreover, Davenport's Puritan congregation and his noble Puritan friends, the Veres, probably exercised a mighty influence. Although, when entering upon his charge, he made proclamation of his fidelity to the Episcopal party, the eye of his superior, the too-famous Laud, then Bishop of London, soon detected Puritan symptoms in Coleman street. Mr. Davenport became speedily identified with the party of reform within the Church. He was partly known, partly suspected, to be a participant in Puritan schemes, and earned thereby Laud's particular animosity. When the latter was greeted by the King on Tuesday, August 6, 1633, as "My Lord of Canterbury," the Puritans, whether in the Anglican Church or out of it, knew that the hour of distress was at hand. Already Davenport, foreseeing the evil, had called his people together, and declared to them that no danger should drive him away

---

[1] Trumbull, I. 89, 492.

if they wished him to stay. What the decision was may be deduced from the fact that, on the day previous to Laud's elevation to the primacy, Davenport fled from the city. During the next two years, the period of "ship-money" taxation, he was sheltered in Holland. Although he was made assistant pastor of the English Puritan church at Amsterdam, and although he was popular among the refugees there, he was soon discontented with the laxity of prevalent notions concerning Church privileges. Returning to England in 1636, he told his friends that, in his opinion, "God had carried him to Holland on purpose to bear witness against that promiscuous baptism which bordered on a profanation of the holy ordinance." But dislike of heresy was not the motive that brought the now staunch Puritan back from peaceful, worldly Amsterdam to perilous England. Already " New England " was a sound familiar to his ears. For seven years he had aided in the colonization of Massachusetts.[1] And now he heard that the Puritan party was giving up all hope of England, that it was planning a most extensive emigration to the New World, and that the leaders, Lord Say and Sele, the Earl of Warwick, Pym and Hampden, were already providing for a new home on their own property at Connecticut. When the younger Winthrop went to prepare the way for the new exodus, it was Davenport himself who assisted in securing Winthrop's lieutenant, Lion Gardiner, then an engineer in Holland. If English Puritanism was destined to build the new Jerusalem upon the American shore, John Davenport hoped to help lay the corner-stone.

He had returned from the Dutch metropolis to England with these sanguine assurances of Mr. Cotton's recent letter delighting his eyes and comforting his soul: "The order of the Churches and of the Commonwealth is now so settled in New England that it brings to my mind the new Heaven

---

[1] Mather says: "His time and money were in that enterprise." Eaton and Davenport were both members of the Massachusetts Bay Company, although the latter's name was suppressed for fear of the higher powers.

and the new Earth in which dwells Righteousness." During the winter of 1636–37, Laud's subordinates reported to him that "Mr. Davenport hath lately been at Hackney, and goeth in gray like a country gentleman."[1] But the primate neglected his recalcitrant vicar, and failed to interrupt the secret activities that attended the inception of a new Colony-State. Davenport and his school-mate, London parishioner and life-long friend, Theophilus Eaton, were able to enclose within the circle of their influence men from so widely-sundered districts of England as Kent, Yorkshire, and Norfolk.

THE FORMATION OF A STATE.

Individually, the company was remarkable. The two founders, indeed, surpassed all their comrades in dignity and influence. But among the associates who sooner or later cast their lot with the colony there were wealthy Londoners, one of them destined to be the founder of three American grammar-schools; there were five ministers; four school-teachers, one of them the first master of Harvard College, and another the first New Englander to publish an educational work; the father of Elihu Yale; and the young Michael Wigglesworth, about to become the lurid morning star of New England literature.[2] The knowledge that rich merchants of the capital were principal members of the company doubtless prompted Laud's vindictive exclamation, when he was informed of the escape of Davenport and his followers to America: "My arm shall reach him even there." The chosen company of adventurers set sail from London in 1637, and, in June, Winthrop recorded their arrival at Boston, "in two great ships." If Mr. Davenport's voyage had been cheered by visions of the paradise at Boston that Mr.

---

[1] Atwater's History of New Haven Colony, 37.

[2] The Wigglesworth family belonged to the Yorkshire contingent, which came over by itself later than the main body, and which was divided, the larger part preferring to stay in Massachusetts.

Cotton had described, he must have been sorely disappointed. He landed in New England to find the colony in turmoil, the Governor, Vane, overriding the counsel of the elders, the orthodox Puritans aghast before rampant Antinomianism, Mr. Cotton himself suspected of heresies, and the redoubtable Anne Hutchinson, the Eve who had wrought all this mischief in the garden. The skill and wisdom of Davenport were instantly made available in confounding the schismatics and in comforting the godly. Not only the minister's learning, but the opulence of the company as well, ensured to the new-comers a warm welcome. Mr. Davenport was named on the committee that was appointed to establish the college at Cambridge. The Massachusetts Colony conferred a magistracy upon Mr. Eaton, and, evidently with a high sense of the value of the bird in the hand, allowed him to pay a rather heavy tax into the colonial treasury.[1] No sooner was the expedition fairly settled upon the Massachusetts shores, than negotiations were begun at Hartford, by letter and by the personal agency of Mr. Edward Hopkins, for the purchase of an extensive tract of country between the rivers Connecticut and Hudson.[2] The only fruit of the business was the loss to New Haven Colony of Mr. Edward Hopkins, who was so well treated at Hartford that in the very next year he represented that town in the Connecticut General Court.

The successful termination of the Pequot War, in the summer of 1637, probably saved the colony from an inland settlement. Before that time Davenport and Eaton could hardly have dared to launch their new ship of state upon the shores of the Sound. The Dutch at one end and the dreaded Pequots at the other were alike dangerous, and it must have been well known that the depredations of the Pequots had already deterred the noble patentees of the Saybrook Colony from risking their august lives within the protection of their

---

[1] Mass. Col. Rec., 1637–1689; New Haven Hist. Soc. Papers, III. 1.

[2] Magnalia, I. 83.

"Owne Forte." But now, in the nick of time, there came to Winthrop, from the scene of the Pequot overthrow, Captain Stoughton's letters, speaking of "the excellent country at Quellipioak River," that surpassed all the "New England region," not excepting the land at the Bay; "and probable it is that the Dutch will seize it if the English do not; it is too good for any but friends." Captain John Underhill must have added the force of his persuasion also in favor of "the famous place called Queenapiok, which hath a fair river, fit for harboring of ships, and abounds with rich and goodly meadows,"[1] for he threw in his lot with the colony when it finally departed thither.[2] Within a few days after Captain Stoughton's return in August to Boston, Eaton set out to view the new Canaan for himself. Winthrop referred in his journal[3] to the departure as though Quinnipiac had been already decided upon as the place for settlement. If Winthrop conversed with men as he did with his journal, his omissions were sometimes as instructive as his expressions. Two years before he had carefully abstained from entrusting to his journal the true secret and scope of Hooker's ambition for Connecticut. Thus, at this time, he regretfully rehearsed the various reasons why the new colony must continue its

---

[1] Cf. Atwater, p. 62. See Massachusetts Historical Collection, XXVI. (Underhill's History of the Pequot War). See also Savage's Winthrop, I. 278 : "July 18, 1637, at Quinepiack, they killed six and took two. At a head of land a little short they beheaded two sachems, whereupon they called the place 'Sachem's Head.'"

[2] The independent spirit of the Puritans crops out prominently in their spelling. Stoughton, Winthrop and Underhill could not agree about the orthography of Quinnipiac, and Stoughton discovered even another variation, "Quillepiage." Davenport and Eaton were contented with "Quillypiac," and Thos. Fugill, the secretary, followed them closely with "Quillipieck." The Articles of Agreement with the Indians, written by Secretary Gibbard, give the reader the choice of "Quinopiocke," "Quinopyocke" and "Quinnypiock." The river Connecticut figures as the "Quintecutt." It was ungracious, indeed, that Connecticut should try to throw the Duke of Hamilton's petition out of court in 1665, on the plea that he had referred to the "Converticu River."

[3] Under date of August 31, 1637. See also Savage's Winthrop, I. 283.

migrations, but ignored the dominant one, which he and every one else understood. Massachusetts and Plymouth had vied with each other in offering inducements for its permanent settlement. Newbury proposed to surrender its whole township to the colonists, and the Massachusetts General Court offered them any place within its jurisdiction that they might choose. But, as Trumbull says, "the principal men desired to be at the head of a new government, modelled in civil and religious matters agreeably to their own apprehensions."

The economic idea was not wanting. The London merchants in the company hoped to live by commerce, and the chief requisite demanded in the search for a location was convenience for trading, with the advantage, if possible, of a good harbor. On the one hand were homes in the midst of friends, in a prosperous colony where the arduous work of breaking the soil had been partially accomplished, and where commerce was already thriving. The reverse side of the picture presented a doubtful journey to a wild country, recently stained by a bloody war and near to the rival Dutch. Yet Davenport and Eaton were able not only to keep their scattered company intact in spirit, but also to draw numbers of their whilom neighbors away with them. The resplendent hope of a prosperous independence led, like a pillar of fire, on the way into the wilderness. Mr. Eaton returned from his quest with the announcement that seven of their number would guard the future home through the winter. On the 12th of March, 1638, Mr. Davenport wrote and, with Mr. Eaton alone, signed a letter of farewell to the Massachusetts General Court, declining finally all proffers of lasting accommodation. The epistle concludes with an eloquent and suggestive commingling of sacred and secular history, hoping that Massachusetts and Quinnipiac shall be "as Joab and Abishai were, whose severall armyes did mutually strengthen them boath against their severall enimyes, or rather they are joyned together as Hippocrates his Twinnes, to stand and fall, to grow and decay, to flourish and wither, to live and dye together." In the

same year the overtures preliminary to the Confederation of
1643 passed between Massachusetts and Connecticut. About
a month later, Old England was planted at the foot of the
Red Hills, and on the 15th of April, 1638, under an oak tree,
Mr. Davenport stood and preached his first sermon at
Quinnipiac, according to certain authorities, from the somewhat ominous text : " Then was Jesus led up of the Spirit
into the wilderness to be tempted of the devil."[1]

Town-Meetings.

The company were soon busy digging in the banks of the
creek and elsewhere the cellars which gave them their first
shelter. The care of crops, and the erection of the "fair and
stately houses wherein they at first outdid the rest of the
country," crowded the next year's space of time. The "Great
Adversary" could have found but very few idle hands among
them for the performance of his proverbial mischief. There
are no traces of courts, trials, taxes, or even of magistrates,
throughout the first eighteen months of their abode at Quin-

---

[1] Matt. iv. 1. Bacon's and Kingsley's emendation for Trumbull's
Matt. vi. 1. Lambert, who perhaps derived his knowledge from Milford
Church Records, gives a much more satisfactory reference to Matt. iii. 1 :
"In those days came John the Baptist, preaching in the wilderness of
Judea." (History of New Haven Colony, 48.) Lambert, whose work is
usually excellent, says also that Rev. Mr. Prudden preached in the afternoon of the same day from Matt. iii. 3 : "The voice of one crying in the
wilderness, ' Prepare ye the way of the Lord and make His paths straight.' "
It is well known that many of the Puritans looked for the speedy coming
of Christ and of the literal Millennium. Doubtless Davenport and his
followers considered themselves a chosen people, but probably not to the
extent that the ensuing paragraph from Lambert's History would imply :
"It is said the New Haven people went still further, and flattered themselves that they were founding Christ's millennial kingdom, which was to
extend from sea to sea, and that their city would be the seat of the empire,
and that Christ would come in person and live with them a thousand years.
But, notwithstanding, it does not appear from the early records that they
ever reserved a building-lot for His palace" (p. 50). (See Magnalia, I. 331.)
That passage has the twang of Samuel Peters.

nipiac, and only the act of October 25, 1639, annulling all former offices and trusts, shows that a magistracy had existed. Throughout this interval the colony probably existed as a joint-stock association of proprietors, subject to such rules and rulers as had been agreed upon, possibly, before leaving England. Who the rulers were would be sufficiently certain, even if Davenport and Eaton had not appeared as the only signers of the diplomatic adieu to the Massachusetts Government. But they did not presume to act without bringing together from time to time the free planters or proprietors of the colony, and, with the legislation of such democratic assemblies, the records of New Haven Town and Colony begin. The exact date and time of New Haven's first town-meeting cannot be known. It was primarily a Fast-Day gathering for humiliation and prayer, but its simple resolution was the Constitution of the new State for more than a year. All that is known concerning it was inscribed upon the opening pages of the Records in June, 1639, in these words: "Whereas, there was a con'. [covenant] solemnly made by the whole assembly of free planters of this plantation the first day of extraordenary humiliation w^h we had after wee came together, thatt, as in matters that concerne the gathering and ordering of a church, so likewise in all publique offices w^h concerne civill order, as choyce of magistrates and officers, making and repealing of lawes, devideing allottments of inheritance, and all things of like nature, we would all of us be ordered by those rules w^h the scripture holds forth to us." Secretary Thos. Fugill explains further: "This covenant was called a plantation covenant to distinguish it from a Church covenant, w^h could nott att thatt time be made, a church nott being then gathered, butt was deferred till a church might be gathered according to God."

In this Plantation Covenant, Mr. Davenport enveloped the kernel of his subsequent colonial polity, but he was sagacious enough to wait for its germination and ripening. Wise men, like Locke and Shaftesbury, tried to make a Colony-State conform to their ready-made Constitution. New England clergymen and traders had a truer regard for both human freedom and human nature. Many of them had had painful reason to study the conditions of constituted powers, and they had begun to perceive, more or less clearly, that the organic law of the body-politic is not a graft, but a growth from within outward. Two English-American colonies of the 17th century formed themselves into compact, self-governing States, without acknowledging any dependence upon any other power at home or abroad. It is noteworthy that these two, Connecticut and New Haven, each perfected its system of government in the most deliberate and leisurely manner.

Connecticut's "Fundamental Orders" were not adopted until the colony was more than three years old, and had successfully completed an offensive war. The founders of New Haven devoted a year to examining, discussing, and testing the machinery of ecclesiastical and civic authority. As the framework of their dwellings was reared in air, the edifice of the State was built in thought. The masons laid down the underpinning of houses and of magistracies, and carpenters at the same time nailed boards and heresies. Dr. Bacon quotes the saying[1] that "the town was 'cast into several private meetings wherein they that dwelt most together gave their accounts one to another of God's gracious work upon them, and prayed together, and conferred to mutual edification, and thus had knowledge one of another,' and of the fitness of individuals for the several places." The majority of the planters were ready to co-operate with Mr. Davenport in establishing the Bible as a code, and a church-membership suffrage; but opposition there was, headed, as Cotton Mather relates, by the Rev. Samuel Eaton. He and the Rev. Mr. Davenport were pitted directly against each other, and, although they were near neighbors, conducted their controversy partly by writing. Perhaps they felt a judicious anxiety for the health

---

[1] Hist. Disc., 19.

of their tempers. Seventeenth-century disputants about the relations of Church and State, though living in a city of huts and cellars on the margin of the wilderness, might be in danger of tilting too earnestly. Mr. Davenport would not hazard collisions, and wrote: "For though much writing be wearisome unto me, yet I find it the safer way for me." Time has been kind enough to preserve one of these arguments of Mr. Davenport. It is composed in the form of an epistle, commencing "Reverend Sir," and was printed at Cambridge, in 1673, under the following title: "A discourse about civil government in a new plantation whose design is religion. Written many years since by that reverend and worthy minister of the Gospel, John Cotton, B. D." Cotton Mather tells us that the name of Cotton is a mistake for that of Davenport.[1]

The mooted point in the "Discourse" was the proposed restriction upon suffrage. The progress of the reasoning reveals what a step in advance of the rest of the world the colonies of Plymouth and Connecticut had taken. Mr. Davenport appealed to the examples of Holland and of England. "In our native country, none are entrusted with the management of public affairs but members of the Church of England, *as they call them.*" He did not admit that his project contemplated a fusion of Church and State. To his mind, each moved independently in its proper orbit, held in place by the immutable power of the Divine Word. He expressly refused to affirm that the "right and power of choosing civil magistrates belongs to the Church of Christ." Mr. Davenport was not a Fifth-Monarchy man, and would have rejected the idea that a divine right to rule was vested in the Church Militant. He insisted directly that the Church and the State must have different officers, different rules, and a different jurisdiction. The Church and its teachers must be supported entirely by voluntary contributions. As a matter of fact, even a deaconship in the Church did thereafter disqualify a

---

[1] Magnalia, I. Bk. 3d, 380; *vide* Bacon's Hist. Disc., 22, 260-350, 34-35.

man for the magistracy.   About 1659, Mathew Gilbert
could become a magistrate only after he had ceased to be a
deacon.   Ten years later, when the colony was merged in
that of Connecticut, Roger Alling, being at the time a candidate for the office of deacon, was elected Town Treasurer.
In view of the prospective diaconate, the election was set aside,
and another Treasurer chosen, May 3, 1669.   In September,
after the sacred mantle had fallen upon him, he was excused
by the town from being any longer Sergeant.   It is interesting to see how, in these minute particulars, the Puritans
obeyed the distinctions of the canon law and the traditions of
the establishment which they had deserted.

Mr. Davenport therefore argued that he would bestow the
franchise upon certain men, not because they were church-
members, but because they alone, being church-members,
could display a certificate of trustworthiness.   His fundamental definitions were arranged with still greater subtlety.
" Ecclesiastical administrations," he said, " are a divine order
appointed to believers for holy communion of holy things.
Civil administrations are a human order appointed by God to
men for civil fellowship of human things.   Man by nature
being a reasonable and social creature capable of civil order,
is, or may be, the subject of civil power.   But man by grace
called out of the world to fellowship with Jesus Christ and
with his people, is the only subject of Church power.   Though
they both have the same last end—namely, the glory of God—
yet they differ in their next ends, for the next end of civil
order and administrations is the preservation of human societies
in outward honor, justice and peace; but the next ends of
Church order and administrations are the conversion, edification and salvation of souls, pardon of sin, power against sin,
and peace with God."[1]

____

[1] It is interesting to trace these political and theological opinions of Mr.
Davenport, and of the Puritans for whom he stood as the type, to a genesis
in the writings of Thomas Cartwright (1572), and of Richard Hooker
(1594–97).   Mr. Davenport avoided, in theory at least, the arrogance of

THE FUNDAMENTAL AGREEMENT.

These passages suffice to illustrate the condition of the intellectual atmosphere in the colony at the time when its second recorded folk-moot met in Mr. Robert Newman's barn, June 4, 1639. Five months before, at Hartford, the Connecticut farmers had erected a State, and now at New Haven, according to the description of Sec. Fugill, "all the free planters assembled together in a generall meetinge to consult about settling civill Government according to God, and about the nomination of persons . . . fittest for the foundacion worke of a church, which was intend to be gathered in Quinipieck." At the outset, Mr. Davenport with a firm hand struck the key-note for the day's actions. He prayed his hearers to "consider seriously in the presence and feare of God the weight of the business they met about, and nott to be rash or sleight in giving their votes to things they understoode nott, butt to digest fully and throughly whatt

---

Cartwright's timocracy, which admonished rulers to "submit themselves unto the Church, to throw down their crowns before the Church, yea, as the prophet speaketh, to lick the dust off the feet of the Church." But Davenport's before-quoted definitions are manifestly the same as these sentences from Cartwright's famous Admonition to Parliament (1572): "No civil magistrate in assemblies for Church matters can either be chief moderator, overruler, judge or determiner. The principal direction of Church matters is by God's ordinance committed to the ministers of the Church. As these meddle not with the making civil laws, so the civil magistrate ought not to ordain ceremonies or determine controversies in the Church, so long as they do not intrench upon his temporal authority." The view of the sequence of events widens here, for this is the spirit of mediaeval canon law masquerading in Presbyterian garb. From the work of Hooker, the judicious, even-tempered champion of the Anglican Church, Mr. Davenport could derive the fundamental principle that membership in the Church and commonwealth must be identical. No one, according to Hooker, could belong to one without belonging to the other. Still more fruitful was Hooker's theory of the foundation of the State in a civil compact and in individual assent—a theory which modern times have somewhat feloniously coupled with the names of Locke and Rousseau. See Hopkins' History of the Puritans under Queen Elizabeth; also Neal, and Hallam (Constitutional History of England, Chap. IV.).

should be propounded to them, and without respect to men, as they should be satisfied and perswaded in their owne mindes to give their answers in such sort as they would be willing they should stand upon recorde for posterity." Mr. Davenport then presented six resolutions, or, as he called them, "Quaeries." In order to shut the door against the possibility of a misunderstanding, the planters voted twice upon each proposal by "holding up their hands," first when Mr. Davenport had read his "Quaery," and secondly when Mr. Newman had written the same "in carracters" and had repeated it to the people. Without a dissenting voice it was agreed that the Scriptures "doe hold forth a perfect rule" for all the duties of men, that the plantation covenant was and should be binding, that all the free planters desired to be "admitted into church-fellowship according to Christ, as soon as God shall fitt them thereunto," and that they were all bound to establish such "Civill Order as might best conduce to the securcing of the purity and peace of the ordinances to themselves and their posterity according to God."

The key-stone of the arch was the fifth Query: "Whether they thatt are in the foundation worke of the Church shall be the free burgesses, and shall alone chuse magistrates and officers, make laws, and elect other freemen out of the like estate of church-fellowship." By way of prelude to the statement of the question, and in order to emphasize its importance, Mr. Davenport delivered a short speech, fortifying his own position with a number of Scriptural quotations.[1] "Then he satt downe, praying the company freely to consider whether they would have it voted att this time or nott." "After some space of silence" Mr. Theophilus Eaton called for the question. There was no negative voice in the vote, nor in its repetition. The free planters of Quinnipiac had voluntarily renounced their sovereign rights, and transformed their democracy into an aristocracy. But the act was not to

---

[1] Exod. xviii. 2; Deut. i. 18; xviii. 15; I Cor. vi. 1–7.

be accomplished without a tardy plea for the supremacy of
the State. "After the vote was past," Mr. Samuel Eaton
stood up to vindicate in that barn his kinship with Hampden
and Vane in Parliamentary halls, and to display a dim sense
of the greater liberties toward which greater Englishmen
were struggling.[1] He granted that freemen and magistrates
alike ought to be God-fearing men, and that in the Church
such men should "ordenaryly" be found; "onely att this
he stuck, 'That free planters ought nott to give this power
out of their hands.'" A debate ensued. One man answered
that the free planters did not lose their freedom, for "in this
case nothing was done without their consent." Mr. Eaton
insisted that provision should be made by virtue of which
"all the free planters" could "resume this power into their
own hands againe if things wore nott orderly carryed." This
was a dangerous point, and Mr. Theophilus Eaton interposed.
He answered "thatt in all places they chuse committyes; in
like manner the compauyes of London chuse the liveryes by
whom the publique magistrates are chosen. In this the rest
are not wronged, because they expect in time to be of y° livery
themselves, and to have the same power." This was likely
to be a convincing illustration to his audience of London
merchants. Mr. Samuel Eaton would say no more after his
brother's speech. When some requested him to give his
opinions at length, he refused, "and said they might nott
rationally demand itt, seeing he lett the vote passe on freely,
and did not speake till after itt was past, because he would
nott hinder whatt they agreed upon." He evidently felt that
the decision had been made before the meeting assembled.
Mr. Davenport related to the company "some former passages betweene them two about this question." In order to
clinch the decision beyond dispute, he put it to the vote for a
third time. Again the hands all signified assent. Then

---

[1] The Records say "One man"; the name was probably suppressed as a
favor to the malcontent. But there is hardly a doubt that it was Mr.
Eaton.

began what modern political parlance terms a "stampede." And some of them professed "thatt, whereas they did waver before they came to the assembly, they were now fully convinced thatt itt is the minde of God." The ground-plan of the State having been thus marked out, the organization of a Church was next in order. "And to prevent the blemishing of the first beginnings of the Church worke," Mr. Davenport advised "thatt the names of such as were to be admitted might be publiquely propounded, to the end thatt they who were most approved might be chosen." This custom will be recognized as still in vogue. The pastor then referred to the knowledge that they had of one another in their "neighborhood meetings," and "to prevent scandals" he urged that the ecclesiastical substructure should be deposited with singular care. The sixth and last Query was now submitted and accepted. It was agreed that twelve men should be chosen who should afterward select seven of their own number to be the nucleus of the new Church and the first burgesses of the new State. The "Records," however, contain eleven instead of twelve names, Mr. Theophilus Eaton and Mr. Davenport leading the list. The following circumstance suggests a characteristic explanation of the omission. It had been agreed that if any of the twelve "pillars" should be esteemed faulty, the objection should be made known. "Noe exception was brought against any of those in publique, except one about takeing an excessive rate for meale, which he sould to one of Pequanack in his need, which he confessed with griefe, and declared thatt haveing beene smitten in heart, and troubled in his conscience, he restored such a part of the price back againe with confession of his sin to the party as he thought himself bound to doe. And itt being feared thatt the report of his sin was heard farther than the report of his satisfaction, a course was concluded on to make the satisfaction known to as many as heard of the sinn."

Verily, the way of the transgressor was hard! And what a shrewd suspicion was it that the rumor of evil would fly farther than the report of atonement! There must be no stain upon the purity of Church or State, if microscopic scrutiny could avail. The six Queries together formed the famous "Foundamentall Agreement," the written Constitution of New Haven Colony. It received the finishing touch at what was perhaps an adjourned session of the same meeting, when it was ordered by all the free planters "thatt all those thatt hereafter should be received as planters into this plantation, should alleo submitt to the said foundamentall agreement, and should sign their names thereto." During the following summer one hundred and eleven names were underwritten. The new machinery of government now stood ready to be set in operation, but never was an enterprise put in motion in a more leisurely manner. As in most of the New England towns, it was felt that the establishment of the Civil Government must wait for the organization of the church, but the temple was not built upon its "seven pillars" until the 22d of August. That day is the third time-mark in the progress of New Haven's constitutional growth. Probably the delay was due to a desire to prove more thoroughly the fitness of the chosen pillars, and to know of the plans and satisfy the wishes of the Milford and Guilford settlers who were still living at Quinnipiac. The Milford church was set upon its seven pillars either on the same or on the ensuing day.[1]

---

[1] The town was favored with the presence of nine clergymen, more than half the number which in later times framed the Saybrook Platform. The opportunities in the New Haven of that day to hear the preached Word were indeed ample. There were Messrs. Prudden and Sherman, of the future Milford colony; Mr. Whitfield, of the recently-arrived Guilford party, and in the New Haven company proper were Messrs. Davenport, James, and Samuel Eaton. Mr. James was one of the first Nonconformist missionaries to Virginia in 1642-43. (See Winthrop's Journal.) The schoolmaster, Mr. Ezekiel Cheever, was also an occasional preacher, as we learn from the Records (I. p. 808) that one of the crimes for which Richard Smoult was "sevearly" whipped was "scofing at the Word of God which was preached by Mr. Cheever." Moreover, Messrs. Hooker and Stone, from Hartford, came to assist in Mr. Davenport's installation. See Bacon's Hist. Disc.

The fourth and final stage in the genesis of New Haven was reached on the 25th of October, 1639, when the colony emerged from its long-continued chrysalis state and became a full-fledged community. The seven pillars, Mr. Theophilus Eaton, Mr. John Davenport, Mr. Robert Newman, Mr. Mathew Gilbert, Thomas Fugill, John Ponderson, and Jeremy Dixon, had met together two months before, and resolved themselves into a Church. Now they assembled again and resolved themselves into a State. Until this time, New Haven was under the provisional government of the joint-stock association. After "solemn prayer," the first act of the new court was to declare that "all former power or trust for mannaging any publique affayres in this plantation, into whose hands soever formerly committed, was now abrogated, and from henceforward utterly to cease." Certain "members of approved churches" were made members of the court, and took an oath of fidelity. The next duty was the election of members of Government. But this was a weighty matter, not to be lightly undertaken. The Roman or Greek would have first consulted the oracles; the Puritan turned reverently to his. Mr. Davenport read and explained the inspired description of a righteous magistracy: "Take you wise men, and understanding, and known among your tribes, and I will make them rulers over you." "Moreover thou shalt provide out of all the people able men, such as fear God, men of truth, hating covetousness; and place such over them, to be rulers of thousands, and rulers of hundreds, rulers of fifties, and rulers of tens."[1] Compare this scene with the surroundings of our modern elections! Do we have a better sense than these men of the divinity that doth hedge true citizenship? Mr. Theophilus Eaton was "by full consent" elected to be magistrate "for the tearme of one whole yeare." In the somewhat churchly language of the "Records," Mr. Davenport "gave him the charge," the first election sermon ever preached in New Haven. He chose an

---

[1] Deut. i. 13 and Exod. xviii. 21.

apposite text, sentences pregnant with the burden of all justice:
"Judge righteously between every man and his brother, and
the stranger that is with him. Ye shall not respect persons
in judgment; ye shall hear the small as well as the great; ye
shall not be afraid of the face of man, for the judgment is
God's."[1] Four deputies were elected to assist the magistrate.
Thomas Fugill, already a "pillar" and a deputy, was chosen
"publique notary," or town clerk. "Marshall" was the title
given to Robert Seely, who performed the duties of a constable.
He was ordered to "warne courts according to the direction
of the magistrate, to serve and execute warrants, to attend
the court att all times, to be ready and diligent in his person
or by his deputy to execute sentences, and in all other occasions to attend the service of the plantation in all things appertaining to his office."[2] It was determined that the yearly
elections should be held in the last week of October. The
fabric of the State was complete. Nothing remained but to
reaffirm more plainly than ever before the essential idea of
their legislation and judicature. "The worde of God shall be
the onely rule to be attended unto in ordering the affayres of
government in this plantation."

Thus the young State turned its feet into a political path-
way which had been, until that generation, untrodden. Of
all the New England colonies, New Haven was most purely
a government by compact, by social contract. Plymouth
had professed at the outset its obedience to the English laws
and sovereign. Massachusetts had a charter confirmed by
royal authority. Rhode Island's democracy had a patent
obtained from the Long Parliament, but it recognized "Our
Sovereign Lord, King Charles," and provided that the civil
government of Providence Plantations should conform to the

---

[1] Deut. i. 16, 17.

[2] This seems to block out quite an amount of work. But it is small and
vague compared with the list of duties of Massachusetts constables given
in Dr. H. B. Adams' Norman Constables in America. See J. H. U.
Studies in Hist. and Pol. Science, I. viii. 26–30.

laws of England "so farr as the Nature and Constitution of the place will admit." Connecticut, indeed, in its Constitution, acknowledged subjection to no earthly power, and its people agreed to "assotiate and conjoyne ourselves to be as one Publike State or Commonwelth."

The free planters of New Haven, in the same spirit of independence, signed each their names to their voluntary compact, and ordered that "all planters hereafter received in this plantation should submitt to the said foundamentall agreement, and testifie the same by subscribing their names." It is believed that this is the sole instance of the formation of an independent civil government by a general compact wherein all the parties to the agreement were legally required to be actual signers thereof. When this event occurred, John Locke was in his seventh year, and Rousseau was a century away. However, as the preceding pages have shown, the freemen of Connecticut and New Haven had certainly not just emerged from the preliminary "state of nature," unless that phrase be understood in the sense of Puritan theology.

A relapse into the theologically-conceived "state of nature" was the peril which ever seemed to Davenport most likely to threaten his tender State. So long as the Church was the avenue to the franchise, Mr. Davenport guarded its entrance as rigidly as the angel with the flaming sword watched the gates of Eden. Davenport confounded the devout man and the good citizen. To so consistent a Calvinist a deep distrust of human nature was inevitable. Humanity, leavened with total depravity, could hope for political, social or intellectual regeneration only through the universal supremacy of the elect few.

Again and again he insisted that purity in the Church was the one and only safeguard of righteousness in the State. Accordingly, his discipline in the Church was deemed severe even for that age. Mather's quaint metaphor was that " Mr. Davenport used the golden snuffers of the sanctuary overmuch." Yet a New England Servetus could have found but scanty charity anywhere outside of the Cave of Adullam at Rhode Island. The Puritans of the Bay Colony, engaged in fierce wrestlings with the adversary in the shape of Roger Williamses, Anne Hutchinsons, Perfectionists and Quakers, looked enviously upon peacefully-orthodox New Haven, and Hubbard wrote: "In their church-settlements, New Haven was exemplary to other plantations, and cannot but have a sweet savor to the present, yea, and to future generations." Hubbard's prophecy was true, if not just as he supposed. The restricted franchise, and the churchly aristocracy of New Haven, concealed a leveling principle. As the will of an English sovereign can transform the meanest subject into a peer of the realm, so the lowliest dweller in the cellars at Quinnipiac could, by admission to church-membership, become a ruler of the State. The day-laborer, the possessor of the good name which is more valuable than fine gold, might be a free burgess, while his neighbor, dwelling in one of the "stately" houses and writing "Mr." before his name, might be forbidden to cast a vote.

It was the democracy within the Church, the belief in the popular right to decide in Church affairs, that finally leavened all our society with our truest freedom. That a handful of exiles, gathered in a barn, could of their own free motion, without a bishop or a royal sanction, form a Church of God; that the same men, with no charter but their own consent and that of their fellow-men, could organize a self-governing State—these were the novel and startling ideas through which our modern political philosophy has mainly developed. In the light of these principles Winthrop and Endicott, Hooker and Roger Williams, Davenport and Eaton, stand forth together as apostles of our liberty.

DAVENPORT'S POLICY.

And yet, though these things have worked together for great good, it is easy to ascribe to the leaders of the colonies more praise than is really their due. Far in advance of their day and generation they were, but even then they builded better than they knew. Endicott was fanatical; Roger Williams was a visionary; and Davenport, even more than the elder Winthrop, was a Puritan who looked backward, not forward. Over the ecclesiastical aristocracy which Davenport and Eaton created, they extended a dual sway like that of the ancient Spartan kings, but without any restraining ephoralty. Davenport's decisions were indeed reasonably and logically formed, but when once determined they were added by him to the stock of positive knowledge, and were upheld with a confidence and persistence that brooked no contradictions and admitted no exceptions.[1] The Rev. Mr. Hooker, at Hartford, was, as long as he lived, no less a dictator. But the flavor of political philosophy at Hartford smacked of Archbishop Langton; at New Haven, of Peter Cartwright and John Calvin. The Father of Connecticut was not only a Calvinistic, ecclesiastical Puritan : he was also a political Puritan. His sympathies were democratic, and his confidence in the people at large transcended the bounds. of his narrow theology. Above all, Mr. Hooker never disregarded his political inheritance. For English kingship he had no favor; to the English ideal of popular freedom he devoted his best endeavors. Mr. Hooker was a Puritan because he was republican; Mr. Davenport, republican because he was a Puritan. For him English laws, precedents and trophies of freedom were swallowed in the gulf of Scriptural legislation. Mr. Hooker sought rather to show that the purposes of English liberty were in accordance with the moral principles of the Bible. The historian Hubbard observed that "soon after Mr. Hooker's arrival, many of the freemen grew to be very jealous of their liberties."[2] Mr. Hooker expressly taught his flock from the pulpit that "the

---

[1] Mather expressed it gently, thus : "They thought him too straight or too high in his apprehensions."
[2] 165.

foundation of authority is laid in the free consent of the people." Mr. Davenport may have seemed to place New Haven upon the same platform, in the "Foundamentall Agreement"; but, in reality, he based his colony upon class distinctions and restrictions. He created an affranchised caste of Brahmans, and the conditions of admission into that order put a premium upon hypocrisy. Nevertheless his work was surely done in a true spirit of love and sincerity. The conclusion must be that he was by nature a believer in might rather than in multitude. Mr. Davenport's mind was fine-grained. He discriminated to a nicety, and abounded in careful reserves. The large-hearted Hooker was strung upon a fibre coarser and tougher; he loved to stand upon the ground among men, and to be visibly their leader. Mr. Davenport's utterances smack of the pulpit. Hooker was endowed with the zeal of a Zwingli, ready to perish in fighting for his cause. He was well fitted to lead sturdy Englishmen into the wilderness. Davenport would have better adorned a Professor's chair at the University. Mr. Davenport resembled in many respects Hooker's Boston rival, the Rev. John Cotton. But it is to be hoped that the New Haven divine, though gifted with a logician's subtlety, was neither so versatile nor so fickle as Mr. Cotton, and that he would not have shifted his allegiance, as Cotton easily did, from Winthrop to Vane and back again. Nevertheless their minds showed the same devotion to dialectics, the same absorption into theological modes and abstractions, the same reverence for dignities.

It is no insignificant fact that the nephew of Davenport attained to high position and fame in the Roman Church. Probably the same traits drove each of the Davenports to such opposite conclusions. The religious instinct that demanded a logical explanation of the universe, the reverence for authority founded upon generalizations of limitless application, the belief in the subordination of classes one to another and of all to a spiritual power, the longing for a consistent unity of truth—such characteristics belong alike to Loyola and to Calvin, and they might lead the same man to a Puritanical Rome, or to an Imperial Geneva. Therefore Christopher Davenport, the Franciscan friar, rested upon the infallible Church, and John Davenport, the Anglican Nonconformist, trusted, with the fierce faith of his time, in the infallible Book of Books.

GOVERNOR THEOPHILUS EATON.

Mr. Davenport was exceptionally fortunate in the friendship and co-operation of Theophilus Eaton. His support meant much more to Mr. Davenport than the assistance of one person only. Besides the score and ten souls who are said to have owned the immediate sway, the *patria potestas*, of Mr. Eaton, he was the leader in a group of six proprietors of the colony, a veritable clan-Eaton. Their shares in the association, together with Mr. Davenport's interest, represented probably at least one-quarter of the whole capital stock of the first adventurers.[1]

Next to Mr. Davenport, Theophilus Eaton was the father of New Haven, and perhaps his impress was as abiding as that of the pastor. There is no need of accumulating evidence to show how Mr. Davenport leaned upon him. Through all their life together, they seem to have acted as one man, without disagreement, or, at least, without public clashing. The colonists revered Mr. Eaton, and his office of Governor was continued from year to year without apparent dissent. His belief in Mr. Davenport's system of "government according to God" was single-hearted and complete. Naturally conservative, his experience in mercantile life as a manager of men served to strengthen his aversion to the turbulence

---

[1] The number of adult males in the first emigration was about fifty. The Eaton group comprised these six proprietors: Theophilus Eaton ; his mother, Mrs. Eaton ; his two stepsons, Thomas Yale and David Yale, father of Gov. Elihu Yale ; his stepson-in-law, Edward Hopkins, a wealthy merchant ; and his brother, Rev. Samuel Eaton. Another brother, Nath'l Eaton, notorious in the history of Harvard College, seems to have come over with this colony.

of English popular forms of government. Hubbard speaks
with disapproval of the disuse in New Haven of jury-trials,
"which was so settled upon some reasons urged by Mr.
Eaton (a great reader and traveller) against that way."
Eaton's life upon the shores of the Baltic probably gave him
that favorable opinion of more summary methods of admin-
istering justice which would be confirmed by his familiarity
as a wealthy Puritan with the subservient juries of Charles
Stuart's venal judges. No finer specimen of the middle-class
Puritan merchant of 1630 came to the New England shore.
He was moderate and dignified, as befitted a man accustomed
to important trusts and financial responsibilities. He was
unceasingly devout, grave and cautious, as became a man who
held himself to be a special and divinely-chosen messenger.
His methodical habits were transferred from the counting-
house to the council-chamber. He did things decently and
in order, and expected the same from others. His custom of
giving commands to underlings, and his highly-developed
sense of dignity, made his utterances sound dictatorial, when
he probably did not intend it. His diplomacy was a failure
on this account. His stilted and threatening phrases offended
the impetuous Stuyvesant. The Dutch Governor at one time
refused to answer Mr. Eaton, but directed his communications instead to Deputy-Governor Goodyear, who seems to
have been officially less impenetrable than his superior.
Stuyvesant complained bitterly that Mr. Eaton was arrogant,
"ripping up all my faultes as if I were a scholeboy, and not
as one of like degree with himselfe."[1] Governor Eaton thus
proves the historic continuity of a type of John Bull, well
known in our own day, impartially condescending, treating all
outside the circle of his own friends as "scholeboys," good or
bad, as the case may be. A plaintiff whom he did not trust
or did not like was sometimes made to appear rather as the
defendant than as the suitor;[2] yet, if his rugged justice varied

[1] Records, I. 521.
[2] "So that it was a vain thing to offer to bear him out."—Hubbard,
329-330.

from the law, it was inevitably upon the side of leniency.
His judgments were sure and speedy, not oppressive. The
reluctance of both Eaton and Davenport to push accusations
of witchcraft is a proof of their elevation above the frenzies
of a common fear. His calm persistence could expand into
obstinacy, characteristic of the race. Swedes and Dutch alike
had as good a title to the Delaware region as New Haven had
to the shores of the Sound, but Eaton and his friends gave up
their claim to the Delaware Bay only with the colonial existence. While Eaton lived, neither Davenport nor himself
lost hope. The Governor held on his way undismayed by
the ill-fortune and impoverishment of the colony, the diminution of his own fortune, and the discontent of his peevish
wife. To her wish that they might return to their native
country, he replied: "You may, but I shall die here."[1] It
was fortunate for the Connecticut Colony that John Winthrop
and the Charter of 1662 were not obliged to contend against
the indomitable energy of Theophilus Eaton.[2]

In domestic life, Mr. Eaton bore himself with a gentleness
that lent a charm to the dignity of his appearance. Mather's
picture of the Governor at the death-bed of his son discloses
how a Roman inflexibility and a fervent, Oriental faith
were blended in the Puritan magistrate. Samuel Eaton was
a youth of promise, a Harvard graduate, already a magistrate,
the pride alike of his father and of the colony. I use the
quaint phraseology of the clerical historian: "His eldest son
he maintained at college until he proceeded Master of the
Arts, the son of his vows and of great hopes. A malignant
fever then raging in those parts of the country carried off
him with his wife, within two or three days of one another.
The dying son looked earnestly on his father and said: 'Sir,
what shall we do?' Whereto with a well-ordered countenance he replied: 'Look up to God.' When he passed by

---

[1] Bacon's Historical Discourses, 109 ; *vide* Magnalia.
[2] See Appendix A, " Mr. Pierson's Elegy."

his daughter, drowned in tears, to her he said: 'God accounts it a charging Him foolishly when we don't submit to Him patiently.' He knew how to weep as if he wept not, for, it being the Lord's day, he repaired unto the church in the afternoon, as he had been in the forenoon, though he was not like to see his dearest son more in this world. Before the first prayer began, the message of his son's death came, yet he altered not his course, but wrote after the preacher as formerly. At the interment, with a very unpassionate carriage and aspect, he did say to the people: 'Friends, I do thank you all for your love and help and for this testimony of respect unto me and mine. The Lord hath given and the Lord hath taken: blessed be the name of the Lord.' Nevertheless, going home to his daughter's sick-chamber, some tears were observed falling from him as he uttered these words: 'There is a difference between a sullen silence or a stupid senselessness under the hand of God, and a childlike submission thereunto.'"[1]

In the pure, white light of such Puritan sincerity, the gibes of Sedley, and the rhyming pasquinades of Butler, shrivel away to contemptible meanness. These were men of the Ironside type, and they faced the King of Terrors as resolutely and as humbly at Quinnipiac as at Naseby. No mistakes in their methods can tarnish the rightful lustre of their intellectual and moral strength. The New Haven that they knew and moulded apparently vanished almost with the expiring breath of its founders; yet a city, like a musical instrument, possesses a tone of its own, and the city at the Red Hills has never lost the calm, conservative habit of Eaton, or the scholastic zeal of Davenport. Through them the names of Hopkins and Yale became a possible accession to the educational nomenclature of New Haven. The institutions that have been marshalled under those names are grander monuments than a city founded, or a creed conserved.

---

[1] Magnalia, I. 149.

CHAPTER II.

EVOLUTION OF TOWN GOVERNMENT.

The settlement of New Haven was made upon a peninsula between two creeks, or arms of the harbor, one of which has become the site of a sewer, and the other of a railway track. The first dwelling-places were cellars or excavations in the bank of the West Creek. These rude shelters were probably protected by boards, sticks and turf, and were not unlike the sod-houses of our own Western country.[1] The town-plot, half a mile square, and bounded by what are now George, York, Grove, and State streets (Neck Lane), nestled between the two creeks, and was divided into nine minor squares, or "quarters," as they were called. On the eight outside squares the principal planters made their homes, while the central section was reserved for a market-place, and is now the beautiful Common, or "Green." Fences divided the quarters, but the house-lots within them were not at first separated. The house-lots were probably proportioned to the amount invested in the enterprise by the owner and to the number of persons in the family; but no record of the allotment of the town-plot is in existence. During the first year or two, the inhabitants of each quarter were, so far as might be, those persons who were bound to each other by ties of vicinage in Old England, or perhaps of blood-relation, so that the absence of partition-lines would relieve the wilderness of some of its terrors. At the ends of the four

---

[1] One of these hovels was for a time the home of the Wigglesworth family, and doubtless aided in forming the sombre imagination of the youthful Michael.

streets intersecting the town-plot,[1] and at the four corners, gates were built in accordance with the order of November 3, 1639: "Mr. Eaton shall appoint the men to make gates att the end of every Streete att the outside of the Towne, with all the outside fences." In 1651, the town empowered the magistrates to press men for the mending of public gates and fences. Mr. J. W. Barber, in his "Antiquities of New Haven," says that, until the close of the last century, a gate about six rods west of York street still closed the lane that has now become West Chapel street. The outside fence was doubtless higher than any of the inner fences. The "Records" allude to it as "The Towne Pale." In the same manner, the town-plot of Milford was planned and palisaded.[2]

Outside of the town-plot there were two aggregations of homesteads, one south of the town-square, between George street and Water street, or the harbor, as it was then; the other situated on the opposite bank of the West Creek. These two divisions were called "The Suburbs," and were counted together as one-quarter in the allotment of land. The house-lots in the suburbs were mostly in the possession of the thirty-two householders, who, at the inception of the colony, were not shareholders or proprietors, and consequently had no rights of commonage. In addition, there were four isolated house-lots on the northern shore of the harbor, east of the East Creek.[3] These were reckoned, for purposes of land-division, with the east central square or quarter of the town-plot.

Late in the autumn of 1638, while the fortunate ones were moving into the newly-built houses around the market-place, the New Haven community first became a landed proprietor. The title was acquired by purchase from the Quinnipiac chieftain representing the forty-seven warriors of his tribe,

---

[1] The four streets were Chapel, Elm, Church, and College streets.

[2] Lambert's Hist. of N. H. Col., pp. 92-96. Here, therefore, was reproduced the "ring-fence" of the ancient village-community.

[3] See map of the town-plot in Atwater's excellent Hist. of N. H. Colony.

and from the sachem Montowese. The bargain included
most of the land now covered by the townships of New
Haven, East Haven, Branford, North Branford, North
Haven, Wallingford, Cheshire, Hamden, Bethany, Woodbridge, and Orange. The English gave, " by way of free
and thankful retribution," twenty-three coats of " English
trucking cloath, twelve alcumy spoones, a dozen each of
hatchetts, hoes and porengers," two dozen knives, four cases
of " French knives and sizers," and, for Montowese's personal
delectation, a coat " made up after yᵉ English manner." A
sort of offensive and defensive alliance was concluded ; and
the Indians promised not to disturb the English by " disorderly hunting ; not to hanker about any of yᵉ English
houses at any time when the English use to meete about the
publique worship of God ; not to be seene on yᵉ Lords day
henceforward within yᵉ compass of yᵉ English Towne ; not to
open without leave any latch belonging to any Englishmens
dore," and not to come armed into town in numbers greater
than six at any one time. Near the village of Montowese, and
in East Haven, there were reservations where the dwindling
tribes still fished and hunted, or, from their fort on Beacon
Hill, idly watched the industrious stranger parcelling out
their ancestral heritage. But even before the time of the
Indian treaties of sale, some restless spirits had strayed from
the village bounds out into the waste. At the close of the
deed from Montowese (December 11, 1638), it is found that
" Robert Cogswell, James Love,¹ and Roger Knapp do hereby
renounce all right to any and every part of the fore-mentioned
land." And thereunto the first two affix their signs-manual ;
but the last makes his mark, a huge interrogation-point.
Thus there was already need of the law of January 4, 1640,
that no one shall purchase any lands from the Indians, or
others, for his " owne private use or advantage, but only in
the name and for the use of the whole plantation." This

---

¹ Records, I. 7. See p. 29 : " Goodman Love is whipped and banished for
drunkenness."

regulation was common to all the colonies, and was always
enforced in Connecticut and in New Haven. The revision
of 1645 forbade the acceptance of land as a gift from the
Indians. Four years later, Mr. William Wells, a prominent
settler of Southold, was solemnly censured because he had
received some land from the Indians "by waye of gift."
Mr. Wells resigned his interest in the land to the Jurisdiction, and declared himself ready to draw a deed to that
effect.[1]

THE SOCIAL ORDER.

The society which formed the new town and State was
distinctly stratified. Along the lines of social structure
various classes can be detected—slaves, indented servants,
day-laborers, householders, admitted planters, church-members, freemen. If it may be allowed to crowd the metaphor
somewhat, the church-members were a vein and not a stratum,
for their body penetrated through nearly all the other layers.
Aside from political privileges, the cardinal difference between
classes was the ownership of land and of rights of commonage. The lower orders, the tenant householders, and, as
time went on, some of the admitted planters, were accorded a
residence by the town, but were excluded, as the Swiss
" Beisassen " are, from any share in the common lands. The
great majority of the planters and freemen were, of course,
commoners, though their frequent assemblage in that capacity
was precluded by the early appointment of a Proprietor's
Committee. About twenty men in the town habitually
received the title of "Mr." Some of these never became
freemen, and two of the most prominent, Crane and Malbon,
did not become freemen until 1641 and 1642 respectively.

The crowd of transient laborers was ever increasing. They
were attracted by New Haven's reputation for wealth, by the
commercial ventures there, and especially by the chance of

---

[1] Records, I. 468.

employment at Mr. Goodyear's "iron-worke," which was established in East Haven in 1655. Moreover, the reports of a more lax administration at "The Manhatos," and in the plantations farther down the coast, were enough to keep a stream of tramps of both sexes steadily flowing southward, and to keep New Haven's marshal busy in superintending the adornment of their backs at the whipping-post. In 1638, Rev. Mr. Hooker complained bitterly to Governor Winthrop that immigrants of good quality were dissuaded in Massachusetts from coming to Connecticut.[1] However, Massachusetts would not care to inquire closely whether obnoxious persons took the road toward the Connecticut and New Haven colonies. Dr. Dwight says: "It is to be remembered that, although the superior classes of the New Haven colonists were distinguished for excellence of character, the peasantry and servants were generally not less distinguished for vice and profligacy."[2] The town contained a number of indented servants, some of them bound out to work as a punishment for misdoing. There were a few negro and Indian slaves,[3] and some white persons were also enslaved as a penalty for arson, sometimes for a term of years, sometimes for life, but they were not sent out of the colony.[4]

THE TOWN-COURTS.

Within such a society as this there were now spontaneously developed the municipal functions of a marshal, a "publique notary" or town clerk, a magistrate and four "probi

---

[1] Conn. Hist. Soc. Coll., I.

[2] Statistical Account of the City of New Haven, 1811, 36.

[3] We read of Anthony, Governor Eaton's "neager," and of Mathew, Mr. Evance's servant. "Time, Mr. Hooke's Indian," testified in the witchcraft trials in 1653, and the Town Records allude to "Captive, an Indian servant of Mr. Malbon."

[4] Only in the case of Mary Betts, who set fire to John Cooper's barn, was the culprit's employer expressly allowed by the Jurisdiction Court to sell her "within the four United Colonies of New England, and not elsewhere, that she may live under publique ordinances for her soules good."

homines," and an assembly of citizens, without even a hint of ultimate reference to higher terrestrial powers. The task is now to observe the expansion of the powers of these simple organs of rule, the differentiation of some new trusts, the creation of others, and the profound modifications caused by a novel and shifting environment. Yet more interesting is it to detect among these phenomena the sudden rise and triumph of a revolt against the universal sway and preponderance of the small magistracy, and the subsequent gradual but firm tendency towards conformity with the local usages of the Connecticut Colony, until the result was assured by the Union of 1664.

The tribunal of last resort, of supreme sovereignty, was the assembly of burgesses, of enfranchised church-members, the New Haven Town-Meeting. The different manifestations of this authority bore to each other a relative proportion which underwent some change at the formation of a colonial government in 1643. Prior to that time, although the territorial circumference of New Haven was continually receding from its centre, the whole domain belonged to the village at Quinnipiac, and was ruled by the magistrates and freemen of that hamlet.

The sessions of the New Haven General Court, as the Town-Meeting was then called, were convened by the marshal's warning at the command of the magistrate. The stated assembly upon the last Wednesday in October for the election of all officers, and also of constables or magistrates for the dependent settlements, was denominated "A Generall Court of Elections," or, more briefly, "A Generall Court."[1] By the latter title also were designated meetings specially warned to consider matters of unusual moment. All free planters and burgesses were expected to attend these courts, but the burgesses alone could share in the legislative transactions.

---

[1] The time for the General Court of Elections was changed to May in 1646.

Half-legislative, half-judicial was the monthly court of the magistrate and his four assistants. This court, which generally sat at the beginning of each month, was described in the records merely as "A Court held at New Haven." It took cognizance of any matters that seemed to Magistrate Eaton suitable for immediate decision without recourse to the whole body of freemen. Its jurisdiction was, therefore, indefinable. It sent drunkards to the whipping-post as a police court; registered wills and administered estates as a probate court; decided civil suits as a superior court, and established a watch, or created a new town-office, as a monthly legislature. These various courts differed from each other, during the first year or two, more in degree than in kind. Perhaps it might be said that at the monthly courts there were no elections. The first judgment from this court was a death-sentence. The procedure involved no inconsiderable stretch of sovereignty, and could be justified only by the exigencies of border-life. A Pequot Indian named Nepaupuck, who during the recent war had assisted in killing several Englishmen at Weathersfield, a town under. Connecticut's jurisdiction, came into New Haven. It was the 25th of October, 1639, the day after the organization of the State. Magistrate Eaton lodged with the marshal a warrant to "apprehend and pinion" the murderer. It appears that stocks were already in existence, for Nepaupuck was secured in them after a rescue had been vainly essayed by his friends. "And the Indian who had attempted his escape was whipped by the marshal his deputy"; although there is no trace of any legal authority for the proceeding. Probably the mere word of a magistrate was then deemed sufficient justification for the flogging of a bad Indian. After a two days' trial the court sentenced the Pequot, "according to the rule in that case, he thatt sheds man's blood, by man shall his blood be shed"; but he was suffered to choose the mode of his own execution. Accordingly, his head was cut off and "pittched upon a pole in the markett-place"—the earliest adornment of the New Haven Green.

So long as Mr. Eaton lived to preside in the Monthly Court, his tone toward the people before him was paternal rather than official. The whole town was his family, and like an Arab patriarch, or a Russian village-elder, he sat to decide the quarrels of his children. Hannah Marsh invoked the protection of the court against Mr. Brewster, who had called her a " Billingsgate slutt." That term was probably not familiar to the ears of Mr. Davenport's congregation, so the Governor proceeded to define the " ordynary acceptation of ' Billingsgate slutt '—namely, that some that were soe called were convicted scolds, and punished at the cuckeing-stoole for it, and some of them were chardged with incontinency."

After examination, wherein it appeared that the words were hastily and angrily spoken, and wherein also Mr. Brewster failed to sustain his aspersions upon Hannah's moral character except by hearsay evidence, the court administered a severe rebuke impartially to both parties. " Mr. Brewster said that he was sorry for his rash speaking." The court reproved Hannah Marsh for her froward disposition, " remembring her that meeknes is a choyse ornament for weomen, and wished her to take it as a rebucke from God, and to keep a better watch over her sperit hereafter, least the Lord proceed to manifest His displeasure further agaynst her." Mistress Marsh, as befitted her station, was even more overcome than Mr. Brewster had been. She said that her frowardnes had been troublesome to herself, and " she hoped it should be a warninge to her for time to come." Mr. Eaton was prolific of these little sermons, and his counsel was invariably received with expressions of humility. No other layman in any of the New England colonies filled a position so unique, with a personal influence so preponderating. His paternal power was carefully fostered and sustained. When the four deputies were chosen in the autumn of 1642, they were expressly told that they might assist the court by way of advice, but should have no power of sentencing. They were to be merely counselors to the

magistrate.   From 1641 to 1645, they retained even this
shadowy authority for only six months at a time, but after
the latter year they were, like other officers, elected annually.
But Mr. Eaton was not left to guide the helm entirely alone.
No limit was set to the possible number of magistrates.   In
the fall election of 1641, Mr. Stephen Goodyear, an enterprising merchant, was made his colleague, and the two men
continued in the chief magistracy of the town, and afterward
of the colony, until 1657, the year of Eaton's death and of
Goodyear's departure.   The only legal chart by which the
magistrates could shape their course was the law of the
Freemen's Fundamental Agreement—that "the judicial lawes
of God, as they were delivered by Moses and expounded in
other parts of Scripture, so farr as they are a fence to the
morrall law, and neither tipicall nor ceremoniall, nor had
refference to Canaan, shallbe accounted morrall and binding
equity and force, and, as God shall helpe, shalbe a constant
direction for all proceedings here, and a gennerall rule in all
courts of justice, how to judge betwixt partic and partic, and
how to punish offenders—till the same may be branched out
into perticulers hereafter."[1]

When New Haven acquired a colonial hegemony, the
position of its magistrates and burgesses was elevated rather
than lowered, although the town's territory was diminished
and its authority correspondingly shorn away.   In the
General Court of Elections New Haven's two deputies were,
in theory, only the equals of the representatives for each of
the five other towns.   But the rank and influence of the New
Haven General Court were materially enhanced when a group
of plantations hailed New Haven as "The Capital."   The
Town-Court, indeed, formed the nucleus of the new government, and furnished it with its most substantial names.
There seems to have been a lack of close distinction between
the powers of a general court for the town and those of a
court for the jurisdiction.   In May and June, 1644, when

---

[1] Records, I. 101.

an Indian outbreak was anticipated, the New Haven Town-Meeting did not hesitate to appoint a council of war for the jurisdiction. Even in the autumn of 1643, just after the colonial confederation had taken place, it appears to have been the New Haven General Court alone that dispatched a military contingent to the assistance of Uncas, and that concluded the terms of combination with the erring sister, Milford. That town, during its short career of independence, had made a breach in the walls of Zion by admitting to the freeman's privileges six planters who were not church-members. To remedy this defect a treaty of five articles was drawn up by the deputies of Milford and by Governor Eaton—to wit: that

"First. In the name of both the church and towne of Milford, it is offered that the six burgesses shall nott att any time hereafter be chosen either deputyes or into any publique trust for the combination;

"Secondly. They shall neither in person, nor by proxi, vote in the election of magistrates;

"Thirdly. None shall be admitted free burgesses hereafter att Milforde butt church-members, according to the practice att New Haven;

"Fourthly. The said six freemen may continue to act in all the towne busines wherein combination is nott interressed;

"Fifthly. They may vote in the election of deputyes to the General Courts for the jurisdiction, which deputyes shall allwayes be church-members."

These stipulations being submitted to the New Haven Court, the last two especially were "seriously considered by the whole Court." "The brethren did express themselves as one man, thatt in the foundations layde for civill government they have attended their light," and they resolved not to "shake the said groundworks by any change in any respect." However, it was probably not forgotten that Connecticut stood near by with open arms; and compromise prevailed.[1]

---

[1] Records, I. 111.

"Nott foreseeing any danger in yielding to Milforde, with
the forementioned cautions, itt was, by gennerall consent and
vote, ordered that the CONSOCIATION proceed in all things
according to the premises."

One considerable right the Town-Court had lost by the
change. It could no longer choose the magistrates for its
own town and the subject towns. Such selections were made
by the Legislature for the jurisdiction out of a list of nominees sent from each town. Henceforth there were usually
at least four magistrates within the bounds of New Haven.
Attendance of all planters and freemen at meetings of the
town was strictly required, and account of absences and
tardinesses was kept, as in modern public schools.

Around Magistrate Eaton's monthly Plantation Court the
trammels of a higher law were, after 1643, more securely
thrown, and the changes in its nature were almost radical.
It was now more frequently called, after the fashion in
neighboring colonies, "The Particular Court." It was ordered
to sit every first "Third Day," or Tuesday, of each month
at nine o'clock in the morning. It was given cognizance of
all civil causes involving no more than twenty pounds, and of
any criminal causes "When the punishment by Scripture
Light exceeds not stocking and whipping, or a fine of not
more than five pounds." But in the *personnel* of the Bench
the greatest alteration for the better had taken place. The
four assistants were now elected judges, equal in power with
the presiding magistrate or magistrates.[1] All the magistrates
in town were entitled to sit with the court if they wished.
A verdict was obtained by a majority vote of the court, ties
being broken by a casting vote in the hands of the Governor,
or of the Deputy-Governor, or of the magistrates who were
present. Appeals from the decision lay to the court of
magistrates for the jurisdiction. Sensible progress had been
made from the earlier custom of according to the deputies the

---

[1] Eaton's Code (1656) provides that the freemen shall choose at least two,
at most four, deputies to the Plantation Courts.—Records, II. 570.

powers of an Advisory Board only. The new law, although it by no means introduced methods of trial by jury, was the first step toward popularization of the courts, toward the advent of greater democracy. At all events it opposed the idea of a one-man power, even upon the bench. The acquittal or condemnation of a criminal by a majority of one in a total of eight or nine votes, and the yearly election of judges, might now be deemed objectionable; yet such was the conservatism of those days of a pure Civil Service that an incumbent was rarely displaced by any power save that of death. The proposal that a body of experienced judges shall supplant the institutions of judge and jury in our higher courts is an innovation that does not lack support to-day. In small and great circles alike does history repeat itself. Such a judicial body would be a clumsy device in a modern city court, and would block, not accelerate, the faithful performance of duty; but the Particular Court of 1643 was relatively a higher tribunal than the City Court of the present time, higher in dignity and the comparative scope of its powers. By Eaton's Code the Plantation Court, which comprised three magistrates, might try any civil cause, and any criminal case which did not involve the death-penalty. At the same time the germ of a police or justice's-court jurisdiction was enveloped in the ability of the deputies, in the absence of a magistrate, to cause the arrest of any malefactor or "suspitious person," and the retention of such persons upon probable cause until the full court should sit. Accordingly, in 1644, the Colonial Legislature voted that the free burgesses of Guilford might elect four deputies and temporarily form a court without a magistrate. The admission of the deputies to judicial power was not accomplished without hindrance in some portions of the colony, as at Stamford.[1]

Naturally the great mass of actions brought before the Particular Court pertained to criminals and to disputed properties. But one class of subjects which often demanded

---

[1] Records, I. 130.

adjudication, and which was characteristic of that day, was the elaborate system of fines, a fruitful source of vexation on the one hand and of revenue on the other. There were fines for absence or lateness at the Meeting, at the Watch, at the Training, and at the General Court. These fines, if unpaid, were ordered and recorded in the Plantation Court. The Town Clerk, the "Clarke of the trained-band," and the Master of the Watch, probably reported delinquents in their respective departments, but for the services in the meeting-house there must have been a sort of monitorial force; perhaps the Deacons performed the labor of supervising the flock. The amounts of the different fines were fixed by law, but varied within the limits at the discretion of the court, or, as Mr. Eaton said, "according to the nature of the sinn, or offence." The maximum penalty for absence from meeting on Lord's days, fasts and Thanksgiving-days, from training, etc., was usually maintained at five shillings, but two shillings were considered a heavy fine.[1] Disregard of the religious ordinances, however, was punished by more than pecuniary inflictions. Suitable discriminations were made between the obligations of the various classes in the community. The General Court of November 7, 1642, voted that any freeman who, after due warning, should fail to appear in the General Courts before the Secretary finished the roll-call, should be fined 1s. 6d.; and that any of the rest of the planters who should be absent after their names were read, should be fined one shilling. The novelty of the first few years had worn away, and attendance at the General Courts seemed, to many, burdensome.

The town was thus assembled half a score of times in the course of a year, and so numerous sessions would be thought irksome now. The fathers were not slow-witted in the invention of pretexts and excuses. Some of them hit upon the

---

[1] Officers were generally mulcted in double the fine of an ordinary citizen. So the law read, and accordingly we find that, December 4, 1644, two Masters of the Watch were each fined ten shillings for neglecting the watch.

obvious plan of staying in the court until after the calling of
the roll, and then departing. It was necessary to prohibit
this under pain of fines in February, 1645. Subsequently
those who desired to be excused from staying sought, and
usually obtained without difficulty, permission from the court
to leave the meeting.

Sometimes the General Court itself took immediate cognizance of absentees and late-comers, as on the 30th of November,
1648, when "Mathew Camfield came late, but the court past
it by, because he was forced to goe looke after some catle."
But most of the derelictions were accounted for in the
Plantation Court, and the magistrate did not often harden
his heart against excuses. A straying cow, inability to hear
the drum, or sickness in the family were apologies usually
powerful enough to parry the blow of punishment. Careless-
ness concerning sanctuary privileges was the only short-
coming that could not hope for absolution.

THE QUARTERS.

Primitive New Haven was an exceptional exponent of
whatever truth there may be in the atomic theory of state-
formation. After town-colonies had gone forth to the right
hand and to the left, the principle of segregation was still
further active among the quarters—the squares into which
the town-plot was divided. One square had been allotted to
Yorkshiremen, another to men of Herefordshire, while Kent-
ishmen and Londoners occupied the remaining sections.
This preservation within the village of former geographical
distinctions nourished the tendency toward minute forms of
local self-government. Therefore the quarters began to
figure as rudimentary political units; the germs, perhaps, of
city-wards, if the fantastic dreams of the founders might
have been realized in a flourishing metropolis.[1] The

---

[1] The impression would be natural that the word "Quarter" was used
solely with reference to the sections of the square town-plot. But there is

institution of a sort of neighborhood class-meeting in each quarter, for prayer and personal testimony, attested the feeling of religious unity. To the quarters, also, the out-land was primarily allotted, and the inhabitants of each square assembled by themselves to determine the manner and means of division in severalty. Some of the common lands were held as the common property of a quarter, and the dwellers within the quarter met from time to time to decide the uses of such commonage. In 1655 the Suburbs Quarter, as a body, asked the town's permission to lease some of their out-land to the Indians for planting. The court refused to grant the request. A few years later, when fears of Indian warfare had subsided, some of the other squares were allowed to make a similar disposal of their common property, to the evident displeasure of the Suburbs Quarter.[1] The practice continued in vogue until the time of King Philip's War. In 1665, indeed, no little scandal arose in town and there was discussion in the Town-Meeting, because some " Indians worked on their lands *in the quarters* upon the Sabbath-day." Moreover, the inhabitants of the quarters were, in a small degree, constituent bodies. For a long time each quarter elected directly officers who exercised supervision over faulty fences and

---

reason to suppose that in 1640 " The Quarter " had a meaning entirely distinct from the mathematical signification of the term. It should be remembered that there were nine quarters, and that one of them, the " Suburbs Quarter," had neither regular shape nor position in the town-plot. In Worsley's *History of the Isle of Wight*, p. 210, is an account, dated 1574, of a lease of a church-house by inhabitants of Whitwell to a certain John Brode, " provided always that if the Quarter (township) shall need at any time to make a Quarter-Ale or Church-Ale for the maintenance of the chapel that it shall be lawful for them to have the use of said house, with all the rooms both above and beneath, during the Ale." (Quoted in Toulmin Smith's *Parish*, p. 497.) So the " Herefordshire Quarter " and the " Suburbs Quarter," in New Haven, may have been equivalent to " Herefordshire Township " and the " Suburbs Township."

[1] N. H. T. Records, II. 225, III. 194; see also II. 384: " At a Town-Meeting, April, 1659. After viewing armes, liberty was given to let lands to Indians for planting in the quarters, the Suburbs Quarter excepted, since many of the proprietors there objected."

straying animals. Through the first century of colonial existence, probably not even "strong watters" caused the authorities more trouble than did the neglected fences. Great unanimity was displayed in making laws concerning the oversight of fences, and there was equal accord in breaking both laws and fences. Pasture seems to have been scarce, and it doubtless made a difference whose ox was gored. In 1644, after the plantation had been "much exercised with hoggs distroying of corne," the General Court ordered that each quarter should appoint its own fence-viewers. In 1647 the municipal ordinance which created the office of "Hayward" proposed that "each hayward shall be payde by the severall quarters which imploye them, as they shall agree." The court assented to the motion, "and it was agreed to movte in the severall quarters to put it in execution." At the same time, and in the same connection, a by-law was passed which lent a certain constitutional dignity to the quarter-moots. "If the quarters have seasonable warning of a meeting, and if any come nott, yett the major part maye agree any course for the good of the quarter, provided it crosses no order of the Courte allreadie made."[1] Again, in the autumn of 1648, "the putting-in catle into ye severall quarters is left to themselves to order." In 1649 the quarter-meetings were ordered to adopt marks for their fences so that the viewers might know each man's portion, a curious attempt to extend the principle of ear-marks for cattle.[2] Although the selection of these officers finally passed under the direct control of the General Court, yet down to the time of the Revolution, fence-viewers, elected in Town-Meeting, were said to be chosen for this or that quarter, some of the district-nomenclature being still the same that it had been in 1640. Even the first grand-list valuation in 1651 was made by officers of the quarters.[3] As population relatively

---

[1] Records, I. 366.
[2] Records, I. 26, 40, 126.
[3] New Haven Town Records, II. 76.

decreased, and as poverty came in like an armed man, the quarters lost their separate importance. The townsfolk forgot locality and lineage, lost sight of the fancy of a city and drew closer together into a compact hamlet.

THE MILITARY ORGANIZATION.

Necessity's first requirement of the newly-founded state was the provision of adequate and organized means of defense. It was foreordained in the nature of things that the settlers of New England must realize to the full their membership in the church militant. The Miles Standish of New Haven was Captain Nathaniel Turner. He had joined the colony in Massachusetts, probably with the understanding that he should use for the defense of the new settlement the experience gained in the Pequot War. The martial organization was doubtless effected provisionally, shortly after the landing at Quinnipiac, and thus preceded the foundation of the state. The little army marches in complete array at once into historic view. In Old England the duty of viewing armor had pertained to the office of constable. In New Haven, the captain properly relieved the marshal or constable of such labor.[1] The order was made November 25, 1639, "Thatt every one thatt beares armes" [that is, all males between sixteen and sixty years of age, if not exempted by office in Church or State] "shall be compleatly furnished with armes—viz.: a muskett, a sworde, bandaleers, a rest, a pound of powder, 20 bulletts fitted to their muskett, or four pounds of pistoll shott or swan shott att least, and be ready to show them in the Markett Place, upon Munday the 16th of this (?) moneth, before Captaine Turner and Leivtennant Seely, under penalty of twenty shillings fine for default or absence."[2] The first intention

---

[1] Johns Hopkins University Studies in History and Political Science, I. viii. 16–21. See Dr. Adams' article on "Norman Constables in America." Miles Standish's authority was more unlimited and unregulated than Captain Turner's. [2] Records, I. 40.

was that such general trainings should occur monthly, and should be accompanied in every alternate month by a view of armor; also, that the squadrons in rotation should profit by a weekly exercise. But relaxation soon set in, and finally it was determined that the general trainings should take place at least six times between March and November, a "strict view" at least once in a quarter, and squadron trainings midway between the general training days. The enforcement of a detailed schedule of fines for various degrees of lateness, absence, and defective equipments heaped up the pence and wampum in the town-treasury.

Captain Turner was not formally chosen to his office until the first day of September, 1640—the same day in which the settlement was christened "New Haven." The Captain was "empowered with the command and ordering of watches, the exercising and trayning of souldiers, and whatsoever of like nature might be needful." Two years later, in August, the official roster was completed by the choice of four corporals, four sergeants, and an "Ancient," and Marshall Seely was confirmed as Lieutenant. In the following month the Captain and Lieutenant were authorized to raise a general hue and cry in case of an expedition against Indians, and no man could refuse the summons to go, though "itt should be to the extreme hazard of his life." "If any shall refuse, the magistrate is to presse him to goe, whether he will or no."

Another reproduction of a time-honored English institution was the Town-Armor. Although every man was required to provide himself with accoutrements, the town was the possessor of certain weapons of war, principally pikes, as early as 1642. But in the General Court's order of November 13, 1643, there is a suggestion of a sort of Town-Armor, such as might be suitable for the seventeenth century. The soldiers expected to go forth soon to battle with Dutch and Indians, and for a protection of English

---

[1] After much fluctuation, the fines for absence or tardiness were fixed at 5s. and 1s. respectively, but the court invariably used its discretion.

ribs from Indian arrows, "itt is ordered thatt every famyly within this plantation shall have a coate of cotton-woole, well and substantially made, so as itt may be fitt for service, and that in convenient time the taylours see itt be done." The coats were made and deposited with the town authorities. In the next generation the Town-Meeting voted that the townsmen should sell these garments for whatever they might bring.[1] That miner of institutional lore, Toulmin Smith, informs us that not only was every man in England bound to have sufficient arms (every weapon was formerly called "armour"), but every parish (town) was bound to have and to keep ready for use a certain amount of armor as its quota towards the national defense.[2] In 1645 the General Court of the town ordered "thatt a chist be made for the pikes, and the great guns putt in readynes forthwith." It is likely that New Haven had already furnished what a later colonial law required of every plantation—viz.: "A partison for its lieutenant, cullars for its ensigne, halberts for its serjants, with drums and pikes." The meeting-house was the arsenal for material as well as spiritual weapons. The chest which held the "Town-pyks" was under the consecrated roof, and as early as September 17, 1642, the court ordered that "when any allarum is made upon the approach of any enemy, every souldier in the towne shall repair to the meeting-house forthwith."[3]

From time immemorial Englishmen have converted days

---

[1] March 11, 1674. New Haven Town Records, III. 176.

[2] Smith quotes from the town records of Kingston-upon-Thames under date of 1598: "To them that wore the town-armour two days, at 8d. a daye—7s." Again, under date of 1603 : "To James Allison and four others for carrying the armour at the coronation, 13s. 4d." (p. 518.) But the general condition of English Town-armor at this time may be inferred from Shakspeare's description of Petruchio's beggarly outfit, which included "an old rusty sword taken out of the Town-Armoury, with a broken hilt, and chapeless." (Taming of the Shrew, Act III. Scene II.)

[3] Records, II. 174. So Toulmin Smith says of the English parish : "In country-places the Town-Armour was kept in the church for security" (p. 518).

for military practice into holiday seasons, and Puritan New Haven was no exception to the rule. Yet it may seem startling that the severe dignity of the court should have lent its official countenance to the offer of a "prise of not more than 5 shillings value for shooting at a marke, three times in a yeare . . . for the incouragement of souldiours in their military exercise." Each town in the jurisdiction was commanded to see that "the souldiours have a good pair of hilts to play at cudgels with, that they exercise themselves in playing at backsword, that they learne how to handle their weapons for the defence of themselves and the offenc of their enemies; and that, in time of their vacancy, they doe exercise themselves in running, wrastling, leaping and the like manly exercises." But this intimated a possible indulgence in unmilitary and unseemly levity. The line must be drawn somewhere, and the General Court drew it at "stoolebale, nine-pines, and quaites." "Such like games are forbidden until the millitary exercise of the day be finished and the company dismissd." Neither the physical nor the spiritual equipment of the New Haven militia was slighted. "The deputies of each plantation must speak to the teaching-elders there to take some fitt opportunities to speak to the souldiours something by way of exhortation to quicken them to a conscieucious attendanc to their duty." It was the happy lot of this carefully-disciplined little regiment that it was not called upon to fire a musket except in defense of other colonies and against distant foes.

The Watch.

The martial organization of the town was rounded out in the spring of 1640 by the establishment of a watch for service in the night and upon days of worship. This, the first police force of New Haven, was regarded as a part of the military, and was under the immediate oversight of the captain. It was so divided that the men of the plantation watched in turn from March to October yearly. Each night-guard was composed of six men and a master of the watch. In 1642 there were in all thirty-one separate watches, comprising two hundred and seventeen men. Every night at sundown the drum was beaten, and within half an hour the master of the watch must be "att the Court of guarde," which stood on the Green. Disorders were forefended by a provision that in forming the membership of each watch, "young and less satisfying persons shall be joyned with another more antient and trusty."[1] That such precautions were needed to prevent light-minded behavior appeared a dozen years later when the watch had become an established village-institution. The watch-house was found to be convenient for loafing and gossip, insomuch that the court was constrained to prohibit any from "sitting with the watch as it had been a custome to doe, whereby they idle away their time." Watching through the night after a hard day's work was undoubtedly a most onerous task for the pioneers in the wilderness. In the hot summer time some drowsiness might be expected. Therefore the suspicion of Dogberry's gentle rule can hardly lurk about the proclamation in August, 1642: "Itt is ordered by the court that, from henceforwarde, none of the watchmen shall have liberty to sleep during the watch." In 1646, in the early autumn, "Mr. William Tuttle and Jeremy Watts are complayned off for sleeping at the watch-howse." Tuttle said he was overcome and sat down on the threshold and slept, while Jeremy was sentinel; but he contritely confessed that he had done wrong, and hoped that it might be for the last time. "Mr. Tutle was fined 2s. 6d., and Jeremy Watts was fined five shillings, yᵉ court desiring it may bee a warning to them both." Several years afterward there was a violent scandal and a profuse outpouring of slander suits, because a certain late-stroller, named Sam Hodgkins, who had himself been fined for sleeping on his watch, had not only found the sentinel asleep, but had looked

---

[1] New Haven Town Records, II. 31.

into the watch-house and discovered the master asleep in his chair and the men wrapped in slumber on the floor and "snortinge." A month later the disquiet was allayed and everybody apparently soothed, but some one kept a watch upon Hodgkins. Erelong the tables were completely turned, and the prying Hodgkins was haled before the court to receive reproof, "because he attendeth not Ordinances upon the Saboth dayes, but, it is said, stayeth at home and sleepeth away his time."

The Sunday watch in and around the meeting-house fell, as in other colonies, to the lot of the town-militia. The first order concerning it was issued September 1, 1640: "Every man that is appointed to watch, whether Masters or servants, shall come every Lord's-Day to the meeting compleatly armed, and all others also are to bring their swords, no man exempted save Mr. Eaton, Our Pastor, Mr. James, Mr. Samuell Eaton, and the two Deacons."[1] After 1643 the squadrons of the trained-band took turns in this guard-service; and in the allotment of seats in the meeting-house, convenient seats were reserved for the soldiers.[2] In 1646 an effort was made to secure thirty-two "planters, householders and sojourners," who would bring their arms constantly and sit in the soldiers' seats, "at all publicque meetings for the worship of God." The endeavor seems to have been unsuccessful. The squadrons continued to present themselves at the sanctuary, and a few of them were deputed to walk the rounds of the town, while one sentinel mounted into the tower.[3] This more active detachment were supposed to keep the matches continually lighted during service, if matchlock guns were used, though such enactments were probably more frequently honored in the breach than in the observance. The whole company was required to be at the

---

[1] Matthew Gilbert and Robert Newman.

[2] Records, I. 119.

[3] Probably after the first few years the outlook from the tower was discontinued, except in times of danger, as in 1649. Records, I. 468.

post of duty within half an hour after the first beating of the drum, with guns ready charged, with match for their matchlocks and flints ready fitted to their firelocks, and with six rounds of ammunition, under penalty of a two-shilling fine for negligence, and of a one-shilling fine for tardiness.[1] The soldiers' benches were popular seats in the primitive New Haven meeting-house. Their stalwart occupants in all the glory of warlike gear doubtless caused thrills of emulous ambition in the souls of the young Wigglesworths, and emotions of a gentler passion in the bosoms of the sisters. There seemed to be also a sense of immunity pertaining to the soldiers' seat that resembled the modern privilege of worldliness overhanging the choir-gallery. But the irreverent songsters of to-day stand in no danger of such Sinaïtic terrors of a monthly Plantation Court, as lay in wait for lightminded listeners in the congregations of 1640. The assertion must be hazarded that no fun in our sanctuaries ventures often to be so furious as that which the walls of the first New Haven meeting-house contained. The General Court of June 16, 1662, hearkened to, and Secretary Gibbard wrote down the story of a most grievous disturbance in the soldiers' seat on the recent Fast Day. One son of Mars had enlivened the service by throwing lumps of lime at another, in return for which the latter with great agility kicked his tormentor. It was also reported from another source that " Mrs. Goodyear's Boy had his head broke that day in meeting, on account of all which a woman said that she doubted the wrath of God would be brought upon us."[2] Previous uncomely behavior by the soldiers upon Lord's days was alleged, and the offenders were ferreted out and punished. These incidents scattered here and there in the records convince us that human nature changes slowly, if at all, and that the popular

---

[1] July 7, 1640, John Morse was fined ten shillings because he shirked his duty of walking the rounds on the Lord's day, but stayed in the meeting-house instead.

[2] N. H. T. Records, II. 437.

idea of a Puritan conventicle deserves modification. Whenever an Indian outbreak was feared the watch was kept with strict fidelity, and even day-watches were maintained; but at other times the laws were loosely interpreted. Due allowance was made for stress of weather. September 2, 1651, the Town Clerk wrote: "The last Lord's-Day at night was so tempestious with winde and raine that the watch could not be carried on."

That the watches and the trainings were esteemed burlensome is testified not only by the number of fines inflicted, but also by the general endeavor to find some pretext as an excuse from serving at all. As a rule, the officers of Church and State were exempted at the outset, but the town-drummer, Robert Basset, who was a black sheep in the flock, could not obtain the coveted freedom from watching until 1649, and even then only through the intercession of Lieutenant Seely. Families living upon farms were allowed to keep one man at home upon training-days, for the sake of safety. If the farmer owned a house-lot in the town-plot he must under any circumstances furnish a man for the watch. Most of the traders gained exemption upon one plea or another, until the undistinguished crowd who were obliged to maintain the watch began to feel themselves abused and to charge the General Court with favoritism. The petition of the ship-carpenters for exemption was finally the impelling cause of an appeal from the court to Governor Winthrop of Massachusetts for advice and for information of the customs there. Winthrop's answer was dated July 14, 1648,[1] and the court accepted it, with slight alterations, as the law of the town of New Haven. Thereby the persons excused from "trayning, watching and warding" were "Magistrates, elders of churches, deacons, deputies, all professed schoolemasters, physitians and surgeons allowed by authority in any of these plantations, the treasurer, officers of the courts and of the military also, as Captains, Leivtennants and Ensignes, mas-

---

[1] Records, I. 464.

ters of shipps and of other vessells above 15 tunn and upward, servants at remote farmes without y° two mile, millers, and such as are discharged for bodily infirmity. But sonns and servants are not freed, except one sonn or one servant to every magistrate and teaching-elder. Seamen and shipp-carpenters must watch as others doe, and trayne twice a yeare. Yet all these persons must have compleat armes in their houses except magistrates and teaching-elders." Under compulsion of circumstances these rules could be temporarily abrogated, as in the perilous days of 1653, when the town voted that "during these hurries and disturbances, none shall be freed from watching except magistrates, elders, and military officers."

In 1644–45, an auxiliary company of artillery was organized. There is a familiar sound in the words: "The court, considering how necessary it is in time of peace to prepare for warre, do give liberty to the company to manage its owne affairs, always providing that it does not trespass against the fundamental agreement." This proviso was a stumbling-block to some of the other towns in the colony, where it occasionally happened that all the church-members were, presumably, more familiar with the Articles of Faith than with the manual of arms, while some of the non-freemen possessed better qualifications for military leadership. The New Haven municipality was never reduced to such extremities and did not unbend the bow by the breadth of a hair; but, in certain other places, the Colonial Legislature was obliged to permit the line to be slackened. The incompatibility of the fundamental law with the highest degree of military efficiency was one prime cause of the disaffection for New Haven's rule that was sporadically exhibited. The town of Southold was especially troublesome. In 1654, there were reports of open rebellion there. One Charles Glover, who was not a freeman, had been chosen lieutenant; and, finding himself in conflict with New Haven law, refused to act further, thus preventing for a time any military practice.

The Jurisdiction Court voted that, inasmuch as the said Glover was understood to have letters of recommendation from the church at Salem, he might assume military command at Southold, "provided that he take the oath of fidellite to be faithfull of the Jurisdiction." But in the next year the court agreed that " If, in any plantation in this Jurisdiction, there be none among the freemen fit for a cheife millitary officer, it shall be in the power of the Generall Court to chuse some other man, as they shall judge fitt, in whom they may confide."[1]

This action was revolutionary, and the fact that Eaton and Davenport were compelled to contemplate such a departure from principle is sufficiently noteworthy. In 1661, in the anxious days of the Restoration, the trumpet emitted a surer tone : " We cannot be perswaded to commit our more weighty civill or military trusts into the hands of either a crafty Achitopell or a bloody Joab, as some abusive medlers do seem to hint unto us in a paper we met withall, though such should seem to be better accomplished with either naturall or acquired abilities above those that are as well lawful as intitled freemen. All planters should come in by the door to enjoy all privileges, and there may be noe disorderly or uncomely attempts to climb up another way."

Captain Turner's absence at Delaware, and his early death in Lamberton's fated "shippe," rendered his captaincy of but little avail to New Haven. The office remained for a long time in abeyance, and a curious glimpse of quaint Puritan character is afforded by the events attending the election of Turner's successor. In 1661, it was proposed in the Town-Court to elect Lieutenant John Nash to the captainship. Whereupon Lieutenant Nash, with much modesty and relnctance, declared that he could not feel a " call of God to that

---

[1] Records, II. 92–98, 109, 145, 177, 404. In the same year Thomas Stevens, of Guilford, was chosen corporal under condition that he proceed no higher in office, because he was not a freeman.

place," that he was entirely unworthy of such dignity, and desired to abase himself. After remonstrances upon either side, "the matter was respited until another time."

Lieutenant Nash then thanked the town for sparing him, and said: "If God shall persuade my heart of his call to this work, I shall be willing to do the town service." At the same time Mr. Wm. Gibbard refused the magistracy in almost identical terms. More than a year passed before Lieutenant Nash could be persuaded to hear his "call." The diffidence of these gentlemen does not look so abnormal when it is connected with the fears of a restored Stuart, of punishment for hiding the judges, and of Winthrop's coming Charter; yet it bears an unwonted and pleasing aspect in these Tammany times.

For a few years prior to the dissolution of the colony, the town maintained a small cavalry troop, whose equipments figure prominently at the close of the second volume of the "Records" in the list of "Town Goods" under the care of the townsmen. After the Union of 1664 the New Haven militia was no longer responsible to the Town-Meeting; the watch fell into desuetude and was revived only by the apprehension of some peril, as during the temporary occupation of New York by the Dutch in 1673, and during King Philip's War.

THE MARSHAL.

The development of the military service suggests the riot-quelling, peace-preserving offices of the marshal. The connection was all the closer in this community because that functionary was also for some time lieutenant of the Town-Army. Three years elapsed before the indefinite promise, made at the outset, of an enlargement of duties was fulfilled. Then it was found convenient to convert his house into a place of deposit: "Oct. 26th, 1642. Itt is ordered thatt whosoever findes any things thatt are lost shall deliver them to the marshall, to be kept safe till the owners challeng them."[1] There was such a large assortment of whippings, finings and summonses that Marshal Seely probably remonstrated against serving as the other officers did, for honor only. Beginning with January, 1643, the marshal's fees from plaintiffs were—for serving a warrant, fourpence; for serving an "attachment," sixpence. Every one warned to the General Court for transgressing its order must pay to the marshal fourpence. Moreover, every unfortunate who was compelled to live behind bolts and bars must pay the marshal, for turning the key, one shilling.[2]

After the formation of a colonial government, the New Haven town-marshal was invariably marshal of the jurisdiction also, and his increased dignities were deemed worthy of a stated salary. This remuneration was fixed in 1644 at three pounds per annum. In the following summer his duty as custodian of unclaimed articles became more lucrative. "The marshall is to cry all lost things that are brought to him to keep, on the lecture-dayes and faire-dayes, and to have one penny for every cry of the partys who shall challeng the things cryed." Of such articles he was enjoined to keep account in a "paper booke," and, if necessary, to cry them twice on lecture-days and for a third time at the fair, "when the greatest concourse of people may be present and hear it."[3] The office of Town-Crier, however, was soon after differentiated from the marshalship. In the spring of 1645, it occurred to some that the severe authority of the marshal might spur delinquent fence-owners to the performance of duty. Many committees had been in vain appointed to view fences, and to deal with the inattentive. In April, after the court had listened to the story of the destruction of a dozen

---

[1] Records, I. 79, 144, 215.

[2] In the Colony of Connecticut the marshal was employed in civil suits; the constables in criminal cases.

[3] The two annual town fairs, one in May, the other in September, were instituted by order of the court in 1644, and discontinued in 1656. This was another limitation of ancestral custom. The traditional features of English fairs were doubtless lacking.

bushels of corn by "hoggs," it was decided that the marshal should warn the guilty quarters to mend their ways and fences. In the following October he was made keeper of the hooks and hinges of the town-gates, "least they be lost." Probably as a measure of economy, the gates were detached through the winter—a custom among thrifty farmers everywhere. In December of the same year, it appeared that the marshal had been dealing with some refractory customers, for it was ordered that hereafter every plaintiff must pay marshal's fees before the writs were served. The only subsequent expansion of the sphere of the marshalship was caused by the partial inclusion therein of the duties usually allotted to tithing-men. The marshal and the military divided between them the services of ecclesiastical police. In 1650, the town voted that there should be a " two-shilling fine upon any one who stands or sits without the meeting-house in the time of the Ordinances without sufficient reason, and the corporalls are desired to goe out now and then to prevent such disorders."[1] Three years afterward, the marshal received what might be called " Letters of Marque," entitling him to seek out and seize all straying boys on the Sabbath and to bring them into church. These obligations upon the marshal and corporals conjointly were several times repeated and somewhat extended. For a few years also, the town-insane were kept at the house of the marshal, much against that officer's will.[2]

<h3 style="text-align:center">The Town Drummer.</h3>

In the absence of more convenient methods of calling people together and of ascertaining the time of day, the town-drummer was a prominent public servant. Inasmuch as his principal tasks at the outset were to give the signals for the summons or discharge of the watch, and to furnish music on training-days, he was regarded as a member of the military and police

---

[1] New Haven Town Records, II. 17.
[2] Records, I. 227, 414.

organizations. Therefore, in 1641, all those who had served in the watch were required to pay " Steven the drummer and Jarvis Boykin nine pence a-peece " for a year and a half's service. But it was the tap of the drum that invited freemen to the General Court, or to any public assembly, and, above all, that relentlessly summoned all the dwellers in Zion to the meeting-house on every Sunday and on lecture-days. The municipal character of such service was so apparent that, one year later, every planter was taxed for the support of the drumstick-wielder. By the spring of 1644, the drummer earned a yearly salary of £5, which was paid out of the town-treasury. This sum was nearly double the marshal's compensation. One year later, the drums were repaired at the town's expense, and £8 of the town's money was appropriated to Steven Medcalfe and Robert Bassett, in return for which " They shall attend all the townes occasions as common drummers for the towne till this time twelve moneths, and maintaine the drums att their owne charge in good plight, and leave them soe att the end of the tearme." In 1647, Robert Bassett shouldered the undivided responsibilities of the position. He was desired to beat the drum twice upon " Lord's-Dayes and Lecture-Dayes upon the meeting-house, that soe those who live farr off may hear them the more distinkly, and he promised soe to doe."[1] His daily task was to drum every evening at sunset, and every morning " halfe an hower before day in the market-place, and in some of the streets "; the last watch was ordered to call him one hour before day, and " to walke with him as a guard while he continewes beatinge." The beating of drums in the daytime for individual amusement was prohibited, lest men should fear an " alarum "—a restriction that may not have seemed so tyrannical to the juvenile generation of that day as it would in this. New Haven stepped to the music of drum-beats until 1681, when the first bell was procured for the use of church and town. However, the town-drummer was not at once entirely super-

---

[1] Records, I. 307, 311.

soded in his office of public herald. In 1686, the bell was sent in care of Mr. Simon Eyre to England for repairs, and it was voted that, three days before a Town-Meeting, "the drum should be beaten around the towne."[1]

Minor Offices, Roads, Fences, and Cattle.

As the years rolled on, the town developed a host of minor officials to offset the original simplicity of its administration. Goodman John Cooper, or Cowper, was distinguished as the first incumbent of a number of inferior trusts. To begin with, in 1643 he was duly confirmed by the New Haven Court in the position of public chimney-sweeper. Every chimney in town that was in continual use must be cleaned once a month in winter, and once in two months in summer. The fee was proportional to the height of the chimney. If any man preferred to do his own chimney-cleaning, and Brother Cooper should find that it was not well done, the latter might do the work over again and exact double pay. Moreover, every householder, under penalty of five shillings fine, was commanded to keep a ladder leaning against his house, of sufficient length to ensure instant access to any part of the roof or to the chimney. But this was intended not so much for Goodman Cooper's convenience as for a precaution against fire. As such it was enforced, as the record of fines proves. Brother Cooper, having borne his sooty honors faithfully for three years, was rewarded with additional dignities. The marshal was too busy to perform the duties of a Town-Crier, and it was ordered that "Bro. Cooper" should cry in the marshal's stead.[2] Brother Cooper seemed to have the true office-holding instinct, and made himself so generally useful that the court, in 1648, questioned

---

[1] New Haven Town Records, IV. 26.

[2] Cooper had two successors in this office. In 1683 the new Sign-Post seems to have superseded the Town-Crier. It served a century, and yielded in turn, but slowly, to the newspaper.

whether Goodman Cooper might not be a suitable person to relieve the town of its distressing perplexities with weak fences and straying cattle. Within a fortnight he was appointed to be the first "Publique Pownder" for the town. It was not intended that he should interfere in any way with the similar officers chosen by the quarters. He supplemented their labors. The first pounds were built—two of them—in 1643, and two Pound-keepers were chosen at the same time. Fence-viewers had been elected by the quarters since the following year. In 1647, also, the quarters had been commissioned to make choice of "Certaine men to be Haywards, each of whom should overlook a convenient compass of ground on every daye, and whoe should take and pound all the catle or hoggs they found there, mending any small defect in any fence, or acquainting the owner with any great breach." Cooper's position, as a sort of town superintendent only, emphasized the neighborhood character of the foregoing services. In addition to his other vocations, he must now spend "Two dayes in a weeke to view all ye fences, and pound catle and swine, and to tell every man whose fenc is defective one every weeke." For compensation he might have twopence on every acre of cornfield "within ye two-mile," and also "that he gitts for pounding catle beside." Brother Cooper made his new office no sinecure, and magnified it so much that he began to despise the humble business of a town chimney-cleaner. He notified the court that his successor in that department must be chosen, but the various town authorities were unable to make the selection. The effort was abandoned in 1658, when the "Townsmen informed the court that they could prevail upon no man to be chimney-sweeper."[1] In one winter Cooper summoned a large proportion of the town for defective fences, and the complaints and fines rained in at the Court-Meetings. But so many and so influential brethren were accused by him of remissness that the court, although encouraging him with compli-

---

[1] New Haven Town Records, II. 284.

ments, wiped out all charges and began anew with clean papers for everybody. Thus originated the first official predecessors of the New Haven Pound-keepers, Pounders, Fence-viewers, and Haywards of the present day.

The fences and roads are said to be unimpeachable witnesses to the degree of civilization among the inhabitants of the adjacent regions. New Haven's ideal of neatness was certainly high, in spite of the occasional inability to determine responsibility for defects, or of the hesitation in acknowledging it. Road surveyors were annually chosen after the autumn of 1644. They were authorized to impress both men and carts for the work of repairing. An attempt was made to create individual pride in the highways by commanding every man throughout the town to repair and maintain the road "before his homelott the breadth of two rodds." A few months later the order was revised so as to include even the footpaths.[1]

The result of all the lawmaking and fining ought to have been a Golden Age of highways perfected; but the improvement was very gradual, and the roads have been fruitful sources of complaint from that day to this. A serious obstacle to free communication and to transportation was the Quinnipiac River. Over the East River, as it was then called, lay the roads to the sister towns of Guilford and Branford, to the village and farms at Stony River or East Haven, and to the rival colony of Connecticut. Therefore, the summer of 1645 witnessed the beginning of the Public Ferryman's official existence. Francis Browne was appointed for one year to provide "A lardge and serviceable cannon or boate, and to attend itt every day from the rising of the sun to the going down of the same excepting Saboth dayes, and other times of solemne publique worship of God." In return for these services he was to have "a little house or shade made att the waterside to worke in," three acres of land in the Oystershell Field (commons), rent-free, and the following fees :

---

[1] Records, I. 148, 227, 231.

> " For not more than three persons   .   .   .   2d. apeece.
> "   between three and six   "   .   .   .   3ob.[1]   "
> "   more than six   "   .   .   .   1d.   "

Not the least agreeable concomitant of the office was exemption from training whenever the ferry demanded his services. This elevated him among the aristocracy. Complaints on account of his absence were entered against him at sundry times, but his plea of the " Ferry's Needs " was always accepted. The fees of the ferry were from time to time regulated by the Town-Court or Meeting, and the ferryman performed his humble but essential duties until after the Revolution, when the Fair Haven Bridges finally rendered his services superfluous.[2]

Supervisors.

The taste for supervising, which was in consonance with the Puritan character, amounted to a passion. It was felt that the State, "whose design is Religion," must permit nothing to remain hidden or unknown. Here was, perhaps, the origin of those traits of exceeding inquisitiveness which fame has attributed to the Yankee character. All appointees must feel a direct responsibility to the municipal power in Court or Town-Meeting. Thence must those also who were only in a secondary sense public servants derive their authority. Therefore, not only was it impossible, as we have seen, that any one should be at once an officer in both Church and State, but the Church was not suffered to choose its menial servants. It was the Town General Court of April, 1643, that formally elected " Sister Preston to sweepe and dresse the meeting-house every week, and to have 1s. for her painos." Four years later a similar court entrusted to Brother Preston the opening and shutting of the " Meeting-House dores." The care of the sanctuary was similarly disposed of by the

---

[1] Records, I. 165.   3 oboll = 1½d.
[2] The first one in 1784 ; the second (Tomlinson's) in 1796.

same authority,[1] until·in the following generation, under the "unhallowed rule" of Connecticut, the Church was reduced to become a dependency of the State.

Some of the Inspectors-General were elected, like the Fence-viewers, annually, but others were chosen at irregular intervals as the town saw fit. At the time when Capt. Lamberton's trade with Virginia and Delaware was beginning, in May, 1640, the court agreed that a measurer should be appointed to "measure all the corne thatt comes into the plantation to be solde, and for that end a role shall be made to strike the bushell with." Subsequently "Brother Peck" was chosen to the office, and compensated by a toll, averaging about one "halfe peny" to every bushel. Brother Peck's official dignity was short-lived, and the law establishing his office and its emoluments was formally repealed in 1646. It had been virtually a dead letter since September, 1643, when the Commissioners of the United Colonies had ordered that, throughout the New England Confederation, there should be but one standard of measures. Shortly afterward the New Haven Court deputed Richard Miles, William Davis and Nicholas Elsey to "See that all the measures in the towne be made according to the stander sent from the Bay."[2] This work was probably accomplished in the meeting-house, July 19, 1644, after which time the Scalers of Measures became a common feature of New Haven's municipal economy.

Sealers of Leather were first elected in 1646. They were enjoined to examine the products of the tanner's craft and to seal such "hydes" as deserved approval. Strangely enough to ears accustomed to modern slang, leather of the first quality was to be stamped "N. G.," poorer kinds were marked "N. F." Fees for sealing were fourpence a "hyde," and twopence a "skine." The New Haven tanners and shoe-

---

[1] "April 23, 1660.—Sister Pecke, the widow, shall sweepe the meeting-house, in place of Sister Preston."

[2] Records, I. 142–144.

makers were but indifferent workmen. One good man after another came before the court to display his shoes full of cracks and unable to keep sole and body together, and to complain of the artisans. There is a pathetic entry at the close of the final orders to the sealers in 1648: "It was propounded to the shoemakers that, seeing hides are now neare as cheape as they are in England, that shooes might be sould more reasonable than they have bine; and the shoemakers promised they would consider of it." What Arcadian gentleness in this interference with the rights of traffic!

DOCTOR AND SCHOOL TEACHER.

It seems strange to find doctors regarded as quasi town officials, but so they were esteemed, and the authorities were more justified in making domiciliary visits upon them than upon the shoemakers. There were several residents who kept drugs and practiced medicine to a limited extent, but whenever a professional physician came within reach, the town endeavored to secure his services by offering him house, lands, furniture, and a yearly stipend. A couple of generations passed, however, before one of these gentry could be induced to remain very long. In 1650, the court stopped at Milford a "Surgion or Phisitian, who was on his way from Plymouth toward the Dutch," and brought him back to New Haven, in order to treat with him about a settlement in the town. A year later a "French Phisitian from the University of Franicer"[1] was in town, and "Mr. Davenport saith that he finds in discourse with him that his abilities answer the testimony given." The court voted to offer the Franeker graduate a house, provisions, and a yearly salary of £10. It was found that such terms would not begin to satisfy the learned Frenchman. Subsequently, "since the town desired it especially on account of Mrs. Davenport," he, or another vagrant

---

[1] University of Franeker, founded 1585, closed 1811. The village of Franeker is in the Netherlands, in the Province of Friesland.

of the same sort, was induced to abide, and he was considered
to be so entirely at the public mercy that, when he wanted to
leave town in December, 1652, the court would not let him
go. But at last the "Towne, understanding that he intends
to take nothing of Mrs. Davenport for what he hath done for
them," accorded him permission to depart if he would.[1]

In the same way was the principal schoolmaster, Mr.
Ezekiel Cheever, also a public officer. After the Town Free
School was ordered, February 25, 1642,[2] he drew from the
Town-Treasury a salary of £20 a year, which was increased
in August, 1644, to £30. Mr. Cheever departed in high
dudgeon for Boston in 1640, and for some time thereafter the
Free School was handed annually by the court from one master
to another. In 1651, the Town-Court elected a committee to
hire a schoolmaster for not more than £40.[3] The court also
specified the items of the teacher's future task: "To perfect
male chilldren in ye English, after they can reade in their
Testament, or bible; to learn them to wright and soe bring
them on to Latin as they are capeable." Three days later
(November 17th) the bargain was struck in the Town-Meeting,
and recorded as follows : "He hath twenty pounds, his chamber
and dyet (at Mr. Atwater's, valued at 5s. per week), 30s. for
traveling expenses, libbertie once a year, in harvest-time, to
goe for his friends, some of his pay to be such as to buy
Books and pay for travel, and, if he be called away to some
other employment for the Honnor of Christ, he may go."[4]
Notice the evident intention to give all "capable" boys a
classical education; while money for the teacher's traveling

---

[1] New Haven Town Records, II. 08, *et passim.*

[2] "Itt is ordered thatt a free schoole shall be sett up in this towne, and
our pastour, Mr. Davenport, together with the magistrates, shall consider
whatt yearly allowance is meete to be given to itt out of the common stock
of the towne."

[3] For Mr. Cheever's interesting career, see Mass. Hist. Soc. Coll., Series
II. 120; Bacon's Hist. Disc., 318; Conn. Hist. Soc. Coll., I., and Mather's
Magnalia.

[4] New Haven Town Records, II. 90, *et seq.*

expenses is a privilege that modern instructors would hardly dare to ask for.

Viewers and Brewers.

The Jurisdiction Court in May, 1654, ordered each plantation to provide itself with "Gagers" of Casks and Viewers of Corn. In Eaton's Code a precarious authority is derived from Deuteronomy and Micah for the enactment that "all Cask used in trade shall be of London Assize," and the salary of each officer is determined. Beyond the occasional elections of these officers, there is but little trace of their activity; and of the officer who ought to have been chosen to keep the Assize of Bread, there is no record. Another class of obscure officials were the Supervisors and Branders of Cattle and Horses. The last-named animal, by reason of its rarity and usefulness, was especially valuable. In 1653, when war with the Dutch seemed imminent, and was indeed ardently hoped for in New Haven, the General Court, "considering how useful horses might be for the service of warr," ordered that no one should send or sell horses out of the jurisdiction without express license from the Supervisors of Cattle. Five years later the court, "having information of some indirect proceedings by some persons," in branding their own horses, renewed the orders that such marking must be done by the Town-Officer, and that horses, when bought or sold, must be registered. The usual fees were attached to the Brander's office, and there is no lack of evidence that the laws were enforced.

For a short period from the first of February, 1647, onward, Mr. Stephen Goodyear was the Town-Brewer. He was authorised by the court to "Brew Beare for this Towne, all others excluded without the like liberty and consent of the Towne." No others applied for such privileges, but it is probable that Mr. Goodyear's right soon fell into abeyance. Rev. Mr. Hooke's beer, which Mrs. Godman was thought to have bewitched in 1655, was brewed within the parson's family.

Finally, the ephemeral office of "Truckmaster with ye Indians" deserves but a mere mention, for its duration was probably very short, and the trade was certainly inconsiderable.[1]

Inasmuch as the Town-Bull was so curious and considerable a feature of the common property of many English parishes,[2] and as New Haven kept common herds, a minute of the Town-Court for January 31, 1649, is of interest: "Mr. Crane desired the Court to consider how good Bulls might be bred, and they which breed them might have just consideration for them; the Town was desired to prepare it against next Court."

There is no record of further decision at that time, but it is probable that the town did take occasional cognizance of such matters. In 1673, there was public action concerning the men "appointed to rayse Bulls," and in 1725 (December 27), the town voted that four pounds should be paid yearly out of the Town-Treasury for three years for the maintenance of the public bulls, and two pounds yearly for the support of the boars. These taxes were to be levied on the "Town Platt." Farmers were exempted.

The Townsmen.

Throughout this multiplication of public trusts the New Haven General Court was gradually shaping the municipal administration in conformity with the experience and example of the other colonies. The most prominent fact in the primitive Town-Government during its first decade was the practically unlimited influence of the Court of the Magistrate and Four, which the absence of the jury served to enhance. Against the restricted suffrage only a small and disunited minority rebelled. But there was a steady and intelligent

---

[1] Mr. Gregson was elected to the office by the Town-Court in October, 1640. See Records. I. 43.

[2] The Parish (Toulmin Smith), 521.

disposition to attribute to the Monthly Court a more subordinate character than it had at the outset. The magistrates' authority and responsibility were limited by the frequent convocations of the Town-Court, by the creation of numerous subordinate officers, and by the formation of a colonial authority. The progressive element in the town directed these movements toward expansion and assimilation, tending always to a democratic diffusion of power, while the conservative party sought rather to sustain the magisterial dominance. The peculiar strength of the position of the magistrate and his four assistants was that those five magistrates, as they might be called, were not only the ordinary judiciary, but also the supreme executive of the town, excepting in those short periods wherein the Town-Court was in session. Such concentration of power was opposed to the practice in Massachusetts no less than to the indirect but potent influence of the rival upon the river.

After the first few years the meetings of the Town-Court became more frequent and important, and the instances of legislative or executive action on the part of the Monthly Court became more and more rare.[1] But the oft-recurring assemblages of the Town-Court with its relentless fines became burdensome and costly. The Town-Court of November 17, 1651, met the demands of the hour, and, doubtless with due consideration of the usages in Connecticut and Massachusetts, decreed the change. "Itt was propounded that there might be some men chosen to consider and carry on the towne affaires, that these meetings which spend the towne much time, may not bee so often. The Court approved the motion, and chose one out of each quarter to this worke—viz.: Francis Newman, John Cooper, Jarvise Boykin, Mr. Atwater, Wm. Fowler, Richard Miles, Henry Lindon, Thos. Kimberley, and Mathew Camfield, which are to stand in this Trust until the Towne Elections in May, come twelvemonth; and they are by this Court authorized to be Townes-

---

[1] Records, I. 74, 190, 464.

men, to order all matters about Fences, Swine, and all other things in the generall occasions of the Towne, except extraordinary charges, matters of Election in May yearly, and the disposeing of the Townes land."[1]

The number of townsmen was soon increased to ten, the idea of district representation being still preserved. "William Russell was chosen for the bankside against the harbor, and the creek as farr as Robert Pigg's." But, in 1653, the number was reduced to seven, at which figure, with some slight fluctuations, it remained. Two years later it was ordered that hereafter they be chosen by "papers, as other officers are, without respect to them that have served before." The townsmen agreed among themselves to meet in public session on the first Monday of every month at five o'clock P. M. "If any of the Townsmen be absent or come not seasonably, they shall pay 2s. 6d." They met in private session at their own pleasure. The place of the monthly meeting was the "ordinary," or tavern, as appears from the notice to that effect January 13, 1659, and also from accusations brought against them in 1675 at the Town-Meeting of extravagant indulgence in "mine host's" liquors at the town's expense. Jeremiah Osborne, ·in the name of the townsmen, reported that they had spent thirty shillings there in the last year, and were likely to spend as much more this

---

[1] The first traces of "Selected Townesmen" and Town Committees upon the records of Massachusetts and Plymouth occur about ten years earlier than this. In Connecticut, townsmen had existed since the formation of the famous Fundamental Constitution. But the name is misleading, for their duties were, at first, magisterial. The General Court ordered October 10, 1639, that each town should choose 3, 5 or 7 of its "cheefe inhabitants" to meet once in two months to try causes involving not more than forty shillings' value, to register wills, and to administer estates. In 1643, the towns were ordered to choose annually seven men who would give to the common lands their "serious and sadde consideration." Seven years later this work was given to the townsmen, and formed the basis of the powers of Connecticut selectmen. So the genesis of the office in Connecticut was almost totally different from that of the similarly-named office in New Haven.—*Conn. Col. Rec.*, I. 37, 214.

year; if the town did not approve, the townsmen would pay it themselves. There the reform movement seems to have rested. In 1654, the town first voted that the townsmen might draw orders on the treasurer in favor of those whom they employed, and that such orders must be presented at the treasury within a month after the work was done.

To the complex web of official life which had been slowly woven around the simple, primal commune, the finishing touch was now given. The fabric of the town, and that of a modern town, was completed. Yet, at first, there was a commingling of jurisdictions between the Town-Court and the townsmen. The latter considered themselves a Standing Committee of the former, unable to act finally in anything without its sanction. They sought the court's permission to do this or that, or the court's approval of their previous resolutions. In the spring following their first appointment, the townsmen, having made a number of orders, published them by reading in the court, and "what was done was by Silence confirmed." The minutes of their meetings for many years were copied into the "Town-Records," not singly, but in the lump, although they ceased apparently to be read over in the succeeding Town-Meeting. As the townsmen gradually grasped the full extent of their authority and opportunity, the sphere of their activities widened. The courts were continually referring this and the other item of business to the townsmen for disposal. Even the care of the town's land, though it had been expressly denied them, was yet in special cases again and again devolved upon them by vote of the town.

CURRENCY AND TAXATION.

In New Haven the wherewithal to eat, to drink, and to wear was always forthcoming. The Church and the town together were watchful to relieve the necessities of the poor. At the outset New Haven probably possessed more ready money *per capita* than any other town on the New England coast had enjoyed, and it alone bore about two-fifths of all the charges of the New Haven Jurisdiction. But even before the period of great pecuniary losses came, the town entered into the same phases of economic experience which its neighbors had encountered. The inability of a limited supply of hard money to cope with the exigencies of isolated colonial life, and with the competition of a vast quantity of inferior currency, was felt rather than admitted. Economic retrogression kept pace with the return to ancient communal forms of land-holding. Within three years the town had reverted almost to the stage of barter. "All comodityes bought and sold among the planters and all worke, wages, and labor henceforward shall be payd for either in corne, as the price goeth in the plantation, or in worke as ·the rates settled by the Court, or in cattell of any sort as they shall be indifferently prized, or in good marchantable bever according to its goodnes."[1] The omission of wampum from this list indicates perhaps an intention to restrict or prevent its use, although in the previous autumn it had been ordered that "wampam shall goe in this plantation for 6 a peny." But, as usual, endeavors to keep out the shell currency were unavailing.

In 1643, the treasurer was authorized to receive in payment of town taxes or rates, Indian corn at 2s. 4d. per bushel, or cattle, or wampum. Two years later the value of wampum was fixed, the white at six for a penny, the black at three for a penny. The legal maximum limit of its use was twenty shillings. Payment of debts within that sum could be tendered half in black and half in white wampum. If any question arose about the quality of the Indian money, Mr. Goodyear, whose business integrity received many such testimonials, was declared the arbitrator between the parties. The debased currency was a serious annoyance to New Haven for a short time only. Tradition, indeed, vouches for some very sharp practice in disposing of quantities of wampum to the Dutch in return for hard cash; but the imputation rests

---

[1] Records, I. 52.

equally upon all the English along the Sound. The local Indian traffic amounted to nothing, and after the time of King Philip's War the "Records" cease to speak of Indian money. The beginning of the end for New Haven was made as early as 1650. Already wampum was as unpopular as the trade-dollars and notched quarters of our own day, and it was put to similar uses. Witness the petition of the Deacons to the court for legislation against wampum: "The Deacons informed the Court that the wampum which is put into the Church Treasury is generally so bad that the Elders to whom they pay it cannot pay it away." A committee was chosen to seek out a remedy. Here was an unpleasant predicament for the Rev. Messrs. Davenport and Hooke! Indeed, this questionable method of disposing of unwelcome currency caused a partial surrender of ecclesiastical independence, and of the principle of voluntary offering which Davenport had established. November 14, 1651, the church-officers were again in despair over the bad wampum that was cast into the contribution, and the court ordered that no planter should henceforth give anything on the Lord's Day but silver or bills.[1] "And whereas it is taken notice of that Divers give not into the Treasury at all upon the Lord's day, it is desired that all such (if they give not freely of themselves) shall be rated according to the Jurisdiction's order, for Minister's Maintaynance." The enforced support of the ministry by a legal rate was henceforth possible, though probably not often actual, and this provision was embodied in the Colonial Code of 1655.

The earliest and only town-ordinance directly affecting the metal currency in use enacted in April, 1643, that "peeces of eight"[2] should be valued in New Haven and its dependency, Stamford, at five shillings; following, as the court vaguely said, the custom at "Matachusetts Bay and some other places." In 1653–54, silver was so scarce that the

---

[1] New Haven Town Records, II. 17, 90.
[2] *I. e.,* of eight rials' value—a Spanish coin.

colonial treasurer was obliged to borrow very small sums of ready money from various persons in order to send to Hartford and Boston the agents who were preparing for the threatened war. If the treasurer could get no silver, he was authorized to procure beaver; or, if necessary, butter; or, as a last resource, Guilford corn.

Taxes were first assessed upon the investments in the Joint-stock Association of Adventurers. Of the earliest recorded tax nothing is known beyond the assertion that it was at the rate of 25s. upon every hundred pounds, in order to defray the cost of the first meeting-house. The sum raised was £500, which shows a taxable amount of about £40,000. With the proceeds of this tax the town proposed to build a " meeting-house forthwith, fifty-foot square." The carpenters were instructed to fell timber "where they can find it, till allotments be laid out and men know their own proprietyes." Only the needs of a public building could receive such consideration, for the prohibition upon cutting timber anywhere upon the Commons without a special license therefor from the magistrate had already been proclaimed, and many subsequent fines attest its rigid enforcement. Subsequently, the town's mark was ordered to be set upon the trees which were suitable for repairing the church, "that no body ele may medle with them." After 1640, a fine of 20s. rewarded the unlicensed felling of trees " where the spruce masts grow." These enactments recall the designation of trees for the royal navy by placing upon them the King's mark.[1] The meeting-house was erected in so slipshod a manner that, within five years, the workmen were called to account before the court. The roof was rotten, and by 1648 the edifice was badly dilapidated, and was strengthened by props.[2]

---

[1] For instances of enforcement, see Records, I. 32, 458.

[2] Records, I. 145, 304, 423. David Peterson De Vries, who sailed by New Haven only two days after the adoption of the " Foundamentall Agreement," wrote in his journal that the English at Rodenberg had 300 houses and a fine church. Distance must have lent enchantment to the

The meeting-house tax was the last assessment of its kind. Before another year had passed away, divisions of land had been made and the incidence of taxation was shifted from pounds sterling to real estate. Annual rates were fixed, October 23, 1640, at fourpence per acre upon meadows and uplands of the First Division, and twopence per acre on land of the Second Division. By 1645 it had been discovered that not every taxable person was a land-owner. It was then determined that all planters in the town "who desire noe land or accept not what is allotted shall pay one shilling a year apeece towards publicque chardges." The three traders or small merchants in town were not land-holders, and formed a class by themselves. They were to be rated from time to time as the "Court shall judge meete." "For they have hitherto injoyed comfortable fruite of civill administrations, having small or noe rates." Mrs. Stolion and Mr. Godfrey were charged at the rate of 20s. a year, and Mr. Leech just twice as much. Their anomalous situation elicited the proposal in the Town-Court that "land should be layd to them" for purposes of taxation only, in order that the ratings might be uniform; but the proposal was "respited."

In the autumn of 1644, the town began its annual contribution for the support of poor scholars at Harvard College. The offering consisted of a peck of wheat, or the value of the same, from every one "whose hart is willing." The largess lost its voluntary character and was regarded as a tax. The Collectors of College Corn were regularly elected town-officers until the end of the colonial existence. It was creditable to the town that such an additional and unnecessary burden was shouldered and carried through the adversities of the

---

mariner's view. Tradition says that Mr. Newman's "Mighty Barn" was then the meeting-house. Perhaps De Vries was misled by the unusual size of some of the houses. Mr. Davenport's dwelling was built, it is said, in the form of a cross. Mr. Eaton's home, built in the form of a capital E, and containing 21 fireplaces, was still larger and more lofty. (See Lambert's Hist. of N. H. Colony, 59, and Vol. III. of Series 2 of the N. Y. Hist. Soc. Coll.)

decade from 1644 to 1654. A reversal of individual fortunes took place meanwhile. The rich men of 1640 were impoverished, and those who owned much land paid larger taxes out of their poverty than others who had accumulated personal property rather than real estate. Discontent with existing arrangements culminated in the Town-Court of March, 1649. Lieutenant Seely moved that taxation upon the basis of landed property should be discontinued. The motion found favor, and was referred to a committee consisting of the Particular Court and ten others, one from each quarter of the town. Soon after, Mr. Theophilus Eaton and Mr. Robert Newman, the Governor and the Ruling Elder, who had been especially afflicted by the failure of the Delaware Company, were freed for the time to come from paying the town-rates. During the summer the committee studied diligently the printed tax-laws of Massachusetts, and were unable to suggest much amendment. In the autumn their advice that those laws be substantially adopted was accepted, and Massachusetts was once more recognized as a more serviceable legislator than Moses. There was a prolonged debate over the exact adjustment of rates upon personal property, particularly upon houses and upon polls. A new committee, again representing the quarters, was elected to make all needful revisions, and to sit as a Board of Relief. General tax-lists first appeared in August, 1651. The court ordered that " all men betwixt this and this day seven-night must bring to those appointed in their several quarters a note of their persons, land, meadow, cattle, houses, and other estate." At the same time the town debated whether it might adopt the Massachusetts law of duties on wines and liquors, but finally concluded that custom-duties now belonged solely to the Colonial Legislature. Thus New Haven swung a little farther out into the stream of New England's common political development. Reform in taxation and the election of townsmen were concurrent phases in the process of assimilation.

CHAPTER III.

THE LAND-QUESTION.

CONTROL OF ALIENATIONS AND DWELLINGS.

The earliest legislative action respecting land occurred immediately after the final organization of the body-politic, and was caused by the removal of most of the Herefordshire settlers to Milford. The town proceeded to buy their town-shares and privileges of commonage. Four men were appointed to "treate with the Hartfordshire men about their lotts, to see if they will part with them, and upon what tearmes." Several, however, retained their possessions in both towns. The virgin soil of the outlying land was not forgotten. The court—that is, the magistrate and deputies, together with Mr. Sam. Eaton and Goodman Andrews—were selected to advise together "about laying out allottments for inheritance." At the next court, three weeks later, the court alone and Mr. Davenport were appointed a Proprietors' Committee to "have from henceforward the disposing of all the house-lotts yet undisposed of about this towne to such persons as they shall judge meete for the good of the plantation, and none shall come to dwell as planters here without their consent and allowance, whether they come in by purchase or otherwise." After the additional enactment of September 1, 1640, which forbade the sale or lease of a lot to any stranger without allowance from the court, the pastor's name was omitted from the committee. Perhaps he foresaw that such questions might easily become burning ones.

Not a foot of ground escaped the notice of the New Haven "Comitty." Even the cellars in the banks of the West Creek were carefully guarded as common property. Mr. Lamberton obtained a "yeard for his cellar by the west creeke, after the comitty had viewed it," and after he had agreed to give what they determined upon, and to sell both house and lot "at what time and to whom the court shall approve of."[1]   In March, 1640, Mr. Johnson made a similar bargain for "the cellar that Thomas Welch lived in to make a warehouse off," but it was stipulated that he should "clayme no propriety in the ground as inherritance."   In the next month, "Henry Akerlye was rebuked for building a cellar and selling itt without leave."   But as the more reputable inhabitants moved into the new houses, certain lewd fellows of the baser sort occupied the abandoned burrows in the bankside, and tales of scandalous deeds in the cellars came to the ears of the magistrates.   On the 2d of December, 1640, Thomas Franck-land stood before the frowning Eaton, charged with drinking strong liquors to excess, with "entertaining disorderly persons into his cellar to drinking-meetings," and with contempt of court.   Thomas found that the magistrate was, as Mather said, "a terror to evil-doers."   The offender was whipped, fined twenty shillings, and deprived of his cellar and lot, "his lott and liberty of staying in the plantation being onely granted to him upon his good behavior."   The decree imme-diately went forth that all families living in cellars should have three months (*i. e.*, to the end of winter) to make some other provision, but that "all single persons are to betake themselves forthwith to some families, except the magistrate see cause to respitt them for a time."   This command was not rigorously executed, for, more than a year afterward, it was again declared "thatt no yong men shall live by them-selves in cellars, but shall at once resort to families whose masters may report concerning them and their conversation." Perhaps this was effectual; there are no more traces of un-comely doings in the cellars.

---

[1] Records, I. 41, 218.

DIVISION OF THE OUTLAND.

After two months of preparation the committee upon allotments began, January 4, 1640, to arrange the first division of the outland. A tract of land extending about one mile from the town in every direction was set apart as "The Two-Mile Square" or "The Upland." Of this upland, and of the meadows around the town, each planter received a share, "according to the proportion of estate which he hath given in, and the number of heads in his family." Five acres each of upland and of meadow were allotted for every £100, but for every head in the family (wherein man, wife and children were reckoned) two and a half acres of upland were bestowed and a half acre of meadow. These divisions were marked out in sections corresponding to the quarters of the town-plot, so that the inhabitants of each quarter might find their new possessions contiguous. A large surface of outland lying northwest of the town was reserved for common pasturage. "The cow pasture shall begin on the hither side of the Beever ponds, and the oxe pasture on the farre side of the Beever pond, and the way to them both to begin att Mr. Tenchea corner."[1] The first of May was designated as the time when cattle should be driven to pasture with a keeper, and it was ordered "Thatt a convenient way to the hay-place be left common for all the towne."

A common field for tillage was yet lacking. "The Necke" was the name given to the peninsula between Mill and Quinnipiac Rivers, whereon the greater part of Fair Haven now stands. Notice the opening clause: "Itt is agreed by the Towne, and *accordingly* ordered by the Court that the Neck shall be planted or sowen for the tearme of seven yeares." Private parties who had broken ground there were warned off, and John Brockett, the town surveyor, was commissioned to "Goe about laying it out forthwith, at the rate of an acre to

---

[1] The corner of York and Grove streets.

every hundred pound, and halfe an acre to every head."[1]   A lot between the East Creek and the Mill River, called the "Oystershell Field," was also reserved as a common, and the magistrates were authorized to "lett it to such persons whose present need requires itt."   Not until the following October (1640) was the work of plotting the meadows finished.   A reminder of ancient usage is noteworthy.   The men who "viewed" the meadows were instructed not to measure swamps, ponds, and creeks.   Compare the Massachusetts regulation that swamps of more than one hundred acres shall lie in common.

At the same time the committee announced a second and concluding division of outland, consisting of the upland lying outside the two miles square.   The wilderness was given away with still greater liberality.   The allotments were made to every planter at the rate of twenty acres for every hundred pounds, and two and a half acres for every head.[2]   The location of individual assignments was determined by the quarters, and the court provided a legal outlet for possible contention.   "To prevent offence as much as may bee, and that all mens sperits be the better satisfied with their allotments, it is ordered that when the planters doe not fully agree among themselves in devideing their lands, all devissions gennerally (the former grants excepted) shall be made by lott thro the towne both in upland and meddow."   The allusion to "the former grants" refers to the special favors that were shown to a few individuals.   These concessions were slight. The leaders of the colony did not intend to countenance partiality or greed.   The Bay Colony granted thousands of acres to private persons, even so many as 3200 acres each to Saltonstall and to the executors of Mr. Johnson's estate. New Haven never offered more than the estimated proportion to any but Mr. Davenport.   "Itt is ordered that Mr. Daven-

[1] Records, I. 26–27, 42.

[2] Such was the order (p. 43).   But an examination of the schedule on p. 91 (Vol. I.) shows that two acres per head was the real rate.

port, pastour of the church, shall have his farme (in the 2nd division) where he shall desire itt, with all the conveniences of upland and meadow and creeks, which the place where he pitches will afforde, though above his proportion according to his desire." Governor Eaton obtained no more than his due allowance, but was permitted to choose the location of a portion of it.[1] Captain Turner and the two deacons were similarly favored, "Thatt they may the better atend their office." Otherwise the lot fell equally and fairly upon all the planters.

Justice and generosity were shown to non-commoners, and the whole history of land-division in New Haven reveals hardly a trace of bitterness or discontent. The suburban quarter wherein most of the non-shareholders lived received its quota of meadow and upland in both divisions without apparent discrimination. Furthermore, there was a sort of general donation to the poor in October, 1640. Several acres of ground, "To be layd out betwixt our pastours farme and the Indians wiggwams," were divided among "The small lotts about the towne." Therefore, at the lot-drawing in 1641, such humble people as " Eliz. the washer," " A brickmaker," and " Bro. Kimberlys bro:," received their shares. Last of all, in the revision of 1645, all residents who had " had noe outland formerly allotted to them," obtained six acres of upland for every single person, eight acres for a man and wife, with an additional acre for " every child they have at present."

The liberality of such legislation shines conspicuous when contrasted with the action of neighboring communities. The

---

[1] Records, I. 42–48, 195–196. Mr. Davenport chose a farm on the east side of the Quinnipiac, in the northern part of what is now Fair Haven Borough. The house in which his farmer, Allen Ball, lived, stood on the site of the house lately occupied by Mr. Andrew Barnes. Subsequently, when Mr. Davenport's descendants came to live upon the farm, they built and inhabited the house where Mr. Chester Bradley now dwells. Governor Eaton's " farme by the brick-kills " was on the west side of the river, probably near the present village of Quinnipiac.

variety of regulations in New England ranges from the
practice of indiscriminate gifts to the restriction of all landed
possessions to commoners. The subjection of the non-
proprietors kept many a New England town in turmoil
until the Revolution, and furnished obscure, but powerful,
aid to the precipitation of that conflict. In more than one
locality, the non-commoners were the Patriots and Sons of
Liberty who drove out the Tory landlords. Jonathan
Edwards wrote in 1751: "In Northampton there are two
parties, like the Court and Country party in England, the
great Proprietors of land and the parties concerned about land
and other matters."[1]

Although Northampton was not at first the least liberal of
the Valley towns, yet, in the early part of the 18th century,
non-commoners and proprietors quarreled violently together
in a town-meeting that lasted through three successive days
and almost all of one night. The majority of towns paid
strict heed to the principle enunciated in the original agreement at Springfield, Mass., in 1636, that each inhabitant
shall receive land, "As we shall see meete for every ones
quality and estate." At Haverhill, land was divided at the
rate of twenty acres for every £200. At Hadley, "In the
divisions of woodland that took place after the meadows were
shared there was much inequality."[2]

Although the towns of the Connecticut Valley and of the
New Haven Colony are said to have been more impartial
than all others, yet no other town seems to have preserved so

---

[1] Judd's History of Hadley, 281.

[2] Egleston's Land System of New England, 34–36 ; and Judd, *quoad antea*,
21. Some Massachusetts towns displayed, in laws at least, a very exclusive spirit :

Watertown, Mass. : " No forrainers coming into the town nor any family
arising among ourselves, shall have benefit of commonage, or of land undivided, but what they shall purchase, except they buy a man's right
wholly in the town."

Also Hampton, N. H.: " No man an inhabitant unless he hath at least
one share of commonage by the first division."

rigorously as New Haven the basis of numbers as well as of estates in a universal land-distribution. Milford and Guilford, New Haven's oldest daughters, were not so free-handed as their mother. The one, after it passed under the sway of Connecticut, divided common lands according to the tax-lists; the other, from the outset, assigned lots in proportion alone to the amounts of investment.[1] The New Haven allotments of 1643 show that William Preston, who headed a family of ten persons, though worth only forty pounds, received twelve acres more of the arable land than David Yale, who was worth three hundred pounds, and was step-son to the Governor.

NEW HAVEN A VILLAGE COMMUNITY.

Sir Henry Maine has defined a village community of the primitive type as an assembly of separate dwellings, each guarded from intrusion, with arable lands divided between the various households. The pastures are partially divided, but the waste is a common heritage.[2] Each of these ancient forms of village life had reasserted itself in 1640, under the shadow of the Red Hills. There stood the homesteads in the compact town-plot. The arable mark comprised the upland with its divided farms, its common tillage in the Nook and Oystershell Field, the fenced pastures in the two miles square, and the common pastures at the Beaver Ponds. The waste was the outlying mark, the wilderness where towns were yet to be. The use to which it was consigned, however, does not, as in the olden time, suggest nymph, nixie, or roving robber. The order of the court in May, 1641, was " Thatt all those thatt have hoggs shall drive them from the plantation about five miles from the towne, and haunt them forth abroade." Additional traces of communal custom crop out in the town's oversight of the common droves, and in the town's determination of the annual seasons for opening and

---

[1] Lambert, 96, 102.
[2] Early History of Institutions, 81.

closing the pasture-grounds. Maine enumerates among the characteristic features of the Teutonic Township the Communal Officer, who watched to see that the common domain was equitably enjoyed by the grazing cattle, or by the woodchopper, and also the custom of "Stint of Common," whereby each commoner's number of beasts was limited.[1] Each one of these Old-World features found its duplicate in our town of New Haven. There were, moreover, herds of cattle belonging not only to individuals but also to the town. The town-flock of sheep existed for a long time, and the first shepherd was Nehemiah Smith, probably an immigrant from the Plymouth Colony, who tended the flock until about 1652. So late as March, 1674, there were three separate common herds, and by order of the court they were daily driven forth "North and Northwest from the Towne into the waste."[2]

But there were other no less prominent tokens of institutional descent besides the marks, the common fields, the primitive customs of meadow and weald. The village pale, the tun, zaun, the hedge; the all-supreme town-moot; the quarters, images of the shadowy tithings; the town-officers, magistrate and four, marshal and captain; the constable; the tithingman; the communal heirship to all its own individual homesteads as opposed to owner's sale or stranger's purchase; the customs of boundary-marking, of keeping public armor, of watch and ward, of hue and cry—each and every one of these bore witness to the unbroken strands of historical continuity. The Puritans are sometimes described as breaking with the Past. Here were the cables, invisible, but stronger than adamant, that bound them not only to England, but to the wooded Germany of Tacitus and Arminius, and even to the far-away Aryan villages.

The common fields of New Haven vanished gradually. The Oystershell Field was leased from time to time. The Neck was by turns a place for tillage, a partly-divided pasture,

---

[1] Village Communities and Miscellanies, 79, 90.
[2] Records, I. 100, 440, and New Haven Town Records, III. 170.

and a sheep-walk.[1] Piece by piece the commonage dropped into the hands of individuals, until now the domain of the Proprietors is represented only by the " Market-Place," the faces of East and West Rocks, to a certain extent by the public parks, and by a portion of land underlying the harbor. The Proprietors' Committee still exists, full of years and honors. It has become a self-perpetuating body, and is one of the few American corporations that can look back over a continuous life of two hundred and forty-five years. Its records are intact. It can boast a full complement of officers, regular meetings, and, a few years ago, it gave ample proof of vigor by successfully resisting, in the courts of the State, a certain manufacturer's attempted encroachments upon land in the harbor.

EVOLUTION OF SUBORDINATE TOWNSHIPS.

In 1640, the town of New Haven could give away farms; she traded in townships. Her competitor upon the river was

---

[1] Records, I. 82, 136, 167, 217, 318, 447, 461, 463.

NOTE.—One portion of New Haven's territory has a singular history of ownership. The Town-Meeting of March 17, 1641, voted that " Thomas Fugill shall have the Iland in the Mill River for his proportion, he being willing to have it when others refused it because it was bad." (Records, I. 49.) From the facts that Allen Ball, Mr. Davenport's farmer, was Fugill's brother-in-law, and had some of the property that was at first Fugill's, and that the island bore for a long time the name " Ball's Island," it seems reasonable to suppose that after the secretary's disgrace and departure, Allen Ball enjoyed the use of the island. But the character of the land did not improve, for Ball's Island lay so long without any individual owner that it was universally regarded as common or town's land. Fifty years ago the town sold annually the privilege of cutting grass upon Ball's Island, and it is said that instances of such action have occurred within twenty years. But in the winter of 1800 some of the property-owners upon the opposite river-banks quietly secured the island for themselves under the provisions of an act of the Legislature bearing the harmless title " An Act to prevent and remove nuisances and obstructions from the channel of Mill River." (Approved June 23, 1860.) To-day the island that in 1641 nobody would have because " it was bad," is worth, with the improvements upon it, perhaps more than seventy-five thousand dollars. Several newspaper articles, in the winter of 1883–84, called attention to the forementioned act.

indigent, but never indolent. Already, Connecticut had planted the germs of five towns upon the shore of the Sound west of Milford. The plantation of New Haven, probably conscious of the impending Federal dignity, as well as of the power that wealth conveys, bestirred itself. July 1, 1640, Captain Nathaniel Turner bought for the town of New Haven the territory of Stamford, immediately adjoining Norwalk, the westernmost purchase of Connecticut. He paid to the Indians therefor, besides the usual quantity of hoes and hatchets, four fathoms of white wampum. This was the first recorded use of Indian money by the English of New Haven. At the same time, two unruly characters named Feaks and Patrick, strange agents for the pious Davenport and judicious Eaton to employ, purchased Greenwich for New Haven. But the superior wisdom of the children of this world was again illustrated. Daniel Patrick had run away from Massachusetts to escape the Puritan rule, and he did not intend to make a second venture. Greenwich revolted to the neighboring Dutch, was incorporated as a town by Governor Stuyvesant, and not until sixteen years had elapsed could New Haven reclaim her errant daughter.

On the first of September, 1640, the plantation of Totokett (Branford) was granted to Mr. Samuel Eaton, Davenport's whilom opponent, and to Mr. Eaton's friends "from olde England," upon such terms as might be agreed by himself and the "Comitty." During the summer, Mr. Davenport journeyed to Wethersfield to attempt the healing of a serious rupture in the church there.[1] His advice that one party should found a new plantation may not have been entirely disinterested. Perhaps he suggested Stamford. At any rate, in October, Stamford was sold to a party of Wethersfield men for £33, upon condition that a fifth part of the plantation might be reserved to the town of New Haven for one year.

---

[1] The church had seven members, and was divided, three against four. The three claimed to be the orthodox church, and the four were plainly the majority. Therefore, each thought that the other should submit.

At the expiration of that time, if that part were yet vacant, the people of Stamford might "Nominate to this Court some persons of their own choyce which may fill up some of those lotts, so reserved, if this Court approve of them." A remaining condition was that the Stamford settlers should "Joyne in all poynts with this plantation in the forme of Government here settled, according to the agreement already made with Mr. Eaton about Totokett."

The church quarrels at Wethersfield were an ill wind that seemed to blow good to New Haven alone. The Rev. Mr. Eaton having decided to stay in England, Totokett was mainly settled in 1644 by Wethersfield people, who left their first home for the same reasons and under the same conditions as the Stamford settlers. The autumn of 1640 saw the English in continuous possession of the Connecticut shore, from the river to the Dutch territory. New Haven meditated a longer flight. Before October her agents had crossed the Sound, and the lands of Yennycock or Southold, on Long Island, became the property of the town of New Haven. It was immediately settled by a portion of the New Haven company, who did not repurchase the title to their farms until nine years afterward.[1] Just as Plymouth's Town-Meeting elected constables for her outlying villages, so, until the formation of a colonial Legislature, the Town-Meeting of New Haven chose constables for the subordinate towns. At the election of New Haven town-officers in the fall of 1641, "Thurston Rayner was chosen Constable for Rippowams (Stamford) to order such business as may fall in that towne according to God, for the next ensueinge year, butt is nott to be established in his office, till he have received his charge from this Court, and testified his acceptance thereof to this Court." In 1642, also, New Haven elected the constable of Stamford, and named John Toustle as "Constable at Yennycock till some further course be taken by this Court, for the settling a magistracie there according to God."

---

[1] June 25, 1649. Records, I. 463.

With such a promising brood of municipalities nestling under her wings, and dependent upon her for the vigor of administrative life, New Haven began to assume the formidable title of "Jurisdiction," and to plume herself on a certain colonial importance. It was the town that entered the Confederation of 1643 as the equal of Connecticut, of Plymouth, and of Massachusetts, for Milford and Guilford were not yet associated. New Haven's township then included the soil that no less than sixteen towns cover to-day.[1] Her borders rested on either shore of the Sound, and swept across the limits of the New Netherlands. The Dutch Director-General, Kieft, attempted to neutralize the threatening advance of the English by securing from the Indians a counter-title to all the lands from Hudson River to the boundaries of Norwalk. The red men appear to have been the only gainers by the transaction. New Haven's last and most extensive purchase brought her into actual collision with her doughty neighbor. The effort to extend New Haven to the shores of the Delaware was remarkable for its boldness and for its utter failure. It engaged the best energies and resources of the town, and its complete collapse was a source of the final ruin of the colony.

THE DELAWARE COMPANY.

As usual, colonization and commercial enterprise went hand-in-hand. The London merchants who led the town had begun at once a traffic with Connecticut, with the Bay, with Virginia, and with the Barbadoes. George Lamberton was trading to Virginia, in his bark *The Cock*, in the winter of 1638–39. He discovered that there was a brisk fur trade along the Delaware, and engaged in it. Such profitable exchange with the miserable Indians along the Quinnipiac was out of the question. The Delaware Company was formed,

---

[1] New Haven, East Haven, North Haven, Branford, North Branford, Wallingford, Cheshire, Hamden, Bethany, Woodbridge, Orange, Greenwich, Stamford, Darien, New Canaan, and Southold.

comprising, among others, Governor Eaton, Mr. Davenport, Deacon Robt. Newman, and Captain Turner. Late in the year 1640, Captain Turner, having successfully negotiated the purchase of Stamford, sailed down the Sound for the Delaware Bay. He was instructed by the Delaware Company to view and purchase lands at the Delaware Bay, and not to meddle with aught that rightfully belonged to the Swedes or Dutch. When the party arrived at Manhattan, Governor Kieft protested against them and their errand. The instructions were shown to him, and the last clause evidently pleased him. He sent word to John Johnson, the Dutch agent at Delaware, to assist the English as opportunity might occur. Johnson obeyed orders, and showed Turner how far the titles of the Dutch and of the Swedes extended. But New Haven's captain paid little heed to boundaries. He bought of the Indians nearly the whole southwestern coast of New Jersey, and also a tract of land at Passayunk, on the present site of Philadelphia, and opposite the Dutch fort Nassau. Winthrop relates that the English could not at first induce the Indians to trade. But a Pequot refugee persuaded the sachem, saying that, though the English had killed his kinsmen, yet the Pequots had been to blame; that the English dealt fairly and would make excellent neighbors. It is to be hoped that the tale is true.[1]

On the 30th of August, 1641, there was a Town-Meeting at New Haven, which voted to itself authority over the region of the Delaware Bay. The acts of the Delaware Company were approved, and "Those to whome the affaires of the towne is comitted" were ordered to "Dispose of all the affayres of Delaware Bay." The first instalment of settlers

---

[1] See Atwater's History, 321. For accounts of the Delaware venture, see Hazard's Annals, 57, 61, 78, 96, 126, 128, *et passim;* O'Callaghan's History of New Netherlands, 231, 268, 365; also Doc. Rel. Col. Hist. of New York, XII. especially; Brodhead's History of New York, 337–363, 387; Winthrop, II. 157, and Trumbull, I. 116, 120; Albany Records, II. 162, *et seq.,* and New Haven Town and Colony Records. See also Annals of the United Colonies.

had previously gone to the Bay.   Trumbull says that nearly fifty families removed.   As they went by New Amsterdam, Governor Kieft issued an unavailing protest, which was met, however, by fair words.   The larger portion of the party settled in a plantation on Varkin's Kill (Ferkenskill, Hog Creek?), near what is now Salem, New Jersey.   A fortified trading-house was built or occupied at Passayunk.   This was the era of Sir Edmund Plowden's shadowy Palatinate of New Albion, and, if there is any truth in the curious "Description," there would seem to be some connection between this fort of the New Haven settlers and Plowden's alleged colony.   "The Description of New Albion," written in 1648, says: "It is now seven years since Master Evelin was there.   At that time Capt. Young and Master Evelin had given over their Fort begun at Eriwomeck within Delaware Bay."[1]

By the 15th of May, 1642, the Dutch had realized the gravity of the situation.   The Director-General and his council solemnly deliberated.

"Having received unquestionable information that some English had the audacity to land in the South River, opposite to our Fort Nassau, an act disrespectful to their High Mightinesses, the Lords States-General," it was resolved to drive the insolent English away.   May 22d, Jan Jansen Van Ilpendam was designated as the man to do it.   His orders were to treat the English most carefully, and "If the English escape or leave the spot, you must destroy their improvements."   Nothing was said concerning the settlement at Varkin's Kill.   Hazard states that, in the summer of 1642, armed vessels attacked Lamberton in the Delaware River, but were driven off.   One obscure author must be his own authority for the story that Van Ilpendam endeavored to capture the English fort, when some Marylanders, who were there, came out and swore so horribly that the Dutch retreated

---

[1] Force's Historical Tracts, II.

in alarm.[1]   Possibly this anecdote reveals the grain of wheat
in " Master Evelin's " bushel of chaff.   This may have been
the only real service ever rendered to England by the vassals
of Lord Edmund, Earl Palatine of New Albion.   Good old
Diedrich Knickerbocker would have vouched for the truth of
the story as it stands.

Meanwhile, John Printz arrived to be the Governor of
New Sweden.   His instructions bore date of August 15,
1642, and ordered him to " Handle tenderly the English
families (about sixty persons) at Ferkens Kill, and to win
them to our Government by underhanded means."   The
means actually chosen were rather rough-handed than underhanded.   The Dutch and Swedes made common cause against
the English.   Each power desired the English as subjects,
but not as independent neighbors.

It seems likely that now[2] the Dutch expedition did burn the
trading-houses, imprison several Englishmen, seize goods and
do damage, as Trumbull says, to the extent of one thousand
pounds sterling.   Governor Printz, on his part, began to
" handle the English tenderly."   Early in 1643, he erected
Fort Nya Elfsborg or Elsinborgh, close by the plantation at
Varkin's Kill.   Lamberton was harassed by demands of toll;
and was finally imprisoned.   The New Haven Records say
that he was decoyed on shore by Governor Printz, who thereupon tried to bribe the English sailors, especially one John
Thickpenny, to swear that Lamberton had planned to levy
war against the Swedes.   The reports of Governor Printz,
which are among the State Documents of Sweden, do not
confess any treachery or suborzation.   They do contain,
however, the minutes of Lamberton's trial at Fort Christina,
July 10, 1643.[3]   The court was constituted of ten persons,

---

[1] Wheeler's " Scheyichbi."   A curious and readable combination of New
Jersey history and of advertisement of Cape May as a summer resort.   It
is said that an old map identifies Eriwomeck with Passyunk.

[2] Probably in the winter of 1642–43, or possibly in the following spring.

[3] From the Swedish Archives, as quoted in History of the Colony of New
Sweden, by Carl K. S. Sprinchorn, translated in the Penna. Mag. of

among whom no English name appears. Lamberton showed that he had bought lands of the Indians near the present Philadelphia two years before the trial. Governor Printz displayed documents that proved a prior Swedish purchase of the same territory. Lamberton, being questioned about the English right to settle at " Varckens Kill," declared that the land there was bought of a chief who represented the sachem of all that country. Printz produced testimony that Peter Hollander, three days before Lamberton's bargain, had bought the whole southwestern Jersey coast of the veritable old head-sachem. The court concluded that the English were trespassers, and that Lamberton must pay double duty on his beaver.

A correspondence ensued between Winthrop and Printz. The latter wrote, under date of January 12, 1644, that he had done his duty to Sweden against Lamberton and the English, who were the aggressors. His report of January 16 shows that he had been sensitive enough to secure and send to Stockholm, from those implicated in Thickpenny's accusations, a denial of that mariner's veracity.

To complete the misfortunes of the English settlers, sickness fell upon them. Their cup of misery was full. Their trade was destroyed, their block-houses burned, together with their arms and stores, their vessels hindered from sailing, their village was overlooked by the threatening guns of the Swedish fort, and their bodies were seized by the pestilence that walketh in darkness along the Jersey coast. New Haven's independent spirit had hardly expected an embroilment with two of the most powerful nations of Europe, and the England to which she might have turned was wrestling with the Stuart. Governor Printz's letter home, June 11, 1644, reads as though he had completed the subjection of the English villagers. Slowly, through the winter and spring of 1643, the major part of them straggled

History and Biography. See the number for December, 1883 ; also Records, I. 106-8.

home to New Haven. Their destitution may be imagined from the following record more than a year afterward (October 2, 1644): "Roger Knap was discharged of his fine which was sett upon his head for want of armes, because the Court was informed that his armes was burnt in Delaware Bay, and, after he came hither he was afflicted with sickness, and so poore thatt he was nott able to buy armes in due time, butt now he is furnished with armes." But the poverty and distress were not confined to the twoscore households who had risked their persons in the enterprise. The ill-starred effort had impoverished the highest personages in the town, and crippled New Haven's best financial strength. There was naturally some dissension between the returned colonists and their employers over the failure of the attempt.

A few hardy vagabonds made the acquaintance of the marshal for accusing Mr. Davenport of trying to conceal his interest in the venture. One Luke Atkinson, among others, expressed the opinion that "Mr. Davenport's name had bin very pretious, but now it was darkned." "For slandering the church and Mr. Davenport, he was fined £40, to Mr. Davenport." But the Delaware Company was not without hopes of redress. Its doleful experience doubtless hastened the first Colonial Confederation, which was formed May 19, 1643, and the organization in the following months of what might be called "The United States of New Haven." Governor Printz's attack upon Lamberton took place probably about the first of July. The whole matter was rehearsed at the meeting of the Colonial Commissioners in September, and the President, Governor Winthrop, was requested to require satisfaction of both the Swedish and Dutch Governors. A brisk paper warfare was commenced, and continued until the treaty of Hartford in 1650. Then Governor Stuyvesant, on the one hand, and the New England Commissioners on the other, agreed that each party should trade and improve in peace at Delaware, "*in statu quo*," and that the entire question, including New Haven's claim of damages, should be referred to Holland and England for adjudication. "*In statu quo*" was a treacherous phrase susceptible of doubtful interpretation. But New Haven was so much in earnest about this pet project, that the obvious risk of danger was outweighed. The question of colonizing the Delaware region was brought forward at once.[1]

"At a Town-Meeting about Delaware Baye, December 17, 1650" (the omission of the title "General Court" is noteworthy), "the Governor said that Divers felt a sense of difficulty in carrying on their family occasions in this place, that the Town held more than could subsist together, and that Delaware Baye is a place fit to receive plantations." The matter was so weighty that no vote was taken, but each man expressed his mind. The mass of opinion favored a renewal of the effort, "Which they hoped would be done, if good foundations, both for Church and Commonwealth, were laid in that place." Early in the next spring the Governor informed the court that, "If Delaware Baye go on, some course must be taken for settling and moulding the Town, according to the General Court's order, both for the satisfaction of them that stay, and of them that go." A committee was chosen to prepare the inevitable Fundamental Agreement. Furnished with this orthodox charter, and relying on the flimsy support of the treaty of 1650, a party of fifty persons set sail once more for the Delaware.

They carried their goods with them, and were armed with a commission from Governor Eaton. Stuyvesant was just then grappling with incipient rebellion caused by his alleged recent treason at Hartford to Dutch interests. His idea of the *statu quo* was therefore likely to be unusually strict. He stopped the expedition at Manhattan, confiscated the commission, imprisoned many of the colonists, and released them only under condition of an immediate return to New Haven, threatening to send them prisoners to Holland if he ever caught them at Delaware. The leaders of the expedition,

---

[1] New Haven Town Records, II. 40.

Jasper Crane and Wm. Tuttle, related the story of their wrongs to the Commissioners of the United Colonies, at New Haven, on the 14th of September. They specified the outrages of the Dutch. New England had been insulted. They themselves had lost more than three hundred pounds. Particularly grievous was it that, were it not for the selfish behavior of the Dutch, "The gospel might have been published to the natives, and much good done." The Commissioners resolved to send a sufficient force for the defense of that country, if, within a twelvemonth, the petitioners would transport to the Delaware Bay, under commission from New Haven, a well-equipped colony with one hundred armed men; and *if*, under all circumstances, New Haven would pay every bill incurred. On the other hand, it was voted that all Englishmen at Delaware should be under the jurisdiction of New Haven.

This was cold comfort. New Haven was resolved upon action, but the southern horizon was black with war, and she was loath to step forward alone. Plymouth was invited to aid in a vigorous attempt to plant a united colony at Delaware, but Plymouth refused. Still persisting, in the same year (1651) New Haven asked Captain John Mason, of Connecticut, to lead an expedition. Under a leader of such courage and military experience, Delaware Bay might have been won for New England, and colonial history have been profoundly changed. Captain Mason desired to accept the offer, but the Connecticut General Court interfered, and prevented a successful issue of the negotiations. During the next three years the New England Confederation trembled on the verge of a war with Stuyvesant. War was declared between England and Holland. Concerted action on the part of the New Englanders would have given New Holland to the Allies, and extended New Haven's limits to the Delaware without any one to gainsay or resist. After the Commissioners declared for war, Massachusetts refused to obey, adopted the *rôle* of a secessionist, and checked the whole proceeding. New Haven, with whom the proposed war was almost a matter of life and death, was justified in adverting to the conduct of Massachusetts as " A provoaking sinn against God, and of a scandalous nature before men." The mutinous schemes of Roger Ludlow and of some New Haven malcontents complicated the problem still more both for Connecticut and New Haven. Finally, just as an army of 800 men was ready to march upon New Amsterdam, tidings came of a European peace, and New Haven's last chance was gone. But the town did not lose hope. In July, 1654, on the day when peace was publicly announced in New Haven, letters were dispatched by the court to the authorities in New Sweden, asserting the " Proprietie which some in this colony have to large tracts of land on both sides of Delaware Bay and River, and desiring a neighbourly correspondency with them both in trading and planting there."

'Late in the fall, between fifty and sixty persons, headed by John Cooper and Thomas Munson, were willing to test fortune again at Delaware. The Delaware Company claimed to have sunk already more than £600, but offered to sell their lands to the emigrants for half that sum, to be paid in four years. There seems to have been some hope that the major part of the town, which was then " Laboring under great discouragement," would incline toward Delaware rather than to Cromwell's offers of foreign settlement,[1] and would migrate to the Bay in a body. But Mr. Davenport said that his health would not allow him to engage in it in person. Mr. Hooke withdrew " Because his wife was gone for Eng-

---

[1] Cromwell's invitation to remove from New Haven to Jamaica was received in the latter part of April, 1656, and fell upon many willing ears. Lieutenant John Nash, in Town-Meeting (May 19, 1656), spoke the mind of " The Generallitie of the Towne that they conceive it to be a work of God, and that persons should goe before "—(*i. e.*, to Jamaica)—" fit to carry on the worke of Christ in Commonwealth and also in Church-affairs. They are free, and will attend the providence of God in it, provided that they hear further encouragement both of the healthfulness of the place and a prosperous going on of the Warr." (N. H. T. R., II. 235.)

land, and he knew not how God would dispose of her." The Governor gave no positive answer. The emigrants endeavored to secure the services of Magistrates Samuel Eaton and Francis Newman. Those gentlemen finally consented conditionally, being evidently in doubt about "The call of God to the work."

In January, 1655, the colonists drew up agreements with the town, and it was voted that "When God shall so inlarge the English plantations in Delaware, as that they shall grow the greater part of the jurisdiction, then the Governor may be one yeare in one part and the next yeare in another, and the Deputy Governor to be where the Governor is not, and the General Courts to be where the Governor resides." John Cooper went before to spy out the land, but he brought back a discouraging report. However, the plan was slowly matured through that year. The enterprise was completely thwarted by a series of untoward events—the conquest of New Sweden by Stuyvesant in October, 1655, the deaths of Mr. Samuel Eaton, and of his father the Governor, and also of Mr. Goodyear, the Deputy Governor. The succession of Mr. Francis Newman to the Gubernatorial dignity, and the increasing uncertainty of English politics, contributed to the same end. But the dream of Delaware was not forgotten.

CHAPTER IV.

THE UNION WITH CONNECTICUT. THE BIRTH OF NEWARK.

The destruction of the English settlements on the Delaware Bay, in 1643, virtually sealed the fate of New Haven as a town and as a colony. The desperate struggles of the next dozen years only enfeebled still more the financial stamina of the town. The only hope of gaining a share in the coveted fur trade was thus extinguished. Furthermore, the undertaking had brought New Haven to the very verge of open warfare with the Dutch. A great Puritan immigration from England was no longer probable. There were dissensions in the Church and scandals in society.[1] The newly-formed New England Confederacy was not a sufficient resource in such an hour of trial. After eight years of effort, New Haven prepared to recede from its original silent assumption of independence, and to ask for recognition from the English Crown.

But allegiance to England in 1647 was not what it would have been in 1637. The Parliament was now triumphant, the King, the prisoner of the Scotch. The Town-Court could listen with complacency to Governor Eaton's announcement that "The Kinges Armes are cutt by Mr. Mullyner for the towne and set upon a post in the highway by the seaside."[2]

The merchants turned to a direct trade with London as a last resort, and freighted Lamberton's "Great Shippe" with a cargo worth £5000. On board went Mr. Gregson, commissioned to procure a colonial charter. Ship, cargo, and passengers all found a resting-place at the bottom of the Atlantic.

---

[1] Even Governor Eaton was scarcely in his grave before incriminating charges were made against him. They were easily shown to be baseless.

[2] Records, I. 369 ; II. 519.

A New Party within the Colony.

The purposes of the original leaders of the colony had failed. The vision of a commercial metropolis on the edge of a wilderness slowly, surely faded away. The financial supremacy within the town passed gradually into the hands of farmers and small traders.[1] The revolution in business was attended by a revolution in political feeling. The men of the newer generation were inclined to disapprove of the strictness of their elders. This younger party was more or less blindly moving toward the subversion of New Haven's peculiar polity, although they generally disapproved of the turbulent demonstrations of a few unruly spirits.

In September, 1648, Mr. Pell, a man of more than average intelligence, who had recently married the Widow Brewster, was summoned to take the oath of fidelity to "The Jurisdiction." He replied that he had taken his oath of allegiance in England and should not do it here. The court, evidently nonplussed, said that no more was required of him than of every one else: "Yett, if he had any grounds against it, he might consider of it." The issue is unknown. No instance of a similar objection is recorded. A much less reputable citizen was the discontented Thomas Langdon, who was haled before the court January 7, 1650, for singing and drinking with young men at his house in the night-time. He was hardy enough to reply: "If we were in old England, we could sing and be merry." He was condemned to pay a fine of twenty shillings. Again, in 1661, several young

---

[1] Not one of the original merchants of New Haven was successful. A few examples will suffice to illustrate the general shrinkage in the estimated values of estate. The estate of

Governor Eaton, reckoned in 1643 at £3000, in 1658 was £1440.
Mr. Goodyear,   "   "   "   "   1000,   "   "   804.
Mr. Brewster,   "   "   "   "   1000,   "   "   605.

Mr. Goodyear was probably not concerned in the Delaware Company. Mr. Isaac Allerton, a pilgrim of the *Mayflower*, came from Plymouth to New Haven, and there closed, in bankruptcy, a long life of commercial activity.

couples were accused of misspending their time in card-
playing at unseasonable hours. One of the culprits, James
Eaton, who afterward held honorable positions in the town,
spoke with great politeness and ability, saying: "Unless all
recreation be unlawful, I cannot see that what I have done is
evil." He was told that "It is contrary to rule, and a worke
of darkness," but the offense was condoned with a lecture.[1]
These remonstrances betray the new influences that were
quietly at work beneath the surface of the town's common
life. The first considerable achievement of the Younger
Party was the introduction of townsmen in 1651 into the
local government. It has already been pointed out that these
new officials antagonized the magisterial element. But two
among the ten townsmen first chosen were entitled to the
prefix "Mr." Here were such men as Jarvis Boykin, formerly Town-Drummer, and Town-Crier John Cooper, who was
probably ignorant of writing.

---

[1] New Haven Town Records, II. 52, 406; also Colonial Records, II. 54–59.
In the outlying towns of the colony the disaffection was greater than at
New Haven, and it seems probable that Roger Ludlow attempted to profit
by it. In 1653, as we have already seen, Connecticut and New Haven
were straining every nerve to bring on hostilities with the Dutch. There
is ground for more than a suspicion that Ludlow at Fairfield was abetting
Youngs at Southold, and ex-Town-Drummer Bassett at Stamford, and
other malcontents who were organizing a promising revolt against the
New Haven Government. It is possible that Ludlow and his party, under
cover of marching against the Dutch, hoped to seize on Manhattan and
the towns on Long Island, and to unite them with Greenwich, Stamford,
Stratford and Fairfield into a new Colony-State, of which Mr. Ludlow
should be the Governor. Thus the Sound-towns would be at once relieved
from the strictness of New Haven, and from the no less unpopular, distant
rule of the river-towns. Bassett headed a rebellion at Stamford in the
Town-Meeting, saying: "Let us have England's laws; for England does
not prohibit us from our votes and liberties. Here we are made asses of,
and bondmen and slaves," etc. Ludlow succeeded in leading his own
town away from its allegiance to Connecticut, and was already at the head
of a little army, when Cromwell's peace with the Dutch and the prompt
action of Connecticut and New Haven put an end to all hostile prepara-
tions, and compelled Ludlow's hasty flight out of Connecticut and into
Virginia.

TERMS OF ADMISSION OF STRANGERS.

It was probably due to the commercial spirit that New Haven was always unusually liberal in the admission of strangers. In 1647, in the midst of wars and rumors of wars, several Dutch merchants petitioned to be admitted as planters, and after debate they were received. But the entrance of foreigners brought new perils. The soil might pass into the hands of aliens, and improper persons might gain a lodging within the town. In May, 1650, a stringent law forbade the "Disposal of any house, house-lott, land, or any part or parcel of the same, to Strangers." No one might entertain a stranger longer than three weeks without permission from the authorities.[1] How carefully this legislation was actually obeyed may be inferred from a vote of the town in 1651. The deputies were ordered to ascertain what inhabitants were not admitted planters, "That they may be called in question and things reduced to order." Governor Eaton's Code of 1655–56 gave the control of all sales or leases to strangers, first to the magistrates; secondly, to the majority of the freemen, and thirdly, to the major part of the inhabitants; but it was provided that residence for a year within a plantation, even without a license, was sufficient to convert a stranger into an inhabitant.[2]

---

[1] In the same year Connecticut, with a natural jealousy of the Dutch Fort and Trading-House at Hartford, enacted as follows: "May 16, 1650. No Foreigner, after September 30th, shall retail any Goods by themselves anywhere in this colony, nor shall any Inhabitant, for one year, retail any Goods belonging to any Foreigner under penalty of half the value."—*Col. Rec.*, 1. 207.

[2] Does not this recall the "Year and a day Town-residence" of the ancient common law? Even the renting of rooms to neighbors was under careful supervision. In 1656, William Trowbridge appealed to the Monthly Court for permission to let his cellar to two shoemakers and a chamber to a saddler. Governor Newman shook his head at the idea of so many young persons under one roof. The Governor had heard that "There hath been a custom of shovel-board in that house of late, and that mens servants do stay there at unseasonable hours." But John Thompson, who was already a lodger there, testified that, "Though there was some recreation used in

No step was taken hastily, yet the wandering stranger was practically sure of eventually becoming a citizen or inhabitant, if he could only secure reputable sponsors. In 1656, Mrs. Finch, of Westchester, came to New Haven and rented a house in order that her lame child might have the benefit of John Winthrop's surgical skill. The town interfered and voted not to let her stay unless some approved person offered himself as her security. Mr. Goodyear and Sergeant Jeffrey performed that kindness for her. Deacon Miles informed the General Court, in 1658, that one Windle, a Dutchman, who had lived in the deacon's family and "Showed a good conversation," desired to be admitted "As a planter with us." "None objecting, it was refferred to the Committee." Such instances might be multiplied.[1]

----

the family," the rumor concerning untimely junketing of servants was untrue. Finally the court decided upon a term of probation, and granted the request until the next meeting of the court.—*N. H. T. Rec.*, II. 310.

[1] Connecticut Colony, in 1659, enacted a general law denying to every inhabitant the right of alienating property unless the offer of sale had first been made to the town-authorities. This was a typical village-community law, such as Russian communes recognize to-day. Cf. Laveleye, Maurer and Maine. Some of the towns that sprang from New Haven legislated more stringently than the parent plantation. Guilford inserted an anti-monopoly plank in her platform. No one could sell or purchase any share in land unless by the consent of the community, or bring into the plantation anybody "not fully approved," or invest more than £500 in town-shares without permission from the freemen. It is said that several persons were fined and whipped for transgressing the second stipulation (Lambert, 103). Southold, in 1654, anticipated Connecticut's law of 1659. "No inhabitant shall lett, sett, or sell any of his accomodacons to any person who is not a legall Townsman without the consent of the freemen, and the Towne shall have the tender of the sale of house or land, and a full month's space provided to return an answer."

Very similar parish-laws existed at the same time in the mother-country. March 13, 1664, the Steeple-Ashton vestry voted as follows: "Item, Whereas there hath much poverty happened unto this parish by receiving of Strangers to inhabit there and not first securing them against such contingencies, and for avoiding the like occasions in time to come,—It is ordered by this Vestry that every person who shall let or set any housing or dwelling to any Stranger, and shall not first give good security for

INCREASING IMPORTANCE OF THE TOWNSMEN.

From the first, the townsmen were eager to assert their control over the transfer and use of land. One of their first orders was that " None but admitted planters shall keep Swine or Cattell within the libberties of this Towne without leave from the Towne, nor shall any Planter let any of his common for Swine or other Cattell to any that is not a Planter without the Townes consent."

Alienations of title that might take place among the planters themselves were not restricted by any general law for either town or colony, excepting that all alienations must be recorded in the "Secretary's booke," and an abstract of title must be obtained from him. As in the Massachusetts, so in the New Haven Colony, each town managed its lands as it saw fit. But the town claimed a strict supervision, and the New Haven townsmen were ever on the alert. They had first assumed control over the sale or lease of town-lots in July, 1656, when " They sent to Mr. Hooke to desire him on ye Townes behalf that, if he sould his house, the Towne might have the refusall of it."[1]

In the following year, Mr. Goodyear was forbidden to sell even a share in the iron-foundry without the town's approval, and when his partner, John Winthrop, sold his right in the iron-works to a couple of Bostonians without consulting the Town-Court, there was great indignation. Subsequently, the assertion of municipal control over Winthrop's right to dispose of his real estate was incidentally the cause of the first serious conflict between the townsmen and the elder leaders of the community.

---

defending and saving the said inhabitants from future charge as may happen by such Stranger coming to inhabit within the said parish, shall be rated to the poor to 20s. monthly, over and besides his monthly tax." There was an enactment of the same sort in Ardley, Herts, so late as 1718. (Toulmin Smith's Parish, 514, 588.) See also the " Poor Laws" in general.

[1] The Rev. Mr. Hooke was then on the point of sailing for England, where he was appointed Court Chaplain to Oliver Cromwell.

In the winter of 1658–59, Winthrop had determined not to become a resident of New Haven, and he wished to dispose of his house and lot. The dwelling was one of the finest in New Haven. Winthrop proposed to lease it directly to Nathaniel Kimberley, an inhabitant of the town, but a man of no especial prominence. Mr. Davenport, in his private correspondence with Winthrop, remonstrated at length: "This way of letting it unto such men will not be for your profit, nor for the townes satisfaction. It will best satisfy them" (*i. e.*, the town) "if you please to give them leave to buy it of you."

The townsmen maintained that the disposition of the property fell within their province, and desired Governor Newman to write to Mr. Winthrop a message similar to the one given to Parson Hooke. Mr. Davenport's coterie, on the other hand, urged the claims of the magistrates to control such alienations of estate. In accordance with this view, Mr. Winthrop announced that he would leave the house in the hands of Messrs. Newman, Gilbert, Davenport, and John Davenport, Jr. But the townsmen, imbued with the spirit of Democracy, resolved that Winthrop's offer intended an infringement of their rights, and that they "liked not that arrangement." They managed to see Winthrop and buy the property for the town.[1] Whereupon their opponents cried out that Mr. Winthrop, a person of high rank and estimation, and of much-needed skill in medicine withal, had been driven away from the town. The whole procedure was rehearsed in

---

[1] The house and lot had belonged to Captain Richard Malbon, and at his death seem in some way to have fallen into Winthrop's hands for disposal. In the General Court, March 9, 1657, it was reported that "Mr. Winthrop already hath Chapmen for Mr. Malbon's house, but is not willing to dispose of it till the Towne refuse." The court voted to buy it for £100, in wheat or biscuit, or in beef and pork, by the Barbadoes market. When Winthrop concluded to live in it himself, the town voted to give it to him; but he refused and paid £100 in goats. The sale was recorded July 7, 1657. (See N. H. T. Records, II. 255, *passim*, and Bacon's Discourses, 326, 376.)

a Town-Court, August 8, 1659. Mr. Davenport said that Mr. Winthrop had always wished to retain liberty to live in New Haven, and he proposed that the bargain should not be consummated, but should be "Stayed awhile, as some stones were come for the iron-worke, which might be an inducement to Mr. Winthrop to come hither." The townsmen replied stoutly that it was not seemly for them to dance attendance upon John Winthrop, and that, if he ever wished to reside again in New Haven, the usual road was open to him. For the first time in the history of the town and colony, Mr. Davenport was defeated. The town voted to approve the action of its representatives. May not these seemingly trivial incidents partly explain Winthrop's forgetfulness, in 1662, of the dignity and the feelings of the New Haven colony?

The immediate result, however, was the enhancement of the municipal importance of the annually-elected representatives of the town, in contradistinction to the magistrates, who generally held office for life. In the next year (1660), the townsmen gained control over the purse-strings. They were empowered to keep account of all "Rates, Fines, Rents, and other incomes of the Towne," and to charge the treasurer therewith; and "The Townsmen and the Court together shall be Auditors."[1] In the following winter, close upon these ominous events, Mathew Gilbert and Robert Treat, leaders of the elder or "Settlers" party, began negotiations with Governor Stuyvesant for an English emigration from New Haven to the Delaware.

THE VILLAGE QUESTION.

During the same year (1659) a land-question of unusual moment sprang up within the limits of the town itself. Mr.

---

[1] Previously the town had, from year to year, chosen as Auditors the court (this refers of course to the Magistrate's Court), generally with one outsider, sometimes with two. But even these auxiliaries were likely to be magistrates.

Davenport took an active interest in it, and for a second time was numbered with the minority. It became a permanent subject of legislation and of bitter discussion, and it was not finally and fully disposed of until more than a hundred years had passed and the War of Revolution had come and gone. The long struggle was between the dwellers in the New Haven town-plot on the one hand, and the inhabitants of outlying farms and incipient villages within the township on the other. The point of controversy was whether or no these dwellers in the mark, these *coloni*, should be allowed to coalesce into municipal units of their own. The farmers did not ask for independent existence, but for the formation of subordinate villages with their own churches and constables. In the town's first debate upon the subject, the lines of opposition were already firmly drawn, and the secretary thought the assembly so important that he dignified it in the records with the special heading of " Villages Propounded." His report is so illustrative of an ancient Town-Meeting, and of the typical Puritan modes of thought, argument, and action, that an almost literal transcription is here presented.

Governor Francis Newman announced the purpose of the meeting. Certain propositions had been received from the farmers at Stony River and Southend, and from those on the farther side of the East River. "They desire a grant of definite parcells of land for to make accommodations for two villages." The East Haven men propounded that the limit of their village-domain might be marked by a fence " from the Red Rocke to the Great Pond '"[1] (Quinnipiac River to Lake Saltonstall), that they might turn their " dry cattell into the commons outside the fence;" and that a special piece of land might be given them (to be included in the fence), where they intended to set their meeting-house. Brother Brackett, the spokesman for the farms (Fair Haven), was bolder and more scientific in his demands. He acknowledged that there were,

---

[1] Here is the idea of the ancient ring-fence.

as yet, only a few inhabitants; " But there is land enough to accommodate a village, whose propositions are as followeth : "

1. The desired boundaries are described.

2. They may pay rates as other plantations do.

3. Every landholder in the village " shall be enjoyned to pay rates in the village, even if not a resident."

Mr. Davenport, who was by far the largest landholder in the last-proposed village, although not a resident in it, delivered a long speech in favor of the petitioners, nearly the whole of which is reproduced in the " Records." " The business is of great weight, both for the honor of God and the good of Posterity. The Saboth ought to be sanctified. Now in this way of Farmes at such a distance, it cannot be kept as a day of holy convocation, and as a day of holy rest in all our dwellings. Let us prevent sin, as we can, in the farmes." If they were brought into a village-form, there might be some officer, as a constable, " to look to civill order." It is a " sad object " to consider how they are deprived of means for the education of their children. But if they were reduced to villages, they might have a teacher. He sought not, as some affirmed, " the destruction of the Town and ffarmes," but he thought that the villages " might be helpful to the Towne " and *vice versa.* If " the new Mill, the Ironworke, and the Villages " might prosper, the " Towne falling into a way of Trade will be in a better state, and the Villages accommodated, and the honor of God in the sanctification of the Saboth and the upholding of the Civill Order provided for. It is the merciful hand of God that His wrath hath not broke out against us more when Sin hath not been prevented at the farmes as it might have been." Governor Newman feared that the provocation of God had been indeed great, most of the farmers being at work " at such a distance that it makes the Saboth a toil rather than a day of holy rest."

It required courage to oppose these two men, but the power of the purse is great in all communities. Sergeant Jefferies said that he was " marvellous willing " that villages should " goe on," but feared that " they will wrong the Towne much by the withdrawal of rates, especially since the ministry of the Colony is so unsettled." Davenport cut short his speech with the sharp retort, "Indeed, if we obey not the voice of the Prophets, God will take away the Prophets." Joseph Alsup was not thereby deterred from remarking that "the Towne" might not be able to maintain a ministry if the villages did not help. Brother Brockit said that the farmers "must move back to the towne," if they could not have villages; and then "the towne must lay rates to support the farmers."

Nathaniel Merriman was the spiteful man who is always present upon such occasions. He threw a firebrand into the midst by saying that, at the first, there were many of them looked upon as men to live by their labor. They had small lots given them, but when "the Towne for their support gave them these lots, it was upon condition that they should inhabit them. And now the Towne would call them off their farmes." He was answered that then the farmers came to town with their families on the last day of the week, and "stayed till after the Saboth," and that the farms were given them that "corn and cattell might be raised;" yet now they need "corne from the towne."

James Clarke was the too-smart young man. He volunteered the information that he could carry corn to the meeting, stay till the "Publique Ordinances be ended," and yet be at home in good time. He was put to confusion by the reply: "It is much to be feared that you do not consider the weight of the 4th Commandment." Governor Newman improved the opportunity for a lecture. "It is grievous that people should depart, as many do, before the publique worship is ended." Upon debate this was found to be the "haynious practise of some Town-dwellers as well as farmers." It was also informed that "sundry are found standing without in the time of publique Exercise, and that the beginning of the Saboth is not attended, and that there is much walking and playing in the Streets by young persons in the evening after the Saboth," which was conceived to be " very prejudiciall to the good of their souls," it being Satan's opportunity to steal the Word out of their hearts. Finally the petitioners were dismissed with the assurance that the town would give them all due encouragement. The whole matter was then referred to a committee. The subsequent report was an adverse one, and the dispute was reopened and continued.

Before the Town-Meeting adjourned, Governor Newman offered a suggestion creditable to himself and implying a rare foresight. It may be called the first instance of official anxiety for the sanitation of New Haven. As in most villages of both new and old England, the cemetery was situated around the church, in the green or market-place. The Governor told the freemen that the present location of the burying-place was a source of ill-health to the town, and propounded that some other place might be thought of and fenced in for a grave-yard.

The townsmen were desired to consider it, and there is evidence that they did so; but the sudden death of Governor Newman and the troubles with Connecticut afford sufficient reason for the total disappearance of the project.[1]

New Haven and the Restored Stuart.

The slow process of local evolution was destined to be now rudely interrupted from without. New England felt no joy at the restoration of Charles Stuart in 1660, and the New Haven leaders, apprehensive of peril, felt the need of a more perfect harmony with Connecticut. Governor Wm. Leete, now the head of the Younger Party, the Rev. Mr. Davenport, and Governor John Winthrop, of Connecticut, who was soon to sail for England, corresponded anxiously about the possibilities of the future. Mr. Davenport insisted that Winthrop should do nothing to prejudice the independence of New

---

[1] New Haven Town Records, II. 331, February 26, 1658.

Haven, and thought, indeed, that he had exacted a promise to that effect. Governor Leete, on the other hand, expressed himself to Winthrop in favor of the union of the two colonies under one charter.

The lowering skies were suddenly made still more threatening, in the spring of 1661, by the advent of Goffe and Whalley, the regicide judges. Obliged to flee from Massachusetts, not daring to stop in Hartford, they found in New Haven security and friends. Men of all shades of opinion combined to aid the fugitives. Mr. Davenport preached to his people from Isaiah xvi. 3 and 4: "Take counsel, execute judgment, make thy shadow as the night in the midst of the noonday; hide the outcasts, betray not him that wandereth. Let mine outcasts dwell with thee, Moab; be thou a covert to them from the face of the spoiler."

The magistrates of the town shut their eyes and stayed their hands when the judges appeared openly in the streets. Governor Leete evaded the demands of the royal emissaries, Kellond and Kirk, for a warrant, and, when pressed by them to acknowledge the King, he replied: "We will wait to see if the King will acknowledge us."

Before the Court of Magistrates, a common citizen of the town indignantly denied, as a slur upon his good name, the report that he had spoken of seeing "*The gentlemen here* three days before the messengers came."[1]

Such sturdy republicanism procured for the obscure town and colony a temporary, but unenviable, notoriety in the court of the second Charles. This New Haven had received tokens of particular favor from the dreaded Oliver; it had never owned the royal authority; it had mocked at the search for the judges; it had done what Switzerland had been unable to do. Letters of alarm and menace from the officers and royal agents at Boston poured in upon New Haven. The colony was too poor to send an agent to

---

[1] Records, Vol. II. 415, May 27, 1661. His name was Edward Parker.

England with golden bribes for the courtiers of Whitehall, and the court bluntly declared that it had not acknowledged the King because it could not agree upon an acceptable form. Mr. Davenport alone wrote to Sir Thomas Temple, at Boston, an unmanly and needlessly subservient letter,[1] to which Temple scornfully referred as "An apollogy from one Mr. Davenport, a minister to me altogether unknowne."

Finally, in August, 1661, New Haven, last of all the colonies, grudgingly proclaimed its allegiance to Charles Stuart.[2]

As time went on, Governor Leete and his friends were seriously alarmed by the animosity in England against town and colony, and feared some especial punishment. They would probably have been disposed to accept the unwelcome provisions of Winthrop's charter in the spring of 1662, if the neighboring colony had not been so offensively violent. Even in 1663, Governor Leete ventured to write to Winthrop in approval of the projected union of the two colonies.

THE HEGIRA TO NEW JERSEY.

Excessively alarming and distasteful were these views to the supporters of the policy of the fathers. Without money, credit, or political affiliations of any importance, they yet clung to the hope of independence, believed the danger from

---

[1] See Mass. Hist. Soc. Coll., Series 3. Vol. VIII. 326-27.

[2] Records, II. 433, August 21, 1661. The proclamation was voted, as though it was a bitter dose, "Seeing now the Bay has done it already." "Although we have not received any form of proclamation by order from his Majestie or Councell of State, for the proclaiming his Majestie in this Colony, yet the Court taking Incouragement from what hath bene in the rest of the United Colonies, hath thought fitt to declare publiquely and proclaime that we do acknowledge his Royall Highness, Charls the Second, King of England, Scotland, France, and Ireland to be our Soveraigne Lord and King and that we do acknowledge ourselves, the inhabitants of this Colony, to bee his Majesties loyall and faithfull subjects. And for the time of doeing it," It was concluded to be done the next morning "at nine of the clocke," and the military company was desired to come to the solemnizing of it. "GOD SAVE THE KING."

England to be averted, and spurned "The Christless rule of Connecticut." Mr. Davenport's feeling toward Leete was bitter. He wrote angrily to Winthrop in 1663, when the charter was already a year old, "As for what Mr. Leete wrote to yourself, it was his private doing, without the consent or knowledge of any of us in this colony; it was not done by him according to his public trust as Governor, but contrary to it."

This repudiation of Mr. Leete was not upheld by the colony. New Haven and Branford supported the cause of the "Godly Government;" but Mr. Leete was continued in his office, and the nominal head of the elder faction, Mathew Gilbert, was, as usual, chosen to the subordinate office of Deputy Governor. Many now began openly to declare themselves citizens of Connecticut and to ignore the New Haven officers and laws. Taxes could not be collected, and the colony, unable to pay even the regular salaries of its officials, was plunging deeper and deeper into debt. The inexorable logic of events was not concealed from Mr. Davenport's understanding, and he sorrowfully exclaimed, "The cause of Christ in New Haven is miserably lost."

The possible overthrow of his plans had been foreseen by him and by the leaders of his party during the quarrel with the townsmen in 1658–60, and, at that time, they had secretly spied out the lands to find a new Canaan.[1]

They turned naturally to the Delaware region, which had already entombed so much of their money. A committee of inspection was sent thither in 1661, and in November Deputy Governor Gilbert wrote to Governor Stuyvesant, thanking him for courtesies shown to the inspectors. He also informed Stuyvesant that Mr. Robert Treat, of Milford, was the chairman of a committee of four, appointed to confer with the

---

[1] Authorities for the following narrative are New York Colonial MSS. IX., as quoted in Whitehead's History of Newark; also the Newark Town Records, Baldwin's Records of Branford, and the New Haven Town Records and New Haven Colonial Records.

Dutch Governor about "Planting under his rule for the enlargement of the kingdom of Christ Jesus in the Congregational Way." Five conditions of willingness to settle under Dutch rule were submitted to Stuyvesant, and he refused assent to all of them, desiring especially to retain control of the election of officers, and the right of appeal to the Dutch tribunals. Whereupon the negotiation slumbered.

But Stuyvesant was anxious to obtain such immigration, and in the winter of 1662–63, Treat, Philip Groves, and John Gregory were bargaining with him again. They found him more amenable to their will, and he obtained time to write home for instructions. June 29, 1663, Mr. Treat wrote to Stuyvesant to inquire if the instructions had come, and complained of hindrances at home to the consummation of the scheme. "Our neighbors seem to hinder and obstruct the matter what they can."

Stuyvesant's instructions had arrived, bearing the date of March 26, 1663, and they urged him to secure the English for subjects by every means and every concession, if necessary. Stuyvesant replied to Treat, July 20, inviting him to come, and reserving only a formal confirmation of officers and the right of appeal in important causes and in capital cases, unless the criminal party confessed. The rapid succession of events checked the transaction with the Dutch at this point. The high-handed discourtesy of the Connecticut Legislature united for the nonce all the New Haven factions in opposition to Winthrop's charter, and through the winter of 1663–64 the warfare of words waxed warm. But Delaware was not forgotten. In January, 1664, amid the throes of colonial dissolution, the General Court for the jurisdiction voted that "The Committee shall treate with Captain Scott about getting a Pattent for Delaware." It appears that New Haven hoped for much from Captain Scott's influence, but the ignominious end of his mission in May, at Hartford, frustrated all such expectations.[1]

---

[1] Colonial Records, II. 499, 541.

The summer of 1664 brought the unexpected surrender of the New Netherlands to the Duke of York. The only avenue of escape seemed closed, and, between the Royal Commissioners and the colony of Connecticut, New Haven felt herself to be between the devil and the deep sea. On the 13th of December, 1664, New Haven, Branford, and Guilford, the only towns that yet held together, voted to submit to Connecticut, "But with a salvo jure of our former right and claime, as a people who have not yet been heard in point of plea."[1] On the 6th of January following, the New Haven Town-Meeting voted to accept the situation, and confirmed the choice of magistrates which had been made by Connecticut.[2]

But yet, in the effort for Delaware, no stone was left unturned. Just one week after the reluctant surrender to Connecticut had been recorded, a letter was addressed by William Jones, magistrate of New Haven, to no less a personage than Colonel Nicolls himself. The history of the great "wrong and injury" of the colony at Delaware Bay was recited. "The Indians of whom we purchased the land there, doe owne our right and much desire the coming of the English." It was hoped that "A further search of our records may be further improved by your honor as your wisdom shall think fit; humbly desiring also that our just claim to the premises, when more fully prosecuted, may be admitted."[3] . . . . "Thus craving your honor's pardon for this boldness, with humble service presented, rests, Your Honor's Humble Servant,　　　　　Wm. Jones."

Appeals to Colonel Nicolls were of course futile. But the grant of all this land between the Hudson and the Delaware to Berkeley and Carteret changed the face of affairs. Governor Philip Carteret arrived and fixed his capital at Elizabethtown.[4] Forthwith, in August, 1665, he sent letters

---

[1] Records, II. 551.

[2] New Haven Town Records, III. 58.

[3] Records, II. 552.

[4] Elizabeth, N. J., was itself descended from the New Haven municipality. See diagram, "New Haven's Family-Tree."

to New England offering to settlers every civil and religious privilege. Mr. Treat and some of his friends immediately visited New Jersey. They bent their steps toward the New Haven property on the Delaware Bay, and selected a site for a settlement near what is now Burlington. Returning by way of Elizabeth, they met Carteret, and were by him influenced to locate on the Passaic River.

It is said that Carteret and Treat drew up a formal agreement in fifteen articles, but the document is not now known to exist. There was probably a reference to it in the record of a Town-Meeting at New Haven, December 4, 1665. "Mr. Jones told the Towne about Delaware. The Articles were read, and *it was said* that a Committee for the ordering of that affayre was appointed."[1] This non-committal statement hides rather than reveals the fact that a hegira of the staunch partisans of the old *régime* was contemplated. Early in the spring of 1666, the remnant of the old New Haven, the New Haven of 1638, under the leadership of Robert Treat and Mathew Gilbert, sailed into the Passaic.[2]

A difficulty with the Indians on account of Treat's failure to deliver promptly a letter which Carteret had given him for their sachem, was amicably arranged through Carteret's aid. There were about thirty men in the company, chiefly from New Haven and Milford, and by the 21st of May, 1666, they felt themselves ready to begin the inevitable Fundamental Agreement.

Mr. (afterward Major-General) Robert Treat seems to have discovered that the pen was indeed mightier than the sword, for the document which was drafted abounded with obscure and stilted phrases. Its superscription was as follows: "In the province of New Jersey, near to Elizabeth Town, and the Town Plotts on the Passaic River, made choice of by friends from Milford and other plantations." Together with agents

---

[1] New Haven Town Records, III. 76.

[2] New Haven Town Records, III., record for April 30, 1666. Mr. Gilbert came back in June, was chosen magistrate, and died in New Haven in 1680.

from Guilford and Branford, it was agreed that all the immigrants should form one township, provided that the Guilford and Branford planters "send word so to be at any time between this and the last of October next ensuing, and to desire to be of one heart and consent [*that?*] through God's blessing with one hand they may endeavor the carrying on of spiritual concernments as also civil and town affairs according to God and a Godly Government." A committee of eleven was chosen to superintend all the details of settlement, and another smaller committee, an inner circle of the former one, was named which would stay within the "Town-Plotts," and receive new-comers. At the head of the committee and at the bottom of this agreement were written the names of Robert Treat and Samuel Swain.

The Branford planters postponed the day of final consideration until October 30. Then they met, and the Rev. Mr. Pierson, Jasper Crane, and twenty-one others, subscribed their names to a more formal Town-Constitution:

"1st. None shall be admitted Freemen within our town upon Passaick River in the Province of New Jersey, but such Planters as are members of some or other of the Congregational Churches, nor shall any but such be chosen to magistracy, or to carry on any part of civil judicature, or as deputies or assistants to have power to vote in establishing laws, in making or repealing them, or to any chief military trust or office. Nor shall any but such church-members have any vote in such Elections; though all admitted Planters shall enjoy all other civil liberties and privileges, and shall have right to their proper inheritance.

"2d. We shall with Care and Diligence provide for the maintenance of the purity of Religion, professed in the Congregational Churches." Upon the margin were inscribed the same texts which Davenport had cited in his Fundamental Agreement, twenty-seven years before.[1]

---

[1] It has been stated that Branford moved bodily to Newark. Such was not the case, although the major part of the inhabitants undoubtedly did go. Mr. Pierson was a more bitter partisan than Mr. Davenport, and the

It was apparent that no interference from Carteret's Government was expected. In November Branford's action was ratified by the others at the Passaic "Town Plotts," now temporarily called "Milford." In June, 1667, the entire force of the little colony was gathered together in their new abode, to which the name "Newark" was applied, in honor of Mr. Pierson's English home. The Fundamental Agreement was revised and enlarged, the most notable expansion being the following article: "The planters agree to submit to such magistrates as shall be annually chosen by the Friends from among themselves, and to such Laws as we had in the place whence we came."

Sixty-four men wrote their names under this Bill of Rights, of whom twenty-three were from Branford, and the remaining forty-one from New Haven, Milford, and Guilford.[1]

Most of them were probably heads of families, and, in all the company, but six were obliged to make their marks. Hence it may be fairly concluded that this expatriated New Haven colony was not insignificant either in point of numbers or of intelligence. It may not be amiss to quote here from the Newark "Records" of 1670 a minute, replete with the Yankee spirit: "Richard ——— is admitted a freeholder, and he hath promised to set about learning to read, which is an encouragement unto us herein."

It may be questioned why the beginnings of Newark should find such a prominent place in the story of New Haven's life.

---

history of his flock was indeed a "moving" one. Without counting the exodus from England to Lynn, Mass., there were three removals within thirty years, and each time in search of a "Government according to God." 1. From Lynn to Southampton, L. I.; 2. Thence to Branford; 3. From Branford to Newark, N. J. The first Lynn emigration was to the western end of the Island, but the settlers were driven thence by the Dutch to Southampton.

[1] As in primitive New Haven, every planter admitted to Newark was obliged to sign the Fundamental Agreement of the town. The last-recorded official enforcement of this act was in 1665. (See the Town Records, and Stearns' History of the First Church.)

It seems to me that, after 1666, the New Haven of Davenport and Eaton must be looked for upon the banks, not of the Quinnipiac, but of the Passaic. The men, the methods, the laws, the officers, that made New Haven Town what it was in 1640, disappeared from the Connecticut Colony, but came to full life again immediately in New Jersey.

New Haven, after the Union, was in the hands of the younger generation that knew not Joseph, or at least hearkened not unto him ; and Mr. Davenport, in old age, removed to die in Boston. Cotton Mather described Mr. Davenport's final discomfiture in words that convey a sort of regretful triumph: " Yet, after all, the Lord gave him to see that, in this world, a Church-State was impossible, whereinto there enters nothing which defiles."[1]

Newark preserved, for a few years longer, that essence, that spirit of political and religious thought which had made New Haven unique. Interlocked as the possibilities of its foundation were with the disastrous experiences of that Delaware Company which was almost coeval with the town and colony upon the Quinnipiac, Newark was not so much the product as the continuation of New Haven. As the branches of the banyan tree lean over to touch the earth, take root, and become themselves towering trees, and in their own turn parent trunks, even though the original stem be dead, so the most ancient town-polity of New Haven touched the soil of New Jersey, and imparted to the city of Newark the first currents of its municipal life. Out of that little settlement upon the Passaic, not only Newark, but nearly a dozen other municipalities surrounding Newark, derive their origin. Such, one might add, has been the unceasing, empire-making labor, not only of one or of many New England towns, but of every home-cluster of the Anglo-Saxon race on either side of the Atlantic.

---

[1] Magnalia, I. 328.

CHAPTER V.

THE WORK OF THE COURTS IN JUDICATURE AND IN LEGISLATION.

The degree of the "blueness" which is supposed to tinge early New Haven history can be determined by examination of the laws, and also by observation of the workings of those laws in the courts. Dr. J. Hammond Trumbull has vindicated the statute-books of New Haven and Connecticut alike from unjust and absurd accusations. But the letter of the law is not so decisive as the spirit of its actual enforcement and operation. The records of the Magistrate's Court of the town of New Haven will reveal the exact measure of harshness and of mercy, of wisdom and of ignorance. The student of the Puritan character must be grateful for the garrulity of the New Haven memorials. Nowhere else is there extant so complete and faithful a picture of colonial administration. The merits and the shortcomings of the peculiar polity of the village as a community, and of the magistrate as judge and lawgiver, are evident on every page.

Without considering the numerous finings for offenses which ranked as misdemeanors in both the State and Church Militant, for the absences, tardinesses, and faulty equipment, it is safe to say that the crimes most frequently charged upon prisoners at the bar were drunkenness, Sabbath-breaking, and lewdness.

DRUNKENNESS.

The sale and use of stimulants were the bane of the village from the first. Mr. Eaton, Mr. Brewster, and others of the gentry, kept a store of liquors in their cellars, and the servants and younger folk managed to indulge in a great amount of

clandestine drinking. The fact of drunkenness was originally regarded as the only criminal feature of the process,
and inquiry into the sale or gift of the liquor was, at first,
not customary, although in 1640 John Charles was forbidden
to draw wine, " Because there hath beene much disorder by
itt." The penalty was at the discretion of the court—stocking,
fining, or, more generally, whipping. The session of Eaton's
court on the 5th of February, 1640, was not unlike the
morning scene in the modern City Court. Five men stood
there accused of drunkenness. The various modes of punishment were all applied, but John Jenner was fortunate enough
to escape the rod by pleading " Infirmyty and the extremyty
of the colde." Disorders continued, and in June, 1645, the
town voted to adopt the license system.

The wholesale trade was not restricted, but thereafter no
person might retail " Wine or strong licquors " without
express license from the Monthly Court. Two men were
licensed to sell, and an ordinary, or tavern, was established.
The business of the ordinary does not appear to have been
lucrative, and pains were taken by the court from time to
time to encourage the innkeeper. Keeping tavern had been
regarded as one of the common rights of the town, and carried
with it a share of land. In 1641, the proprietors' committee
were ordered to lay out " Meadow and upland for an inne."
Four years afterward, when Wm. Andrews was first actually
licensed to keep the ordinary and to retail liquors, twenty acres
of upland were assigned to the inn " To put strangers' horses
in." " If Andrews dye or leave, the land shall still goe to the
Ordinary for the use aforesaide." Subsequently meadows for
pasture and hay were allotted in the same manner.[1]

---

[1] This assignment of land to the innkeeper as a sort of perpetual fief for
his office, recalls a custom in more than one English parish. Some
portions of the common field were frequently christened with the name
of a trade. The tradition of this custom has sometimes caused a popular belief that no one can legally own a certain lot who does not follow
the trade associated with it by name. (See Maine's Village Communities, 126.)

At first there were no discriminations enforced between Indians and white men with reference to intemperance, and Indians seem not to have been punished for drunkenness alone at any time. But the red man early manifested his fatal weakness for firewater. It was reported in the Town-Court of May, 1654, that some Indians had been seen drunk, and "The Court feared that it was on Mr. Goodanhouse's vinegar." Eaton's Code of 1655–56 sought to check the sale of stimulants to Indians by rigorous precautions. The Monthly Court kept a very close watch upon the use of liquor, and occasionally inquired even into the consumption of liquors within the family circle. Dutch traders in the town who could not speak English were obliged to answer before the court through their interpreter for furnishing "Strong Watters" to customers—a circumstance which shows perhaps a kind of underground traffic among people of the baser sort.

Governor Eaton came into the court-room on the 7th day of December, 1647, with a burden upon his mind. "The Old Serpent" had brought a reproach upon him. It had been noised abroad in the town that "Anthony, the neager," the Governor's servant, had "gott some stronge watter" and had been seen drunk. The report reached Governor Eaton's ears. He rehearsed the story in court, and lamented that the knowledge of this new temptation of Anthony could not have been kept "within the compasse of the family," where Anthony might have received family correction. The "neager" was summoned to testify. He said that, "being sent for suger to Mr. Evanc his house," he did not refuse the invitation of Mathew, Mr. Evance's servant, to drink ; but "Mr. Evanc his neager poured somewhat out of a runlett, and gave it hime, and went awaye, and he drunke not knowing what it was, and after hee had drunke, hee was light in his head after hee came abroade." Mathew was also present in court, and "Conceived that Anthony dranke at one aboute the quantetie of two wine-glasses." The court gravely considerod the matter, and concluded that, as this was Anthony's first offense, and "Possibelly hee might not know what he drunke till afterward, it being given him in such a vessell as is used to drinke beare out of, and hoping it will bee a warning to hime for time to come," no public corporal punishment should be inflicted for this time. "But, as the governers zeale and faithfulnes hath appeared (not conniving at sinn in his owne family), so they leave it to hime to give that correction which hee in his wisdome shall judge meete." So Anthony went home to take his lesson in private.

The sin of drunkenness invaded the more select circles also, and polluted even the precincts of Mr. Davenport's carefully-guarded temple. James Heywood, a member of the Church, went on board of a Dutch ship, and drank "So that he had not the use of his reason, nor of his tongue, hands, or feete."[1] He was promptly cast out of the Church. April 6, 1647, he was brought before the Monthly Court to receive secular punishment. Governor Eaton informed him that his sin was aggravated "With many circumstances," and asked what he had to say for himself. Heywood replied in a very humble and contrite speech: "I owne my sinne and take the shame; the hand of the Lord is justly out against mee, so that I doe justifie the proceedings of the Court in what God shall guide their harts to."

The Governor's summing-up, a fine specimen of its kind, is preserved: "Drunkennesse is among the fruits of the flesh both to be witnessed against both in the Church and Civill Court, and its a brutish sinne and so to be witnessed against. A whip for the horse, a bridle for the asse, and a rodd for the fooles backe, and his sinne is more heynous as he was a member of the Church. But it hath not been brought to mee that this man hath bin guilty of drunkennesse, nor is it fownd that it was an appoynted meetinge for drinkinge, but he, being called, drank an excessive quantitye, w'h caused these efects. I leave it, therefore, to the Courts judgment, whether

---

[1] Records, I. 806.

they shall find it a disposition to drunkennesse, or an act onlye."

The soft answer turned away wrath. The court decided to spare Heywood's back at the expense of his purse. He was condemned to pay to the town "Fivety Shillings."[1]

Robert Bassett, the Town-Drummer, filled a peculiar position in the community. He was a roving, lusty Englishman, somewhat reckless of the higher powers, a ringleader in the merrymakings among the lesser folk, and strangely out of place in a Puritan "State, whose design is Religion." Besides being a competent workman, he seems to have enjoyed a monopoly of the drumming-talent in the town, and hence could and did indulge himself in ways that would have cost another man a scarified back, or a ticket-of-leave. The records of the court upon August 1, 1648, afford a ludicrous picture of a spree at Bassett's house on the previous Friday.

Ten men, mariners and shipbuilders, had resorted to Robert Bassett's after sunset, and, like Falstaff of old, called loudly for sack. The jovial drummer, nothing loath, supplied them. "The miscariage continewed till betwixt tenn and eleven of the clocke to the great provocation of God, the disturbance of the peace, and to such a height of disorder that strangers wondered at it." Secretary Francis Newman was so shocked and indignant that he dilated upon the subject in the "Records" to his own evident relief and for our behoof. "No man without speciall licence is permitted to retayle

---

[1] A still worse scandal grieved the Church at Milford in 1657 and 1659. William Hast, who was not only a church-member, but sergeant in the military company, was arraigned before the Court of Magistrates at New Haven for smuggling liquors into the colony and for drinking to excess. The indignation waxed great against him, the more because it was reported that people in Virginia, where he traded, pointed at him and said: "This is one of your church-members." The court was actually enraged. "You have a blacke eye; whether it came by drinking, you best know. . . Shall wickedness be suffered, and is there no balm in Gilead (as we may say)?" He was put in the stocks, threatened with whipping and with guardianship, and bade to remember, "That the Divell is your keeper in your present state."

strong liquours in small quantities, much less to use his house or cellar as a tavern for company to come in and spend their money in drinking wine or strong liquours; onely if a merchant will drawe out a pipe or pee, he might sell either to neighbor plantations, or to the inhabitants of New Haven a runlet, case of glases, or by the gallon for his private use." But Robert Bassett lavishly provided six quarts, "By which means some of the company brake into quarrelling and divers other sinful miscariages." The owner of the pinnace grew tipsily jocular, and hailed the boatswain as "Brother Loggerhead." "They fell first to wrestling, then to blowes, and theirin grew to that feirenes that the master of the pinnace thought the boatswain would have pulled out his eies; and they toumbled on the ground down the hill into the creeke and mire, shamfully wallowing therin." The owner of the pinnace, being sore afraid, ran about the streets, crying, "'Hoe, the Watch! Hoe, the Watch!' The watch made hast and, for the present, stopped the disorder; but in this rage and distemper the boatswaine fell a-swearinge, 'Wounds and Hart,' as if he were not onely angry with men, but would provonke the high and blessed God."

The owner of the pinnace, who had aroused the guardians of the peace by his outcry, returned to Robert Bassett's house in the hope, probably, of quieting his perturbed spirits with more sack. But "Bassett thrust him out of dores, thretening, as Thomas Toby relates it, to make him sucke as long as he lived, which words argue distemper and are used by drunken companions; so that the disorder was verey great and verey offensive, the noyse and oathes being heard to the other side of the creeke."[1]

Verily, a fearful revel this, to intrude upon Mr. Davenport's visions of millennial glory! Robert Bassett might have expected to undergo a heavier penalty than the five pounds fine which was imposed upon him. Nevertheless, during the next year he found it convenient to remove to Stamford.

---

[1] See the whole long report, Records, I. 393–96.

Upon the kindred vice of tobacco-using but little notice
was bestowed. The only objection to its consumption was
apparently grounded not on a dislike for the drug itself, but
upon the fear of danger from fire. In 1646, and in 1655, it
was ordered that " Whosoever shall be found taking tobacco
within the streates, yards about the howses without the dores,
neare or abonte the towne, in the meeting-howse, or body of
the trayne-souldiers or any other place where they may doe
mischiefe thereby, shall pay sixpence a pipe or a time; but,
if he be a poore servant and hath not to paye, and his master
will not paye for him, he shall sit in the stockes one houre."[1]
Although the habit was thus confined to the fireside, and was
evidently regarded with disfavor, yet the admission of the
commercial value of the weed cropped out curiously in 1654.
Four men petitioned the General Court of the town that they
might have twelve acres near the Shepherd's Pen, on the west
side, for the planting of tobacco. There was a disposition to
grant the request, " Knowing," in the words of one speaker,
" the benefitt of Tobacco for trade so long as they employed
it to no other use." But some objected on account of the
danger from the use in town, and the petition was not acted
upon.[2] But that the consumers of nicotine in the town were
not only numerous, but bold, might be inferred from a
monthly court entry. October 7, 1662, " John Tharpe was
sharply witnessed against for taking Tobacco in the meeting-
honse."[3]

SABBATH-BREAKING.

It is written that Israel fell because it forgot to reverence
its Sabbaths. New Haven heeded the warning to guard
zealously her holy days. By the adoption of the Mosaic
Law, Sabbath-breaking was made a capital offense, and

[1] Records. I. 241 ; II. 146.
[2] New Haven Town Records, II. 179 ; III. 6.
[3] Connecticut absolutely prohibited the use of tobacco except by medical
authority.

Eaton's Code confirmed that statute with the provision, "If the sinn was committed proudly and presumptuously." The Mosaic Law overshot its mark. The magistrates shrank from applying so severe a penalty. Between law and practice, therefore, there was wide discrepancy until 1648, when the town enacted a by-law that moderated the Mosaic stringency into closer conformity with English usage. It was proclaimed in the Town-Court that some persons had recently taken too much liberty in secular employment on the Sabbath. The court thereupon ordered that the Sabbath from sunset to sunset should be holy time: "Whoesoever shall do any ordinary outward occasions, either upon land or watter, extraordinary cases, works of mercy and necessitie being excepted, shall suffer such punishment as the perticuler Court shall judge meete."[1] The court and community gave a wide interpretation to the term "Sabbath-breaking." There was a family group of allied offenses. Besides abstention from sanctuary privileges, and secular employment upon the Sabbath, the conduct in church, the behavior toward the ministers, even remarks about the Church individually or collectively, were all under surveillance and subject to judicial investigation. The pages of the court records which tell of these proceedings indicate what was really the highest degree of New Haven's Puritanical austerity.

At the second court held in New Haven, two servants of John Cockerill adorned the whipping-post for stealing money out of their master's chest on the Lord's Day in meeting-time—a great aggravation. In 1645, about the time of Secretary Fugill's disgrace, there was a series of scandalously irreverent acts in town, and even within the Church. Bamfield Bell amused himself by singing certain profane songs, as Brother Wm. Payne deemed them. But Bell retorted upon Brother Payne's reproof with "You are one of the holy bretheren that will lye for advantadge." There were two

---

[1] The irreverent conduct of Blayden and of Reekes, hereafter described, provoked this legislation.

witnesses to the story in court, and Mr. Evance testified that it was Bell's "Constant frame to reproach those that walke in the wayes of God. The centance of the Court was that he should be severely whipped."

The first one to suffer a severe punishment for "Doing his own will on the holy day" was Wm. Blayden, in 1647. He had, however, given previous offense by staying away from both court and meeting. He pleaded that his clothes were wet through on Saturday, that he was unable to light a fire, and that consequently he was obliged to lie abed all day Sunday. The court brushed aside his plea somewhat roughly. "The truth appearing to be noe other than a profaine neglecting, yea, dispising the ordynances of Christ through sloathfulnesse, the judgment of the Court was that he be publicquely whipped, as he is the first profanely breaking the Saboth, worshipping not God, nor wayting for a blessing from him onn himselfe."[1]

A few months afterward, a ship which traded to the Barbadoes for Mr. Richard Malbon and his son-in-law, Mr. Perry, was grounded in the harbor. On Sunday, the wind, shifting, blew in a high tide, and the vessel floated. Messrs. Perry and Malbon consulted over the necessity of warding off possible danger from the ship. Mr. Perry, feeling perplexed, betook himself to Mr. Davenport for advice. "Mr. Davenport tould hime hee should leave it to God's providence, the Saboth was a day of rest, and therfore hee ought to rest." But Brother Perry found it hard to rest when his property was in jeopardy, and he gave orders that some might go to see what state the vessel was in, but that nothing should be done "Without apparent necessitie." The upshot was that before the next court stood Mr. Larabee, a seaman, and Steven Reekes, captain of the ship, charged with "Hauling the ship to or towards the neoke bridge upon the Sabothe, which is a laboure proper for the six days, and not to be undertaken on the Lord's-day."

----

[1] Records, I. 173, 334.

All the circumstances were rehearsed and examined. The court—doubtless Governor Eaton—preached the usual discourse to Captain Reekes, and by way of conclusion, "Considering the persons that they are strangers, and thinking they did not doe it out of contempt, but ignorantly, they agreed for this time (the failing being acknowledged and amendment promised for time to come) to passe it by, but if any of our owne take libbertie heareby, the sentence will bee heavier on them." What mirthful derision would greet the relation of this aneedote by Captain Reekes to the mariners of Virginia and Barbadoes!

But such incidents disclosed to the men who conducted New Haven's fortunes a tendency which to them was no laughing-matter. Only the stronger moral fibres can withstand the strain of adversity. The weaker ones bend and break. By 1645 the adventurous enthusiasm and the charm of novelty had alike vanished from the new settlement. The Puritan, chafing against the discomforts of frontier life and the goads of misfortune, viewed each successive mishap as a divine reproof for sins committed. At each reverse, therefore, the watch over the graceless members of the community was more strictly kept, and the inquiry went forth: "Are there Achans among us?" Church and State were anxiously sifted to find the accursed thing that provoked the wrath of heaven. At such times, therefore, the court manifested the highest degree of interference with individual liberty.

SPIRITUAL DISCOURAGEMENTS.

The deepest spiritual discouragement that the town experienced was in the years from 1645 to 1650, after the failure of the Delaware Colony, and coincident with Lamberton's equally unfortunate final voyage. Thomas Fugill was a "Pillar" of the Church and State, a member of the Proprietors' Committee, a deputy magistrate, the secretary of the town and of the colony. As secretary of the town he

had recorded all grants of land, including those which had
been specially made, some of them being in his own favor.

In November, 1641, the town had voted that he might
have "24 acres, his share of the 2nd Division, in land at the
foot of West Rock." The charge was made that he had taken
more than his due, but no attention was officially paid to the
rumor until February 24, 1645, when the Town-Court appointed a committee to examine Fugill's copies of the
"Orders," and to mend those that were defective. The result
of the revision was that in February, 1646, the Town-Court
ordered a survey and measurement of Fugill's land at the
West Rock. The surveyor reported to the Town-Court in
March that Secretary Fugill had reserved for himself 52
acres 13 rods of land, which was 28 acres 13 rods above his
proportion. Fugill had been his own surveyor, and had
relied upon his eyesight alone in running his fence-lines.
Moreover, he had taken land where he was by law forbidden,
and he had omitted from the records clauses that restricted
his choice of ground.

After the defects in the records had been ascertained,
Fugill tried to restore the missing clauses by interlineations,
and offered to swear that no deception had been intended.
The knavery was clearly proven, but Fugill evaded admission
of guilt with a pertinacity and an ingenuity worthy of a
better cause. The trial thus far had been before the Town-
Court, a primitive kind of impeachment. At this stage the
meeting remembered its non-judicial character, and adopted
the strange step of appointing a committee, which included
the Monthly Court, to consider the prosecution of the case
before the Court of Magistrates.

The tribunal of the Church also took prompt cognizance of
the charges, convicted Fugill, and excommunicated him.
The Court of Magistrates found him contumacious, and
forbade his selling goods or estate until he had appeared
before their court, or the New Haven Monthly Court.
After he was tried and sentenced by the latter authority to

pay £20 to the town and to surrender illegal acquisitions, he betook himself to Massachusetts, and so disappeared from view. The cutting off of Fugill from the Church initiated a succession of excommunications and clerical censures.

Already in May, 1645, Mrs. Eaton, wife of the Governor, had been cast out for entertaining heretical opinions about baptism, similar to those of Roger Williams. She was not even allowed to enter the meeting-house, was alienated at least for a time from her husband, and was threatened with banishment. In the next year, William Preston was excommunicated for lying, and the Widow Potter also for some obscure cause, probably on account of behavior in a romantic attachment for one Edward Parker, a young man of whom the elders and magistrates did not approve. These instances, together with the censure of Mr. Ezekiel Cheever in 1649, upon a number of trivial charges,[1] belong to the history of the Church, and are mentioned in the court records but incidentally. They may serve here as illustrations of the common mode of thought and action.

The Church could not lay its hand upon those outside its pale, yet it doubtless seemed that the purification of society in general was as important as that of the Church. The climax of interference by authority was attained when, in June, 1646, three ladies, non-church-members,[2] were arraigned before the Monthly Court upon the vague charge of "Severall miscarriadges of a publique nature." There had been a preliminary hearing before Governor Eaton and Deputy Governor Goodyear, so that those gentlemen were practically accusers. The indictment against Mrs. Brewster contained fourteen counts, and, as in the other accusations, the evidence was furnished mainly by servants, one of whom, Elizabeth

---

[1] He was accused of holding his head in his hand during sermon-time, of being discontented with recent actions in Church and State, etc. It is significant that Mr. Cheever was one of Secretary Fugill's chief persecutors two years earlier.

[2] Excepting, possibly, Mrs. Brewster.

Smith, was then under trial for lewdness. The system of espionage betrays the same repulsive features, whether in a frontier village or in the Court at Whitehall. Mrs. Brewster was taxed with expressions of dissatisfaction with Mr. Davenport's prayers and sermons, with expressions of sympathy for Mr. Fugill, Wm. Preston, and for Mrs. Eaton. The three defendants had been all friendly to Mrs. Eaton. Mrs. Brewster had assured Mrs. Eaton that only a General Court could decree banishment, and that if matters were carried so far, Mrs. Brewster and other women would take Mrs. Eaton's part and they would all be banished together. Mrs. Brewster even had the hardihood to say that they would all flee to the Rhode Island Adullamites. Mrs. Brewster answered in court to this that she spake in jest. The court informed her that " To harden one agaynst the truth who already lyeth under guilt may not passe under a pretence of jesting." Further, Mrs. Brewster had called Elizabeth Smith by many unsavory names, as indeed the occasion seemed to warrant; but Mrs. Brewster would confess only to using the word " Harlot." She was told that " such rayling landguadge is uncomely and sinfull; Micaell the Archangell durst not carry it soe with the Divell, though he had matter enough against him."

Worst of all, Mrs. Brewster had befriended the unfortunate Parker and Widow Potter in their unsanctioned yearnings, and had advised them to take one another in the presence of witnesses if the magistrates refused to serve them, and had instanced two parties in the Bay Colony who had so done. The court reprimanded Mrs. Brewster, especially for her familiarity with " Widdow Potter, an excommunicate person." " Mrs. Brewster at first seemed to justifie it, saying her pastour in England *admired* that none of the sisters went to one Mrs. Bennett, cast out of a neighbour church for obstinacy in error, to reclayme her in a way of love." Governor Eaton intimated that the " Pastour in England " might be a myth, but that it was certainly forbidden to eat and drink with excommunicated people. Whereupon there arose much discussion whether Mrs. Brewster, while apparently drinking sack with the proscribed widow, had or had not really swallowed any of the liquor.[1]

Mrs. Brewster was accused of referring to the "Contribution"—the custom of walking up to the deacons' seat and depositing there the money-offerings or pledges for the support of the church—as though it savored of Popery, calling it "The Masse," and "Going to the High Alter."[2] She was also charged with selling wine in small quantities and to the detriment of the innkeeper. She retaliated by showing that she had sold liquor to three of the magistrates before her. One of these arose in his place and informed the court that "Mrs. Brewster had said she would prove him a lyar, which he hoped she could not do." The two other defendants were confronted with similar accusations; one because she had said that the angels of the Seven Churches of Asia mentioned in Revelation were spirits and not teaching elders; the other, because she had refused to join the Church, alleging as a reason the number of liars in it.

In each case Governor Eaton discoursed with much fluency, eloquence, and orthodoxy, telling the last offender, "That uppon such a grownd any might have declyned Christs famyly

---

[1] This stern application of the Apostle's command against unbelievers and evil-doers was not peculiar, of course, either to New Haven or to New England. Excommunicated persons were not only excluded from the table: they were also shut out of the church. In the assignment of seats in the meeting-house in 1646, no place was allotted to the Governor's wife, and Lechford's *Plaine Dealing* says: "At New Haven, alias Quinapeng, where Master Davenport is pastor, the excommunicate is held out of the meeting at the doore if he will heare." (Massachusetts Historical Collection, 3d Series, III. 78.)

[2] Touching this custom, a vote of the parish of Steeple-Ashton, Wiltshire, in 1610, is of interest: "It was agreed that every man should bring in their rate to the communion-table, that the churchwardens might not be too much troubled in the collection of it." (Toulmin Smith's Parish, 512.) When Mrs. Godman was suspected of witchcraft, she was forbidden to come to the "Contribution."

because there was a theife, a divell in it, and might have
reproached that primitive pure church at Jerusalem, because
Ananias and Saphira were found out and punished for lyinge."
But all three of the women answered in a bold and forward
manner, which, as the secretary wrote, "Offended the whole
Court." In conclusion, the New Haven Monthly Court
decided that it had caught a trio of Tartars, and it referred
the cases to the Court of Magistrates.[1] These were New
Haven's Anne Hutchinsons, and they seem, on the whole, to
have fared better than their Massachusetts prototype.[2]

QUAKERS AND WITCHES.

Rarely was such rash language as Mrs. Brewster's used in
Mr. Eaton's dignified presence by any, unless perchance by
"Quakers, Ranters, or other Herriticks of that nature."
The "Cursed sect commonly called Quakers" did not often
vex the good people of New Haven. There were none
resident within the town, and the inducements extended to
visitors of that sort were not alluring. One Edmund Barnes,
in 1659, "A marriner and Quaker," left his ship in the
harbor and came ashore to take an airing. His Quakerism
seemed to scent the air, for it was discovered with astonishing
celerity. Sailor Barnes was speedily bundled back upon
shipboard, where the master promised to keep him and to

---

[1] The outcome is unknown, for the first volume of Colonial Records
(1644–1668) is not extant. It contained records of criminal cases, some
of them (e. g., that of Plain, of Guilford) being very disgraceful; and it
is conjectured that the second generation of officials, perhaps at the time
of the Union, destroyed the volume out of regard for the good name of
the colony.

[2] The penalties affixed by law for such heretical actions and vagaries
were more puerile in Massachusetts and Connecticut than in New Haven.
By Connecticut's Code of 1650, any one speaking disrespectfully of the
Church must pay £5, or stand upon a lecture-day for two hours on a block
four feet high, displaying on a paper pinned to his breast these words:
"An Open and Obstinate Contemner of God's Holy Ordinances."

carry him away. There were only six trials for Quakerism in the colony, and most of these originated in neighborhood quarrels rather than in any desire for ecclesiastical purity.[1] Although Massachusetts and New Haven were the two colonies that were Puritan after the straitest sort, yet the latter's judicial history was never stained by the life-blood of Quaker or of witch. The extreme penalty, under New Haven law, for Quakerism was "Boring thro the tongue with a hot iron," but it was never inflicted. Probably the New Haven magistracy would have been loath to apply to witchcraft the Mosaic penalty of stoning to death, if the exigency had arisen, but they prudently avoided the possibility of such perplexing necessities. In the decade between 1650 and 1660, the witchcraft mania raged in Connecticut Colony, especially in New Haven's neighboring towns, Fairfield and Stratford, where narrow-minded Roger Ludlow exerted an evil influence. But when Ludlow, in 1654, came within reach of New Haven justice, he was obliged to pay fifteen pounds for calling a woman a witch, and ten pounds more for accusing her of falsehood.

In the same year there was a determined effort on the part of some of New Haven's leading citizens—the Atwaters, the

---

[1] Four of these trials emanated from Southold, one from Greenwich, and one, that of Edmund Barnes, began in New Haven. One man was whipped, and one Humphrey Norton was whipped, branded, and banished. He had already been exiled from Plymouth, and had seen fit to testify at Southold, where he had taken refuge. His trial, however, took place before the New Haven Plantation Court, March 10, 1658. His various writings were read in court, "Wherein are severall Horrible Errours and Reproaches, *if not more.*" Mr. Davenport occupied the whole morning in refuting Humphrey's tenets before a great concourse of people, "The said Humphrey making much hinderance to Mr. Davenport, and using a boisterous, bold manner." In the afternoon, Humphrey attempted a reply to Mr. Davenport's sermon, and "Uttered Abominable, erroneous, reproachful, and Wicked speeches." "Some of the bystanders cried out that he ought not to live, and looked for the earth to open and swallow him," but, fortunately, certain of the elders were enabled to silence him. (New Haven Town Records, II. 284.)

Lambertons, and even Mr. Hooke, the colleague of Davenport—to hound to death for witchcraft a woman whose sharp tongue had rendered her obnoxious, and therefore suspicious to her acquaintances. Elsewhere such notable persons might have secured the doom of the unfortunate object of their enmity, but Eaton and Davenport were uninfluenced, and Mrs. Godman, the suspected individual, died peacefully in her bed some years afterward. Subsequently a man and his wife were banished from the town under suspicion of witchcraft, but their worst enemy seems to have been a character of general unworthiness.[1]

With the advent of the second generation, judicial severity diminished faster than judicial curiosity. Two men, who travelled in 1654 from Milford to New Haven on Sunday afternoon, were not fined, but ordered to make apology in the "Public Assembly after exercise, both here and at Milford." Five years afterward, Sam Clarke, who was accused of "Hankering" about men's gates on Sabbath evenings to draw out company to him, was merely exhorted to remember that he who, being often reproved, hardeneth his neck, shall suddenly be destroyed, and that without remedy.[2]

One generation passed away. The freemen of New Haven, in Town-Meeting assembled, voted "To seriously recommend to the town authorities and to heads of families the proposal of the Reverend Elders that Horse-Racing on Lecture-Days ought to be prevented," and that children and servants should not be allowed to frequent the ordinary or any

---

[1] New Haven Town Records, II. 209, 218. Nicholas Bayly and wife.

[2] What individual opinion of the sanctity of holy time was, may be seen in the course of an exceedingly virulent quarrel between the Widow Hitchcock and Sergeant Richard Beckley. The widow affirmed that she had seen, on the Sabbath, Beckley's children playing, picking blackberries, and stealing the "Indians' Beans."

Beckley indignantly repelled the charges, and said: "If these are true, they were not fit to live in the woods nor in the Commonwealth." The court observed by way of conclusion that "The poyson of Asps" was under the widow's lips.

private tippling-houses on such days, either with strangers
or others. The town unanimously returned hearty thanks
to the reverend elders for their pious and great care to
"further religion and reformation among us in these declining times."[1] Nevertheless, at the same time, it was no
unheard-of thing that men and women who lived seven or
eight miles from the town, should walk into meeting on
Sunday morning, and walk home again at night, carrying
each way babies in arms. If the extravagances of judicial
inquiry among New Haven Puritans had originated in
Pharisaism, or in wilful tyranny, they would deserve some
other meed than smiles of amused surprise. But honest-
hearted fidelity to an exalted ideal of righteous living
partakes of a sacred nature, whatever the modes of its mani-
festation may be. In New Haven modes were transformed,
but the ideal scarcely changed. Conformity to the political
standards of Connecticut aided in substituting the might of
moral suasion for the strong physical arm of the law. The
absolute Sabbath-rest and uniformity of action that Davenport had imagined were forgotten, and the Sunday laws were
kept furbished for the arrest of indecorous travellers, or, as
now, for the protection of some rural orchard and the restraint
of greedy publicans. But, as the town advanced toward the
quiet seed-time of the eighteenth century, the ideal of life was
chastened and spiritualized by those influences of moral and
intellectual independence that culminated in the great awakening of 1741. Upon such a people a clerical Munchausen
was able to cast the stigma of a Draconian Blue-Law.

LEWDNESS.

Lewdness, like Sabbath-breaking, was a term which covered
a multitude of sins. The New Haven magistrates stamped
as " Unholy dalliance " all manner of unauthorized commu-

---

[1] May 2, 1692. New Haven Town Records, IV. 63.

nication between the sexes, from the weightier matters of the
law down to occasional osculation and frivolous conversation.
The sneer is sometimes heard that the Puritans were strict in
dogma, but lax in morals. The criticism is unjust. The
serving-people who caused the scandal of that early day
were, as a rule, not Puritans, unless mere living in a Puritan
community could make them so. The real Puritans were no
more hypocritical than are devout people of our own day.
With one exception,[1] the founders of New Haven, the real
fathers of the community, incurred no stain of lechery.
There seems to have been, within the town, no practice of
"bundling," a custom which was in vogue elsewhere both in
Old and New England, and if one allusion possibly points
to such an act, the reference shows that punishment was
severe and swift.[2] Throughout the first generations occasional instances of certain and wilful immorality among
the better families of the place occur among the children and
youth, and seem to arise from the dreariness and exposure of
frontier-life, or from contact with servants.

The dependent laborers, the wandering sailors and home-
less young men (the tramps of that day); above all, the
broken-down roisterers and desperadoes of Merry England,
and the persons with weak wits—these were fatal obstacles to
the Puritan's hope of a Godly Church within a righteous
State. They belonged to that floating scum of ne'er-do-wells
who were the curse of both New England and Virginia, and
who were whipped out of one plantation into another, from
the Piscataqua to the Carolinas. England, so anxious to
retain upon her own shores the Hampdens and Eatons, interposed no obstacles in the way of the vagabond who longed
for the license of the New World's forests. Toward rude
settlements this graceless strain of English blood has always

---

[1] William Potter, planter and church-member, convicted and hung for
bestiality.

[2] The case of Wm. Harding. See Records, I.

llowed, as our own Western frontier can testify. Such elements in society the Puritan tried to repress or banish. Our dealings with similar problems are necessarily characterized by our greater forbearance; but, as a result, our jails and asylums are crowded; our slumbers are scarcely defended by bolts and bars, where the Puritan slept with unlatched doors; and we shrink from sending our children to the common school for fear of a moral contamination which we are practically powerless to avert. The debauchery of young children by vicious servants was, as it is now, one of the worst and most prevalent vices. The New Haven courts discovered and punished it. It was worth while that every such offender should be chastised, even if the process did include some absurd inquisitions into trivial occurrences. Those who suffered for alleged bestiality seem invariably to have been feeble-minded folk who readily admitted their guilt. For believing in the possibility of such monstrous births as are gravely recorded, the people of that age cannot be seriously blamed.

Against the harboring of strangers the rules of the town were sufficiently strict—perhaps too strict for observance; but when a suspicion of loose living attached to any sojourner, the laws were enforced with sudden energy. So, in 1657, the marshal was ordered to see that "John Benham carry away the woman whom he brought from Westchester (as it is said wife to one Knap in Virgenia), for she hath given offense here; or he will be liable to answer what damage doth come thereby." The court had a very unfavorable opinion of married people who lived apart. Wm. Gibbs's case is typical of a class. In July, 1655, he confessed to the court that he had a wife in England. The court lectured him upon the danger of exposing both himself and his wife to sin, and ordered him to go to her at once under pain of a fine of twenty pounds for delay. In August he was still in town. The court summoned him to appear, and demanded with asperity his reasons for lingering.

Over the social relations between young people of different
sexes the court and community watched with vigilant care,
and here at sundry times the patriarchal theory of their
village life was most quaintly asserted. Maids who loved
not wisely but too well were almost sure, under Puritan
justice, of speedy marriage with their untrustworthy swains,
and both offenders were equally certain of beginning their
married life with a sound whipping. However, compassion
for the weaker vessel was stronger than regard for the
inviolability of the law; so that erring damsels frequently
escaped the whip by the plea of bodily weakness, certified to
by some wise woman. With the increase of poverty and the
decrease of commerce, the troublers of Israel departed to
more flourishing settlements. At the same time the tales of
revolting depravity disappeared from the records. The rigor
of the law was now generally reduced to the restraint of unseemly conversation among light-minded youth. The most
ludicrous meddlings with domestic concerns occurred after
the death of Governor Eaton, when the political and social
tension was gradually relaxed, when the lash of justice lost
its sting but retained its resounding noise. The official mind,
sworn to administer the law, was continually perturbed by
cases of wilful dancing, card-playing, and other worldly
amusements. Local legislation against fast-riding shows that
horse-racing had begun to amuse the populace. When a
definition of "Fast-riding" was demanded, "It was thus
explained that if it was faster than a hand-gallop it was a
transgression of this order."[1]

Two years before the union with Connecticut, the young
men of New Haven were in turmoil throughout one autumn
on account of the suit of Dorman vs. Johnson for slander.
The kernel of the matter was a jocular anecdote related by
Johnson. He had heard Dorman praying in the swamp for
a wife, and saying, "Lord, Thou knowest my necessity, and
can supply it. Lord, bend and bow her will and make her

---

[1] New Haven Town Records, III. 87.

sensible of my condition." The court fined impartially all the participants in the affair, and witnessed sharply against the evil habit of unseasonable joking. One young jester incurred severe reproof because he drew upon paper a mock astrological chart, muttered gibberish at the stars, and asked the gaping onlookers if they would like to see the devil.[1]

But by far the most laughable criminal suit on record was summoned before the court on May-Day, 1660.[2] A certain Mrs. Murline or Moline had in her family three grown-up children, Jacob, Maria, and Susan. To the abode of the Murlines, Sarah Tuttle, daughter of a prominent settler, wended her way in quest of thread. As might be expected, the three damsels fell a-talking about the recent marriage of Mr. and Mrs. John Potter. Some highly-flavored jokes were concocted, which, as Mother Murline testified, "Much distressed her, and put her in a sore strait." Jacob happened to overhear the badinage. Coming into the room, he confiscated Sarah's gloves and refused to surrender them except in consideration of a kiss duly given and received. "Whereupon," saith the horror-struck chronicler, "they sat down together, his arm being about her and her arm upon his shoulder, or about his neck, and he kissed her and shee him; or they kissed one another, continuing in this posture about half an hour, as Maria and Susan testified." Mr. Tuttle tried to prove that Jacob had endeavored to steal away his daughter's affections, which would have brought Jacob under the operation of a severe colonial statute for that case made and provided, "But" (the chronicler again) "Sarah being asked if Jacob had inveagled her, she said 'No!'"

The court was deeply exercised by the affair, told Sarah that she was a "Bould Virgin," and read a warning lecture, to which Sarah demurely answered, in what seems to have become the cant reply in that court, "She hoped God would help her to carry it better for time to come." They were

---

[1] New Haven Town Records, III. 19.
[2] *Ibid.* II. 375.

each fined twenty shillings. Sarah's fine was not paid until two years later, when, upon Mr. Tuttle's assurance that his daughter had much amended, the court remitted half the penalty.

METHODS OF CIVIL PROCEDURE.

The civil jurisdiction of the Monthly Court is of the least interest to us, excepting as its records incidentally shed light upon methods of procedure. There were no professional lawyers in the town, but there are several instances of representation by attorney. Mr. Pell, one of the village apothecaries, not infrequently pleaded the causes of others.[1] One of the most striking features of primitive New Haven jurisprudence is the continual resort to arbitration. As among older village communities, the elders of the hamlet exercised a sort of judicial power by a unanimous consent, and even the court itself seemed anxious that disputes should be settled, if possible, out of court. In 1639, at the time of the State's foundation, two worthy citizens were at variance, and the court gave them a month in which to agree, promising consideration of the question if it was open at the expiration of that time. A few months later, by a curious usage, not only was a Board of Arbitrators appointed, but two others were chosen to represent, before the board, the original litigants, although the latter were both residents.[2]

Perhaps the ordinary methods of civil procedure were well exemplified in the course of the suit of Evance vs. Captain John Charles in 1646. It was alleged that the gross negligence of Captain Charles had caused the loss of Mr. Evance's shallop, with a cargo of peas and Madeira wine, in the course of a voyage to Guilford and Saybrook. The disputants first chose four arbitrators. The arbitrators, disagreeing, referred the matter by consent to an umpire of their own selection.

---

[1] It should be noted that advocates were employed upon each side in 1654, in the suit of Staples vs. Ludlow for slander and defamation.

[2] Records, I. 26, 38, 41, 200, *et passim.*

The contending parties, not satisfied with the umpire's decision, appeared before the court. Mr. Evance's statement was naïve. "He further acquaynted the Court that at the first hearing of the said losse he apprehended it as an afflicting providence of God, immediatelye sent for his exersise, but, since, being fully informed of the fore-mentioned negligence, he sued for £100 damages." Thereupon occurred an incident which speaks volumes for the honor of New Haven's judges. Governor Eaton and Mr. Goodyear rose, and saying that they were both pecuniarily interested in the wine that had been lost, desired and obtained liberty to leave the Bench, "That they might neither judge, speake nor sit in court while a cause wherein themselves were concerned was in hand."

Witnesses were put on oath, and freely summoned for either party to a cause, if necessary, by the authority of the marshal. Conversation between the judges, the witnesses, and the parties interested was allowed, so that the progress of a cause bore some resemblance to a modern debate.

The Monthly Court of New Haven enjoyed a probate jurisdiction. Observing, by the way, that the first recorded will was Nathaniel Axtell's, made January 27, 1640, "Before his goeing into olde England," one finds but little that is unique or remarkable in the Probate Records. However, the provisions concerning apprentices and the partition of estates may deserve a passing glance. No laws to govern apprenticeship were specially enacted by the town, but the customs adopted were eminently wise and liberal. Early in 1640, Mrs. "Higgingson," widow of the Rev. Francis Higginson, teacher of the famous First Church at Salem, Mass., died in New Haven, intestate. There were eight children, and the endeavor was to give them equal shares. The good education that the older boys had already received was accounted equal in value to a half-share, in this case £20. The value of the farm in Massachusetts was to be equally divided between the seven brothers, but the daughter obtained no land. Instead, she received her mother's old clothes, the forty pounds, and the reversion to the remainder of the estate when debts and the other portions had been paid. One of the younger sons, Charles by name, was apprenticed to Thomas Fugill for the term of nine years. "And the said Thomas Fugill is to finde him what is convenient for him as a servant, and to keepe him att schoole one yeare, or else to advantage him as much in his education as a years learning comes to."

Here, again, the New Haven Court was ahead of the times. No such care for the education of apprentices was known to the common law of the mother country. These regulations were dictated by that republican sense that placed the school-house by the side of the church on every village green.[1] Nowhere else in the records were the conditions of indenture so fully described, so that it cannot be known how closely the precedent was followed. But it is probable that the status of the father made some difference with the treatment of the child.

In 1646, Roger Allen received the young John Potter, "For to learne him his trade, to give sutable apparell, and 5s. at the end of his time."

The court maintained a close watch over the matrimonial speculations of the widows of deceased planters, and invariably stepped in to secure the property of the first husband's children from the hands of the stepfather.[2] Inventories were taken, appraisals made, and creditors satisfied by the order of the court in the most methodical manner. If a will was made, it is noteworthy that the testator often constituted either the Church or "Our dear Pastour" one of the legatees, and Mr. Teach even provided that his little son might be left as a ward of the Church and Mr. Davenport together.

---

[1] Records, L. 26–29. Kingsley's Historical Discourses, 40. Blackstone, Bk. IV., Chap. XIV.

[2] Records, I. 262, 279, 460.

LEGISLATION CONCERNING TRADE AND PRICES.

It is sufficiently notorious that government in the seventeenth century, whether in large or small communities, was not administered upon a principle of *laissez-faire*. But New Haven, during her brief commercial day, made remarkably rapid strides toward an unusual freedom and equity in economic transactions. Sumptuary laws neither town nor colony ever had. In 1641, an elaborate industrial law was introduced determining righteous rates of wages, prices, and profits. Here, at least, there was no reference to Moses, but the instinct of busy English village life inspired every line. Wide outlooks and previsions were not wanting, betraying the hopes that stimulated Eaton and his compeers. It was ominous, however, of the future that, after a year's experience, the first calculations appeared to have been made upon too generous a scale. The second schedule reduced the major part of the rates by about one-third of their previously estimated value. "Comodityes well bought in England shall nott be solde here by retayle above 3$^{d.}$ in the shilling for proffit; if bought from ships, the advantage shall not be above 3ob.[1] in the shilling by retale nor above a peny by wholesaile." The coasting trade was given a wider loophole, a timely encouragement to local enterprise. "Comodityes bought and brought from the Bay, Conectacutt, Virgenia and other places to be moderated in prises according to the adventures and nature of the comodityes." A day's work in summer was fixed at not less than ten hours; in winter, at not less than eight. The wages of master workmen must not be more than two shillings in summer, or twenty pence in winter. Ordinary laborers, such as "Plaisterers and haymakers," must sell the sweat of their brows in summer for not over eighteen pence; in winter for no more than fourteen. "Itt is ordered that, if any workeman take more than is appoynted for worke and wages, he thatt gives itt and he

---

[1] Records, I. 142, 144. An obolus = a half-penny.

thatt takes itt shall, each of them, pay a dayes work fine and the informer shall have the fourth part." Compare this with the statute 5 Eliz., c. 4, by which a person paying more than the legal wage was liable to ten days' imprisonment, and the person receiving less, to confinement for twelve days. The New Haven Court once inflicted a fine of 40s. upon a workman for transgressing the aforesaid law, but nothing was said about the employer.[1] When "Fatt venison sould by the English" must be exchanged at the rate of two and a half pence per pound, starvation could not be an imminent danger. "Dyett for a laboring man with lodging and washing" was reckoned at four shillings sixpence by the week. In these regulations New Haven followed the guidance of her neighbors in New England[2] and the traditions of the parent country. Comprehensive laws stating wages and prices have burdened European statute-books down to our own day, but ten months' experience in 1641 convinced New Haven of their uselessness. Properly enough, the same General Court that voted to establish a free school also ordered "Thatt the lawes formerly made concerning wares and workes shall from henceforwarde be voyde and of no force, till the court see cause to the contrary."[3] But no New Haven court saw cause to revert to such clumsy law-making, until the finanoial stress of the Revolutionary period drove men to all sorts of questionable makeshifts. In time of war, as in 1653 and in 1673, the town forbade freedom of export, and there are instances of

---

[1] Records, I. 51.

[2] One of the early laws of the Connecticut Colony was an "Order about worke and wages." It was repealed in 1640, re-enacted in June, 1641, and continued in force until March 20, 1680.

[3] Records, I. 61, February 26, 1642. An act of 8 George III. fixed the rate of wages for tailors, and the Spitalfields Act of 1773 (repealed in 1824) did the same for silk-weavers. A German Imperial decree of 1869, and an ordinance of September 4, 1871, provide that each magistrate shall fix the rate of wages in his own district.—(See Roscher, Political Economy.)

some municipal interference in particular cases, but no more general legislation was attempted.

MAGISTERIAL INTEREST IN TRADE.

The magistrates and other chief men of the village constituted a Standing Board of Arbitration, to whom, sometimes in their official, sometimes in their private capacities, each separate grievance was referred. The accusations were generally made by citizens against traders. The latter seemed to have little reason for complaint. The wise men of the village invariably sought to check slack workmanship and extortionate dealing by remonstrances only. Yet to a New Haven artisan of that day a domiciliary visit from the sedate Davenport and majestic Eaton, attended by a half dozen other dignitaries, must have been an ordeal indeed. The courteous recommendation by the court to the shoemakers in 1648 has already been noticed. A still more noteworthy incident occurred four years later:

"The Magistrates and Elders were desired to speak with the Doctor, and see if they cannot settle a more moderate price for his visiting of Sicke Folkes than he has yet taken."

Some natural discontent at the prosperity of the foreigners who had been allowed to settle and to trade in New Haven took the shape, in 1656, of a "Complaint that the Dutchmen lately admitted do sell things excessive deare." Their worst fault, however, seems to have furnished the second ground of complaint: "They doe not attend y[e] publique meetings on y[e] Lords daye as duly as they should, so Mr. Davenport, the deacons, and the Townsmen were desired to meet this afternoon and speak with them."

The third Monthly Court held in the town had licensed Peter Brown to be the public baker, "So long as he gives no offence in itt justly." During the hard times of 1647–49, there was murmuring in the town about the diminutive size of the baker's loaves. Governor Eaton proposed in court

that an assize of bread should be established. He inquired
who had any book that described the usual sizing of bread.
John Brockett said that he owned one, and he was desired to
lend it to the Governor. This was one of the first deliberate
reversions to English example, and may be classed with a
contemporaneous enactment that nails must be sold in town
at the rate of six score to the hundred.

The outcome of Governor Eaton's study of John Brockett's
book was embodied in the colonial code. Three lawful kinds
of bread were enumerated, the penny white, the penny
wheaten, and the penny household loaf.

When wheat was worth three shillings per bushel, these
loaves must weigh respectively 11½, 17½, and 23 ounces. A
sixpence's increase in the value of wheat warranted a proportional lightening of the loaves. Six verses from the Old
Testament justify the officer appointed thereunto in seizing
loaves of light weight, in confiscating one-third of them for
himself, and in distributing the rest to the poor of the place.[1]
Of the enforcement of this law in New Haven there are no
proofs. There was a complaint in 1655 by Mr. Allerton and
others that the baker and miller of Milford furnished bad
"Biskitt and Flower," whereby "The place lyes under
reproach at Virgenia and Berbadoes, so as when other men
from other places can have a ready markit for their goods,
that from hence lyes by and will not sell: or, if it doe, it is for
little above halfe so much as others sell for." The Colonial
Court sent for the Milford miller and baker, but did no more
than read them a lecture.[2] In 1647, with a similar jealousy

---

[1] Lev. xix. 36; Deut. xxv. 15; Prov. xi. 1 and xx. 10; Amos viii. 5–6.

[2] The Eatons, Goodyears and Allertons had no intention of degenerating
into chapmen, and they, at first, abandoned the petty traffic of their town to
three obscure persons. One of these, a Mrs. Stolion, kept one of those
mercantile museums still common in New England villages, and known in
later days as a "Yankee notion store." In the autumn of 1646, she
quarreled with Captain Turner over an incompleted barter of cloth for
cows, and the result was that Mrs. Stolion's business methods were
thoroughly discussed in court. Captain Turner deposed that he was

for the reputation of the settlement, the court summoned James Hayward and reproached him severely for reporting in the Bay that New Haven was poverty-stricken and a costly place to live in.[1] Hayward's words were probably true, but the prevalent idea of " Fidelity to this Jurisdiction " could not tolerate such freedom of speech.

In 1662, Jacob Murline turned this official anxiety to foster trade to good account for himself. He had not repented of his evil ways, for he was found guilty of extreme lewdness, and sentenced to be severely whipped. Murline was engaged in trade with the Dutch, and he escaped punishment altogether by the ingenious plea that, if he were flogged, the Dutch would not trade with him, and that, therefore, the commerce of the town would be injured; " For the Duch do not treat a person whipped as the English do, but look upon him as though he were a dog."

In August of the same year, New Haven was on the alert

" Discouradged from proceedinge on account of the dearnes of her commodities and the excessive gaynes she tooke." Naming some instances of her exorbitant prices, " He left it to the consideracion of the court whether she had not done him wronge in complayning of him, and if she might not be dealt with as an *oppressor of the commonweale*." The village fathers responded that they would not permit extortion in the " Commonwealth," and asked for evidence. Captain Turner demonstrated that her profits on cloth reached 150 per cent. She had charged ninepence apiece for " Primmers " which cost but fourpence here in New England. (An unfeeling woman, to grind the faces of the poor with the " New England Primer " !) She paid out wampum at the legal rate of six for a penny, but refused to take it except at seven for a penny. Messrs. Goodyear and Atwater affirmed that her price for " English mohejre " was double the value in English markets. " She sold thridd at the rate of 12s. per pownd, which cost not above 3s. 6d. in olde England. Her charge for needles was a penny apiece, but they could be bought in England for 12d. or 18d. per hundred." The upshot of the inquiry was its reference to the Court of Magistrates, but there is no further trace of the suit. Mrs. Stolion baffled all further investigation by going to her long, last account in the next spring (Dec., 1645). See Records, I. 174–176.

[1] Hayward or Heywood, the man who had been excommunicated and fined for drunkenness.

to secure two merchants who had recently arrived in the Bay Colony from England. Mr. Davenport said that "They would bring ships from England, and would get what we can manufacture here; and then" (a pathetic reminder) "we must remember that these Londoners do not know the state of a wilderness." The town made generous offers of land.

REVIVAL OF THE COMMON LAW AND ENGLISH USAGE.

In the name of Moses, the New Haven Court set aside English precedent and the jury trial. But this act was not by any means entirely due to religious theories. The desire for independence on the one hand, and for sober, practical simplicity on the other, favored the adoption of the Mosaic Code. English laws implied secular and clerical hierarchies. English law-books the settlers did not have, or at least they had no time to examine and re-arrange such law-books. The Bible presented a code whose provisions were universally known, and whose authority was above question. Its usage as a statute-book, with reasonable modifications, was for these busy pioneers a dictate of common sense. The extent to which the reasonable modifications were actually introduced is not always understood or fairly stated.

It is true that throughout all their initial deliberations there was no public mention of England's king nor of England's laws. The "Freeman's Oath," which was adopted, pledged allegiance only to "This Jurisdiction," and to the "Civill Government here established."[1] Even the Governor's oath of office lisped not a syllable of subjection to any earthly power. The conflicting claims of Royalist and Puritan noblemen and of the Crown cast but a light shadow over the land. England, weakened by faction, was far away, and New Haven, strong in the anticipation of the coming Puritan

---

[1] Hubbard asserts (p. 329) that the New Haven settlers took "What help and strength they could from the Massachusetts Patent." The assertion seems to rest upon no foundation at all.

nation, which could confront, if necessary, the parent country, assumed the tone of an independent republic, acknowledging no king but God, no laws but those of its own choice.

Nevertheless, it is equally true that New Haven's law and customary usage conformed far more to Sir Edward Coke than to Moses. Let it not be supposed that English inheritance yielded easily to the example of Israel. The democratic assembly, the folk-moot, the vote by show of hands, the decision according to the will of the majority, were traits of English common life that antedated prelacy and the kingship. What but the inherent force of English traditions impelled the selection of four deputies, no more, no less? What were the magistrate and his four assistants but the " Reeve and four best men " whom Alfred and De Montfort knew?[1]

Moreover, the capstone of Davenport's whole polity, the restriction of the suffrage to members of the Established Church of New Haven, was but an imitation of English theory and law, and both Davenport and Eaton are yet on record in acknowledgment of the fact. The employment of committees in public administration was a prominent characteristic of New Haven's primitive government. The committee-system finds but little place in Deuteronomy, but committee-rule is of ancient date among the hamlets of England, and lies, indeed, at the roots of representative government there.

After 1650, capital offenses in Connecticut and New Haven were identical, except that burglary and Sabbath-breaking might, under certain conditions, be punished in New Haven with death. Five capital crimes by Moses' law were omitted from the New Haven Code, although only one of them could be called "Ceremoniall." One offense, treason, was inserted, although Moses did not recognize it.[2]

---

[1] " The communaltie of Gavelkindmen ought not to the Summonce of the Eire, but onely by the Borsholder and foure men of the Borowe."— Lambard, Perambulation of Kent, (edition of 1596), 571.

[2] Capital punishment must or could be inflicted in New Haven for idolatry, witchcraft, blasphemy, murder (wilful, unpremeditated, by

Roughly speaking, New Haven's criminal laws were Mosaic or Biblical in origin; its civil code and administrative acts were English in pattern; while in many cases the comparison of precept with precedent and the requirements of colonial life evoked indigenous legislation. To the last-named sources must be mainly attributed the federative principle in the colonial government, the regulations concerning stray cattle and swine, concerning wolves and other wild animals,[1] concerning Indians and the education of the youth.

The unwitting recurrence to ancient forms of government and land-tenure is noticed elsewhere. But the opening paragraph of Eaton's Code was quoted from Magna Charta; the formalities of entering or appealing a suit, of levying an attachment, of escheats and replevins, were borrowed bodily from the common law. Weights and measures were ordained "According to the use in London"; assises of bread were established; and all casks were ordered to conform to the London Assise, with a very flattering reference to a verse in Deuteronomy which speaks of a "Perfect and just measure." It was the force of the common law that made twenty-one years the age of maturity, that punished arson by a servant with sale into slavery, and that authorized the decoration of a condemned thief's neck with a halter as a punishment. Imprisonment for debt was impossible, except in case of

---

"Poyson, or other wicked Practise"), bestiality, sodomy, adultery, manstealing, perjury to take away life, treason and misprision of the same, marriage within the Levitical degrees (reckoned as incest), unprovoked smiting of parents or rebellious conduct to the same, presumptuous Sabbath-breaking, burglary on the Lord's day (upon the third conviction), and rape, at the discretion of the court. The Mosaic law made these offenses capital (except treason), and, in addition, sexual intercourse at the period of uncleanness, disobedience to priest or judge, false prophesying, prostitution in a priest's daughter, and marriage by a lewd woman under pretense of virginity. Murder, bestiality, and sodomy, were, so far as is known, the only crimes for which the supreme penalty was actually imposed in New Haven.

[1] Blackbirds were at one time public enemies.

bankruptcy.   It is curious that detention and sale of debtors were justified solely by allusion to a decree of King Artaxerxes, mentioned in the book of Ezra (Ezra vii. 26).

The law of inheritance was of a composite character.   The "Third Part" was the dowry right of the widow; the eldest son, however, by reason of Deuteronomy xxi. 17, received a double child's portion, but the General Court might alter this at will; if there was but one child, the estate was separated into thirds and the final third divided by the Monthly Court between widow and child either equally or as it saw fit, the right of appeal being reserved.   These usages recall Blackstone's description of common-law provisions from the time of Edward III. to that of the Stuarts, both by reason of the general likeness and of the few points of dissimilarity that resulted from the substitution of a Town Court for a royal one.[1]

It is fair to say that the idea of the English city was more influential in New Haven than in any other New England settlement.   Many of the yeomen in the company came from the famous shire of Kent, countrymen of Wat Tyler and Jack Cade.   But the assembly was guided and inspired by a mercantile spirit.   The knowledge of English municipal and urban life was no less potent in New Haven's educational arrangements than in the encouragement of trade.

The schools, public and private, which were always maintained at New Haven, probably found their prototypes and models in the Collegia which existed, or had existed, in the mother-towns of Ashford, Coventry, and London.[2]

But the little State in the wilderness far outstripped its ancestral patterns.   No school-system like that which Davenport and Eaton planned and upheld then existed elsewhere in

---

[1] Blackstone, II. 492–93.

[2] Lenham, Egerton, Charing, and Ashford were among the towns and villages of Kent known to be represented in the New Haven company. The use of the name "Greenwich" is also noteworthy. The settlers of Guilford were nearly all men of Kent or of Surrey.

Now or Old England. The foundations of the New Haven State included these three fundamental principles of a public education—the absolute freedom of elementary instruction, compulsory education for all children, and a higher education to be at least partially supported at the public expense. In the latter half of the nineteenth century New Haven has been able to reach once more the standard of 1639.

The town-plot itself was also a witness to New Haven's inheritance. The New England village, indeed, was usually clustered around a church standing upon its bit of green. But New Haven here again showed the city idea modifying the rustic village-common. The skilful precision with which New Haven was laid out around its central market-place elicited at that time universal admiration. What common-squares of old London, and country-borough greens, were there represented! It can hardly be estimated how many towns from that day to this have reproduced the New Haven square with its central green.

CHAPTER VI.

NEW HAVEN A CONNECTICUT TOWN.

1664–1700.

The unconditional surrender of New Haven Colony to Connecticut, December 13, 1664, was confirmed by the New Haven Town-Meeting on the seventh of the following January. A sign that old things were passing away may be seen in the vote of the 26th of December, that the Town-Fort, " Which is against George Pardee's house, being rotten, may be disposed of." Throughout the year, 1665, the town gradually adapted conditions to circumstances. In March, the first summons to a Connecticut General Assembly was received, and John Cooper and Lieutenant Munson were elected to be the first deputies of New Haven as a Connecticut town.[1]

The last echoes of the recent angry struggle were heard in the resolution that the town would support Mr. Leete in his legal controversy with Bray Rossiter, the leader of the late malcontents in Guilford, and in the following vote: " The Towne was acquainted that Connecticut expects we should beare our part of the charges of the Pattent. It was debated, and concluded that we judge it not righteous nor reasonable that we should beare patent charges.'"[2] The effect of the protest does not appear. Disinclination to kiss the rod was only natural.

---

[1] This session was deferred until April. John Cooper and James Bishop, who were then elected, were really the first New Haven representatives who *sat* in a Connecticut General Assembly.

[2] Records, III. 65–66. The date of the vote was May 1, 1665. All quotations from records are now from the New Haven Town-Records, unless otherwise specified.

On the first of May, townsmen were chosen to the number
of six, which had become customary; but, in July, the list was
increased to seven, in accordance with Connecticut usage, and
the whole body was re-elected for security's sake. In compliance with the new statutes two constables were selected.
The service of a marshal was continued until 1670, about
which time that office appears to have been quietly dropped
throughout the colony. Messrs. Jones, Gilbert, Nash, and
Bishop, who had been elected by the late Connecticut Assembly to be magistrates in New Haven, took the oath of their
office in the fall Town-Meeting. A new title had been adopted
in May for Mr. Jones, "Who was chosen to call the Town
together, and to be Moderator in Town-Meetings." James
Bishop was continued in the office of Secretary or Town
Clerk, much to the regret of those who, in after years, have
tried to read his marvelous chirography.

CHANGES IN CONSTITUTION.

These unwelcome innovations, the Connecticut laws, were
admitted into the town and read at a General Court, August
14th, by Assistant and Moderator William Jones. The court
then proceeded to frame such enactments as the change of
laws rendered needful. It was ordered that a Monthly Court
should be held as formerly, "If occasion require, on the first
3d day of the weeke in every month, for tryall of all cases
that may be tried by this Court without jury, and in October,
December, March, and June, there shall be juries if any cases
require it."

"3s. 4d. must be payd for every action, beside the jury-
fees, when the jury is called. Defendants shall have three
days warning unless they agree otherwise."

A suspicion that the golden age of Arcadian rule was over
might lurk behind this order: "The Townsmen shall see that
at least one roome of the prison be made safe for prisoners."
The same officials were charged to oversee the repair of the

roads and the engagement of a schoolmaster. Already the
restricted suffrage was a thing of the past, and on the third
of October, 1665, the first New Haven jury was selected.
The panel comprised six men—John Gibbs, Henry Ruther-
ford, John Cooper, William Andrews, Henry Glover, and
Thomas Munson, Foreman. Nothing of permanent interest
was submitted for their deliberation. This was the first
County Court of New Haven, but the separation of Connecticut into four counties was not consummated until the
next year, when New Haven attained the minor dignity of a
county-seat.

December 20, 1665, the year of first things closed with the
first coroner's jury, again of six men, who delivered upon the
body of Henry Morrill a verdict of suicide. A probable
reason for the rash act appears about a year afterward, when
Goody Morrill was fined 3s. 4d. for " Provoking and striking
an Indian." The magistrates improved the occasion for
dramatic effect by " Declaring themselves ready to doe justice
as well to Indians as to English." The minutes of the criminal
trials now begin to disappear from the town records. Perhaps the last one (or among the last ones) was the trial of
Jonathan Lampson, in 1671, for giving " Cydar to an indyan."
His ingenious plea that there was no law against "Giving
Cydar " did not save him from a fine of twenty shillings.

The Monthly Court and its deputies were now things of
the past. In place of deputies, Connecticut's usage required
for each county three or more commissioners, who were
forerunners of the justices of the peace, and were styled
" Justices of the Peace and Quorum." They were associate
judges with the colonial assistants, or magistrates, and were
elected by the Legislature. They no longer represented any
town, but yet New Haven sometimes nominated candidates.
In the Particular Courts, the town-courts of Connecticut
(abolished in 1666, but reorganized in 1669), the towns were
by law represented by two selectmen, who were to sit with
the assistant and commissioners. The selectmen probably

did not magnify this part of their office. Out of these courts the justices' courts were developed at the close of the century. A few other changes appear in the official roster of the town. The Secretary masqueraded under the new title of "Recorder." Two Road Surveyors filled an office which was revived in 1666, after a long interval, and a board of four Assessors was elected under the clumsy name of "Listers for the estates of men." There were usually three constables, two for New Haven, and one for the "Iron-worke," as East Haven was called.

When New Haven Colony gave up the ghost, Connecticut seems to have taken no action respecting the collection of duties at the port of New Haven. The town gave no sign for a year. Then it ventured, July 9, 1666, upon its own responsibility, to appoint Wm. Holt, "To take notice of the customs of wine and strong liquors." This drew attention, and, in 1668, the Recorder wrote that the County Court, by order of the General Assembly, had appointed James Bishop to be the first Collector of the Port for the Colony of Connecticut (June 29, 1668).

Compared with the modern practice, Town-Meetings, now rarely called "General Courts," were very frequent, and the townsmen were still accustomed to submit often to the community, for its approval, the reports of their own monthly meetings. There were three Town Election-days in the year— apparently an unthrifty arrangement. One occurred in the spring, near the end of April, when the great number of officers were filled; one, in September, to choose deputies for the fall meeting of the Assembly; and one, in November, for the election of constables. As the town came together in mass to elect its local officers and to frame its local laws, so, every spring, the freemen of the town were summoned, with all the other voters in the colony, to the grand festival of the General Court of Elections at Hartford. Out of a theocracy New Haven had fallen straight into a pure democracy. In May, 1670, on account of the increasingly cumbrous character of this custom, the Assembly enacted that henceforth freemen might be represented at Hartford by proxy. Laws were passed regulating the local proxy-takings, or elections, as they practically were. Henceforth the spring session of the Town-Meeting, wherein delegates to the Legislature were selected, was divided into two distinct parts. In the morning, after the choice of the deputies, the remaining time was devoted to taking the proxies of the freemen for the coming election at Hartford of Governor, Deputy Governor, and magistrates or assistants. The afternoon was set apart for the discussion and determination of purely local business.

In the first year of this classification of the growing public business, the custom of "Reading the minutes of the last meeting" is mentioned as though it were a new habit (1671). The freemen sometimes made this election-day a very busy one, and the meeting sat until far into the evening. Abuses crept in. Many went away as night came on, and the few who remained passed important laws, or one party tried to tire out another by a long sitting. In 1701, some local Solomon moved, and it was voted, "That no Town-Meeting shall continue after the Sun is no longer in sight, and the Moderator shall determine when that is." This implicit reliance on the moderator's fairness and eyesight lasted until 1713. Subsequently, this Town-Meeting was made to cover two days, the first, called "Proxies' Day," being devoted to the election of officers, the second to the transaction of town business. The number of freemen in the town immediately after the union with Connecticut cannot be stated, nor can it be known how large an accession to the body of voters was caused by that event. There seems to have been little active compliance with the requirements of Connecticut registration. A feeling of bitterness made the oath of allegiance to that colony a stone of stumbling and rock of offense. The Connecticut Council, in 1664, voted not to press the "Actuall swearinge of freemen at present." The substantial fruits of victory having been gained, it was wise to refrain from

flaunting the symbols of triumphant authority. But in May,
1666, the Assembly sent "Mr. Shearman to give the freemen's oath to any who would take it." He administered the
oath to just nine men. However, the colonial records of
Connecticut show that in October, 1669, the "Constobels"
reported ninety-one freemen in New Haven. This indicates
a population of over five hundred.

In the year 1666, while the New Haven Phoenix was
rising to life again in New Jersey, the town of New Haven
was performing the last kind offices for the late colony by
straightening out its somewhat tangled financial affairs. On
the 26th of February the four resident magistrates were
chosen "To meet with some from other plantations of the
late colony, and to issue Captain Manning's business, to audit
the accounts of the late Jurisdiction with Roger Alling, and
to settle the distribution of the late Jurisdiction's stock."[1]
The magistrates reported, in March, that the other towns
desired some return for the money which they had formerly
contributed to the colony-school, now extinct, and which
sums, as they conceived, had inured to the benefit of New
Haven. The justice of this claim seemed to be conceded.
The town was now the custodian of two cannon which had
once maintained the honor and power of New Haven Colony
against Dutch and Indians, by pointing peacefully out over
the waters of the harbor. In a spasm of reckless generosity
the town voted to the other towns all its right "In the two
great gunns." But there were sharp Yankees in the other
towns also, and, in July, New Haven agreed to pay £30 to
its ancient comrades.

---

[1] *Vide* Colonial Records, II. 66–75. Captain Manning's vessel and
tackling were seized by the colony in 1664, on account of the captain's
alleged treasonable trade with the Dutch. The property was ordered to be
sold in May, at Milford, to the highest bidder "by an inch of a candell."

THE HOPKINS GRAMMAR SCHOOL.

The short-lived colony-school, which had expired amid the stormy quarrels of 1662, had been based partly upon the Hopkins bequest, of which Mr. Davenport was the sole surviving New Haven trustee. It was to be the Harvard of the Quinnipiac Colony. When that hope, like all others, failed, and Mr. Davenport prepared to depart from his transformed Zion, he made one last effort for the cause of education in New Haven, and succeeded. There was a disposition on the part of the town to be contented with the town's free school, wherein George Pardee 'taught, and, at the court's desire, "Payd particular regard to the children's manners." Nevertheless Mr. Davenport was resolved that his town should not lose its share of the Hopkins estate, but should develop into a seat of learning. Perhaps his determination was not weakened by the obstacles that the Connecticut authorities threw in his way. In April, 1664, eight months before New Haven surrendered to its neighbor, Mr. Davenport appeared in the court and recited his discouragements. "The magistrates of Connecticut layd a restraint upon the estate until they had a coppy of Mr. Hopkins' will and an inventory was taken; after this was done, they would have a coppy of the will attested from the Probate Court in England; and after that, they kept on the restraynt because Mr. Winthrop was in England; thro' Mr. Dally, he dealt with Mr. Winthrop, who promised that, as soon as he came over, it should be set at liberty; yet not until this Spring is it free."[1]

After recounting the arrangements that the trustees would make with Hartford, Hadley, and Harvard, he besought the court to secure New Haven's share to the town by the speedy establishment of a grammar school. The words of Davenport never fell upon deaf ears in New Haven. The magistrates, elders, deacons, and deputies were appointed a committee to manage the matter. The result was "The Hopkins

---

[1] Records, III. 37.

Grammar School." Its yearly support from the town was
£30, and Mr. Davenport paid from the Hopkins bequest £10
more. The school was feeble during the first years, when the
town was changing rules and rulers, but Mr. Davenport,
though evidently aging fast, watched over it with unre-
mitting zeal. Into the Town-Meeting of February 7, 1668,
he came, and made some querulous remarks about the
attendance at the school. He threatened the withdrawal
from the town of his portion of the Hopkins estate unless
the children went to the school, "To be taught for the fitting
them for the service of God in church and commonwealth."
Whereupon " Roger Alling declared his purpose of bringing
up one of his sons to learning," and six other good men made
similar statements. " And Mr. Augur said that he intended
to send for a kinsman from England." The schoolmaster,
Mr. Samuel Street, " Declared that eight were now in latting,
three more would be, in summer, and two more before next
winter." Probably Secretary James Bishop's knowledge of
" latting" was slight and shaky. Mr. Davenport seemed to
obtain satisfaction from what was said, and proceeded to urge
that " The town should endow the school with a farm, which
the town debated."[1] Before Mr. Davenport left the town, a
few weeks later, he made sure that New Haven should not
lose the funds which he had hitherto held in trust.

On the 18th of April, 1668, Secretary Bishop busied him-
self with copying upon the records the document by which
John Davenport, with a wealth of words, did "Give, Graunt,
Enfeoffe, and Confirme the said sum of £412, and the said
moiety or halfe part of £500," to a self-perpetuating Board
of Trustees, consisting at that time of " Mr. William Jones,
Assistant of Connecticut Colony, Rev. Mr. Nicholas Street,
Teacher of the Church of Christ at New Haven, Messrs.
Mathew Gilbert, J. Davenport, Jr., and James Bishop, Com-
missioned Magistrates, Dea. Wm. Peck, and Roger Alling."

---

[1] Records, III. 118. A school, endowed from the commonage, was,
apparently, a project in 1638–40. Oystershell Field was for this reserved.

The conditions were that John Davenport should retain the full "Power of a negative voice, while it shall please God to continue him in this country, or any part of it," and that the rent of the Oystershell Field, and of Mrs. Eldred's town-lot, should be always devoted to the use of the school. Comforted perhaps by the thought that he had thus secured one blessing to New Haven which neither Time nor Connecticut would be likely to take away, Mr. Davenport left the town forever. His educational mantle fell mainly upon the shoulders of Mr. William Jones, whom we find, in 1675, scolding the town roundly because it had suffered its school to lapse for a twelvemonth. In the next year the town was warned by the County Marshal to answer before the County Court for not sustaining a grammar school. In July, 1677, Mr. Jones preached the same sermon more sharply, and this time he wielded the peremptory mandate of the highest power. "It is a shame to the Town that now for three years there hath been no Grammar School here. . . . . But now the General Assembly hath required that the Town shall provide for such a school." So the town voted that the grammar school should be recommenced, and appropriated £20 per annum for that purpose.[1]

The time came when the town acted without such sharp stimulus. It was voted, December 16, 1728, that the Commons, known as the Oystershell Field, should be given freely into the hands of "The Hopkins Committee," "To be improved for the educating of children of Congregational or Presbyterian parents only, and no other use whatsoever forever hereafter." The lands might be sold with the consent of the major part of the proprietors, "The money being improved as aforesaid, and to no other use whatsoever."[2] For two full centuries town and school have grown together, and although newer institutions have overshadowed the ancient foundations, age defeats not usefulness. New Haven's Grammar School

---

[1] Records, III. 184, 201.
[2] *Ibid.* IV. 417.

still proclaims the good deeds of Edward Hopkins and of John Davenport. But in view of the fore-mentioned theological rancor, intended to endure "Forever hereafter," it must be admitted that, for almost a century, there was a steady decline from liberal theories of education such as the founders of New Haven had cherished.

Governor Eaton's Code of 1655 required all parents and guardians to " Endeavor, that all their *children and apprentices*, as they grow capable, may, thro God's blessing, attain at least so much, as to be able duly to read the Scriptures, and other good and profitable printed books in the English tongue, being their native language; and, in some competent measure, to understand the main grounds and principles of the Christian Religion, necessary to salvation."

Deputies, constables, and other "Publick Officers," were ordered to watch for infractions of this law, which were punished by fine upon fine. But, if the parent or master were obstinately delinquent, "So that Children or Servants may be in danger to grow barbarous, rude, and stubborn, thro ignorance, the Court of Magistrates may take such Children or Apprentices from such Parents and place them for yeares; Boyes till they come to the age of one and twenty, and Girles till they come to the age of 18 years, with others, who shall better educate and govern them." This passage embodies the desire of Eaton and of Davenport. Five years later, when the General Court legislated upon the subject, a less exalted ideal was apparent. Of apprentices and girls nothing was said, the latter probably being instructed in the "Dames' Schools"; but the following amendment is an intimation at once of educational progress and of restricted benefits: "To the printed law, concerning the education of children, it is now added, that the sonnes of all the inhabitants within this jurisdiction, shall (under ye same penalty) be learned to write a ledgible hand, so soone as they are capable of it." (May 30, 1660.)[1]

---

[1] Colonial Records, II. 576, 583.

THE MINISTER'S TAX.

The terms of the juncture with Connecticut had dissipated the one legal bond of union between the Church and State in New Haven; but the way was paved for the substitution of another. The first prophet of the inevitable was Magistrate Jones. Recalling, perhaps, the bad wampum that had been cast into the plate for the Church Treasury, he proposed in Town-Meeting, November 11, 1667, that the elders should be made public officials, since their maintenance had been for ten years a source of scandalous trouble, and their living was at present so unreliable.[1] The town gave the proposal honorable burial by voting to consider it merely. But, ten years later, March 13, 1677, Deacon Peck, the Church Treasurer, was constrained to make the same motion in Town-Meeting, and for the same reason. It must be set down as one of the paradoxes of human nature that a Puritan community was backward in paying its minister, except under compulsion. Deacon Peck's facts were cogent arguments. The town assented to his motion, and voted to raise yearly for the elder's support a tax of twopence halfpenny in the pound. Where the Church had once been ruler, it was now the client. Henceforth the elder was a public functionary, and it was announced that the minister's tax must be handed by every man to Deacon Peck.

There was a young man named "John Tompson," who discerned that, under this law, men were no more likely to crowd Deacon Peck's gate than they were before. On the 24th of April, he therefore "Informed the Town-Meeting that Collectors of the Minister's tax ought to be appointed, who should make it their business to gather the same; otherwise men would not pay their quotas any more promptly than

---

[1] "*Resolved*, A sume of £200 shall be given to both yᵉ Elders in winter wheat @ 5s. per bushel, in summer wheat @ 4 and 6, pease @ 3 and 6, Indian Corne @ 2 and 10, porke @ 3½ a pound, and beef @ 2½d. per pound."

before, and the law would be practically invalid." John
Thompson's wisdom and valor were greater than his discretion; the rulers thought he ought to be seen and not heard.
Although he was plainly in the right, he was severely snubbed.
The court informed him that he was wasting his breath, and
that important business must not be obstructed by his
unnecessary proposals. However, it was soon discovered
that the "mouth of the babe" had, for that time at least,
spoken sagely. In December, Mr. Jones made the same
statement, and to him the town listened. "The Townsmen
had heard that there were not the necessary supplies brought
in for the minister's subsistence, which was not well among
such a people." Deacon Wm. Peck and John Chidsey were
authorised "To make up the rate, and to deliver it to the
ministers, and to prosecute such as fail in the payment."
John Thompson got his revenge by helping, through many
years, to make East Haven a thorn in the flesh to the parent
town.

When the "Rev. Mr. Pearpoint, a godly man, a great
scollar, a man of good parts, and likely to make a good instrument,"[1] was settled over the New Haven Church in 1684, he
obtained from the town, besides the twopenny tax, a home-
lot, a new house on it, and a five-hundred-pound right in
commonage. The minister's tax of twopence in the pound
was mentioned by itself as late as 1692, but it was doubtless
reckoned with the other taxes, and paid into the town treasury rather than into the pockets of Deacon Peck and John
Chidsey, for the town at that time voted to pay the minister
the lump-sum of £120 in wheat, rye, corn, peas, pork, and
beef, and to supply him with firewood.

The subjection of the Church entailed, as practical consequences, some additional burdens upon the town. To its
honor be it said that the town did not shirk them. In 1684,
the townsmen reported that the "Widow Banister had

---

[1] So read the recommendation of Rev. Mr. Moody, of Portsmouth, N. H.,
noted for his conflict with Sir Edmund Andros.

formerly been releeved by the Church Treasury from the deacon; but now, there being no Church Treasury, shee must be supplied from the Towne." And it was so done.[1]

TITHINGMEN, JUSTICES OF THE PEACE.

There were no tithingmen in New Haven before 1678. We have seen that order in the Church was preserved in earlier times by the marshal and corporals. But now the marshalship was extinct, and "Watch and Ward" was not what it once had been. December 16, 1678, the town commissioned "William Payne and Samuel Hemingway to take a stick, or wand, and smite such as are unruly, or of uncomely behavior in ye meeting, and to acquaint their parents."[2] Possibly these gentlemen performed such services during the remainder of their lives; at any rate no such office was filled again until 1723, when the word "Tithingman" is first mentioned, and when yearly elections to that office began. December 16th of that year, seven tithingmen were chosen in Town-Meeting—two each for the First Society, for West Haven, and for East Haven, and one for North Haven.

The municipal government during the colonial period received but few more additions. The local judicature was rounded out by the first election of justices of the peace (two of them) April 29, 1701, and the consequent first establishment of justices' courts. The first grand jury was drawn on the 20th of December, thirteen years later.

DIVISIONS OF LAND.

After 1668, the picturesque animation of the old colonial time died away. The power of initiation no longer rested exclusively in New Haven hands. The terrors of the wilderness were far removed. Dutch foes were conquered, and,

---

[1] Records, IV. 2.
[2] *Ibid.* III. 210.

save for one short period, Indian enemies were too distant to
be feared. Commerce was almost abandoned, and the former
homes of the Eatons and Goodyears had become the domiciles
of gain-loving, unambitious farmers. The town had once
busied itself with defying the New Netherlands, and with
planning to control the Delaware Bay. Now, as a quiet
Connecticut village, townsmen and freemen officially debated
and wrangled over the allotment of swamps, the improvement of roads, and the orthodoxy of ministers. Many pages
of the records at about the time of the Union are covered
with reports concerning the town mill. The first one, upon
the Mill River, becoming unsatisfactory, a new one was
planned at the Beaver Ponds, and the citizens made the
matter a burning question for some years. In 1691, it seems
strange to read that the town proceeded to elect a miller, and
chose for that position a certain Samuel Tod.[1]

The enforced attention paid to agriculture soon revived the
question of land distribution, which had lain dormant for
more than twenty years. In 1668, much of the outlying
territory within the township was still the public waste, and
was even partially unexplored. Within three years, those
who could not find room in the village and along the shore
began to push out toward the growing plantation at " The
Iron-worke," or up the river to North Haven, where Major
William Bradley, a friend of Cromwell, had made a home,
probably in 1649. About 1670, the settlement of Wallingford, then called " New Haven Village," was begun, and New
Haven officials began to wonder how far to the north their
township extended. The first survey of the northern boundaries was induced by speculation whether or no a great
"Swamp, called Lebanon," fell within the town limits.
September 9, 1672, the townsmen were desired to "Consider
of and appoint some suitable persons to run the Line for a
tryall to see how farre twelve miles will reach from the sea

---

[1] Records, IV. 36.

northward into the woods."[1]   New Haven surely had not
been over-curious concerning the exact extent of what she had
gained in 1638, in return for hoes, hatchets, and knives.
Not until this line had been surveyed did the ancient custom
of perambulation appear in New Haven.   The first record of
such an observance is on the 2d of April, 1683, when the
townsmen "Desired Sergt. Winston to give Milford, Wallingford, and Branford notis that the perambulation be made"
around all the common boundaries with New Haven.   The
landmarks were heaps of stones.[2]   Thereafter such perform-
ances were occasional occurrences.

The rapid increase of the remote farms and parishes soon
suggested to the parent town a timely appropriation of the
enlarging value of its public domain.   In the spring of 1672,
a committee of twelve was chosen in Town-Meeting "To
consider about stating such lands as may stand for towne-
commons for ye future, and also for the purchasing of such
lands of ye indyans as are within our towne-bounds yet un-
purchased, and also what lands may be fit for another
division, and how to be divided to men for proprieties and
improvements."[3]

During the next generation there was a rush for the undivided lands which gradually degenerated into a scramble.
The committee reported the basis of the Third Division in
March, 1675.   "Sutable tracts for a standing common," were
reserved, especially between Mill and West Rivers.   "All
orderly approved and admitted planters" got a share—to every
£100, twenty acres, and four acres to every head.   "But as
the estates were, in the beginning, rated at much above their
present value, they are abated one-third.   If the abatement

---

[1] Records, IV. 169.

[2] Records, IV. 444.   In bounding the Indian land at Morris's Cove,
mere-stones are mentioned.   This ancient word is still in use at New
Haven.   (See City Year Book, 1875.)   It is the name of the stones which
mark the building-lines in the streets.

[3] Records, III. 165, 184–86, 224–26.

would make any estate too small, nevertheless any such shall receive 20 acres."

The proprietors were careful to avoid any collision with the town by recognizing its paramount authority. The acts of their Assembly "To consider of the common fields and fences" were submitted to the Town-Meeting, April 27, 1675, and obtained its approval. King Philip's War interrupted proceedings, and when that was ended, it was agreed that two hundred acres should be divided among the soldiers in the late war according to the terms of service. In 1680, the Third Division was completed.

The "Records" now contain more and more frequently-recurring accounts of individual applications for land, which were almost invariably granted. The first conservative note of alarm was raised by Sergeant Eliazar Brown, December 26, 1698, who protested "Against any further disposal of undivided lands."[1] In March he had only three supporters. With the beginning of the eighteenth century, public divisions became numerous. The Fourth Division, in 1701–7, was signalized by the speedy repression of a spirit of mild exclusiveness among the proprietors. In 1702, they voted that the proprietors of 1683 should be the proprietors now, and that future purchasers could claim no interest in undivided lands. In the next year, the town decided that every inhabitant should receive the allotted share, but that the representatives of the original purchasers might receive two additional acres for every £100. The natural outcome was that seemingly all New Haven rose up for additional acres and fractions of acres by right of a large assortment of grandmothers, cousins, and aunts. There was a fifth, a sixth, a seventh, and an eighth division, the last one in 1722; but, between the fifth and the sixth, the Connecticut Legislature confirmed all the town-lands to the proprietors of New Haven. Henceforward the undivided commons were referred to as the "Sequestered

---

[1] Records, IV. 101.

Lands."[1] Each division brought with it a new allotment of
land as a public common. In 1721, the "West Rocks and
the Blew Hills" were designated to "Lie in common forever,"
and *to be used, if they might be, as sheep-pastures*, the former by
New Haven, the latter by the Northeast Village.

The Indian Reservations.

It is to be observed that one of the duties of the committee
of 1672 was to secure the Indian lands which were pur-
chasable. The Quinnipiac tribe had two reservations, one
near the Cove, the other upon the river, near the former home
of Sachem Montowese. Their numbers were dwindling,
their abode was frequently shifted, and a tendency was
evident among them to live by themselves among the English.
Their feeble grasp upon their lands was watched by covetous
eyes, especially as the land-fever became hot. Assistant
William Jones apparently secured Montowese's reservation
for himself in 1668. The Records refer to it but gingerly.[2]
The Indians certainly had land enough left to them, for, in
1671, they petitioned the town that some of their friends and
relatives "might sit down with them."[3] In 1682, great discontent was reported among the Indians because, in the
recent Third Division, their lands had been marked out for
them in severalty. This discontent, together with an untimely indulgence in drunkenness, ruined the Indian landed
interest of New Haven. In April of the next year (1683),
divers of them drank firewater and paraded noisily through
the town. In·the language of the "Records," "For their
delinquency and breach of law" they soon found themselves
in durance vile. Having no money with which to cancel

---

[1] Records, IV. 208, 223, 244, 340, 347.

[2] Records, III., September 7, 1668. Mr. Jones drew several plums that
year. In March, he had been voted by the town a salary of £20 yearly,
the half-year to begin at Michaelmas and end in May. How did such
Babylonish chronology manage to slip into Puritan records?

[3] Records, III. 162, 230, 238.

their fines, they were in a quandary, until a bright thought
in the mind of Thomas Trowbridge finally effected their
release. They had land and needed money. Goodman
Trowbridge had money, but wanted land. What could be
easier or more natural under such circumstances than an
exchange of goods? So Mr. Trowbridge got his deeds of the
Indians' lands, and the red brethren got out of jail; but
when they reflected upon the transaction, they became angry,
made the plea of "fraud," and declined, at first, to give up
the property. In May, the town voted to make Mr. Trowbridge's quarrel its own, "In order that all Indian claims of
land in our township may be at an end."

In 1706, a committee was again empowered to purchase all
the Indian lands that were yet unbought, thus showing that
Thomas Trowbridge had not acquired the whole of the
reservation. However, the Indians were still there seventeen years later. Some unruly spirits had been asserting the
doctrine of "squatter sovereignty" upon the Indian territory, and the ensuing commotion reached the ears of the
Town-Meeting. There was a debate about ejecting the trespassers, but it is impossible to tell whether that was done.
It was about this time that the last sachem of the Quinnipiacs was frozen to death while in a drunken stupor, and the
town seems to have been inclined to doubt the utility of
entertaining such worthless subjects.

But faith in missionary work was still strong enough to
flicker. A committee was chosen "To consider whether the
land *belongs* to the Town or to the Proprietors, and whether it
may be advisable to secure by Bill the land to the Indians
for encouraging them in the Christian faith." In 1725, a
committee was authorized to sell the Indian land to four
planters, and, six years later, a vote was recorded that fifty
acres in Waterbury should be purchased for the Indians in
behalf of the proprietors. It seems, therefore, that the company

---

¹ Records, IV. 361, 494.

of proprietors had taken the Indians under its protection, and it probably removed them, or the majority of them, to Waterbury. There is no direct evidence of such an exodus, but, with one exception, nothing more is heard of the Indians or their lands until 1765. The sole exception was in the year 1753, when the Records show that some Indians visited the town, and seemed to obtain, as their right, a piece of ground for planting.

In February of the year 1765, some of the Quinnipiacs made an unexpected and probably disagreeable appearance, and demanded the right to plant certain grounds.[1] Two of New Haven's most noted citizens, Roger Sherman and Samuel Bishop, Jr., were appointed to search for the Indians' title to any planting-land. The report was that the proprietors had reserved about thirty acres as planting-ground for the Indians, if it was wanted; but that, in course of time, the land had been sold and the money turned into the treasury. It had been placed by itself in the accounts as "Indian money." The town voted an appropriation out of that money to enable the committee to put the Indians in possession. There are a few allusions to the further progress of the affair, but the exact result is unknown. Probably a compromise was reached; the name of Roger Sherman is sufficient guarantee that no injustice was done. This incident closes, so far as we know, the chapter of New Haven's dealings with the aborigines—a history honorable alike to the town as a corporation, and to the two colonies to which that town in turn belonged.

THE VILLAGE CONTROVERSY.

By far the most prominent question of municipal interest, and the one most hotly contested throughout this century of the town's existence, was one which had been inherited from the ancient *régime*—the question of villages and village

---

[1] Records, IV. 528, 561.

growth. The first phase of this contest, in 1659, and the seeming quietus which the project shortly after received, have been described. The eldest and, for a time, the most flourishing of the suburban settlements were those two of which mention has been made, and which were afterward known as East Haven and Fair Haven. The former village was then usually referred to as "The Iron-worke." The first suggestion of working in iron was at a General Court of the town, March 16, 1655. "Mr. Goodyear desired if any knew of any Iron-stone about this Towne, they would make it knowne, that, now Mr. Winthrop is here, he may be gotten to judge of it, and if it prove right and that an iron mill might be set up here, it would be a great advantage to the Towne."[1] Later the town voted to give "140 dayes work" to Winthrop & Goodyear toward making the "Damm beyond the farms at Stoney River," and about the same time the jurisdiction exempted the "Persons and estate employed in the iron-worke" from rate-paying. In two years Mr. Goodyear was so impoverished by the venture that he was freed from the town-rates. He wanted to sell his share, and the town voted that the purchaser must be one of whom the town approved.[2] John Winthrop felt himself, however, somewhat independent of New Haven control, and, without asking anybody's permission, leased his interest in the furnace to Messrs. Clark & Paine, of Boston. A town-court was summoned hastily, and Mr. Winthrop's heinous deeds were rehearsed and considered. It was declared that, if such acts were allowed, Mr. Goodyear might do the same, "And so the trade may be carried to other places, and a disorderly company of workmen brought in here." It was resolutely affirmed that no sale or lease should be made without the town's license. It is probable that Clark & Paine complied with the town's requirements, for they kept the iron-work in operation until about 1679, when, as tradition saith, an epidemic sickness

---

[1] Records, II. 208, 270, 277.
[2] Colonial Records, II. 178.

carried off the principal workmen, and the enterprise was abandoned.[1] But the town was as careful, after the Union, to exclude unwelcome characters, even from the villages, as it had been under the former rule. In 1665,[2] the town cautioned the "Masters of the iron-worke to admit no workmen without a certificate of good character from some known good person."

After the failure of 1659–60,[3] the would-be villagers, like the rest of the population, forgot their schemes of local independence until the political excitements of 1662–65 had subsided. Farms within the New Haven township that sought for separation from the old town might do so for two different motives. They might desire the more pretentious honors of complete municipal freedom. Such an intention the parent village would be likely to obstruct and resist. But the smaller settlements generally aspired only to the honors of a "Parish," or "Village," as they were wont to term it. The privileges of a parish were an independent church and school, and were not so difficult to obtain.

Again, the villagers might seek only to hold, as proprietors, the strictly-defined territory of their village, and possess their own commons, with the right to enlarge or diminish them— always within the limits of the village. To become such a community was the petition, in 1667, of Fair Haven, or, as the Records term it, of "The village on the sides of the East River." The court and townsmen were appointed to determine the boundaries, and, in 1670, the Articles of Agreement were read in Town-Meeting. It was voted to give the designated land freely to the villagers.[4] But the village did not grow as it had been expected to, perhaps because the tide of local emigration suddenly turned northward. In 1669, the town

---

[1] See Dodd's East Haven Register, and Atwater's History of New Haven Colony.

[2] Records, III. 68–69.

[3] See before, III.

[4] Records, III. 99, 155, *et passim*.

appointed a Board of Trustees to regulate the affairs of the new village above the plains. The place was called New Haven Village, but grew so rapidly that in 1670 it was incorporated as a town, by the name of Wallingford. The trustees, however, governed the town for two years more. After this there was a long lull in the activities of village-founding.

Public Benevolence.

It is pleasant to notice at this period practical sympathy with the distresses of other towns, and even of distant individuals. Our private, public, and corporate benefactions sometimes cover an extensive field, when fire or flood, in almost any corner of the world, has suddenly inflicted suffering. New Haven, in February, 1666, like other New England towns, heard the cry of ejected Nonconformists in England. The town voted that a subscription should be made "For the saints that are in want in England." Two summers afterward there was trouble nearer home. "Mr. Jones proposed that the towne helpe Guilford about their hay, for so many were sick there; and the towne showed itself very forward to helpe some." The care of the poor became, as we have seen, an additional duty for the townsmen, of especial importance after the Church Treasury was abolished. We find the town paying £3 that Goody Graves might go again to Stonington for the perfection of her cure, and the townsmen resolving that Lieutenant Mansfield and Thos. Trowbridge should go to Goodman Beamont's to inquire after the condition of the goodman and his dame.

Again, there is a substantial indication of a danger once universally dreaded, now happily forgotten: "The towne was informed of the request of Thos. Lechfield of Boston, whose wife is a captive in Algiers, and who craves the charitable benevolence of well disposed persons for a help to her redemption. And generally persons spake as willing to be helpfull if persons were appointed to gather it."[1]   When contributions were made in grain and meat, the labor of the solicitor was not light.   Money had been scarce for years, and the methods of payment were rendered more complex by the existence of diverse estimates of valuation.   In 1662, the town had signified its willingness to pay £60 yearly for the instruction in "English and arethmatick."   A dozen years later, Geo. Pardee, the schoolmaster, was hired for " £18 yearly out of the treasury at ye antient townes price, and the benefit of the house, barne, and home-lot, formerly Mr. Evances; or, if the price be altered to the merchants' price, then the salary shall be £16 per annum out of the treasury."[2]

Indian Wars.

War sets the most difficult problems in finance, and a generation was now come which was doomed to hear of little else but wars and rumors of wars.   The records of New England towns are filled with beach-marks of the martial tides.   New Haven waited for no initiative.   The tone of its utterances upon foreign affairs might have befitted some little city-republic of ancient Greece.   In the last days of July, 1673, the Dutch fleet recaptured New York.   The news sped quickly up the Sound.

On the 4th of August, Deputy Governor William Leete, recently admitted as a planter in New Haven, adjured a hastily-summoned Town-Meeting "To consider what we must do for our security in this time of danger, the Dutch having taken New York with such a considerable force, as is reported."   The town appointed watch and ward by day and night at South End, as well as at home, and, in case of an alarm, the great guns were to be fired.[3]   The patrol was, ere long, dismissed, and the town rested for two years, until the

[1] Records, III. 227, April 26, 1681.
[2] *Ibid.* 178.
[3] *Ibid.* 173.

opening horrors of King Philip's War. A good idea can be
gained of the widespread affright at that time by the precautions taken in so distant a town as New Haven. The
wrestle between fear and economy is a relieving touch to the
picture. It was the 2d of July, 1675,[1] when Mr. Jones
described to the shuddering Town-Meeting the massacres at
Swanzy and elsewhere. "When the great mischeeff by the
Indians upon the English in those parts was understood,
every one was warned to keepe arms ready; those who lived
abroad at farms should not straggle in the woods, and, at
sign of danger, they should gett together, or come into the
towne." Mr. Jones swelled the rising fear by the information
that "Philip, ye Indian" (on the margin, "Metacom, or King
Philip"), "is a bloody man and hath been ready formerly to
break out against the English, but hath been restrained."

For the time being, the lazy, besotted Quinnipiacs were
viewed in the glamour of imaginary war-paint. The magistrates paid them a solemn visit. The red men "denied any
knowledge of Philip's motions, or any liking for them. They
said that they had none gone that way." Moreover, they
promised to stay at home, and, if any strange Indians appeared,
to inform the English and not harbor the intruders. In
September, the town ordered that farmers should work in
companies. The news of the disaster at Bloody Brook, and
of the partial burning of Springfield, caused a complete panic.
The Town-Meeting almost resolved itself into a garrison.
The town must be palisaded. Fortifications were to be
placed at the ends of all the streets, and at the four angles of
the town-plot. Several houses that occupied points of
vantage were designated as block-houses, to be fortified.
All the brush within half a mile of the town-plot was to be
cut down, that no lurking foe might find a shelter. But, by
the end of October, the committee in charge of the defence
was obliged to report discouragements. Fortifications were

---

[1] Records, III. 153.

found to be expensive, and the worthy burghers were more
ready to pass resolutions than to contribute days' labors or
to pay taxes. Goodman Harriman's house had been fortified,
and a sentry-box placed on the roof. He complained that
"The sentinells, in their rounds, had done great damage to
the shingles, and he looked to the towne for compensation."

In the spring of 1676, the progress of the war was most
unfavorable to the English, and the frenzy seized upon the
town again in March. Assessments and damaged shingles
were at once forgotten. The Indians were coming in a body
down the Connecticut River, and planned to go along the
coast to New York, destroying everything in their path.
They were already on the way and moving toward Hartford.
The palisade was but partially completed, and the brush in
the outland had not been cut. Trenches must be dug and
breastworks thrown up. Every one must have a gun and a
fixed quantity of "powther." None of the local Indians
should come into the town or into any English house.[1] The
evidences of fear disappear from the Records as suddenly
as they came. Within a month the Narragansett power was
broken, and, in 1679, the sale of the wood for the unfinished
palisade was ordered for the benefit of the town. In that
same year, a rascally, drunken Indian succeeded in scaring
the town—for a few days only—with his whiskey-begotten
fancies. That was the end of apprehension of peril from the
surrounding wilderness.

Two years later, indeed, the Town-Meeting was informed
that "Maj. Robert Treat had been here and spoken of a
great body of Indians gathered up y⁰ Hudson. He feared
that the blazing starr in the winter, and reports of Guns and
Drums heard by some, and y⁰ Earthquake, forewarned some
great judgment or changes neare." The Records, however,
do not reveal what reception Mr. Treat's prognostications
received beyond the pithy sentence, "It was refferred to a

---

[1] Records, III. 188, 190, 194, 213, 227.

committee." This was the favorite means of disposing of
any proposition before the New Haven Town-Meeting, but
it seems doubtful whether this committee was to investigate
Indians, or the comet, or the earthquake, or all together.
The result of their toil was never recorded.

VILLAGES AGAIN.

The year, 1679, saw also the revival of the village project.
The compact with Fair Haven or "East-Side" Village, which
had been hanging fire since 1670, was reaffirmed, with the
ominous proviso that all the grants should be void if a
ministry was not supported. Samuel Hemingway, the re-
cently-elected tithingman, petitioned that Stony River, South
End, and the Iron-work "Might bee one village, and might
have a minister of their own." Townsmen and Town-
Meeting alike favored the petition, and the village was soon
an actual fact.[1]

But the East Haven brethren were ambitious. Although
nothing had been said about their desire for town-privileges,
and although they probably made no application at this time
to the General Assembly for incorporation, they met together
August 4, 1684, and chose town officers "So farr as they had
power." They reported their proceedings to the New Haven
Town-Meeting, which granted its confirmation. The offices
filled were those of "Selectmen, Collectors, Listers, Constable, and Recorder." The incumbents were all elected by
East Haven, with this stipulation, "If the towne of New
Haven shall appoint them." This is believed to be the first
and last instance wherein a subordinate portion of a town,
with the consent of the whole town, but without authority
from the Legislature, assumed the functions of municipal
sovereignty. For the time being, it made New Haven Town
a little colony again within the larger colony. Administra-

---

[1] Records, III. 211, 213; IV. 6, 86, 88.

tion, police, and taxation were entirely abandoned to the East Haven settlers. It may be that their small number of inhabitants was a reason for not applying to the Assembly for incorporation. There were only four men in all the offices. This abnormal state of affairs did not endure. Before 1687, both the village and the townlet had given up the ghost.

Through all this period the increasing activity of the townsmen is noticeable. It is they who constitute the committees by whom proposals made in Town-Meeting are examined. The Town-Meetings recur less frequently, and the records of the townsmen's meetings, many of which are preserved, contain more and more proofs of efficiency. The first erection of that venerable New England institution, the "Sign-board," fell in New Haven to the lot of the townsmen. In March, 1683, "The townsmen desired Capt. Munson and Sergt. Dickerman to mack and sett up a sing-post (!) according to law somewhere in the market-place neare the meeting house, and doe it with speed."

At the same time, the townsmen exhibited a laudable zeal for the promotion of intelligence and morality. "The Townsmen agreed to goe to all the inhabitants of the towne and farmes to see how the children are educated in reading the word of God. Lieut. Munson and John Chidsey took the square of the towne, John Cooper, Sr." (he made his mark himself), "and Lieut. Moses Mansfield, all the west side of the East River and so down to Goodman Dorman's, Sergts. Winston and Dickerman, the subburbs, and the west side of the West River." Perhaps there was need of such a secular inquisition. The influence of the Church was beginning to undergo a great declension. A curious sign of the utter reversal of former conditions lies in the record of March 17, 1684: "The Town voted that the *Church might manage* sending a messenger to Rev. Mr. Moody."

THE TYRANNY OF ANDROS.

Mr. Moody's name suggests that of his persecutor, Governor Andros. New Haven and all New England were now confronted with a question more critical than that of village and village-exemptions. The Stuart tyranny which the Puritans had once beaten down, and which they had fled to America to avoid, followed them to these shores. The attacks upon vested rights, in which the city of London had already lost its charter, had been more bold and sweeping since the closing years of Charles the Second's reign. The ambitious Dudley and the spiteful Randolph had compassed the ruin of the Massachusetts charter, and it was evident that the same despotic policy was to prevail in the colonies as at home. It was advised by the Connecticut Assembly that each town should survey its territories, and procure a charter for itself from the colonial authority. New Haven took the initial steps in the work during the month of June, 1685. In July, the first writ of *quo warranto* was issued against the Governor and Company of Connecticut.

While the contest was pending, "New Haven's Patent" was read in Town-Meeting, April 27, 1686.[1] The document is a lengthy one. The town-boundaries were marked, as usual, by trees and stones. The town is granted, "In the year of our Lord God, 1685," to three magistrates and three townsmen in trust, by the "Governor and Company of Connecticut Colony, in accordance with his late Majesties gracious charter in the 14th year of his reign . . . . . to be held according to the tenor of East Greenwich in Kent, in free and common soccage." The patent was signed January 6, 1686, "In the first yeare of the reigne of our soveraigne Lord James the Second of England, Scotland, France and Ireland, King, Defender of the Faith," etc., by Robt. Treat, Governor, and by John Allyn, Secretary. Thus, by process

---

[1] Records, IV. 81-88.

of law, Connecticut rooted its famous charter among the local institutions of its people and awaited the coming storm.

In 1703, just after Anne, last of the Stuarts, ascended the throne, Governors Dudley and Cornbury repeated the assault upon Connecticut's charter. The Legislature repeated the tactics of 1686, and issued "Confirmations" of the New Haven and other town-patents. The Indian treaties, the patent, and its confirmation are, therefore, New Haven's documentary evidences of title to its territory. Barring the dramatic scene at Hartford which made the Charter Oak famous, Connecticut escaped close contact with Governor-General Andros's rule, "which," as Randolph boasted, "was as arbitrary as that of the Grand Turk." New Haven's records mention merely that the "Lawes and Orders sent from Boston by his Excellencies command" were read and published. The suspension of the General Assemblies relieved the freemen from the necessity of choosing deputies. Otherwise, the Town-Meetings, except for a short time in 1688, occurred as often as usual. For the first time in the town's history, permission was granted that John Osbell and John Hancock, single men, might live by themselves "Until the Towne see fit to alter it." A fulling-mill on the site of the iron-work, and two sawmills, the first ones in town of which there is any record, were authorized, and an extensive system of roads was planned.

On the 18th of April, 1689, Sir Edmund Andros and his council were prisoners, and the Boston streets were filled with enthusiastic adherents of William of Orange. New Haven Town-Meeting assembled on the 3d of May, and the scribe, in his joy and fear, produced this cumbrous sentence: "After the opening of the town-meeting, and prayer made for direction from God in this dangerous juncture, the Towne were informed of the late dissolution of the Government at Boston, by the Governor, Sir Edmund Andross, his resignation of the same; with surrender of the Castle and ffort into other hands intrusted till further order from the present powers in England; and this chang hastened by the discovery of a dangerous plot against Boston to destroy that place, as we are credibly informed, which great overture hath occasioned and necessitated the ffreemen in all or most places in this colony to choose their Deputies to meet together in y' usual place and at the usuall tyme of Election to consider together what to doe, and to have the proxies of the freemen ready, if need be, in order to the Reassuming & Settlement of Government, according to charter, to prevent anarky and confusion, and the Daungerous effects thereof, especially when we have grounds or cause to suspect Indian, or other enemies. The printed declaration from Boston was publiquely read."

The trying times of the French and Indian Wars were now begun. Liesler's well-meant imprudence in New York, and the savage massacres upon the Mohawk frontiers, brought Connecticut face to face with the impending struggle. That half century of warfare which was to draw the colonies together, and to develop the military skill of a Washington, commenced its long discipline. New Haven was, as usual, ready to act with independence. One month before the Assembly ordered such a course, the town instituted a military watch, and voted that "A flying army should be fitted out." In view of the recent revolution, it was deemed adviseable to administer again the freeman's oath to the 90 voters within the town. Iu 1669 there had been 91 freemen. The diminution must be accounted for by the loss of Wallingford, yet as that subtraction had occurred a score of years before, the growth of New Haven was certainly very slow.

LOCAL ENACTMENTS.—INTEMPERANCE.—FUNERAL CUSTOMS.

A quaint witness to the paucity of population, or to the disregard of Sabbath-going, is found in the vote of the Town-Meeting, in 1692, that the "Deacons shall fill up the empty seats in the meeting house with as suitable persons as they can."[1] In the same year, as military ardor was now mounting high, a species of warfare was declared against some lowly domestic enemies. First the geese were attacked. A long series of annual regulations was begun with the order that "Geese shall not be allowed to graze on the Commons within or without the Towne after the end of March, for that they are found noxious to the food of cattle." Next, a vigorous campaign against weeds in the streets was instituted. Barberry bushes, "Sorrill," and "The poysonous stinking Weeds that infest our Market-place," were subjects of annual by-laws, and, in 1725, several persons paid five-pound fines for disregarding these regulations. This lesson of municipal neatness was not driven home, however, for in the next year the town repaid the fines.

After 1690, there was a steady increase in the consumption of liquors, and licenses for the sale of intoxicating drinks were profusely voted by the town. The Town-Meeting-days were festivals of dissipation.

In October, 1701, the Connecticut Legislature met for the first time in New Haven. The additional demand upon New Haven tavern-keepers' liquid resources which was created by the grave and reverend magistrates and deputies may be gauged by the vote of the Town-Meeting, in the preceding September, authorizing five more men to "Sell Rum only while the Court sits." Chief articles of import were liquors and molasses, the latter article being chiefly used in the production of that once-renowned beverage, New England rum. The only customs-revenue in the colony was raised upon wines and liquors. There was good reason, therefore, for alarm at the prevalence of intemperance. The consumption of liquors was carried to the most objectionable excess in connection with the time-honored custom of feasting at funerals. Such relics as this of the "merrie England" of yore

---

[1] Records, IV. 60. The vote may mean that the war had drained the honor-seats on the men's side of most of their former occupants.

are usually forgotten in the modern conception of the grim
Puritan. But to the correction of this abuse the healthier
public sentiment of the community was finally forced to
address itself.

"Oct. 29th, 1694, Whereas, some inconvenience is observed
in the use of Rum, or Strong Drinke at Funeralls, the Town
recommend it to the inhabitants that may, from tyme to tyme,
be concerned that they would use their liberty and prudence
in laying down that custom for the future, only as there may
be need of some Refreshing in a private way for persons
living remote."[1] This delicately-phrased advice reminds the
modern reader what a wide chasm separates the funeral
customs of our grandfathers from our own, and how near the
last century was to primitive humanity. Here was a time
when the wake-feast for the dead was as common among
Englishmen as among their despised Irish brethren. Sometimes the edibles and potables were furnished to the pall-
bearers alone, but more often to all who came. Bells were
tolled for the dead—a custom which has not wholly ceased.
The procession was entirely on foot, headed by the men walking in couples, and completed by the women in similar order.
In the centre was the bier, a platform with legs eighteen
inches high, and belonging to the town. A hearse was
not used until the close of the 18th century. Upon the
bier was the coffin wrapped in a pall. There is a reference
to this shroud in the record for December 19, 1715, to the
effect that "Mr. Jonathan Atwater has freely offered to the
town a cloath to be servisable at Funeralls, the said Cloath to
be kept at the house of Ensign Isaac Dickerman, and when
upon any occasion fecked from said house, to be carefully
returned thither again." In the cemetery the grave was dug
by friends, and by their hands, after the ceremony, was filled.
Upon the mound the bier was left standing until another
death gave it a new resting-place.

---

[1] Records, IV. 74.

CHAPTER VII.

NEW HAVEN, A CONNECTICUT TOWN.

1700–1784.

The opening years. of the 18th century were signalized by
a small mining mania, more unremunerative than the earlier
iron-working enterprise had been. One Mr. Rosewell, in
1699, hoped to start a slate-quarry near the town, and, a few
years later, some imaginative souls beheld the Blue Hills
stored with all kinds of mineral wealth. There were thought
to be valuable iron-mines there, and, in 1721, the New Haven
proprietors actually leased to a New York company the
"Copper mines in the Blue Hills" for a twentieth part of
the ore.[1]

Already people had begun to introduce into the meeting-
house a fashion of building private pews which would be
exempt from the periodical "dignification." In March,
1701, the town voted that "Seating in the meeting-house shall
bee according to Office, Civil, Ecclesiastic, and Military, and
according to Rates." Human nature reveals one of its
ludicrous weaknesses in the need of the ordinance that no
one should advance his rates in order to obtain a more
dignified seat in God's house. Still another enactment
must command the sympathy of many modern sufferers.
"The Constables are desired to take notice of the persons
that open the Meeting-house windows in the tyme of public
worship." Shortly after, boys were forbidden, under penalty

---

[1] Records, IV. 118, 337. Should not the impetus to these efforts be
traced back through the minds of men to the time when adventurers
expected to pick up nuggets of gold on the shores of the New World, and
royal charters stipulated for a part of all the precious metals?

of twelvepence, "To play within 20 rods of the meeting-
house, for the meeting-house windows are often shamefully
broken."

THE QUARREL WITH EAST HAVEN.

In 1703, the village quarrel broke forth afresh. East
Haven now numbered a population of 200 souls, with a
grand list of £2,560, and began to feel strong enough to
resume the independence that had been laid aside since 1685.
In December, 1703, East Haven voted to "Take up the
Village-grant" which had been formerly received from New
Haven and from the General Assembly. A committee of
seven was chosen to manage the affairs of the village, and
the matter was favorably considered by the Assembly of
1704.[1] So long as the petition was only for the privileges
of an ecclesiastical parish, New Haven made no opposition,
although the new village was a combination of the two
hamlets that had made the previous appeals.[2] The official
account of the rural attempt to find a minister shows the
quaint, old-time reverence for the college-bred man. Jacob
Hemingway was born in the village, the youngest son of
Tithingman Samuel Hemingway. In 1703, he had just
received his diploma at the new college in Saybrook from the
hands of the Rev. Abraham Pierson. "At a meeting of the
village, Nov. 20th, 1704, voted, to seek to Sir Heminway
that he would give them a taste of his gifts in order to settlement in the worke of the ministry." Not long afterward
they were so much pleased with the "Taste of Sir Heminway
in preaching the Word," that they made him an offer of
settlement. The thrifty youth made answer, "That Sir
Heminway doth comply with their motion, God's grace
assisting, and does accept the proposition, and desires some
consideration with respect to wood." He got it. But that
November village-meeting took one more step which naturally

---

[1] Dodd's East Haven Register, 57, 60, et passim.
[2] i. e. East Haven and Fair Haven.

excited the jealous temper of New Haven, and originated an eighty years' contention. They advanced a claim to all the undivided town-lands adjoining the village-limits and between the river Quinnipiac and the Branford line; and furthermore, they proceeded to divide them. To New Haven this seemed an act of grand larceny, and, in the next month, the "Selectmen were ordered to look into the business of our neighbors at the ironworks, concerning their village, and make a report thereof." In the following spring (April 24, 1705) they reported; and New Haven Town voted that the former grant of a village had lapsed, that New Haven did not grant and never had granted any common, undivided land to the present village, and that all dwellers without the village-bounds must pay for the support of the ministry in "New Haven plott." A confused wrangling ensued. New Haven attempted to dispose of the common lands, and was met by East Haven with a counter disposition.[1] New Haven attempted to tax the village, and was resisted. The General Assembly tried to pacify the belligerents, and failed.

In 1707, East Haven petitioned the Assembly for town-privileges, and obtained a most equivocal document, capable of both an affirmative and negative interpretation. East Haven construed it as a town-charter, and acted accordingly. New Haven, whose deputies had probably inspired the discreditable sophistries of the document, rejected East Haven's construction as absurd, and tried to veto acts of independence. At this juncture, tradition imputes a decisive influence in the struggle to the Rev. Gurdon Saltonstall, who had just been elected Governor of Connecticut. He took up his residence upon his wife's property in East Haven, but, instead of siding with his neighbors, used his overwhelming influence against them.

" The people of the village kept large flocks of geese; many of which found their way to the Furnace Pond, and frequently passed over to the Governor's farm. The Gover-

---

[1] Town Records, IV. 156, 188, 191.

nor, vexed by this invasion of his rights, proclaimed a defensive war, attacked and routed the feathered army, and made a great slaughter among them. The owners of the geese were in turn greatly offended. And such was the effect upon the minds of the inhabitants generally, that, at the next election for Governor, not a single vote from East Haven appeared for Saltonstall."[1] Geese once saved Rome, but they ruined East Haven; forthwith the Assembly passed a series of acts which, if not repealing, at least nullified the charter of 1707, and reduced East Haven again to the footing of a parish.[2] New Haven Town-Meeting voted, December 25, 1710, that, so long as East Haven kept a ministry and school, it need not pay New Haven rates for those ends; but that every other point would be contested. The mode of procedure in establishing a Church upon a legal basis, and even the phraseology used, testify to the persistence, at this late day, of Davenport's example and opinions. In 1709, the village requested, and the Legislature accorded, permission "To embody into a Church-State with the approbation of the neighboring Churches." One year afterward the village met together and chose seven men to be the "Pillars" of the Church. When another year had elapsed, the Church was gathered to its pillars (October 8, 1711), and "Sir Heminway" was regularly ordained.

The conflict of secular authorities waxed and waned until 1717, was resuscitated in 1752, and from that time was prolonged until after the Revolution. Through the greater part of this time East Haven chose officers annually, but acted with New Haven in public business and in the election of deputies. The unneighborly strife affected other than the contending parties. East Haven became the pioneer in a

---

[1] Dodd's East Haven Register, 48.

[2] The General Assembly of this period displayed more than one symptom of moral obliquity. The Legislature which met at New Haven, October 14, 1708, appropriated £50 to keep "Doggs in the northern frontier towns of the Colony to hunt after the Indian enemy."

division of the whole outlying township into ecclesiastical
parishes. The records of the First Church and Society of
New Haven, the Mother Church, begin with the first of
July, 1714. In December of the same year, West Haven
Village, or Parish, was spoken of. In the next spring, the
bounds were marked out, and a quarrel, miniature by comparison, ensued because West Haven thought the parent town
too miserly (April 26, 1715). The next spring witnessed
the differentiation of the parish of North Haven, then called
"The Northeast Village." The boundaries were described,
and it was voted that the "Inhabitants be allowed to support a ministry as soon as they can."

YALE COLLEGE.

In the autumn of 1716, the scattered members of Yale
College were gathered together and united at New Haven.[1]
The hopes of Eaton, Hopkins and Davenport were finally fulfilled. The references in the Town Records to the college are
few and meagre. There is only the bare mention of the material

---

[1] In Vol. III. of O'Callaghan's Documentary History of New York (p.
117) is a letter which makes some positive assertions concerning the foundation of Yale, and which throws a side-light upon ministerial influence
in Connecticut. It was written (November 9, 1705) to the Secretary of the
Society for the Propagation of the Gospel. The author was Colonel Caleb
Heathcote, of Westchester, an ardent Episcopalian, as will appear, and
subsequently Receiver-General of Customs in North America. "The chief
argument of Connecticut people against the Church has been the ill lives of
the Episcopal ministers, and now the Society has taken away the ground of
that. No sooner was the Society formed than the people of Connecticut,
doubting of maintaining their ground without some further support, they
with great industry went through their colony for subscriptions to build a
College at a place called Seabrook. And the ministers, who are as
absolute in their respective parishes as the Pope of Rome, argued, prayed
and preached up the necessity of it, and the passive-obedience people, who
dare not do otherwise than obey, gave even beyond their ability. A THING
WHICH THEY CALL A COLLEGE was prepared accordingly." Colonel Heathcote further related that most of the "Connecticut folk are little better
than heathen, not having been baptized nor admitted to communion."

inducements which the town held out to allure thitherward
the infant institution. December 24, 1716, the proprietors'
meeting voted to give eight acres to the college, and individual
proprietors offered forty acres more. The trustees at the time
made a judicious acknowledgment of the fact that New
Haven was the highest bidder for the possession of the building school. Their memorial to the Legislature, in 1717,
states, as reasons for preferring New Haven, "The con-
veniency of its situation, agreeableness of the air and soil, and
the cheapness of commodities; whereunto may be added the
largest sums of money by far, subscribed by particular
gentlemen for building an house for the school in said town."[1]

THE WALPOLEAN LETHARGY.

From this time onward New Haven Town shared in the
lethargy that fell upon the English world during the peaceful
administration of Walpole. The official records afforded but
few glimpses into the world outside. The town filled up the
spheres of its local life, and, like all the great and small
colonial units, unconsciously husbanded its strength for the
struggle that was to follow.

February 2, 1719, "The Town by a full vote granted an
half-quarter of an acre of land in the Market place at the old
prison-house to build an house upon for his Majesties service,
according to the order of the last January County Court, and
to be laid out by the Townsmen." This building was erected
near the southwestern corner of the green, at the intersection
of Chapel and College streets.

There arose a feeling that public affairs should be conducted with greater decorum. Those were the days when
many men were snatching at bits of unoccupied land, and

[1] It has sometimes been overlooked that Governor Saltonstall would
strongly desire the settlement of the college at New Haven. He was a
resident of the town, and would not be likely to forget the needs of his
son, who was ready to enter college in 1721.

mining frenzies were frequent. It was voted, therefore, in 1721, that "Any one, speaking in Town-meeting without the Moderator's recognition, shall forfeit two shillings"; further-more, that the "Townsmen provide a great Chair at the charge of the Town, for the use of the Town." Luxury[1] had entered into the high places. The paternal functions of government were sometimes curiously exemplified. In December, 1725, "It was voted that the Inhabitants of the Town that are Husbandmen shall axletree their carts five or six inches wider than they now are by the first of April next."

In 1731, doves were put under the ban along with the barberry bushes. "The Town being of the opinion that the Doves are more hurtful than profitable, vote that the Select-men repair to the owner of Doves in this Town, and inform the said owner that the Town expects they should destroy them, the said Doves."

Through the first half of the century, and until long after the Revolution, the small-pox was often a source of general alarm and of public expense. In 1732, the townsmen were actively engaged in preventing the spread of the disease, and public pest-houses were demanded. The first one was built on Oyster Point in 1752–53.

In these days, too, the Records begin to show disagreeable signs of the existence of another pest—slavery. The slave-trader, and even the kidnapper, were about their fiendish work. One Michael Roger, a sailor from Jamaica, and a free man, was . in peril of their clutches, and escaped by the testimony of Captain John Hinman, of New York, with whom he had sailed. In Roger's behalf was offered also a certificate, copied with many flourishes into the Records, and signed by "Paul Richard, Esq., Mayor of New York." Traces of the "peculiar institution" are yet more numerous in the news-papers of the day. The Connecticut *Gazette*, for instance, in 1761 contained such advertisements as this: "To be Sold, Several likely Negro Boys and Girls, arrived from the coast

---

[1] Records, IV. 341, 405, 409, 427.

of Africa. Samuel Willis, at Middletown." In 1763, several similar notices appeared.[1]

Throughout the first half of the 18th century the currents of popular thought and interest flowed in ecclesiastical, not in political channels. The excitement deepened and culminated in 1741–43, when Whitefield's preaching led to the disruption of the Church in the controversy between the New and Old Lights. The Church at New Haven, and most of those in its immediate vicinity, had always been severely orthodox. Mr. Davenport's Church, in 1665 and afterward, was firmest of the firm against the heretical, half-way covenant, and the oft-proposed "Presbyterianizing" of the "Congregational Way." The same Church shut its eyes to the great awakening. It strongly opposed the doctrines and measures of the enthusiastic New Lights, and strongly supported the tyrannical law by which itinerant preachers could be punished as common vagrants. It is well-nigh impossible for us to imagine the dismay and anger that met the demand of a minority of thirty-eight members to be allowed separate worship. The town, as well as the Church, was divided against itself, and for nearly twenty years the two parties were to each other as heathen men and publicans. But the dispute left upon the body politic only slight traces of its existence, and the Records of the town practically ignore the strife. Perhaps the first recognition of the existence of the two Churches is in 1761, when the selectmen are ordered to divide a number of copies of the Saybrook Platform between the committees of each Society.

THE SALE OF THE TOWN'S POOR.

During the last French and Indian wars, appear the first signs that the care of the poor and helpless was considered

---

[1] It should be said that, in the files of the New Haven journals (kept in the Yale Library), the advertisements of runaway slaves, which were very numerous during the Revolution, seldom refer to cases of punishment as a means of detection. I have noted but one such case

burdensome. We hear no more of individual townsmen commissioned to make visits of friendly inquiry and sympathy to the houses of the poor. Primitive solicitude had given way to official conciseness. The first record of guardianship assumed reads as follows: "We, the Selectmen of the Town of New Haven, by and with the advice of Civill Authority in said Town, agreeable unto the laws of this Government, took Susannah Nesbit, an Idle Person, with her estate and Credits into our care" (May 13, 1746). After 1750 the wealth of New Haven increased rapidly, and her commerce was large. Yet, as in modern times, commercial prosperity was accompanied by depression of the lower classes and by great poverty among them.

The familiar cry for State employment was raised, and in December, 1763, the town voted that "The Selectmen lay out £6 in the purchase of junk to employ poor and idle persons in labor."[1] In the same year the town-poor were sold at auction to the lowest bidder. The town authorized its townsmen to make any satisfactory disposition of the paupers, and this is the way in which it was done. The notice appeared in the *Gazette* under the inappropriate date of July 4: "We the subscribers, Selectmen of the Town of New Haven, do hereby give notice . . . . that there will be a Vendue on the second Monday of August next at the State House in said Town at four of the clock in the afternoon, where those persons which are maintained by the Town will be set up, and those persons who will keep them at the cheapest rate may have them. Also a number of Children will be bound out until they are either 14 or 21 years of age, if any persons appear to take them.

> "John Mix, Wm. Greenough,　　　⎫
> "Thomas Howell, Amos Hitchcock, ⎬ Selectmen."
> 　　　　　　　　　　　　　　　　　　⎭

At the same time agitation was commenced for a public workhouse; but nothing definite was accomplished until

---

[1] Records, IV. 556.

four years later, when money was voted and application made to the County Court for the creation of a county workhouse at New Haven (1767).

The First Post-Office.

The increase of wealth, and the exigencies of a Continental alliance against French and Indian foes, induced a closer mercantile connection between the colonies, both North and South. In this way New Haven entered the sphere of Franklin's influence. Wherever Franklin moved he dropped the seeds of union, and not the least of his good works was the intercolonial post-office. It is probable that New Haven, as a way-station, partook of the benefits of the monthly mail-trip, begun in 1672, from New York to Boston and back again. The famous jurist, Andrew Hamilton, also set on foot, in 1683, a scheme for a weekly mail from Boston to Philadelphia;[1] but there seems to be no official record of New Haven's participation in these services. After Franklin made the tour of the colonies to perfect arrangements for post-routes, the mail-service of the towns along the coast took the semblance of completeness and regularity. In 1754, James Parker, of Woodbridge, New Jersey, was appointed by Benjamin Franklin to be the first Postmaster of New Haven. Mr. Parker would hardly satisfy modern ideas of official fidelity, for although he was Postmaster at New Haven, his residence was still in Woodbridge.

The working partner of the firm of J. Parker & Co. was John Holt, who, in the year of Parker's appointment, established the first printing-office in New Haven.

The first production of the type was the laws of Yale College, printed in Latin, and published probably in December, 1754. In January of the next year was issued New Haven's first newspaper, the *Connecticut Gazette.* This journal could boast of two columns on each page. Its size was about 14

---

[1] See Hinman's Antiquities of Connecticut, 152.

by 9½ inches, and it was sold for "Two shillings sixpence lawful money per Quarter," including postage.

Sometimes the routes that Franklin had mapped out did not permit quick transmission of the mails, and, if need arose, a special postal service was maintained by subscription. Such was the case during the Seven Years' War, in 1758, when J. Parker & Co. offered to subscribe £5 toward the support of a "Post to Albany during the Summer," so that news from the army might be speedily received. John Holt retired from business in New Haven in 1762. The *Connecticut Gazette* lived for two years more, and was then discontinued. But in the summer of 1765, "Benj. Mecom, at the Post-Office, New Haven," revived it. His spirit was accommodating enough to deserve success. He offered a weekly twopenny paper at 8s. 8d. a year; and all kinds of "Provision, Firewood, and other suitable country produce will be taken as pay of those who cannot spare money, if delivered at the Printer's dwelling-house, or at any other place which may accidentally suit him." He announced that the price would not be increased when the "Stamp Act takes effect, if sufficient encouragement is forthcoming." Mr. Mecom assured the public that he had engaged correspondents, and had sent for three sorts of "English Magazines, the Monthly Review of New Books, and one of the best London Newspapers." He thought that "These, with American intelligence from Nova Scotia to Georgia, and from Canada," would provide continually a "Stock of Momentous Materials."

First Oyster Laws.

The revival of business drew official attention for the first time to the development of what has since been one of New Haven's leading industries, the oyster-trade. The Town-Meeting in February, 1762, enacted the first oyster laws. The matter was a subject of annual legislation for many years afterward, but the provisions of the first regulation were typical of all.

"Whereas many persons have made a practice of catching and distroying the oysters in the harbor of New Haven in the months of May, June, July, and August, which is to the great detriment of the inhabitants of New Haven; which to prevent, voted that no person shall be allowed to rake up and catch any Oysters in the harbor of New Haven or the Cove, from the first day of May to the first day of September, under a proportionate penalty of twenty shillings per bushel; but the Selectmen may allow any person to catch a small quantity of Oysters in case of sickness or necessity." The same penalty was affixed to carrying off oyster-shells, and a committee of five was elected to prosecute "Breaches of this Vote." Violations of the law were sometimes punished, but always with a lenient hand.

SKETCH OF THE TOWN'S COMMERCE.

The enlargement of both domestic and foreign trade and the increase in wealth and population were sudden, and immediately consequent upon the termination of the Seven Years' War, and upon the removal of the hostile menaces from Canada and the Ohio Valley.

Until the decade, 1750 to 1760, the commercial interests of the town stagnated. Twenty years after the union with Connecticut, New Haven had a larger number of taxable polls than any other town in the colony, but its grand list, £13,127, ranked third, Hartford and Windsor each showing a larger total. Out of twenty-seven ships in the colony, with a tonnage of about 1050 tons, New Haven could boast of only five small vessels, with a total tonnage of 134. There was a handful of small merchants in the town, most of them trading with Boston, New York, and the West Indies. The staples of commerce with the islands were, of course, liquors and sugar.

A large proportion of the produce found its way to Boston to pay for English cloth and manufactures, but the remainder went to Madeira for wine, or to Barbadoes for rum and molasses. There was some export of lumber, but the town exercised a jealous control over the trade. Only upon petition and after a permissive vote by the town could pipe-staves be exported. The town denied such a petition in 1691. In 1695–96 and in 1698, the town gave liberty to ship pipe-staves for a few months only. One man was allowed to export three thousand pipe-staves, provided that he procured no more, either from the commons or from his own property.[1]

The first result of the crusade by Dudley, Randolph, and the New York Governors against the New England charters was to tighten the chains of commercial restriction. The navigation laws had been practically disregarded, but now the day of lax colonial administration was over. Under pressure from England, Governor Leete, in May, 1680, reluctantly took as a bitter dose the "Oath of Trade and Navigation." In the next year, as in duty bound, he made the following report to the Commissioners of Customs at London. His anxiety lest he overestimate the resources of his colony, and his care to allay governmental suspicions, are amusing and possibly disingenuous. He would probably have used different language to persons intending immigration.

"After above forty years' sweating and toyle in this wilderness, we have had neither leisure nor ability to lanch out in any considerable trade at sea, having only a few small vessells to carry our corne, hoggs, and horses unto our neighbors of York and Boston to exchange for some cloaths and utensills wherewithall to worke and subdue this country. Likewise some of those comodities are carried to the Barbadoes and those Islands to bring in some sugar and rum to refresh the spirits of such as labor in the extream heat and cold. We have appointed customers or collectors in our severall counties to take speciall care that these acts of trade and navigation be duly observed and kept, the most aptest persons we could

---

[1] Records, IV. 55, 76.

pitch upon for that affaire, tho this work is yett novel and unknown to them, thro want of experience. We shall be ready to grant Mr. Randolph such aid as shall be requisite. Jan. 24th, 1681."[1] At about the same time, Governor Leete reported to the Privy Council, apparently with a feeling of thankfulness, "We have no need of Virginia trade, most people planting so much tobacco as they spend."

The New York Governors invariably represented New Haven as a resort of smugglers, and the Board of Trade always inquired about that charge in its communications to the Connecticut authorities. The Lords of Trade, writing to Governor Hunter, say:[2] "In the latter end of October, 1707, one Capt. Bollews of New York went from Curaçoa with dry Dutch goods to New Haven, near the Sound of New York, the most convenient place to run goods."

In 1720, New Haven's shipping was just where it had been forty years earlier; while, in 1745, the whole trading fleet of the town consisted of two coasters and one West Indian vessel.[3] To show the miniature character even of this small commerce, Mr. Trowbridge relates that, in 1745, the ketch *Speedwell* sailed to the Azores with a cargo worth £90 4s. 6d.—in which valuation the sixteen quarts of rum for the master's use were included.

At this time there were about 225 buildings and 1400 people in the town. Scarcity of good money was, of course, an ever-present difficulty. About 1680, pine-tree shillings from the Massachusetts mint began to circulate in the colony. Madam Knight, in 1704, sojourned a while in New Haven, and jotted down in her journal that the people had four different prices for commodities, according to the manner of payment. First was "Pay," in kind, at a value set by the General Court fifty per cent. higher than money-price;

---

[1] Hinman's Antiquities of Connecticut, 190.

[2] O'Callaghan, Col. Doc. of New York, V. 160.

[3] Dr. Dana, as quoted by T. R. Trowbridge, Jr., in New Haven Historical Society Papers, III.

second, " Pay as Money," in kind, one-third cheaper than the General Court standard; third, "Money," a mixture of many coins, good, bad, and indifferent, chiefly pieces of eight rials, or Bay shillings, with some wampum; fourth, "Trusting." After 1709, the colony had a paper currency of its own, with all the usual attendant evils, and possibly the sudden prosperity of the period about 1760 was partially due to the prohibition by the English Parliament, in 1751, of the issue of bills of credit. In 1756–58, Connecticut called in all her bills of credit, paying one-ninth of their value and repudiating all the rest.[1]

Flax was then one of the staple products of the New Haven region, and advertisements in the papers stated that cash or flaxseed would be received in payment. The exports from New Haven in 1760 amounted to an inconsiderable sum in value. For the year ending May 1, 1774, the exports were worth $142,000, and were made up as follows: Flaxseed, 150,000 pounds; wheat, 15,000 bushels; rye, 20,000 bushels; Indian corn, 33,000 bushels; oxen, 2000; horses, 1400. The imports for the year had about the same value. About thirty ships sailed out of New Haven Harbor to engage in foreign trade, and the grand list of the town showed a total of £73,210. It was by far the wealthiest and most populous town in the colony.

THE APPROACH TO THE REVOLUTION.

From oyster laws, from restraints upon unruly geese, and from the marking out of new highways, the drowsy Town Records suddenly wake up to the din and the confused alarms of the Stamp Act and Boston-Port-Bill time. The familiar story of the growth of disaffection and of consequent revolt can be readily deciphered from the official milestones

[1] New Haven Historical Society's Collections, Vol. I. Bronson on Connecticut Currency.

that dot the road to revolution. The New England Town-Meetings stood near the heart of the insurrection, and New Haven conformed to the usual type.

For the sake of comparison, it is instructive to notice the reception in 1761 of the news of George the Third's accession. The Governor received dispatches officially announcing the death of the "Late Most Gracious Sovereign," and on the 22d of January, having assembled a militia force, the Council, and many of the notables of the colony, he proclaimed upon the New Haven Green that the "Imperial Crown of Great Britain, France and Ireland, as also the supreme dominion of the Colony of Connecticut, had solely and rightfully come to the high and mighty Prince George, Prince of Wales." The Governor and company thereupon acknowledged their "Faith, Constant Obedience, Affection," etc., "Beseeching God, by whom Kings and Queens do reign, to bless the Royal King George the Third with long and happy years to reign over us. . . . . God save the King." There was a general signing of the proclamation, three huzzas, the discharge of twenty-one cannon, and a grand dinner for the dignitaries at Mr. Beers's tavern, where the healths of His Majesty, of the Royal Family, of the King of Prussia, and "Other loyal healths," were drunk. The militia also were refreshed with grog, so that we may well believe the ancient scribe who wrote: "The whole was conducted and concluded with great decency and order and great demonstrations of Joy." Apparently, the loyal enthusiasm vanished almost with the dinner and the grog.

The year 1763 saw the determined effort by the Bute and Grenville administration to crush the illicit West India trade of the colonies. The answer from New Haven may never have been heard, but it was firm. The Town-Meeting which took the first revolutionary step was held on the anniversary of Washington's birthday, February 22, 1763. "The Committee appointed in consequence of a letter from the Selectmen of the Town of Boston to the Selectmen of this

Town to consider of some measures to be agreed upon for promoting Economy, Manufactures, etc., report:

"That it is their opinion that it is expedient for the town to take all prudent and legal measures to encourage the produce and Manufactures of this Colony and to lessen the use of Superfluities and, more especially, the following articles imported from abroad, viz.: Carriages of all sorts, Horse-Furniture, Men's and Women's Hats, Men's and Women's Apparel ready-made, Household Furniture, Men's and Women's Shoes, Sole-Leather, Gold, Silver, and Thread-Lace, Gold and Silver Buttons, wrought Plate, Diamond, Stone and Paste-Ware, Clocks, Silversmith's and Jeweller's Ware, Broad-cloths that cost above ten Shillings Sterling per yard, Muffs, Furs, and Tippets, Starch, Women's and Children's Toys, Silk and Cotton Velvets, Gauze, Linseed Oil, Malt Liquors, and Cheese; and that a subscription be recommended to the several Inhabitants and Householders of the Town, whereby they may mutually agree and engage that they will encourage the use and consumption of articles manufactured in the British American Colonies, and more especially in this colony, and that they will not, after the 31st day of March next, purchase any of the above enumerated articles imported from abroad after the said 31st of March, and that they will be careful to promote the saving of Linen Rags and other materials proper for making paper in this colony. The foregoing Report being considered by the Town was by a full vote approved of and accepted." "Protection" was patriotism then.

During 1764 the colonies waited to see what was in store for them, and encouraged each other in peaceful resistance while Grenville elaborated new schemes of taxation and repression and prepared the Stamp Act. Upon the threshold of the struggle there is an interesting record of an event in the world of commerce. Mr. Trowbridge relates that the brig "Derby of Derby" arrived from Dublin with twenty tons of coals and thirty-eight Irish servants—probably the earliest importation of each article. What became of the coals cannot be told; possibly that was a luckless consignment. But Israel Boardman, of Stamford, advertised, January 5, 1764, "A parcel of Irish Servants, both Men and Women, just imported from Dublin in the brig Derby, and to be sold cheap."[1]

The next glimpse at New Haven reveals the New Haven of 1765. The Stamp Act had passed. Jared Ingersoll, of New Haven, the representative of the colony at the Court of King George, after laboring zealously by the side of Franklin to prevent the passage of the Act, accepted, by the advice of Franklin, the office of Stamp Distributor for the colony. Mr. Ingersoll reached home in the first part of the year 1765, and the supplies of his office were in New York by summer-time. Crowds gathered around his house in a threatening manner, and burnt him in effigy. Some of the more imaginative minds remarked upon the identity of his initials with those of Judas Iscariot. Ingersoll issued a notification that he did not expect to force stamped paper on anybody, and desired the citizens to think more how to get rid of the Stamp Act than of the officers who were to supply them with the paper; to learn something about the nature of the office before they became so angry at it. On the 6th of September the cooler heads and the authorities in the town felt obliged to curb the riotous feeling against Ingersoll by semi-official proclamation. On the 17th, the Town-Meeting voted that its representatives in the General Assembly should labor for the repeal of the Stamp Act, and, in the presence of Mr. Ingersoll, the meeting resolved "That the Freemen present earnestly desire Mr. Ingersoll to resign his Stamp-Office immediately."

Ingersoll arose and courageously said that he would not resign except in accordance with the will of the General Assembly. Two days after, Mr. Ingersoll, on his way to Hartford, was waylaid at Wethersfield by a large force of

---

[1] Barber's Antiquities, 113.

men, the majority of them being "Sons of Liberty" from Eastern Connecticut, and was forced to resign his office.[1]

What the state of affairs in the town was during the winter of 1766, can be best told in the record of the Town-Meeting, February 3: "Taking into consideration that a due execution of the laws is absolutely necessary for maintaining Justice, Peace, and Good Order, and that, for several months past, there has been a total suspension of the execution of the Laws in Civil and Probate Matters in this Colony, the Courts, Magistrates, Justices of the Peace, and other officers having for some reasons wholly declined proceeding therein, which obstruction of business has been attended with considerable inconvenience and will be attended with very bad and dangerous consequences, Therefore, the said Courts, Magistrates, and Justices, especially the Honorable Superior Court by way of example to the others, together with the respective Officers of such Courts and the Practitioners at the Bar are hereby requested to proceed and transact their usual business, *agreeable to the laws of this Colony.*" After a recital of disorders in the town, "Threatening to the Public Peace and dangerous to the Civil Society," the meeting voted to stand by the officers of government with all care. The vote stood 226 against 48. Thus New Haven joined in the general defiance of the English Parliament; for this vote was intended as advice to the officers of law to disregard the stamped paper in the discharge of their duties.

A fortnight later the Stamp Act was repealed. Through the next few years the Revolution ripened beneath the surface with but little official aid. Reference to newspaper literature

---

[1] Hollister, II. 188; Barber's Antiquities, 114; Town Records, IV. 560–565. As Ingersoll rode toward Hartford at the head of his cavalcade of captors, he was questioned about his feelings. He replied that he had now a clearer idea than ever before of the passage in Revelation which speaks of Death on the pale horse and hell following after him. If the newspapers of the day are trustworthy, Ingersoll was treated for a year or more as a sort of prisoner of war. Even his private letters were taken from him at New London and used against him.

shows the progress of "independent" ideas, and reveals what some of these disorders were that had alarmed the sober burghers. The noisy section of the townsfolk was mainly "patriot," and was incensed against the two Grand Jurymen who tried to suppress the nocturnal assembling, whooping, and burning in effigy.

Barber quotes a letter written in June, 1766, by Benedict Arnold to "Mr. Printer," in which that hot-headed youth vindicates himself for having administered justice according to Lynch's Code to an offender. Arnold was a merchant and ship-owner. One Peter Boole, a sailor from a ship which Arnold owned, made, or tried to make, a complaint to the officers of the New Haven Custom-House against Arnold for smuggling, whereupon Arnold and some of his friends gave the informer an informal thrashing at the public whipping-post. The antagonism between patriots and conservatives, and the influence of the latter party in the town, are shown by Arnold's question, " Would so great a number of people in any trading-town on the Continent (New Haven excepted) vindicate, protect, and caress an Informer, a character particularly at this alarming time so justly odious to the Public ?"[1]

The news of the repeal of the Stamp Act reached New Haven on the 23d of May, and a universal jubilation ensued, "All" (according to the veracious printer) "without any remarkable indecency or disorder." The kernel of disturbance was touched in this way, " Business will soon be transacted as usual in this loyal Colony."[2]

In 1768, a letter from the selectmen of Boston recommending "some measures of economy" was received, and referred to the local selectmen for consideration. Into the ensuing

---

[1] In 1769, Admijah Thomas asked public pardon in the newspaper for "Informing that Timo. Jones, Jr., was 'running of Goods.'" He may be the same one who in September, 1769, was carted, pilloried, tarred and feathered for informing.

[2] The *Connecticut Journal.*

non-importation agreements the majority of the merchants in the town entered heartily. Yet there was a strong opposition, and the patriot leaders were obliged to hold frequent assemblies to sustain the enthusiasm and coerce the unwilling ones. In the summer of 1770, many of the New York merchants renounced the agreement. Shortly after, Roger Sherman presided over a meeting of traders, merchants, and other inhabitants of New Haven, which resolved to keep the agreement and to transfer trade from New York to Philadelphia and Boston. September 10, 1770, the town elected eight representatives to a convention of the colony, which assembled at New Haven on the 13th, for the purpose of encouraging non-importation and domestic manufactures. The Convention enumerated the articles that might be imported from Great Britain without incurring public odium. The list begins ominously enough with " Powder and Shot."[1] Jared Ingersoll had recovered the esteem of his neighbors, for his name appears with those of David Wooster, Roger Sherman, David Austin, and James A. Hillhouse, upon a committee of 38 members chosen to consider the " Commercial Interests " of the town of New Haven.

In the midst of the unsettled times, the people of New Haven found leisure to desire urban dignities. The first move toward incorporation as a city was made December 9, 1771 : " Whereas, a motion was made to the town that this town might have the privileges of a city, and that proper measures might be taken to obtain the same," a committee of eighteen was elected, headed, as usual, by Roger Sherman, and comprising the most influential men of the place, to " Judge of the motion what is left for the town to do with regard to

---

[1] The remaining articles were : "German Steel, Hemp and Duck, Wool-Cards, Card-Wire and Tacks, Impliments for Cloathiers' Trades, Fish-hooks and lines, Tin-plates, Hatters' Trimmings, Salt-peter, Sickles, Bar Lead, Pins and Needles, Copperas and Allum, Brimstone and Sea-Coal, Sheep-Shears, Shoemakers' Awls and Tacks, Sheet Copper, Apothecaries' Drugs, Paper Moulds, Books, Chalk, and Salt."

the same, and report thereupon to the town." The clouds of war prevented further action.

True to the traditions of the town, a strong conservative party formed itself in New Haven, and, in 1772–3, it seems to have been in the majority.[1] The violent spirit of the Sons of Liberty doubtless led to some unpleasant outbreaks, and the records for those years contain a number of solemn adjurations for the establishment of virtue and good order. The spirit of restlessness could not fail to animate a party which counted Benedict Arnold among its leaders. In March, 1774, the same month in which the Boston-Port Bill passed the Parliament, New Haven was engaged in leading a forlorn hope against the assertion of Connecticut's jurisdiction over the Wyoming Valley, and against the claims of the Susquehanna Company. New Haven urged the submission of the conflicting claims to the King in Council—a course which was ill-suited to the temper of the time, and which, as Trumbull says, was made by many a subject of banter and ridicule.[2]

But all these minor notes of discord were soon buried in the clash of a greater contest. Hollister bears witness that New Haven led the State in sympathy for Boston. It was probably not long after Postmaster Elias Beers received the documents describing the embargo that was laid upon Boston, that Daniel Lyman presided over a Town-Meeting called to express New Haven's sentiments. "May 23d, 1774, Voted, that we will to the utmost of our abilities assert and defend the Liberties and Immunities of British America, and we will co-operate with our sister towns in this and the other colonies in any Constitutional measures that may be thought most conclusive to the preservation of our invaluable rights

---

[1] Records. V. 19, 96, 84.

[2] New Haven men were prominent in the Middletown Convention, which met to oppose the Wyoming project. The town voted to adopt the remonstrance of that Convention by a vote of 108 to 90. This was in April, and the unexpected closeness of the vote caused a heated discussion in the newspapers.

and priviledges. For the maintenance of Publick Peace and
support of Generall Union, which at this time is so absolutely requisite to be preserved throughout this Continant,"
eighteen prominent citizens were named a Committee of
Correspondence. A copy of the transactions was forwarded
to Boston.

On the 20th of June, the town voted "That a General
Congress is desired as soon as it may be, and that a general
annual Congress would have a great tendency to promote the
welfare and happiness of all the American Colonies." About
a month after the first Continental Congress did assemble,
the town appointed a committee to receive and transmit "Subscriptions for the relief of the inhabitants of the town of
Boston that are now suffering in the common cause of
American freedom."[1] The selectmen were instructed to buy
powder and build a powder-house with the £100 of "so-
called" Indian money. It is noteworthy that the proceeds
of the Quinnipiac Reservation of 1638 survived to be shot
against the English soldiers of 1775.

New Haven during the War.—Committees.

[2]As soon as the news of Lexington and Concord reached
New Haven, Arnold, who was Captain of the Governor's
Guards, paraded his company[3] before the place where the
selectmen and the other authorities were in session. His
demand for ammunition was refused, and Colonel Wooster

---

[1] Records, V. 44, October 18, 1774.

[2] In the Conn. Gen. Assembly that met at New Haven in the fall of
1774, the Ticonderoga expedition was planned. The campaign was mapped
out by certain members, especially by Mr. Parsons, Mr. Silas Deane,
Gen. David Wooster, and Samuel Wyllys. These gentlemen, and others,
borrowed upon their own security the necessary funds from the Colonial
Treasury. They dispatched a scout to investigate the feasibility of the
undertaking, and were, in short, responsible for the risk and the success of
the enterprise.

[3] 2d Co., Gov.'s Foot Guards, was organized December 28, 1774. Arnold
was the first captain.

(as he was then) went out to persuade him to wait for proper orders. Arnold answered threateningly, concluding, "None but Almighty God shall prevent my marching." The supplies were forthcoming. Arnold and his company were in Cambridge by April 29, but most of the soldiers returned after three weeks' service.[1] All the towns that contributed to this first Revolutionary uprising were paid by the State with scrupulous care. It was ordered that New Haven should receive the sum of £238 1s. 11d.

The various committees that Revolutionary exigencies called into being practically ruled the town in many departments. New committees were evolved at each successive step. Still there was no diminution in the number of regular town-offices that were annually filled. The official force of the town comprised seven selectmen, nine listers, eleven tithingmen, collectors of town and country rates, constables, grand jurymen, surveyors of highways, the customary cohort of fence-viewers, sealers of weights and measures, packers, branders, key-keepers to the pound, a town-clerk, a treasurer, a leather-sealer, a gauger, an excise-master, pound-keepers, and a committee on encroachment on highways, a body which was by no means inactive in those days.[2] The selectmen were ordered to call Town-Meetings at the desire of the Committee of Correspondence, but, after November, 1774, the functions of the latter committee seem to have devolved upon the "Committee of Inspection." This committee was first chosen November 14, "In accordance with the eleventh article of association entered into by the late Continental Congress at Philadelphia," and it was voted that the major part of the committee, probably for convenience in assembling, should be within the limits of the First Society. With laudable impartiality a by-law of the same year ordered that, among the selectmen, one must be in the First Society,

---

[1] Hinman's Conn.'s Part in the War of the Revolution, 23; Hollister, Hist. of Conn., II. 165; Barber, 120.

[2] Records, IV. 584–86.

one in White Haven, one in the Church, and one in Fair Haven.

The public business grew so great and important that, in 1775, as a war-measure, the number of selectmen was, with permission of the Legislature, increased to thirteen. November 6, 1775, there was a carnival of committees. To one was entrusted the erection of a beacon on Indian Hill; to another, of a fort at Black Rock; to another, the procurement of floating defenses in the harbor; to another, the enforcement of the following resolution: "Voted, that every person who looks upon himself as bound either from conscience or choice to give intelligence to our enemies of our situation, or otherwise take an active part against us, or to yield obedience to any command of His Majesty, King George the Third, so far as *to take up arms against this Town*, or the United Colonies, be desired peaceably to depart."[1]

This vote was probably the immediate cause of an odd communication which the town received on the same day from five men who represented the Sandemanian Church. These men had formerly allowed themselves to be numbered among the patriots; but now they stood forth to contradict their previous apparent acquiescence. They had been influenced by the fear of man; they trembled before God for their great wickedness therein; and they avowed themselves to be really true to God and King. Afterwards nine followers of this creed signed a long letter to the Committee of Inspection, in which their position was sustained solely upon religious grounds and by Scriptural quotations. It appears from this document that one of their number was already in prison, but political principles of every sort were ignored by them. The imprisoned man was regarded as a martyr to religious conviction.[2]

---

[1] Records, V. 54–57. The October session of the Assembly had ordered that thirty men and a lieutenant should be stationed at New Haven until winter set in. Hinman, Conn.'s Part, etc., 191.

[2] Hinman, Conn.'s Part, etc., 588, 591.

The Committee of Inspection, supported by dominant public sentiment, ruled the town with rigor throughout the year 1775. The newspapers of that year tell of citations before the committee for buying and selling tea, for calling " Gage an honest man " and declaring that " Whigs are liars," and even for "Speaking slightly of the money emitted by our Assembly." The indications are that the culprits generally confessed and submitted. One cannot but feel that " Francis Vandale, from Old France," had fallen upon evil times indeed. December 13, 1775, in the midst of proscriptions, sieges, and invasions, this itinerant Kelt announced to the inhabitants of New Haven that he " Intends to open a Dancing School in this town and also teach the French language. He is a Protestant, provided with good certificates, and has given entire satisfaction *in those necessary arts* at Cambridge, Boston, and New Port."

Some question probably arose about the authority of Town Committees to exercise such supreme authority over opinion as they had so far done. In accordance with Congressional recommendations, the Legislature, sitting at New Haven in October, 1776, declared Connecticut to be a free and independent State, and enacted a Statute of Treasons. Petitions from New Haven were at this time presented to both Governor Trumbull and the Legislature, entreating that certain obnoxious Tories might be arrested by authority of the State, and, if possible, removed into the interior. Six men were tried and two were found guilty.[1] They were banished to " Eastbury in Glastonbury, there to remain at their own cost until further orders, and were not allowed to receive or send letters which had not been perused by the civil authority."

---

[1] One of them, Ralph Isaacs, was prominent enough to be a member in 1771 of the committee to consider about incorporating New Haven as a city. The other, Abiathar Camp, was a devout Episcopalian. He asked permission to attend the nearest church of his creed, which was at Middletown, but the request was denied. (Hinman, Conn.'s Part in the Revol., 241, 566.)

The seriousness of the situation had become evident to all, and enlistments were rapidly hurrying to the front the more ardent sympathizers with the patriot cause. Strenuous efforts were put forth to keep the whole weight of the wealthy and influential town of New Haven in the right side of the scale. Governor Trumbull, on the first of August, 1776, addressed an urgent appeal to "The Civill Authority, Selectmen, Committee of Inspection, and all Military Officers in the Town of New Haven," which was sent to the Rev. Mr. Whittlesey, and read by him immediately after service. All the forementioned dignitaries were exhorted, as they valued life, property, liberty, and country, to exert all their influence and power in forwarding the enlistments within their respective spheres of influence.

There were, however, signs of cooling ardor during this year. Thrift was sometimes a counter-agent to zealous patriotism. The October Assembly had ordered each town to furnish sundry articles needed for military use, including one tent for every £1000 in the Grand List. But the militia of New Haven had received permission to remain in the place as a Home Guard. The Town-Meeting of December 16 therefore voted that New Haven would be excused from providing the tents, etc., "As the militia of this town are not ordered to march forth."[1] Earlier in the year there was a quaintly worded witness to the watchful care which the authorities, although surrounded by the menaces of war, extended over the minute details of local administration. " March 4th, 1776. On complaint that the town of Wallingford were a-going to send Rhoda Woolcot into this place as one of the poor of the town, Voted, that Mr. Thos. Mansfield go to Wallingford, serch out the truth of the matter and make report."[2]

---

[1] Records, V. 67.

[2] This is extracted, not from the Town Records, but from the Records of the selectmen's meetings. Their transactions had long ceased to be reported in the occasional Town-Meetings, and their own Records are

Financial burdens were more onerous than ever, and the
little finger of taxation at that time was heavier than the
whole body of a tariff now. The history of the corporate
action of New England towns at that juncture is the story of a
struggle to sustain the economic life of the American cause. In
January, 1777, the town sanctioned the prices which had been
affixed to sundry articles by the recent Legislature. " Those
who do not accede, upon conviction before the Committee of
Inspection, shall be deemed enimies to this country and treated
accordingly." The town even took a step in advance of the
General Assembly, and elected a committee of its own to
enlarge the list of fixed prices within New Haven's limits.
Every volunteer for the war was offered two pounds as bounty-
money, and the men were to receive annually, " for three
years, if they stay so long," one pair of good strong shoes,
one pair of good yarn stockings, and one shirt. It was
promised also that the selectmen would care for soldiers'
families, and the pledge was fulfilled. A tax of one shilling
in the pound was imposed. The selectmen performed some
notable acts this year. They introduced public inoculation
for small-pox into the town, and they were requested to send
to the " Pest-houses as fast as they are emptied of soldiers
all such as shall receive the Small-Pox voluntarily."[1]
Another unwonted task of theirs was to distribute one

quite concise and non-communicative. In the New Haven Town-Clerk's
office are several long, narrow volumes, containing the minutes of selectmen's meetings during the Revolutionary time, and their accounts of
payments and distributions from 1776 to 1805. Timothy Jones, Jr., was
First Selectman during a large portion of that time.

These books are full of information concerning prices in those days and
concerning the supplies that the town furnished to soldiers, to soldiers'
families, and for the war.

[1] The results seem to have been unfavorable. January 18, 1779, it was
voted, " That the Town will not allow Inoculation to be set up in this
Town under any restrictions or regulations whatever." This law continued in force until December 27, 1784, when Dr. Lewis Morgan received
from the town liberty to inoculate. There were also subsequent prohibi-
tions. Records, V. 67, 69, 78, 98, 140.

hundred and thirty-three bushels of salt among the members
of the "Societies," taking heed that no Tories received any.
The close of the year witnessed the best action of all. The
meager reports of the selectmen's meetings fortunately preserved the testimony of this deed. "December 1st, 1777.
Voted, that Mr. Darting's three negroes, Tim, Cloe, and
Tim, be free^d. and Tim^o. Jones, Jr., be desired to write a
certificate for that purpose." It is likely that "Mr. Darting"
represents, with a clerical error, Mr. Thos. Darling, a prominent citizen of Tory proclivities, and a political antagonist of
Roger Sherman.

THE ARTICLES OF CONFEDERATION.

The New England Town-Meeting of one hundred years ago
had a high regard for its own opinion. Witness the dignity
and attention with which New Haven criticised the Articles of
Confederation of the United States of America. In December, 1777, the town examined that pulseless simulacrum of a
Constitution, and appointed a committee almost as large as
the Congress to formulate and deliver the opinions of the
town. That committee presented a voluminous report
January 5, 1778. Their verdict was hostile, and the town
accepted their conclusion. The first objection censured the
extreme particularism of the Articles, but from a novel standpoint. The committee disapproved of that "Clause in the
4th Article prohibiting any State from laying any Duty,
Imposition, or Restriction on the property of any of the
States." They agreed that no State should have power over
United States property, but saw no reason why the property
of one State should not be treated as the goods of an individual
are treated. They proceed with the strange conjecture that,
under this provision, some State may buy up or otherwise
secure a needed article and make a corner in the markets,
while the State which is the natural producer of the article
cannot prevent the removal of its own fruits. This was

State's Right against States' Rights, out-Heroding Herod.
The next criticism is more creditable to its authors: " We
object also to furnishing troops in proportion to the white
inhabitants only, as we hope the time may be when the black
man may be a freeman, and the owner of property and then
he ought to bear his share of military burdens."   There is no
record of any debate upon this statement, and yet slavery
existed in New Haven for more than a generation afterward.[1]
Probably the number of slave-owners was small.

But the committee very wisely placed the seal of its
severest condemnation upon that part of the " 8th Article
which directs the support of a common treasury by a tax on
land and its improvements within each State."   They pointed
out that a State dowered with an extensive territory might
be really poorer than a smaller State whose wealth was not
largely derived from agriculture, and they expatiated upon
the difficulty of making fair appraisals.   In this respect the
honorable committee was surely considering the general welfare rather than that of Connecticut or New Haven.

The fate of war descended upon New Haven on the 5th and
6th of July, 1779.   General Tryon's attack was unexpected
and the disaster was great.   There is need only to sketch the
familiar picture—the attack in two directions, the resistance,
stout enough to defend the town from conflagration, but not
from capture and sack, the solitary President of Yale " Exercising the rights of war " with his musket, the gathering of
the neighboring militia, the panic-stricken flight of the non-
combatant inhabitants.   One does not like to forget the
fugitive Mrs. Potter, who rushed along the North Haven
road tightly grasping a junk of salt pork, selected in the
moment of terror from among all her treasures ; nor the two
other women who ran, one swinging a bunch of tallow-dips,

---

[1] At the close of the eighteenth century New Haven County had 800
slaves—twice as many as any other county in the State contained.
Within ten years the number in New Haven County had shrunk to about
280.

which melted in the sun, and the other carrying in her arms
a cat, although her children were forgotten. More akin to
our purpose is the portrayal of the economic distress that
resulted within the plundered region. Money was given by
the State to those towns which had been invaded. The Committee of the Legislature in the following winter computed
the total damage to New Haven at £24,893 7s. 6d.—which
was one thousand pounds greater than the estimate of the
sufferers themselves. Afterward there was a large addition
to this sum on account of damages in the parishes of East
and West Haven.

The valuation was purposely based upon the price-lists of
1774, except in the case of necessities and rarities like rum,
wine, salt, and tea.[1] The reversion to the ante-bellum basis
is noticeable, for, only a few months before, the authorities of
the town and of the State were vying with each other in
support of the New Haven Convention of January, 1778.
That convention had been called, in accordance with the Act
of Congress, November 22, 1777, in order to regulate the
price of labor, manufactures and produce, imports, and the
charges of innkeepers. The general character of their scale
of values can be seen in the recommendation—which became
a law—that "The price of labor should not exceed an advance
of 75 per cent. over the rates of 1774." The depreciation of the
currency in 1779 can be inferred from actual prices entered
at that time in the private cash account of David Judson,
of Stratford.[2] One and a half "Hard" dollars cost sixty
dollars, one and a sixth pounds of tea were worth thirty-five
dollars, a pistol was procured for the round sum of one
hundred and fifteen, and even a pair of garters cost four
dollars.[3]

---

[1] Hinman, pp. 612, 626–7. The last application from the town to the
State in behalf of sufferers by the invasion was in the winter of 1784.

[2] New Haven Historical Society Papers, Vol. III.: Prof. Baldwin's article
on The Convention of 1778.

[3] The following prices are extracted from the selectmen's accounts with
soldiers' families in 1778:

If it is proper to judge by frequency of legislation upon
the subject, the high prices of liquors were deemed most dis-
tressful in New Haven. Only a month after the British
invasion, the town voted that "As some persons have sold
Rum at an exorbitant price or have with-held it entirely, the
Town disapproves of a greater price for good West India
Rum than $32.00 per gallon by retail, and New England
Rum in proportion, and will treat with proper contempt all
who sell for more, or refuse trade." This resolution was
made very pointed, for a committee was named with the sole
duty of reporting the "Sense of the meeting" to Capt. Elijah
Forbes.[1] Illicit trade with the British and Tories upon
Long Island was another source of frequent disquietude to
the town-authorities. So great was the possible profit that
the traffic could not be entirely suppressed, in spite of the
danger of confiscation at either end of the route. June 22,
1779, the town enjoined it upon the selectmen to stop the
trade to Long Island. In the next June a vigorous resolution was accepted by the town and circulated for signatures,
pledging the subscribers to abstain from trading with Long
Island and from using articles that came from thence.

At the same time the town again followed the example of
its superiors in throwing water against the wind. "Voted,
that we will receive the new Continental money, or Bills of
Credit lately emitted by this State, equal to Gold and Silver
in all payments, and that we will freely sell all such articles
as we have to dispose of for such money."[2] In order to
clinch this beyond possibility of withdrawal, tellers counted
the voters and reported 264 for, to 8 against, the motion.

	£ s. d.		£ s. d.
6 Loads of Wood	57	5 w. of Rye Flour	0 14 2
1 qt. of Rum	2 5	9 " " Beef	2 2 9
" " " Molasses	1 7	27 " " Pork	15 6
1 lb. of Tea	4 7	3 " " Sugar	4 7

[1] The particular limit of the value of West India rum was rescinded
within ten days.

[2] Records, V. 110.

A committee was appointed to visit absent citizens, and to record their votes and names. The new bills were scarcely emitted before they fell 50 per cent. of their face value. In this year the town was offering heavy bounties to volunteers, £4 10s. to three-months men, and to six-months men £12. Taxation was frequent and burdensome. A tax of sixpence in the pound was levied in November, 1780, and in the next January another of one and a half pence. In times of such scarcity the lot of the town-poor was unusually unfortunate, and it is honorable to the town that, in 1782, there was reluctance to sell them, as heretofore, to the lowest bidder. A committee was appointed by the Town-Meeting, December 9, to provide some plan for the care of the poor, and one which might prevent the "Idle and Strowling from spending their .time from door to door." But the humane attempt failed. In January the selectmen were again ordered to "Sell the town-poor that they may be supported in the cheapest manner."

In April, 1783, New Haven heard the news of the cessation of hostilities and of the immediate prospect of full independence. There were the wonted salutes, parades, dinners, and divine services, and there was a "Very ingenious Oration" by Tutor Elizur Goodrich, of Yale College. But there were two features of the celebration which were significant for New Haven. The hymn of thanksgiving was sung by "The singers *of all the congregations* in consort"; and a "Liberal collection was made for the poor of the town, to *elevate their hearts for rejoicing*."[1]

Treatment of Tories.

The all-important question of local interest became, "What shall be done with the Tories, and with the property of Tories, present or absent?" The town of New Haven found especial difficulty in answering this readily, for the

---

[1] It is too probable that "Elevating their hearts," being interpreted, meant "Quenching their thirst."

reactionary or doubtful elements within it were numerous,
and comprised some of the more prominent families. At no
time was this more apparent than during the British raid.
The troops of King George were guided to the town by a
representative of one of the leading families of the place,
and, in the Town-Meeting that was convoked after the
departure of the English, it was " Voted, that the Town
resents and disapproves the conduct of those who stayed in
Town during the late incursion of the enemy, without sufficient reason." A committee was chosen to examine all such
persons for the causes of their conduct ; and, more significant
still, certain commissioned officers were requested to " Inquire
after those who lately neglected to fight against the enemy."
On the 16th of August, 1779, the committee presented a long
account of what they had accomplished. They had accepted
a large number of excuses, but a yet larger number they
thought to be insufficient. They advised, however, that
these delinquencies be overlooked for this time on condition
that the culprits behave themselves hereafter. The committee gave it as their opinion that a number of individuals
had lied to them, and they found five men guilty of treasonable practices. Jared Ingersoll, of Stamp-Act fame, had occasioned scandal by entertaining some British prisoners who
passed through the town on their way to an exchange, and a
new committee was appointed to investigate that. We may
be sure that Mr. Ingersoll was reminded of the Jersey
prison-ship. This bare recital of official procedures readily
suggests the jarring conditions of New Haven society through
the Revolutionary period, the majority, uncertain of its strength,
not daring and generally not wishing to use extreme measures,
yet suspicious and watchful ; the minority, possessing a degree
of wealth and social influence, despising their opponents,
malicious and selfish. When the happy consummation of the
war was finally attained, the status of the Tory population
under the new *régime* offered everywhere a complicated
question, delicate in its nature and difficult to determine.
The popular sentiment, not only in Connecticut, but through-

out the country, was most hostile to the Tories. In the spring of 1783, the New Haven Town-Meeting declared itself emphatically against "The return of any of those Miscreants who deserted their country's cause, and joined the enemies of this and the United States of America during the late contest." In Northern and Eastern Connecticut the feeling toward the Loyalists was rancorous. But, during the year 1783, a portion of New Haven's patriotic opinion upon this subject underwent a radical conversion. The city-project of 1771 had now revived, and the co-operation of the considerable Tory element was desired. New Haven's commercial interests and a political amnesty seemed to go hand-in-hand. To the work of conciliation a few leading minds devoted themselves.

The scheme for incorporation was part of a wider municipal movement. As the war was closing, the struggle of the parishes against the parent town was renewed, and speedily resulted in the dismemberment of the township. That sturdy rebel, East Haven, found allies in 1780. On the 8th of May, New Haven Town-Meeting appointed special agents to oppose the application of Amity and Bethany for town-privileges.[1] But North Haven and Mount Carmel[2] followed the example of their sister parishes. The town made a virtue of necessity and voted, February 12, 1781, its consent to the four petitions. In December a committee was appointed to divide the town. Its report of January 7, 1782, defined not only the boundaries of the aforesaid petitioners, but of the long-stubborn East Haven also, and sketched a plan for the equitable adjustment of financial responsibilities.

Since such local problems required solution, the argument rapidly gained force that immigration and assistance from all quarters for the embryo city should be welcomed without too many troublesome questions. Every effort was made to guide and to soften public opinion concerning the proper treatment

---

[1] These parishes, partly in New Haven and partly in Milford, were united under the town-name of Woodbridge.

[2] Now Hamden. The name should have been Hampden.

of Tories. The columns of the newspapers were not infrequently used in defense of a lenient policy. In the autumn
of 1783, a petition for incorporation as a city received two
hundred and fourteen signatures. The petitioners averred
that "Want of a due regulation of the internal police"
obstructed the normal growth of New Haven's commerce;
also that wharves, streets, and highways ought to be commo-
dious for business, and to be kept continually in good repair.
The Connecticut Assembly postponed its decision in the
matter until the January session (1784). On the fifth of
that month the Town-Meeting requested its representatives
to "Exert themselves that the Act for incorporating a part
of the Town of New Haven be passed with all convenient
speed." A high rate of speed for those days was attained.
The Act became a law on the eighth, three days later.

Not until the formation of a city government had been
successfully achieved was the dangerous topic of Tory citizenship again brought officially before the town. The Town-
Meeting of March 8, 1784, just a year after the "Miscreants"
had been denounced, submitted the question to a committee
for adjudication. Pierpont Edwards was the prime mover of
the committee, which reported promptly to the same Town-
Meeting. These various proceedings had probably been
forecasted and provided for, inasmuch as the document was
voluminous and elaborate enough to have emanated from a
National State Department, if there had been one. It reviewed
ancient and modern history, picking up apposite illustrations
along the route, enlarged upon the sovereign powers of each
State under the Confederation, and then concluded that, by
"Express provision of the Statutes of Connecticut, each town
has the exclusive right of admitting inhabitants."

"Furthermore, since by the Definitive Treaty and by
the Recommendations of Congress founded thereon, a Spirit
of real peace and philanthropy towards our Countrymen of
the aforesaid description [Loyalist] is most strongly incul-
cated, and since the great National Question on which these
persons differed with us in sentiment, is settled authorita-

tively in favor of the United States, it is our opinion that, in point of Law and Constitution, it will be proper to admit as inhabitants, such Tories as arc of fair character and will be good and usefull members of Society, and faithfull citizens of this State, but that no persons who committed unauthorized and lawless plundering or Murder or have waged war against these United States, contrary to the laws and Usuages of Civilized Nations,—should be admitted."

The closing paragraphs of this prolix production evince intermingled pride and wisdom, and a sharp lookout for the main chance withal.

"In our opinion no nation, however distinguished for prowess in arms and success in war, can be truly great, unless it is also distinguished for Justice and Magnanimity. None can properly claim to be just who violate their most solemn treaties, or to be magnanimous who persecute a conquered and submitting enemy. Altho, when the distresses and calamities of the late war are fresh in our recollection, we may think a persecuting Spirit justifiable, we must, when reason resumes her empire, reproach such a line of conduct and be convinced that future generations, not being influenced by our passions, will form their idea of our character from those acts which a faithfull historian shall have recorded, and not from our passions of which they can have no history. As this Town is most advantageously situated for commerce, having a Spacious and Safe harbour, surrounded by a very extensive and fertile country which is inhabited by an industrious and enterprising people, fully sensible of the advantages of trade; and as the relative and essential importance of this State depends on the prosperous extent of its agriculture and commerce, we think that the proposed Measure will be highly expedient.[1]

"John Whiting,   David Austin,
Jonathan Dickerman,   David Atwater,
Jonathan Ingersoll,   Pierpont Edwards,
James Hillhouse,   Sam. Huggins."

---

[1] Records, V. 144.

The town accepted this report immediately, and patriotic President Stiles wrote in his diary, with evident disapproval, " This day Town-Meeting voted to readmit the Tories." Thus New Haven began to hide the wounds that war had made. The remedy of mutual toleration and forgetfulness banished all the scars of conflict from the official records of the town, but doubtless the healing process was more protracted and painful among the deeply-injured tissues of society. How has history repeated itself upon a larger scale since 1865!

FINAL DIVISION OF THE TOWNSHIP.

In the following year (March 28, 1785) the town set the seal of finality, so far as it lay within its power so to do, upon the newly-created towns of Woodbridge, East Haven, North Haven, and Hamden. Some of them had already gained legislative recognition. In December, the sole remaining parish, West Haven, received the permission of New Haven to apply for town privileges, but, chiefly through the opposition of Milford, the town of Orange, in which West Haven is included, was not formed until 1822. Thus the once-spacious township of New Haven shrank to very nearly its present proportions.

THE CHURCH THE GERM OF THE TOWN.

The parish question in New Haven has here been traced for more than a century. No institutional evolution can be more instructive or more common than this differentiation of townships. The investigation prepares a reply for the query, " What has made the town?" The whole history of the New Haven township unites in the answer, " The Church." Just as an English community is said to derive the title of " city " from its possession of a cathedral church, so the New England settlement won its municipal honors by right of its meeting-house. No town upon our shores cherished its Church-organization with greater fidelity than did New

Haven; and New Haven held all her children strictly to account, first of all for a church, and for a school which was in essence but another form of the Church. A Church-Meeting, the antecedent of a Town-Meeting, is the primary lesson of our municipal development.[1]

The growth of parishes and of new townships, and the consequent alienation of lands, reduced the jurisdiction of the proprietors and their committee to a shadow. However, until the close of the Revolution, the proprietors had from time to time exerted a more or less vigorous influence. After the formal land divisions had been concluded, the proprietors successfully asserted against the town a sole guardianship over the Indian Reservation. It was the proprietors also who contracted for royalties from the copper-mines in the Blue Hills, and who gave land to the college and to the grammar school. It was a vote of the proprietors in 1770 which first allowed a separate society to erect its church-edifice on the Green[2]—a vote which may have been remembered against the proprietors when the first city charter was drawn.

The increase of non-Congregational religious bodies was another characteristic of the latter part of the century under consideration. The multiplication of churches affected the town's official life by the contest for satisfactory territorial lodgment in which the upstarting societies were forced to engage, but more by the political strifes that sprang up in the path of religious differences. As the Church was the parent of the town, so did the creeds and customs of opposing churches beget the political parties of the Revolutionary time, and, indirectly, those of our own day.

So wide was the chasm made between what might be called "The Established Church of the Commonwealth" and all dissenting organizations, that opposition in religious belief

---

[1] See Appendix B, The Town of Naugatuck.

[2] The Fair Haven Society, whose meeting-house was built nearly on the present site of the North Church.

necessarily included opposition in almost every corner of
society and politics. New Haven's famous Episcopal schism
of 1722, therefore, heralded the introduction of a new element
into the political life of Connecticut. The rupture in the
First Church, which followed the great awakening of 1741,
aided in diversifying the political landscape only as it
encouraged the existence of a few Sandemanian, Methodist,
and Baptist sectaries. These people shared in the political
fortunes and discomforts of the Episcopalians, but were, in
general, not numerous enough to deserve a separate consideration. Because, therefore, the Episcopalians and the sectaries
of Connecticut were religious Ishmaelites, they arrayed themselves against the dominant public opinion of the colony as
soon as a political question arose sufficiently comprehensive
to warrant the division. The New Haven Episcopalians
were naturally prominent in a colony where Episcopalianism
had always lacked that official support which the representatives of royalty in other colonies had been able to bestow.
When, therefore, the relations with the mother country were
subjected to political discussion, the Loyalist sentiment of the
colony, animating many of the richer, more aristocratic and
conservative inhabitants, centred upon the New Haven
region,[1] and especially upon the Church of England there.
President Stiles wrote of the New Haven Episcopalians in
1784, "They are all Tories but two." Heretofore sectarian
animosity had sought a political expression in squabbles
over land, or over the personal merits of individuals. Now
there was a worthy subject for controversy in which both
religious and political sympathies were concerned. Party
lines were slowly drawn which, under changing names and
conditions, have run forward continuously to the present day,
both in New Haven and in the State.

---

[1] Cf. Curtis' History of the Constitution of the U. S., II. 408. Colonel
Humphreys wrote to Alex. Hamilton, under date of September 16, 1787,
that the New Haven Loyalists, in his presence, "half in jest, half in
earnest," drank the first toast at dinner to the Bishop of Osnaburg, as a
possible and desirable candidate for the American throne.

CHAPTER VIII.

THE DUAL GOVERNMENT.—TOWN AND CITY.

1784–1886.

Town-Born vs. Interloper.

The incorporation of New Haven City, like most progressive measures, was achieved in the face of no little opposition.
City privileges must have been deemed Grecian gifts in those
days, for the dispute over the same subject in Hartford was
still more animated and prolonged. The change in New
Haven was wrought out through friction between several
strongly-defined elements in society. The staid, conservative
families and the younger, enterprising business men who
together made the town, rallied in two camps, which were
described in the local vernacular as "The Town-Born" and
"The Interlopers." This odd division seems to date from
the days when New Haven's commerce revived, perhaps
about 1760. Those who had breathed the air of New Haven
at their first entrance into this world, sometimes looked
askance at the influx of bustling traders, shippers, and professional men not "to the manner born"; while those
individuals whose ancestry had sat in Robert Newman's
barn, and had worshipped from generation to generation in
the First Church, perched aloft upon social summits that
have not yet been entirely leveled. These people were
grieved by the destruction of their quiet town-life, by the
intrusion of a rabble of sailors and workmen, and, above all,
by the insurgent spirit of unrest that came with the ships and
strangers. The interlopers, on the other hand, were most
directly responsible for the new commercial activities of the

place. Among them were ambitious, aggressive, and broad-minded men, ready to promote progress in municipal as well as in personal affairs. The number of inhabitants in New Haven in 1748, the township including the half-dozen outlying parishes, was about 1400. The official records of Connecticut in 1756 attribute to New Haven a population of 5085. An increase of 3600 in eight years was, at that time, a very prosperous growth. In 1774, the inhabitants numbered 8022. The average annual increment from 1724 to 1748 was 20; between 1748 and 1774 it was nearly 255. The augmentation of wealth during the latter period outstripped that of the population. Compared with the former two decades, the amount of tonnage in the port had increased over forty-fold, and the value of exports had been multiplied by 470.

Such were the results of the re-infusion of the commercial spirit into the veins of Eaton's torpid town. However, it is not supposed that the business interests of the community were helplessly dependent upon sharp social distinctions. Not all the town-born eschewed business enterprise, neither did the life of the place spring wholly from young and imported blood. The feeling between town-born and interloper became an instinct, an inherited sentiment, powerful in politics and society, but often almost entirely dissociated from original conditions. Instances are not wanting of the outcropping of this old antipathy from beneath the deposits of years of social growth. Sometimes the interests of the town-born were very sternly sundered from those of the interloping element. Mr. Trowbridge relates that one Capt. Brown, being compelled by stress of storm to throw overboard some portion of his cargo, ordered that the goods of interlopers should be selected for the libation to Neptune, but that the consignments to town-born people should be saved.

Leaders of the interloping element before the Revolution were men like Benedict Arnold, Col. David Wooster, the hero of Danbury, James Hillhouse, the most public-spirited and generous of citizens; above all, Roger Sherman, the foremost man in New Haven, if not in the State, throughout one generation. It is safe to say that while he lived he was the head and front of every species of good work for his adopted home. Sherman, Wooster, and Hillhouse were interested, in 1771, in the movement toward the formation of a city, and, when the close of war afforded once more an opportunity for domestic improvement, Roger Sherman was the central figure around which the progressive elements in society clustered. Starting in life as an apprentice to a Massachusetts shoemaker, he became a member of the Connecticut Council, a Judge of the Superior Court, a member of the Revolutionary and Continental Congresses, wherein he belonged to the committee that reported the Declaration of Independence, a member of the United States Constitutional Convention, a Representative and afterward a Senator in Congress under the Constitution. Among the prominent leaders of that era, he enjoyed the rare honor of affixing his signature to the four most important documentary expressions of the new national unity, "The Address to the King," "The Declaration of Independence," "The Articles of Confederation," and "The Constitution." Throughout the latter part of his career he was dowered with "pluralities" like a mediæval prelate. At his death, in 1793, he was a United States Senator, a Judge of the Superior Court of Connecticut, and Mayor of the city of New Haven. To that infant city, indeed, he maintained a relation quite comparable to that which subsisted between the ancient town and its Governor, Theophilus Eaton. Mr. Sherman's unsympathetic character, however, could not command that universal allegiance which waited upon the Puritan patriarch.

First Phases of City Politics.

The distinctions of Patriot and Tory intersected society and envenomed the neighborhood animosities. The town had officially promised, as we have seen, to forgive and forget, but the diary of President Stiles shows how beneath the surface the poison rankled.[1] A combination of interlopers, business men, and Tories, the latter probably actuated by political motives mainly, was most actively interested in the fortunes of the new city. Out of about six hundred adult males then living within the city limits, the selectmen certified that 343 were qualified[2] to be freemen. About one-fourth of the latter number failed to take the oath, so that there were only 261 qualified citizens at the time of the first election, February 10, 1784. The poll for Mayor showed 249 votes, of which Roger Sherman received 125—just enough to elect him. Thomas Howell, deacon of the First Church, received 102 suffrages, while 22 freemen preferred Thomas Darling, who was probably the choice of the extreme Tories. Deacon Howell, who was, like Sherman, an interloper, was elected to be Senior Alderman. Three other Aldermen were named—viz.: Samuel Bishop, Deacon David Austin, and Isaac Beers, the bookseller. Provision was made, as the law required, for a City Clerk, two Sheriffs, a Treasurer, and for twenty Councilmen. About one hundred citizens completed the election of the latter on the third day (February 12), when the new officials were formally inducted into office. Inasmuch as the charter directed that the municipal year should begin in June, the forms of election were repeated on the following first of that month. On the day after the close of the February election, Dr. Stiles sketched a bird's-eye view of the political situation.

"The city-politics are founded in an endeavor silently to bring Tories into an equality and supremacy among the Whigs. The Episcopalians are all Tories but two, and all qualified on this occasion though despising Congress govern-

---

[1] See Prof. F. B. Dexter's excellent paper on New Haven in 1784.

[2] Suffrage was limited to those who held personal estate worth at least £40, or real estate renting for £8 per annum. Loyalty to Great Britain might also be a cause for disfranchisement.

ment before; they may, perhaps, be forty voters. There may be twenty or thirty of Mr. Whittelsey's meeting added to these.[1]　Perhaps one-third of the citizens may be hearty Tories, one-third Whigs, and one-third indifferent.　Mixing up all together, the election has come out, Mayor and two Aldermen, Whigs; two Aldermen, Tories.　Of the Common Council, five Whigs, five flexibles but in heart Whigs, eight Tories; Sheriffs and Treasurer, Whigs, but one flexible." Evidently the arrangement was not quite satisfactory to the " inflexible" President of Yale.

THE FIRST CHARTER.

The Act of January 8, 1784, which was New Haven's first city charter,[2] had incorporated the inhabitants of that portion of the town of New Haven which lay between the Quinnipiac and West Rivers, and between the Mill River meadows and the harbor, under the title, "The Mayor, Aldermen, Common Council, and Freemen of the City of New Haven." We have seen that twenty Councilmen were at first elected. The number of Councilmen was, however, a fluctuating quantity.　Twenty was fixed by the charter as the maximum limit.　The list was soon reduced to ten, it was increased to twelve, then to fourteen, and in 1853 the original membership was restored. The city legislature comprised the Councilmen, the Aldermen and the Mayor.　Under the name of the Court of Common Council, it was empowered in general terms to regulate local affairs, to afford security to property and person, and to provide for the convenience of trade.　The city was not divided into wards, so that the legislative body was not based upon a neighborhood constituency.　The Aldermen were chosen, practically, as assistants to the Mayor, and the chief functions of both Mayor and Aldermen were

---

[1] Mr. Whittlesey was pastor of the First Church.

[2] The text of the Act can be found in Conn. Private Acts, I. 406, and in the City Year-Book for the years 1876–78.

judicial. In conformity with venerable English usage, the City Court was the Mayor's court, wherein that official and the two Senior Aldermen presided. The other two Aldermen were Judges in reserve. The new City Court wielded a jurisdiction like that of the Court of Common Pleas in all civil causes originating within the bounds of the city, except such as concerned land-titles. At least one of the parties to a suit must be a resident of the city. The criminal jurisdiction of the court was confined to offenses against the city ordinances. Justices of the Peace for the town still dispensed the ordinary criminal justice. The Mayor and his four Aldermen bear a definite resemblance to the magistrate and deputies, the Reeve and Four, with whom New Haven started in 1639. The ancient institutional stock of the five elders clung tenaciously to the New Haven soil.

Finally, all the freemen, in full City-Meeting assembled, were the ultimate arbiters of all municipal questions. This purely democratic assembly alone could levy taxes, and elect officers. Its ratification was absolutely essential to every by-law enacted by the Mayor and Common Council. Even then no by-law was valid until it had been published for three weeks successively in "Some public newspaper, in or near said city." This arrangement seems sufficiently clumsy, but the most remarkable check yet remains. Any by-law of the city might be repealed within six months after enactment by any Superior Court holden in New Haven County, if the said Superior Court judged the by-law to be unreasonable or unjust.[1]

Such pains were taken to prevent arbitrary municipal rule; yet in one instance the charter itself trod closely upon vested privileges. The city was empowered to exchange or sell the

---

[1] The English "Municipal Corporations Act" of 1882 provides that an order of a borough-council for the payment of money may be taken to the High Court of Justice by writ of *certiorari*, and may there be wholly or partly disallowed or confirmed, with or without costs, as pleases the court.

northwestern portion of the Green, in order to secure other land or highways, or another Green. These clauses were intended to notify the Proprietors' Committee that its authority over the public square was henceforth vested in the city, and that the proprietors could no longer vote away building-sites upon the Green. However, the remainder of the Green was confirmed as a common or public walk, to remain so forever, never liable to be laid out in highways or to be appropriated to any other purpose.

Jealousy of corporate action and the assertion of State legislative supremacy were distinctive features of this early charter. Public sentiment in 1784 regarded a city as a hot-bed of aristocracy, and a single executive officer, whether local or national, as a possible Julius Cæsar. The successive obstacles to the full habilitation of a city ordinance, the ratification by the citizens, the three weeks' publication in a newspaper, and the possible veto by the Superior Court, would check in our day not only the centralization of power, but also the transaction of business. In 1784, " Thou shalt not go slowly " had not become an American eleventh commandment.

The State Legislature reserved to itself ample oversight in the affairs of the new municipality. The Mayor, although elected in the first instance by the people, held his office during the pleasure of the General Assembly—a reservation which tended to make him Mayor for life. This tenure of the Mayoralty endured until 1826—a period of forty-two years. During that time New Haven was ruled by four Mayors, two of whom died in office and three of whom enjoyed an aggregate term of thirty-eight years. During the forty-two years next ensuing after 1826, the city has elected eighteen different Mayors. Moreover, the election and tenure of Probate Judges were both subject, until 1851, to the General Assembly. In the *personnel* of the town government the establishment of the city wrought no change, and the functions of town officers were altered, if at all, in amount, but not in kind.

DESCRIPTION OF THE CITY.

The city proper of New Haven, in 1784, was the small nucleus of the town, and situated at the edge of the harbor; but the city limits included Davenport's original town plat and the two miles square, with the common fields and pastures. Although General Garth, in 1779, had thought New Haven too fine a place to burn, it was but a straggling village of 3350 inhabitants. In its centre was the unfenced, unkempt Green, marked by wagon-ruts and disfigured by weeds and bushes. Against this unsightly growth, as well as against the nomadic geese and swine, the village fathers had long waged an unavailing paper warfare. In the southwestern corner of the Green, nearly opposite the New Haven House of our day, stood the old County House and Jail, removed in the spring of 1784, at an expense of £30, across the street into what is now the College campus. Near them the old State House, erected in 1717, was situated, and was now perhaps used by the grammar school. The building which had superseded it in 1763, "The New Brick State House," formed with the First and the " Fair Haven " Congregational Churches a line of edifices upon Temple street. The only other churches in the city were the " Blue Meeting-house,"[1] or " White Haven Church," at the southeast corner of Elm and Church streets, and the Trinity Episcopal, on Church street. Two college-buildings, South Middle and the Athenæum, held the Yale of that day, though the first college-edifice was still standing, much dilapidated, in the southeast corner of the campus. Doubtless the sight of a college and a jail thus jostling each other caused more than one jocular remark in the hamlet. Student-life was boisterous then, and was destined to become more so.[2]

---

[1] So called on account of the color of the paint used upon it.

[2] For Dr. Manasseh Cutler's impressions of New Haven in 1787, see Appendix C.

MUNICIPAL IMPROVEMENTS.

A multitude of good works followed upon the new order of municipal duties. The first city tax of one penny in the pound was decreed.[1] The first by-law forbade the erection of buildings without a permit under a penalty of ten pounds, the heaviest fine which the Council was allowed to inflict. There was a flavor of antiquity in the agreement that meetings of the City Council should be called by "Posting notices on each corner of the eight central squares." In addition a bell was to be rung, and proclamation of the day and hour made, at each corner. By September this method of convocation was deemed inadequate, and the City Clerk was instructed to notify members of the government whenever the Mayor ordered a meeting. The tolling of the State House bell summoned the annual City-Meetings on the first Tuesday of every June at nine o'clock A. M.

As soon as the first municipal year was fairly begun, the Council labored vigorously at its work of construction. It was determined that New Haven's trade should be as honest as official supervision could make it. In July, by-laws were passed creating a large number of inspectors and gaugers.[2]

---

[1] Taxes upon the dollar were not laid until July, 1799, when the rate was fifteen mills.

[2] The City Government, during its first quarter century. Elected by the freemen of the city: The Mayor, tenure of office at pleasure of General Assembly; 4 Aldermen, term one year; Councilmen (not more than 20), term one year; Sheriff, City Clerk, Treasurer, Tax Collector, each, term one year; Gaugers of Molasses, Rum, and other Spirituous Liquors; Inspectors of Pot and Pearl Ash; Inspectors and Cutters of Hoops, Staves, Heading, and Ready-Made Casks; Inspectors and Cutters of Plank, Boards, Clapboards, Oars, Shingles, and Scantling; Weighers of Hay; Inspectors and Measurers of Wood; Inspectors of Wheat, Rye, Indian Corn, and Flour; Inspectors and Packers of Beef, Pork, and Fish; Pound-keepers; Inspector of Tobacco; 6 Fire Wardens (after 1788); Board of Health (after 1794).

Elected by the Court of Common Council: 144 Jurors of the City Court; City Attorney (after 1808).

Articles offered for sale must bear the stamp of official
approval. Even prices of board and lodging were fixed
by law. There were enactments against nuisances, against
obstruction of highways, and against disregard of sanitary
precautions. One of the earliest ordinances provided for the
establishment of a public market. The ordinance was from
time to time suspended until, in the next year, two city
markets were built by subscription, one on the southeast
corner of the Green, the other where the present city market
stands. All retailing of meat and vegetable products elsewhere, between sunrise and eleven o'clock of the forenoon, was
forbidden under penalty of twenty shillings. A long and
bitter controversy arose over the merits of a public market
as opposed to individual peddling, or the old-fashioned street-
market in wagons. The city was never contented with the
conclusion that had been reached, and, after much trouble
and ill-feeling, the market law was formally repealed in June,
1826. President Dwight, who was a zealous champion of
the city market, called its overthrow "A striking example of
the power of habitual prejudice."[1]

In June of the initial year the charter was found lacking
in an unexpected quarter. The little village-city felt unable
to extend a suitable welcome to distinguished aliens. So the
needful legislation was procured from the General Assembly,
and the "freedom of the city" was soon after bestowed
upon the "Hon. William Michael St. John de Crevecœur,
Consul-General to His Most Christian Majesty for the States
of Connecticut, New Jersey and New York"; also upon his
children and upon his wife, "Mehitabel." In the following
spring, the "freedom" of New Haven was again granted to
a handful of dukes and princelings. Among the company
were the Duc de la Rochefoucault, the Marquis de St. Lambert, and M. de la Custelle, *avocat du parlement*. To welcome

---

[1] He says: "There is something very remarkable in the hostility of the
New England people to a regular market." (Travels, I. 195.)

and convey these honored and honorable strangers, all the half-dozen carriages in the city must have been required. Public vehicles were heavy responsibilities in those days, for every professional carter was compelled not only to carry a license, but also to give a surety of one hundred pounds.

The city was disposed to foster immigration, and an elaborate welcome was prepared for visitors of a lower degree than the French nobility. A City-Meeting, held September 23, 1784, appointed a Committee of Hospitality, consisting of Charles Chauncey, Pierpont Edwards, James Hillhouse, Timothy Jones, Jonathan Ingersoll, David Austin, and Isaac Beers, Esqrs. Their duties were "To assist all such strangers as shall come to the city for the purpose of settlement therein, in procuring houses and land on the most reasonable terms, and to prevent such persons, so far as possible, from being imposed upon with respect to rent and the value of houses and lands, and to give them such information and intelligence with respect to business, markets, commerce, mode of living, customs and manners, as such strangers may need; and to cultivate an easy acquaintance of such strangers with the citizens thereof, that their residence therein may be rendered as agreeable and eligible as possible." If this programme was carefully followed, the home-seeker must have thought New Haven a true Arcadia. Yet working-men of the better sort were not attracted, unless President Dwight's opinion of his fellow-citizens was untrustworthy. While he extolled the intelligence and virtue of the community in general, he branded the artisan and laboring classes, both white and black, as abnormally vicious.

In the autumn of 1784, suitable names were ordered for the various roads, ways, and alleys within the town-plot, and the first year of urban existence closed with an application to the General Assembly for. wider powers, especially in respect to the laying out of highways. In the next year the State of Connecticut, in the exercise of its sovereign powers, established a mint at New Haven, and issued coinage therefrom until 1787.[1]

Contrary to the usual custom, neither town nor city was inclined to waste words over the Constitution of 1787, probably because there were few malcontents. The town recorded its desire for a convention of ratification, and appointed Roger Sherman and Pierpont Edwards delegates. There was no other official reference to the momentous change from a confederation to a nation, but public sentiment, as voiced in the journals, was enthusiastic in its support of Federalist principles.

The town began to feel pricks of conscience about disposing of paupers at a yearly auction, and, in 1785–86, the Town-Meeting declared that "The Town's-poor should be kept by themselves at one place, unless some of those who now have them offer to keep them at a manifestly cheap rate." There were then thirty-seven paupers, costing £12 per week, exclusive of clothing and doctors' bills. Three years later, when it was temporarily the fashion to let out most of the town's yearly expenses by contract to some one individual, there were but £270 paid for the support of the poor.

Both town and city discussed the erection of a workhouse until 1791, when it was built. The Town-Meeting of June 25, 1792, adopted what it called "The Workhouse Byelaws," which had been prepared by a committee. Any assistant, or justice of the peace resident within the town, might send to the workhouse for not more than three months, "Rogues, vagabonds, sturdy beggars, lewd, idle, dissolute, profane and disorderly persons, all runaway stubborn Servants and children, Common Drunkards, Common Night-

---

[1] A Connecticut copper cent from this mint, found in the basement-wall of the Hartford City Hall, bore on the obverse side the head of the Governor (probably Gov. Huntington), with the words "Autori. Connec." On the reverse were a female figure holding an olive branch, and the inscription "Inde. et Lib., 1787."

walkers, Pilferers, all persons who neglect their callings, misspend earnings and do not provide for their families, and all persons under distraction unfit to be at large and not cared for by their friends or relatives." Such a motley company might be punished, if need were, by the master of the house, upon the approval of his superiors, by " Fetters or Shakles, by whipping on the naked body not more than ten stripes at one time, or by close confinement without food and drink." Upon release, the criminals might claim two-thirds of their earnings, minus the cost of commitment and support. Criminals, paupers, and lunatics continued to be thus housed under one roof until the middle of the next century, when the growing scandal shocked the better class of citizens into action.

The Fire Department.

The fire department of the city made its humble beginning in January, 1788, when a " Fire Engine " was ordered at the expense of the city. Frequent legislation for three years finally gave the control of the department to six Fire Wardens, under whom the entire male population of the city between the ages of 16 and 60 was enrolled. To begin with, there had been but two fire companies, of seventeen men each. Practice with the engines in " Washing and Playing " was ordered on the first Saturday of every April, July and October. Every one must attend with bucket or pail under peril of a two-shilling fine. Ministers, and the President, tutors, and students of Yale College were alone exempted. Moreover, the Fire Wardens were empowered to appoint four sackmen, " Respectable freeholders, each of whom on every alarm of fire shall take with him to the said fire one or more sacks and shall take care of all property necessary to be removed from danger of fire." There was one clumsy check to the extensive power of a Fire Warden : no building could be destroyed, in order to prevent the spread of fire, until the consent of the Mayor, Aldermen, and the body of Fire Wardens, or the major portion of them, had been obtained. No part of the city organization was so frequently tinkered as the fire department. Rigid rules fettered the action of the householder in minute details, and heavy fines were imposed—on paper. The fines were also inflicted, generally to be remitted at the next City-Meeting. Not only the erection of a stove, but even of a stove-pipe, without the permission of the Fire Wardens, was strictly prohibited. Oddly enough, the city re-enacted almost the same laws that had been framed in the same town in 1640, forbidding the kindling of bonfires in the street, or the smoking of tobacco within four rods of a building, and also enjoining the stated cleaning of chimneys. But the anti-tobacco legislation could not be enforced, and all the regulations brought neither safety nor satisfaction until the modern day of steam and electricity.

Danger from fire was no more dreaded than danger from small-pox. That scourge visited the community, as it had done thirty years before, with the revival of commerce. Both town and city moved to erect a small-pox hospital. A strict quarantine was maintained against all comers from New York. The town voted that "Laben Smith, who has come into the harbor with passengers from New York who do not belong to this Town," might land them on the east side of the harbor, provided that "They make off in a stage, and do not endanger the Town."[1] When it was announced in Town-Meeting, August 29, 1794, that a vessel was coming up the harbor, Mr. Adee was sent at once to the waterside, commissioned by the meeting to prevent any boat from landing. At the same time three physicians were elected health officers for the port. The city followed suit in the ensuing spring with the establishment of the first Board of Health. The mind of the city was especially exercised about the East Creek, which had become a receptacle of filthy drainage. The Board of Health consisted of ten persons, under the style and title of "The Health Committee of the City of New

---

[1] Records, V. 347.

Haven." It had full power to abate nuisances, and to improve, as it saw fit, the sanitary condition of the city. Through the labors of this committee, the local authorities obtained from the Legislature power to establish a quarantine for foreign vessels. The community became both unhealthy and impoverished. Although the trade of the place grew rapidly, the city felt the weight of the financial pressure that was universal in the nation. It was very difficult to secure adequate taxation. As a sign of the times, the path to the Treasury was more and more securely hedged in. In 1790, the City Clerk was constituted the sole drawer upon the Treasury, and his orders must first be certified by the Mayor. At the same time it was provided that, so often as there was no cash in the Treasury, the Treasurer should number and register each bill that was presented, and should pay the same in the order of presentation. Both town and city were indebted, apparently, even for the running expenses, and every new street or turnpiked road might be the occasion of fresh borrowing. In 1802, the town-tax was five cents on the dollar, and a committee, of which Noah Webster was a member, was alarmed by a debt of $3,000.

All the work of the Board of Health was performed at its own expense. Most of the public improvements of the time, in the way of adornment or of more efficient sanitation, were dependent upon private funds and private energy. One of the very first acts of the City Government, in February, 1784, was to vote that " Any gentlemen who might agree to defray the expense" could enclose the southeastern part of the Green so as to admit footmen only, "Sufficient room being allowed for carriages before the public buildings." In the same independent way roads were improved, streets opened, and meadows diked and drained.

ADORNMENT OF THE GREEN.

First and foremost in these enterprises were two public-spirited and wealthy citizens, David Austin and James

Hillhouse. To them principally were due the rescue of the Green from its primitive savagery, its enclosure within fences, and its adornment with trees. Not the least of the improvements was the institution in 1796 of the Grove Street Cemetery, which was then a sort of wonder of the world, and the abandonment of the old burying-ground in the rear of the Centre Church—an improvement first proposed by Governor Francis Newman, in 1659. Yet the acts by which the city granted permission for these labors concluded significantly, " Provided the same be done without expense to the city." There was active opposition to the whole procedure, not only within the city, but in neighboring towns. The rejection of the graveyard on the Green seemed to the more ignorant and conservative classes both expensive and sacrilegious, and it was urged against Mr. Hillhouse in a political canvass twenty years afterward.

However, there is evidence that, after the beautifying was completed, the city repented and made a small contribution. The gentlemen who had been most active in the reform were appointed as a sort of Park Commission, their chief anxieties being due to Yale students and to geese. Against the latter bipeds a ponderously-framed law was proclaimed: " No goose or gander shall be allowed to go at large within the limits of New Haven town, unless such goose or gander be well-yoked with yoke 12 inches long, under penalty of impounding such goose or gander ; and goose or gander taken damage feasant shall pay five cents poundage fee." In 1798, with the consent of the town, the Legislature extended the limits of the city toward the East and West Rooks. Already the care of the poor was the chief burden upon the town. The first annual balance-sheet was entered in the " Town Records " for December, 1799, and out of a total expense of £630 the town's poor cost £514. The item had doubled in ten years.

With the opening year of the nineteenth century, the City Clerk was first instructed to act as the Clerk of the Common

Council.[1] The state of the public finances was constantly growing worse. The City Court was supposed to derive support from the fines imposed therein, but the penalties were not carefully collected. A partial remedy for the defect was found in 1803, when the Common Council was empowered to appoint a City Attorney.[2] The supply of water furnished another troublesome question. A proposition to build an aqueduct was first debated in City-Meeting in 1804. Two years later, the consent of the General Assembly was received, and a committee, headed by Noah Webster, was elected to manage the construction of an aqueduct. But poverty prevented the successful termination of this effort, and compelled the city to tolerate the inefficient service of creeks and wells. Unavailing were all endeavors to improve the quantity and quality of the water in the East Creek.

Public Letters to the Presidents and Others.

A most peculiar feature of New Haven Town-Meetings at this period were the eloquently-worded manifestoes upon public affairs. Events of unusual interest and importance could hardly fail to evoke a sermon or an eulogy from New Haven. In 1793, five long resolutions assured Washington that his policy of neutrality " Merits our warmest approbation and support," and that " We will exert ourselves to promote a conduct friendly and impartial towards the nations of Europe," etc., etc. In 1796, New Haven told the National House of Representatives its opinion of Jay's Treaty: " We view with great anxiety the opposition now attempted against the treaty. . . . We avoid declaring what our decision might have been, had this treaty been submitted to our determination. For us it is sufficient that we discover in it no principles subversive of our Constitution."

---

[1] July 7, 1800.

[2] In 1815, the appointment of a City Attorney was, by law of the State, vested in the City Court, and it has so remained.

At the close of John Adams's term of office, New Haven welcomed the homeward-bound ex-President and reviewed his administration with eulogistic words. Federalism reigned supreme in New Haven. "We view with abhorrence all attempts made in our country to mislead public opinion, to inspire distrust, to awaken a spirit of needless discontent, and to deprive magistrates, who have long and faithfully served the public, of their most grateful reward, the esteem and approbation of their constituents." Naturally enough, the community was soon embroiled with Thomas Jefferson, and favored him with frequent communications. His appointment of an aged citizen to the Collectorship has become a part of national history, but the most fruitful cause of correspondence was the embargo, or, as it was occasionally called in this vicinity, the "dambargo."

This measure completely killed a commerce which had not entirely succumbed to the unfavorable conditions of the Revolution. In 1787, 7,250 tons of shipping were registered in the port, and the amount had increased in 1800 to 11,000 tons. In 1790, the trustees of the famous wharf thought themselves justified in setting up a three-thousand-dollar lottery for the extension of their property, and they instructed Mr. Lyman, the taverner, "To increase hereafter at their meetings the quantity of his sling and toddy."

About 1792, the New Haven Bank was incorporated with a capital of $80,000, and the Chamber of Commerce began to meet in "Ebenezer Parmalee's front room, on the first floor." There were three shipyards, and, in the South Sea fleet, about a score of ships, three of which registered over 300 tons. The most famous of these was the *Neptune*, which, in 1799, brought home from a voyage around the world a cargo of tea, silk, and china, upon which the net profits were $240,000, and the duties upon which amounted to $67,000, or $20,000 more than the entire civil-list tax of the State.

The "Orders in Council" began the work of destruction. The brig *Anne*, bound homeward from a Danish port, was boarded twice by the French cruisers and three times by the English. Everything edible was removed, and the captain, remonstrating with a French officer, was told to eat pine shavings, "good enough food for Yankees."[1] If New Haven ships did not bring home many victuals, they were not so scantily provided with beverages; for, in a couple of years, there passed through the Custom House two million gallons of rum, gin, brandy, and wines altogether. It seems strange that any of the ships should have been meddled with, since they were provided with a formidably polite document which was called a "Municipal Letter," and which invoked in their aid the influence of the Mayor of New Haven.[2]

The year 1807 was marked by two events of memorable import in New Haven's development. The First Methodist Church and Society were enabled to buy a lot for building purposes, and the embargo was declared. The former sig-

---

[1] New Haven Historical Society Papers, III.: Ancient Maritime Interests of New Haven, by Thos. R. Trowbridge, Jr.

[2] The following is a copy of a "Municipal Letter":

"Most Serene, Most Puissant, High, Noble, Illustrious, Honorable, Venerable, Wise and Prudent Lords, Emperors, Kings, Republics, Princes, Dukes, Earls, Barons, Lords, Burgomasters, Schepens, Counselors, as also Judges, Officers, Justiciaries, and Regents of all the good Cities and places whether ecclesiastical or secular who shall see these patents or hear them read, We, Samuel Bishop, Mayor, make known that the Master of the Catherine of 84 tons burthen, which he at present navigates, is of the United States of America, and that no subject of the present belligerent powers has any part or portion therein directly or indirectly; and as we wish to see the said Master prosper in his lawful Affairs, our prayer is to all of the before-named and to each of them separately where the said Master shall arrive with his vessel, they may be pleased to receive the said Master with goodness, and treat him in a kind, becoming manner, permitting him upon the usual tolls and expenses in passing and repassing to pass, navigate, and frequent the Ports, Places, and Territories to the end to transact his business where and in what manner he shall think proper. In which We shall be willingly indebted.

  (Signed)   "SAMUEL BISHOP,
                 Mayor."

nalizes a turning-point in the long and unequal struggle between the Orthodox Puritan and his dissenting brethren, the brunt of which, in New Haven, was so long borne by Trinity Church and by the inconsiderable band of Sandemanians. The embargo (December 22) resulted finally in the transformation of New Haven from a commercial to a manufacturing town. During the year 1808, seventy-eight vessels were shut into New Haven harbor. In August, Elias Shipman, Noah Webster, David Daggett, Jonathan Ingersoll, and Thos. Painter, Esqrs., by order of the Town-Meeting, prepared and forwarded to Thomas Jefferson a "Memorial" of about 4,500 words, "Respectfully representing" that the embargo ought to be modified or suspended. One may note the orthodox economy of this paragraph: "We are disposed to foster the growth of manufactures as rendering the people independent of foreign nations for articles of consumption, but, in a country containing immense tracts of uncultivated land, we question the policy of forcing into existence manufactures less congenial to the habits of our people than agricultural pursuits. Manufactures that are adapted to our society will best thrive with unrestricted commerce." This faithful re-echo of the new economic gospel of that day should be read in connection with Jefferson's letter in the same year to his staunch supporter, Abraham Bishop, Collector of the Port of New Haven. The President has heard that "Col. Humphreys, in your neighborhood," makes the best fine cloth in the United States; and, inasmuch as he desires to wear homespun at the "New Year's Day Exhibition," he requests Collector Bishop to forward a suit, and says that he will deposit the price of it "with any member of the Legislature here."[1]

Jefferson returned, in September, a characteristic answer to the memorial, alleging that no one knew better than himself the inconvenience caused by the embargo. He referred the

---

[1] New Haven Historical Society Papers, I. 148.

petitioners to the " Legislature " as the only authority competent to prescribe the course to be pursued. New Haven had its share, in the following winter (1809), in persuading Congress to defeat the Administration upon the question of limiting the duration of the embargo. The Town-Meeting of January 28 adopted a long series of resolutions breathing out the spirit of the subsequent Hartford Convention.[1]

" We will submit to national laws, consistent with the principles of the federal compact, and not repugnant to the spirit of the Constitution and to the fundamental principles of a free government."

" When the rulers of a free people transgress the limits of their authority, it is the right and duty of citizens to manifest a sense of injury and to seek redress."

The town solemnly declared the embargo to be a violation of the Constitution, quoted the Declaration of Independence, used such ominous expressions as " The insidious stratagems of peace become more terrible than the sanguinary operations of war," and " We must oppose the torrent of oppression." Finally there came an appeal to the Governor and Legislature to meet and take measures for the protection of rights. Subsequently the device of non-importation was found to be the same demon under a new name, and the town frequently cried out against it. The last memorial (in 1814) represented New Haven as " Already reduced to poverty and wretchedness."[2]

---

[1] In the winter of 1814–15. It assembled on the 14th of December, 1814.

[2] New Haven's share in the war of 1812 was not entirely confined to memorials. Mr. Trowbridge has related a laughable account of one privateering venture. In 1812, the sloop *Actress*, 60 tons, Capt. Lumsden, was fitted out in New Haven harbor as a privateer. In the Gulf Stream a big English ship was sighted, which was pronounced a tea-ship, and a veritable prize. Much elated, the crew of the *Actress* cleared for action, and were already drinking Jamaica rum in honor of their anticipated fortune. Capt. Lumsden arrayed himself in a resplendent blue suit, with red facings, and a cocked hat, lent him by Jeduthan Bradley, a Foxon militia captain. Capt. Lumsden hailed, and was answered, " The *Spartan*,

DOWNFALL OF FEDERALISM.

It would not be reasonable to suppose that these rebellious declarations were supported by the unanimous sentiment of the town. The unwavering Federalism of the official utterances was anything but popular in the taverns around Long Wharf, where the toast to " Free Trade and Sailors' Rights " was greeted with the greatest enthusiasm. But the minority in the town comprised more stable elements than sailors and laborers. We have seen how the Tory Episcopalian freemen came forward to assist actively in the formation of the city government. The freemen of whom these men were representatives, the freemen who, for one reason or another, were dissatisfied or at variance with the most flourishing Church in the community, fell easily into opposition to the first National Administrations, with which the major part of Connecticut heartily sympathized. Those men, therefore, who at first fought Federalism because they wanted to see the Government fail, " Who," as President Stiles wrote, " despised the Congress-Government," and most of whom despised also the New England Puritan idea, formed, together with those who antagonized Federalism on account of State pride or excess of republican zeal, the nucleus of the Anti-Federalist party in New Haven and in the State. But Toryism soon died away, and ecclesiastical heat availed only to keep alive the seeds of future political dissension. In the middle of President Madison's first term, the Democratic-Republican minority in Connecticut began to assume a more aggressive form, and in New Haven the omens of a new political birth were soon perceived.

---

of London." The name was ominous, for it belonged to a powerful frigate known to be on our coast. But, reflecting that this was a tea-ship, Lumsden said, " Consider yourself a prize to the U. S. privateer *Actress*. Send your papers aboard." The Britisher humorously asked Lumsden if he " Really expected a great ship like this to strike colors to such a little fellow." Lumsden swore, and threatened to fire, whereupon the *Spartan* displayed its sixty guns, and a voice said, " Come to our gangway, and we'll hoist you in."

The insolence of England, the prolonged supremacy of one party in the State and of another in the nation, the rights and wrongs of the various sects, the lack of a written Constitution for the State[1]—all these causes helped to produce and animate a body which first found an abiding mouthpiece and oracle on the 1st of December, 1812. Upon that day Mr. Joseph Barber issued the initial number of the *Columbian Register*.

In the spring election of 1813, New Haven gave the Administration ticket 59, out of 225 votes. During the two following years there was no contest, but in 1815 the *Register* took the lead in appealing to denominational jealousies, and, from that time on, the fight waxed warm, and extended from New Haven throughout the State. The minority adopted the name "Toleration Party," and professed to maintain the broad principles of equalization of all creeds before the law, and of equal rights for all men. The Toleration journals were filled with letters addressed to "Congregational Hypocrites," to "Downtrodden Episcopalians and Methodists." It was asserted that only Congregationalists had been elected to office, that Yale College and other Congregational institutions had been aided by public money, and that Episcopal schools and charitable foundations had been slighted and ignored. One indignant churchman informed the town through the columns of the *Register* that his vote would not again be cast for Governor John Cotton Smith. The Governor had deliberately walked across the Green to his boarding-place, when he might have accompanied some of his associates to Trinity Church to hear the Bishop preach.

The Federalist papers at first affected to despise the agita-

---

[1] A convention of Jeffersonian leaders at New Haven, Aug. 29, 1804, ventured to make the first noteworthy assault upon the venerable charter of 1662. Of what stupid tyranny the ruling party was capable may be seen in the fact that every justice of the peace who attended that convention was impeached before the next General Assembly.

tion. The *Journal* said that the Federalist party was in no new danger from Episcopalian votes, " Because two-thirds of the 2,000 Episcopalian voters in the State are and always have been Democrats." But the apathy of the *Journal* was of short duration. In the election of 1816, the Toleration ticket was partially successful throughout the State. Hartford and New Haven for the first time gave Democratic majorities, and the latter town elected Wm. Bristol as its first Democratic Representative to the Legislature. It was a stunning blow to the New Haven gentry, and it evoked the following lamentation—written, as the *Register* said, " By a half-fledged scribbler in the prostituted columns of the *Journal* "—" O Shame ! Triumph of Apostacy and Delusion ! In this Federalist Town of New Haven, where four-fifths of the Freemen are friends of order and steady habits, prejudice, apostacy, and fanaticism are triumphant. The result of the election this day furnishes the fullest evidence that moral depravity and personal debasement form no barrier to political delusion and sectarian prejudice. Oh, Shame ! Judgment hath fled to brutish beasts, and men have lost their reason." [1]

In the following year, there was a slight reaction in the town. The Federalist ticket received thirty majority, which the *Register* attributed to illegal votes cast by students and tutors from Yale College, and to " The unexpected exertions of four Congregational clergymen who attended and *voted at the polls throughout the day.*" But, in general, the Toleration-ists went on from victory unto victory. Having gained possession of the State, and of most of the local boards as well, they declared in favor of a written Constitution to replace the ancient charter of 1662. The Federalists were put upon the defensive, and in a hopeless cause, for the tide of republicanism had now acquired an irresistible force. In New Haven they seem to have absented themselves from

---

[1] The vote in New Haven was : Dem., 868 ; Fed., 280.

the Town-Meeting of December 29, 1817, which voted
almost unanimously that the town's representatives should
urge the immediate formation of a written Constitution.
The *Register* said proudly that about two hundred voters
attended, " Mostly mechanics," and it pilloried unmercifully
a young Federalist lawyer who had ventured to ask that
assembly, " Where are our most respectable citizens? Why
are they not here?"

In the summer of 1818 (July 4th), the Federalists of New
Haven made a last vigorous effort to elect their own men to
the Convention which was about to frame the new Constitution.   One of their nominees was the Hon. James Hillhouse,
the beautifier of the Green and of the city.   Alluding to Mr.
Hillhouse's agency in the removal of the graves from the
Common, the *Register* exclaimed: " He is the most desperate
and ferocious prosecutor of desperate' and ferocious deeds.
God forbid that the destroyer of the sepulchers of our fathers
should ever receive the suffrages of their sons."   The Democratic candidates were successful by a poll of 300 to 250, and
in the next autumn the town ratified the new Constitution by
a vote of 430 against 218.[1]   New Haven Federalism was
ended.   The following eight years were years of political chaos.
The Democratic body alone was a well-drilled, compact body,
obeying without hesitation the commands of its half-dozen
leaders.   Only upon the question of slavery could an opposing majority be mustered in the town.   Not until 1826 was
the Whig party, which followed the standard of Clay, able to
win its first victory in New Haven.

SLAVERY AND ABOLITION.

In the year after the adoption of the State Constitution,
the town delivered, for the first time since the Revolution, an
official utterance upon the subject of slavery.[2]   The trumpet

---

[1] Records, VI. 62.   In October, 1818.   The Convention met in Hartford
in August, 1818.

[2] December 27, 1819.   Records, VI. 71, *et seq.*

gave no uncertain tone. The slave-power was seeking to
gain both Florida and Missouri for degradation, and New
Haven recorded its verdict substantially thus: "The existence of Slavery in the United States is, in the opinion of this
meeting, an evil of great magnitude. It is the high and
solemn duty of the government of this free and enlightened
nation to prevent by all constitutional means the extension
of Slavery. It is therefore

"*Resolved*, That, in the opinion of this meeting, the Congress of the United States has the undoubted right to prohibit the admission of Slavery into any State or Territory
hereafter to be formed and admitted into the Union;

"*Resolved*, That, in the opinion of this meeting, the admission of Slavery into any such State or Territory would be
opposed to the Genius and Spirit of our government, and
injurious to the highest interests of the nation;

"*Resolved*, That the Senators and Representatives from this
State in Congress be respectfully and earnestly requested to
use their most strenuous exertions to prevent the further
extension of Slavery in the United States."

So said the town! Meanwhile the City-Meeting said not a
word about the Missouri question. It was fixing the weight
of loaves of bread at "The New York Assize," and the
prices of the same by statute at 6¼ and 12½ cents—legislation
surprisingly similar to Eaton's Assize of Bread in 1655.
However, the time came when the city did speak, and to a
very different purport from that of the foregoing.

In 1831, a number of Abolitionists, some of them residents of New Haven, subscribed funds for the establishment
in New Haven of a college for the education of negro youth,
and the promulgation of anti-slavery sentiment. Forthwith, as when, in Ephesus of old, a reform was proposed,
the city was in an uproar. Mayor Dennis Kimberley[1] called
a City-Meeting on the 10th of September. It was a crowded
gathering, and adopted a long list of fiery preambles and

---

[1] He was a Whig.

resolutions which declared that "The propagation of sentiments favorable to the immediate emancipation of slaves, and, as auxiliary thereto, the contemporaneous founding of colleges for educating colored people, is an unwarrantable and dangerous interference with the internal concerns of other States, and ought to be discouraged; also that Yale College, schools for females, and other educational institutions already existing in this city are important to the community, but the establishment of a college in the same place to educate the colored population is incompatible with the prosperity if not the existence of the present institutions of learning, and will be destructive of the best interests of the city." Wherefore the Mayor, Aldermen, Common Council, and freemen of the city of New Haven mutually pledged themselves to resist the establishment of the proposed college by every lawful means. The Bourbons prevailed, and the project was abandoned. Not long afterward the chivalrous citizens of Canterbury, Connecticut, declared war on Miss Prudence Crandall because she was willing to teach "Niggers." Wm. Lloyd Garrison, referring to "The proscriptive spirit," wrote: "The New Haven excitement has furnished a bad precedent; a second must not be given, or I know not what we can do to raise up the colored population in a manner which their intellectual and moral necessities demand." Ten years later (1841), the town of New Haven appropriated $150 for a school for colored children, and, in 1842, there were two such schools.[1]

Municipal Growth.—Sects.—Administrative Changes.

During the rapid upspringing of the Democratic party (1810–17), and amid the birth-throes of the new Constitution, political excitement seems to have checked even the

---

[1] Records, VI. 197. The captives of the famous *Amistad* were brought to New Haven in 1839.

normally slow development of New Haven's municipal government. But with the winter of 1818–19 the symptoms of growth appeared again. Pressure of business caused the differentiation of a Board of Relief from the office of the selectmen. An increasing desire for official regularity in the place of previous easy informality manifested itself in a by-law by virtue of which the Common Council for the first time elected a sexton, a leader of the hearse, bell-ringers, and other officers necessary to the service of burial.

The 6th of July, 1820, was a red-letter day in the calendar of the First Methodist Church and Society. Their ambition to place their church by the side of its Congregationalist neighbors and within the jealously-guarded limits of the Green was gratified. The City-Meeting placed the seal of its final approval upon an ordinance permitting the Methodists to build an edifice upon the northwest corner of the public square.

Throughout the year the city government was engaged in framing a rudimentary Police Department. Night-watches were established, consisting of three superintendents and a score of watchmen, although the enabling act of the Legislature allowed seven superintendents and fifty watchmen.[1]

---

[1] That the city could exist thirty-six years without a regular force of this sort would seem to argue either Arcadian simplicity or alarming insecurity. The actual condition of affairs was probably a mixture of both. President Dwight, writing in 1810, depicted New Haven as a model Happy Valley, where disturbances were unknown, where private contentions hardly existed, and where ungirt Peace ruled alone. But one burglary had been known in fifteen years. However, he adds, "This good order of the inhabitants is the more creditable to them, as the police of the Town is far from being either vigorous or exact." At the risk of involving the worthy President in contradictions, it is worth while to compare another of his paragraphs with the foregoing. After dilating upon the excellences of the various social elements in New Haven, he says: "The one considerable exception is the class of labourers. By this term I intend those men who look to the earnings of to-day for the subsistence of to-morrow. In New England almost every man of this character is either shiftless, diseased, or vicious. The local and commercial circumstances of this Town have allured to it a large (proportional) number of these men; few of whom are very industrious; fewer, economical: and fewer still, virtuous." (Travels, I. 188–I. 196.)

The work of renovation was continued into the year 1821.
The Fire Department was remodeled. The Fire Wardens,
who had held the entire responsibility, were now empowered
to elect a Chief Engineer and five Assistant Engineers.
Hereafter the Chief Engineer could order the demolition of
buildings, in order to prevent the spread of fire, without wait-
ing, as formerly, for the consent of the Mayor and the
majority of the Aldermen. The charter and its numerous
amendments were consolidated, and the Legislature recast
the charters of all the cities in the State into one Act. In the
same year a Baptist society followed in the path which the
Methodists had hewed out with such difficulty, and effected
a territorial lodgment. In the annual Town-Election, tithingmen were chosen for the Baptist and Methodist, as well as
for the Congregational Churches. Not until 1833 were the
first tithingmen elected for the Episcopal Church,[1] and the
Universalist and Roman Catholic Churches received this
token of official recognition in 1836.[2] In 1849, the town met
for special ballot, because it had omitted the election of tithingmen for the Society of Mishkan Israel, or, as the Town
Records put it, of "Miskin Israel."[3] The rapid increase in
the number of congregations must have rendered the choice

---

[1] Trinity Church had not needed tithingmen, if its worshippers were
generally as choleric as the one mentioned in N. H. Hist. Soc. Papers,
II. 38. Spying a little boy who was inclined to conduct himself
frivolously during the service, the devout Churchman rushed up to the
offender with the words, "You damned little rascal, how dare you behave
so in a church? You thought you was in a Presbyterian meeting-house,
didn't you, hey?"

[2] In this year each political party was accusing the other of sharp
practice in choosing a large number of tithingmen, who were by that
means qualified to become voters, and hence, it is to be supposed, party
workers. The trick had been in vogue for five or six years. At first the
Democrats had employed it successfully, but latterly the Whigs had beaten
the former at their own game. It is satisfactory to see that, in 1836, each
side was ashamed of the usage.

[3] The Town-Meeting was by law obliged to elect at least two tithingmen
in each congregation.

of tithingmen not only troublesome, but farcical. At the Town-Meeting of November 8, 1865, one hundred and twenty-five tithingmen were elected for thirty-one churches. After that year the selection of tithingmen was relinquished to the separate churches. The North, or United Church, still elects yearly two tithingmen, and other churches may do the same.

The Farmington Canal was an Old Man of the Sea for New Haven. It cut deeper into the financial prosperity of the place than into its soil. The Town-Meeting, which enthusiastically approved of the project, was appropriately held on the first of April, 1822. A few years later the city sunk in the Canal one hundred thousand dollars of borrowed money. The principal result of the investment was the rise in the rate of taxation to seventy mills on the dollar.

Moreover, in connection with a system of extensive borrowing, this extraordinary rate continued year after year. It was the inflation-period alike of nation, State, and city. In 1840, the tax was eighty mills on the dollar, while in 1846–47 the high-water mark was attained of ten cents on the dollar for ordinary city expenses, and an extra rate of two, in the second year three, cents on the dollar to pay for the fence around the Green. The town-rate during the same period was usually from two to three cents. It should not be forgotten, however, that these excessive rates were levied under Connecticut tax-laws upon an extremely small valuation of both real and personal property. Had the assessed valuation been more nearly equal to the real one, the same sums of money might have been raised by a really moderate tax. There seems to have been some distress caused by taxation, but it probably resulted from unfavorable conditions of trade, banking, and the currency, rather than from heavy rates. There was some very peculiar and happily unique tax-legislation by the City-Meeting of 1824. In order to provide the means for preserving the city from fire, the assessors were ordered to levy taxes principally upon the property of those citizens who had the most to fear from fire.

The Democratic phalanx, which had taken possession of the town under the standard of "Toleration," had been arbitrarily managed; and, during the second quarter of the century, the Whigs were generally predominant[1] in town and city. The growth of manufactures, encouraged by the long European wars, made Clay's "American System" popular in the community. But the political conscience of either party was then in its feeblest state. That insurgent, obstinate Democracy which we may call Jacksonism, asserting, against itself, unquestioning fealty to the will of a leader, infected both parties. As a result, almost every vestige of eighteenth-century aristocracy was gradually effaced. In 1826, the rising tide of Jacksonian Democracy left its mark upon the New Haven city government. An important amendment to the charter was obtained from the Legislature. The Mayor's term of office was hereafter limited to one year, and he was to be elected, with all other officers of the city, by ballot. Thus the chief officer of the municipality first became directly responsible to his constituents, and the hand of legislative authority was further removed. Hitherto the city offices had been generally held until death or old age incapacitated the incumbent. Under the new *régime*, offices were political prizes, and rotation was the order of the day. The peaceful atmosphere, which had previously seemed to linger even in the pages of the records, disappeared.

Henceforth the progress of urban development is more confused, more rapid, more tentative. The coming of the steamboat (1815) and the opening of the Canal (1828–1835) promised to make New Haven a distributing centre, and the necessity of improved means of local transportation seemed imperative. The roads of the town and streets of the city were in a wretched condition. The office of City Street Com-

---

[1] Their sway was practically unbroken, after 1834, until the dissolution of the party during Pierce's administration.

missioner had been created in 1818, and the Council had
then ordered sidewalks on the principal streets, but the City-
Meeting, three days later, vetoed the ordinance.

Not until 1834 was there a Superintendent of Sidewalks,
with orders to see that the sidewalks were leveled and properly paved at the expense of the property-owners. There
was persistent opposition. Although private individuals
had used pavements since 1809, a number of citizens who
were satisfied with the " good old times " seemed resolved to
sustain Dr. Manasseh Cutler's observation, in 1787, that the
streets were not paved and probably never would be. After
some years the city overrode the most violent protesters.[1]
More sympathy will be felt with the opinion of the people,
in 1833, relative to an Act of the Legislature authorizing the
selectmen of the various towns to sell for purposes of dis-
section the corpses of friendless paupers. The town strongly
repudiated this Act, and instructed its selectmen to bury at
public expense all such paupers who might pay the debt of
nature in New Haven. In 1835, both town and city revised
and improved their by-laws. Most of the changes and
amendments related to contested or defective elections, or
prescribed more rigidly the order of proceedings at the
annual elections. For some years thereafter, the names of
all freemen of the city who voted at the annual meeting were
copied into the city records. The First Selectman was still
the most important officer in New Haven, if size of salary is
any criterion. He received five hundred dollars a year,
while the Mayor was content with two hundred dollars.

The arrangement of the City Court, which had existed
since 1784, began to create dissatisfaction. Mayors and
Aldermen were now selected for political considerations, and
it was probably seen that a good partisan might not be a

---

[1] It is related that Wm. Lyon, who lived between Orange and State
streets, on Chapel street, when the city finally paved in front of his
dwelling, took long steps across the pavement and walked in the street,
declaring that " God's soil " was good enough for him.

learned judge. Therefore, in 1842, another amendment to the charter[1] divested the Mayor and the Aldermen-Judges of all judicial power and bestowed the same upon a new officer, called the City Recorder, who was to be annually chosen by the Common Council, and who was to receive one hundred dollars per annum. This curtailment of the Mayor's powers was made good in another direction. By virtue of his office he was placed at the head of the Police Department. The Recorder's Court had the same jurisdiction as its predecessor. But there were conflicting interpretations of the real meaning of the Act creating the Recorder's Court, so that Aldermen-Judges were still elected, and could sit as side-judges with the Recorder. In 1857, this usage was approved by a vote of 661 to 561.

It had been voted, in 1836, that the City Watch should serve both day and night. Three years later the labors of the watchmen were, perhaps, somewhat lessened by the return of the Fair Haven territory to the jurisdiction of the town government. In 1842–3, the watch was costing the city about two thousand dollars a year, and, apparently for no other reason than this, there were determined attempts to abolish the department altogether. In June, 1842, such a motion was defeated by only three votes in a poll of two hundred and seventy-five. One year afterward the City-Meeting (October 14, 1843) actually instructed the Common Council to discontinue the watch, and from that time until 1848 the city remained practically unguarded. An inadequate night-watch was employed, and in January, 1845, on account of depredations by students and others, the Mayor and Aldermen were commissioned to increase, at their discretion, the number of night-watchmen. Finally a series of incendiary fires frightened the people back to complete sanity.

---

[1] In 1841, a series of letters appeared in the *Palladium* clearly and forcibly criticising the construction of the city government. The advice of this writer was almost literally followed in the next year.

A WINDFALL FROM WASHINGTON.

The resources of the town received a very material accession in 1837, as a consequence of folly in high places. On the 17th of January, the town voted that it would accept its proportion of the United States surplus deposited with this State, in accordance with the conditions imposed by the Legislature, appropriating the interest of such moneys to educational purposes. New Haven's share was the respectable sum of $27,427.67. It was forthwith loaned upon New Haven real estate, and the "Town Deposit Fund" has figured in each annual budget since.[1] Although this windfall was blown into New Haven's lap by a Jacksonian Administration, the town does not seem to have cherished Democratic statesmen very warmly. John Tyler was a Democrat, if he was anything. A City-Meeting was convoked June 17, 1843, to provide for his reception in New Haven, and a proposition to set apart $500 for his entertainment met this response:

" *Whereas,* It is expected that the President of the United States will pass through this city on his way from Bunker Hill to the Capitol; therefore,

" *Resolved,* That we recommend to the citizens generally to manifest in such manner as shall best accord with their own sense of propriety their respect for the office; nevertheless, without considering the embarrassed condition of the Treasury, the occasion does not require any pecuniary appropriation, or any action of the city in its municipal capacity."[2]

This was very cold comfort, especially when compared with the enthusiasm manifested a few years later (in 1848) over the prospect of a possible call from Henry Clay. The Mayor, at the head of a deputation of eleven citizens, was appointed

---

[1] Records, VI. 168.

[2] Jackson himself, in 1833 (June 15), met with a very ceremonious welcome to New Haven, and the *Herald* put " Jack Downing's Letter " side by side with the account of the President's reception.

to "Respectfully urge the venerable and illustrious statesman
to come from New York to New Haven as the guest of the
city."

But this was lukewarm when placed by the side of the long
and well-written resolutions adopted upon the death of John
Quincy Adams.

THE LIQUOR TRAFFIC.

With the beginning of the year 1840 the wires were laid
for a temperance agitation, and with reason. Previous to
that time the town had maintained a special license system.

January 10, 1840, free rum was introduced in the following by-law: " Voted, that all persons be allowed to sell Wines
and Spirituous Liquors in the town of New Haven during
the current year." This law was re-enacted from year to
year. The results were naturally seen in the receipts of the
courts and in the town balances. At the close of the fiscal
year of 1839 there had been a balance in the treasury of
$3,000; the grand jurors' fees for prosecutions amounted to
$27; and the town tax-rate was at two cents. In 1843, the
balance in the treasury was $301; the jurors' fees were nearly
$1,000; and the town tax-rate had risen to three cents.

The state of affairs thus indicated could not fail to attract
notice, and especially the attention of Mr. Charles B. Lines,
a citizen of sleepless energy and abundant interest in public
affairs. During 1843 and 1844 he conducted a brisk agitation in Town-Meetings for an abolition of the free-sale system.
The question was transferred to legislative halls from 1845
to 1854, and finally a law was procured, essentially prohibitory in its intent, by virtue of which the towns might permit
the sale of liquor through certain prescribed agencies, but only
for sacramental, medical, or chemical purposes. Mr. Lines
thereupon appeared in Town-Meeting, July 25, 1854, with a
motion that all existing permissions for liquor-selling should
be revoked, that the selectmen should hire some one agent to

sell whatever liquor might be needed, and that they should be empowered to draw from the treasury for that purpose. Jonathan Stoddard, Esq., moved to table these resolutions, and his motion was carried by a vote of 803 to 671. The meeting then adopted a series of resolutions offered by Stoddard, to the effect that the selectmen might draw six and a quarter cents for the purpose mentioned, that the appropriation should take place in 1860, and that the money should be used in "The faithful execution of the law."

The first act had thus ended with the discomfiture of the temperance men; but Mr. Lines was not dismayed. Perhaps the fact that the town-tax had mounted to five and a quarter cents on the dollar aided him. On the 22d of August, 1854, he renewed his motion. Stoddard again opposed him and carried an adjournment for one year by a vote of 1,115 to 1,050. September 20, Mr. Lines repeated his motion, omitting the restriction of the selectmen to one agent. It was agreed that the town should take a day to ballot on the question. The 27th of September was fixed upon, and Mr. Lines was successful by 1,640 yeas against 1,407 nays. From that autumn until the spring of 1857, the report of the Town Liquor Agency was a feature of the annual Town-Meeting and of the annual Town-Budget. The books of the agent are preserved now in the Town Clerk's office, several neatly-kept volumes, in which the quarts or half-pints are entered opposite the purchaser's name, in the proper column of "Sacramental, Medical, or Chemical." It is perhaps needless to say that the "Medical" column is filled to overflowing. The Town Liquor Agency had another name in the mouths of the citizens, as appears by the action of the town on the 28th of November, 1856: "Voted, that Lucius Gilbert and Judson Canfield be a committee to investigate the affairs of the Town Agency, or Maine Law Grog-Shop, and report to the Selectmen." The Prohibitory System had been put on trial and had failed. The last sale of liquor in the "Maine Law Grog-Shop" is dated in February, 1857.

Light in the Streets.

Modern improvements were the order of the day in New Haven from 1840 to 1850. Steamboats had already come, and the Canal had impoverished the city. In 1848, the liberally-inclined citizens made up their minds to illuminate their ways with gas, and succeeded in forcing the city to do it by a vote of 182 to 80. The step was creditable to New Haven enterprise, for, at that time, Trenton, New Jersey, was the only other small city in the country which had put gas into its streets. The taxpayers who objected to the measure laid much stress upon the injury that the gas would work upon the trees, and in July, 1850, a committee was actually appointed to confer with the "President and Directors of the New Haven Gas Company with a view to ascertain what measures, if any, can be adopted to preserve the shade-trees of the city from the destructive action of the gas."

A High School.

During these years the schools of town and State were undergoing radical transformation, and were recovering from the low estate into which they had fallen in the earlier part of the century. The movement toward better things began in New Haven in 1844, when the First School District presented to the town resolutions advocating some provision for higher instruction and the formation of graded schools. The Town-Meeting consigned the subject to a committee, and the project ripened. In 1854 and 1855, graded schools were organized, and in the latter year the town elected its first Board of School Visitors. The re-organization of the New Haven School District under a Board of Education was completed in 1856.[1] Already official action by the School Society

---

[1] The towns were originally the educational units in Connecticut. But some of them were large, and contained outlying ecclesiastical parishes. In 1712, such parishes were allowed to direct their own schools. In 1717, they were authorized to lay taxes and choose school-officers. This was, practically, the formation of school-districts within the towns, although

in 1850 and 1852 had called into being the germ of a high
school, in connection with a grammar-school. The germ
became a developed organism in May, 1859, when the Hillhouse High School was established. In the same year the
familiar title, "Acting School Visitor" was dropped, and
"Superintendent of Schools" was substituted in its place,
but the duties of the office remained the same as before.
Since that time the increase of schools and of population has
promoted the gradual but steady enlargement of the Superintendent's responsibilities. The new school-system was
destined to struggle long for emphatic popular approval.
After seven years an unmistakable verdict was given. In
the spring of 1866, the Board of Education voted to recommend the discontinuance of the high school. In June, after
a thorough discussion, New Haven, as a School District,
decided to maintain the school by 1,170 votes against 419.

THE ERA OF RAILWAYS.

In our day of material forces widely subjugated to man's
use, there has been no industrial revolution more momentous

---

the selectmen were still the supervisors of all the schools. Moreover,
many of these parishes became towns, and, in general, the school-district
seemed to owe its genesis to the Church Society rather than to the town.
By the school-law of 1766 further subdivision of the towns into school-
districts was encouraged. The substitution of district for town-authority
was completed in 1798, and henceforth the town as an educational unit
was entirely superseded by the School Society. Supervision was transferred from the selectmen to specially-appointed officers, and the free high
schools, which had been by law maintained in New Haven and in the other
county towns, were no longer required.

The first backward step up this long-descending track was taken in
1838, by the creation of a supreme authority over the educational system
of the State. With some fluctuations of fortune, the centralizing influences have increased in strength from that day to this. A statute of 1856
allowed any town to abolish its districts and to revert to the original plan
of managing the schools as town-institutions. (See "Revised Statutes
of Connecticut"; and "Public Schools in Connecticut," by Henry R.
Sawyer, A. M., published in *Education* for Sept.–Oct., 1886.)

than the one wrought by the introduction of railways. Not
every town discovered the evils as well as the advantages of
railway-influence so quickly as New Haven did. The first
cars that ran in the city were on the Hartford Road in the
spring of 1839. In 1848, both the Canal Railway, as far as
Plainville, and the New York and New Haven Railway
were opened to the public, the former in January, the latter
in December. It was expected that the Canal Road would
be speedily completed to Springfield, Mass., and citizens of
New Haven who were inclined to be Micawberish expected
something to turn up that would be very big indeed. Over
the bed of the ill-starred Canal wealth would at last begin
to roll into New Haven. But the New Haven and Hartford
R. R. Co. had no mind to allow a parallel line, and it fought
its rival over every inch of ground, and with every weapon
that the arsenals of the law could furnish. The Hartford
Road made common cause with the owner of a bit of farm-
land which was included in the Canal Road's "lay-out" at
Simsbury. This man could "Neither be bought nor scared"
out of his comparatively valueless possession, which was
generally known as "The Peddler's Lot." The final result
was that the Canal Road never reached Springfield, and was
almost fatally crippled at the start. Indignation at New
Haven was at white heat, and, as usual at such times, Mr.
Charles B. Lines came to the front in the City-Meeting,
December 22, 1849, with nine long and fiery resolutions.
The flame of anti-monopolistic feeling in these resolutions
burns brightly enough to shed no little light in our own day.
" . . . . A railroad monopoly would be more odious than
the steamboat monopoly from which some of our citizens have
suffered so much. Therefore,

"*Resolved*, That the recent attempt by the New Haven
and Hartford Company to stop this important public work
at the very moment of its completion, after nearly a million and
a half of dollars had been expended upon it, and when only
one hundred rods remained to be finished, not less than the

stealthy manner in which the attempt was made, is an act of cunning and high-handed oppression, of doubtful legality, unworthy of honorable men, disgraceful to a corporation, and from the effects of which we appeal to the Legislature for relief."

Mr. Lines, always running a-tilt against the champions of evil, turned from rumselling and corporate selfishness to break a lance, or, more literally, to shoot bullets against the slave-power in Kansas. Times had changed since the day when a City-Meeting resolved to prevent the foundation of an "Abolitionist" college in New Haven. Meetings were held in the North Church to raise money and buy rifles for free-soil emigrants[1] to Kansas, and Mr. Lines became one of the leaders of a New Haven company which settled the county and town of Waubonsie.[2]

The Needs of the Poor.

The day had now come when the moral sense of the community was shocked by the housing of criminals, paupers,

---

[1] Rev. Henry Ward Beecher gave them a parting address in the North Church, March 22, 1856.

[2] The community, therefore, was inevitably sundered to the very bottom by the Kansas quarrel. On the one hand, subscriptions were openly solicited for the purchase of "Kansas rifles," and on the other the *Register* spoke of 30,000 Connecticut Democrats ready to take up arms, if need be, to maintain the rights of the South. In the Presidential election of 1856, the town polled a large vote, out of which Fremont secured a small majority. In the following year, the Republican leaders imitated the ancient custom of the town, and opened an epistolary fire directly upon President Buchanan. A large assembly of citizens, in Brewster's Hall (July, 1857), addressed to the Chief Executive a memorial embodying their views of his duty to Kansas. Buchanan replied to them under date of August 15, 1857, and the memorialists rejoined September 22. The rejoinder was signed by many well-known men, among others by Rev. Drs. Nath'l W. Taylor and Leonard Bacon, Pres. Woolsey, Gov. Dutton, Mayor Skinner, Gen. Wm. H. Russell, Charles Ives, Eli Blake, James F. Babcock, and the Sillimans. The whole correspondence exhibited the points of the controversy in clear and vigorous rhetoric, attracted wide attention, and contributed largely to the formation of public opinion.

and lunatics under one roof. The Rev. S. W. S. Dutton forcibly impressed upon the Town-Meeting of November 20, 1849, the disgrace of such an usage. A committee, consisting of Messrs. Dutton, Wm. H. Ellis, Oliver Smith, Chas. B. Lines, and Prof. Benj. Silliman, was appointed to " Devise provision for the insane, disabled, and dependent poor, whom our laws consign to the Workhouse." Mr. Lines moved that the selectmen should be instructed to " Remove immediately to the Insane Retreat at Hartford the insane persons now confined in the Almshouse." The motion was approved, and the removals were made forthwith. One year later (November 26, 1850), the committee reported that the old house had no conveniences nor sanitary advantages, and that the refractory could be confined only in small dungeons underneath the chapel. The committee recommended the erection of a new Almshouse for the exclusive use of the " Virtuous Poor," and the town accepted their counsel. It was the moral and material renovation of this period, rather than any sectarian feeling, which led the city to give to the Methodists, in 1848, five thousand dollars on condition that they would move their church-edifice away from the Green. The newly-developed solicitude for the city's beauty was curiously exemplified in the following ordinance: " Resolved, that that part of the Green now occupied by the Methodist Episcopal Society shall not be occupied by the students of any institution, or by any other individuals as a play-ground for playing ball or any other game of amusement."

THE CITY-MEETING.—CHARTER OF 1857.

The services which the water in the Canal had occasionally rendered in extinguishing fires probably emphasized the idea, in 1850, of a contract with the New Haven Water Company for a sufficient supply of water at all times for such purposes. This led to negotiations in 1852 for the purchase of the water-works by the city. A vote in 1852 to buy the water-works

was immediately succeeded by a counter-agitation, which was
successful in the next year. The water-supply was abandoned to the care of the private projectors, but the subject was
not laid away to rest before 1856, and ended in successful
lawsuits against the city. The City-Meetings held to decide
the matter were tumultuous, and were open to suspicions of
chicanery. The tellers were unable to count the votes, and
the Mayor was unable to preserve order.

Such disorders turned the public attention toward additional reforms in the government. In 1853, the city was
divided into four wards, and the ward organization was
still further perfected in 1857, when the four wards were
replaced by six. But the centre of discussion was the cumbrous institution of the City-Meeting. It was plain that
the size of the city rendered government by such a democratic assembly difficult, if not impracticable. Yet so great
was the distrust of the few by the many, that the City-Meeting in 1849 forbade the appropriation by the Common
Council of more than one hundred dollars without the
approval of a City-Meeting called for that purpose.

There was good sense enough in the city to repeal the law
shortly afterward, but it was a sign of rapid progress that,
in the spring of 1854, the following motion prevailed in
City-Meeting: "Resolved, that the Mayor, Aldermen, and
Common Council be requested to digest a constitution or
plan of government for the city of New Haven to be submitted to the citizens, by which all the powers now vested
in the municipal corporation, styled 'The Mayor, Aldermen,
Common Council, and Freemen,' shall be vested in a representative body, or bodies, to be chosen by electors residing
in the city of New Haven; and that the same be prepared
and submitted in season to be passed upon in City-Meeting,
and, if approved, to be carried to the Legislature for its
sanction."

The motion was the germ of a new charter which received
legislative sanction in 1857. The Mayor and Common

Council were no longer fettered, as they had been, by the City-Meeting,[1] and the duties of the Council were materially increased. Among the various propositions for reform, the plan of abolishing the two-headed system of Town and City-Government did not escape consideration. Both town and city, the former leading the way, appointed committees in 1852 to confer together upon the feasibility of uniting the two jurisdictions under one administration. The only result of the conference was, perhaps, the discontinuance of the separate Town-Meeting for the election of town-officers. This alteration was adopted November 12, 1855. Henceforth town-officers were elected by districts, at voting-places designated by the selectmen. The practical effect was to make town and city voting-places the same so far as the city extended.

Town-Officers.

The Town-Agent, measured by his present duties and powers, is a modern growth upon the ancient trunk of town-government. But though the special importance of the office is of recent date, its beginnings can be traced far back in the town's history. The general power to sue for the town was bestowed upon the townsmen in December, 1700. Even before that time the oversight of the poor had been enrolled among their responsibilities. Throughout the eighteenth century the townsmen, as a body, performed such offices, or delegated the labor to some of their own number. In the first years of the nineteenth century, the town at its annual meeting usually divided the Town-Agency between two of the selectmen, and, for the first time, bestowed upon each the title "Town-Agent." For example, in 1800 the First Selectman, Jeremiah Atwater, was appointed an agent to sue

---

[1] The provisions were: " Within 60 days from the passage of a bye-law the Mayor *may* call, and, upon written request of 7 Common Councilmen and of 20 other freemen, he *shall* call a City-Meeting to approve or reject said bye-law." But from this date the City-Meeting slumbered.

and to be sued for the town, while Thomas Punderson, the
Second Selectman, was chosen the Town-Agent to take care
of the poor. The usage varied; sometimes the First Select-
man was not a Town-Agent, and sometimes the Board of
Selectmen, as a body, was Town-Agent. Subsequently the
Board of Selectmen appointed as Town-Agent one of their
own number, usually the one who was also named First
Selectman.

Political complications caused each party to adopt, in 1878,
the custom of designating upon the town-ticket the candidate
for Town-Agent, thus ensuring a direct election by the
people. This is a device intended to render the office more
popular in its character, and also more secure to the party
in power. The law of the State seems to give the Board of
Selectmen a choice in the matter; but the present incumbent
of the office and his party-friends have refused to permit the
board to vote, alleging that the popular election is sufficient.
Since 1848 the Town-Agent has received a larger compensation than any other town-officer. Since that time, also, the
great increase in the foreign-born population has added
largely to his responsibilities. The annual distribution of
considerable sums for what is called "Outdoor Relief" is
virtually under his control. These facts have given the
Town-Agent a certain hold upon a large body of voters, and
have made him an influential factor in town-politics.

The Town-Clerk, after 1847, earned two hundred dollars
per annum, an increase of one hundred per cent. upon his
previous compensation. The salary of the First Selectman
was raised in 1848 to eight hundred dollars,[1] while the Mayor

---

[1] In December, 1818, the selectmen were first authorized to draw pay for
the time devoted to the public service. Down to the time of the Civil
War, the selectmen cared for all the highways throughout the town, yet
Captain Beecher, through the greater part of his sixteen years of service,
received but five hundred dollars a year, and furnished his own horse and
wagon. His predecessor, Squire Mix, furnished the same, and obtained
only a dollar a day.

and City Clerk, six years later, were drawing but five hundred dollars each. With the approach of war-times, salaries rapidly rose, until they attained more nearly to the modern standard. In 1860, the Mayor and City Clerk respectively obtained one thousand, and eight hundred dollars.

CITY-IMPROVEMENT.—POLICE AND FIRE DEPARTMENTS.

In this year the first steps were taken toward a city-sewerage system. The attention of the authorities was forcibly arrested by a suit which Samuel Peck brought against the city for damages on account of municipal neglect to provide sewers. The city could previously boast of a few small sewers, but there was no adequate provision for drainage; and not until ten years after this, during Mayor Lewis's first administration, was the sewerage system made thorough and complete. The spirit displayed in the Common Council in 1861, over the construction of the George-street sewer, may explain some of the hindrances to prompt and effective action.

It was ordered that, in accepting bids for building the sewer, "No contract should be made with any person not a citizen of New Haven, and that the whole work, so far as practicable, should be in the hands of New Haven citizens." Councilman Healey tried to add a provision that each laborer employed should be paid at least one dollar a day.

From the time of the introduction of railway traffic and competition (in 1848) until the breaking out of the war was a period of active expansion. Increasing business demanded a more practical administration of public affairs. Hence came those attempts which have been recounted to divide, define, and restrict official functions, to simplify and improve antiquated methods. Yet progress was, after all, exceedingly slow. The forward step was taken painfully and, as in the case of the city-sewerage, with tedious delay. No straw shows more plainly the adverse direction of the prevalent wind than the fact that, until 1851, horses and cows were pastured in the streets within the city-limits without much efficient hindrance from the authorities. But in that year the energy of one man, James F. Babcock, caused the adoption of a stringent by-law which was finally successful in abating the nuisance. Three or four years earlier it had been a recognized custom to entrust scavenger-duty in the gutters to swine, and the constables who served orders for the demolition of pig-pens within the city-limits are said to have seriously endangered their chances for re-election thereby. Mr. Babcock might not have been so successful in his crusade against vagrant cattle, had not the same year of 1851 witnessed the replacement of the old Department of the Watch by a more modern Police Department. This reform, and the transformation of the Fire Department, were the two most important municipal changes that immediately preceded the war. The City Government and the Legislature concurred in 1861 concerning the organization of a new police force, under a board of six Police Commissioners, with terms of three years each. In June, 1862, Chief-of-Police Pond made his first annual report. The police cost the city that year ten thousand dollars. Chief Pond objected to the Legislature's restriction of the number of policemen to twenty, and it seems that the obstacle was soon removed.

The Fire Department was remodeled at the same time and upon the same plan. A board of six Fire Commissioners was created, and the Chief Engineer and his subordinates placed under its control. The new companies were, of course, paid for their services. The former volunteer companies had become centres of political influence, not always of the better sort, and in some cases they even wielded a degree of social power. They were disbanded in the summer of 1861, and in June, 1862, the commissioners entered upon their duties.

In connection with the development of the Fire Department, mention may be made of a remarkable petition which was presented to the Common Council in 1865 by Henry

Peck, Theodore D. Woolsey, *et al.*[1]   The petitioners besought that a mutual city-insurance system might be adopted whereby every building within the city-limits should be insured by the city.   The property-owners were to be "Taxed at an amount not to exceed in any instance what was paid to the insurance companies."   The request was supported by elaborate calculations of the profits of insurance companies which might thus be saved to the citizens.

The petition was referred to the Fire Department Committee of the Common Council, who reported favorably upon it, alleging that 12½ per cent. upon a total valuation would cover all losses and leave a profit to the insurers.   The danger of a great fire in the city was not regarded as imminent enough to render the scheme impracticable.   The Common Council, after delay, instructed the committee to apply to the Legislature for an act authorizing the city to become its own insurer, but stipulated that no such act should take effect until it had been ratified by a City-Meeting. Nothing more is heard of the proposal.   This was the most noteworthy spurt of socialism in the whole course of New Haven's municipal career.   Nothing could be more directly opposed to the general tenor of the political philosophy of the community.

In the Civil War.

When the war-cloud of 1861 began to hide from view all matters of municipal and local interest, New Haven, as in 1776 and 1812, contained a strong conservative party opposed to bold measures and desiring pacific discussion.   A petition from New Haven was forwarded to Congress, in 1860, asking for peace-legislation, in order to satisfy the border slave-States.   When the echoes of the guns fired upon Fort Sumter reached New Haven, the *Register* said, "Henceforth these States pass into two Republics instead of one." ·

---

[1] The late Hon. William W. Boardman is said to have been chiefly responsible for the project.

After Bull Run there was much ill-suppressed feeling upon both sides in the city, and some of the more outspoken friends of the South were kept under surveillance. On the other hand, there was prompt support of Lincoln's administration by the more loyal portion of the population. Volunteers speedily offered themselves, and meetings of the citizens chose committees to procure supplies and forward the work of enlistment.[1] Persons securing recruits were paid by the citizens' committee three dollars for each recruit. The city appropriated money for bounties, and for the support of families of volunteers.

In the spring of 1861, a Home Guard was formed with about four hundred members, some of whom afterward saw service at the front. In 1862, the call for 300,000 volunteers aroused earnest effort in New Haven. A bounty of one hundred and seventy-five dollars was offered. The first Town-Meeting to take official cognizance of the necessities of enlistment was held on the 5th of August, 1862. Resolutions offered by the "National Committee" were adopted, beginning "Whereas, the President of the United States has called for 300,000 volunteers to aid in putting down a causeless war," and enabling the treasurer to borrow $75,000 for the payment of bounties. The issue of town-bonds to the value of $180,000 was also authorized. But the enlistments were not numerous enough, and, in State and nation, men began to speak of a "Draft." New Haven's quota was 662. Up to September 1 there had been 319 enlistments. Resolutions offered in the September Town-Meeting to facilitate the coming draft were opposed by Mr. James Gallagher, and were rejected.

Partisan feeling became so violent that it was deemed best to send a committee from New Haven to Washington to

---

[1] See Crofut & Morris's Military and Civil History of Connecticut during the War of 1861-65. The first citizens' mass-meeting to consider the perilous state of the country was held in Brewster's Hall in 1861, on the historic date of the 19th of April.

request the arrest and confinement of all persons discouraging the enlistments. In the summer of 1863, the draft came, and, for a short period, New Haven was threatened with riot. The same party-violence that shed blood in the streets of New York during those dreadful July days appeared in New Haven also, but was overawed by the firmness of the authorities. On the 23d of July, the Town-Meeting passed by-laws to relieve the harsher features of the draft. The principal amelioration was in the vote that the town would hereafter purchase exemption for any conscript whose family necessities required his presence at home. In January, 1864, the selectmen were authorized to pay three hundred dollars to set free any citizen from enrollment. The town was generous with money during this year, and voted large sums for the purposes of the war.

No picture of official action can do justice to the share that New Haven as a whole took in these troublous times. The reactionary and even disloyal element left its impress necessarily upon the record of municipal effort, and yet New Haven was liberal with money and supplies, and the stream of contribution ceased only with the close of hostilities. To-day, the town counts high upon its roll of fame the honored names of such heroes as Theodore Winthrop and Alfred H. Terry.

Recent Charters.

The charter of 1869 marks a culminating point in New Haven's constitutional development. In size, spirit, and organization it began to be in reality a modern American city. Prior to that time it was a more or less thriving, overgrown village. Between 1850 and 1880 the city's population increased threefold, its grand list eightfold. With the formation of a paid fire department and of a police force worthy of the name in 1861–62, the municipality put forth signs of maturing strength, and commenced to reach upward and outward for a wider sweep.

Old forms of administration were outgrown and outworn, while experience gradually demonstrated the full range of municipal rights and duties. The charter of 1869, as usual, extended the sphere of the City Council's activities, but its most important provisions affected the judiciary.

The Recorder's Court was amended out of existence. In its place, and in place of the old-fashioned Justice's Court which had up to this time been the Police Court of the city, was substituted "The City Court of New Haven." Jurisdiction, therefore, was granted to it in both civil and criminal cases. The sole power of choosing the two judges of the new court was lodged in the General Assembly. As before, the City Attorney was to be the appointee of the court, but he no longer performed the duties of legal adviser to the city. That service was transferred to the corporation counsel, henceforth the best remunerated officer in the city government. The annual city-elections were hereafter to be held on the first Monday in October, and the municipal and calendar years were made coterminous. At the same time the city extended its boundaries by annexing the Fair Haven peninsula between Mill and Quinnipiac Rivers—an act which was consummated on the 5th of July, 1870. The town replaced its loss, eleven years later, by the annexation of territory to the eastward, whereby it gained completer control over the waters of its harbor.

The growth of the city necessitated a readjustment of the ward system. Ten wards were created in 1874, and the number was increased in 1877 to twelve. It was a slight counterbalance to these advances that, in 1873, New Haven unwillingly lost its honors as a capital, while Hartford regained the position that it had held in the 17th century.

The fifth and latest city-charter, that of 1881, has placed the city election upon the first Tuesday in December. The hope was that thus the quadrennial excitements of national party strife might be excluded from local elections. The charter of 1881 was intended also to improve the arrange-

ment of the various departments, especially by ensuring
equal representation of the two political parties upon the
Boards of Commissioners. The previous influence of un-
scrupulous partisanship in departmental administration
made the need of some remedial effort seem urgent.

Conservative Influences in the Community.

The gradual growth of municipal power has exhibited in
succession many slowly-shifting phases. Though changes
must be, yet, through them all, come glimpses of a typical,
fundamental conservatism. For nearly a quarter of a millennium the town and region of New Haven have preserved
a local character, a well-defined individuality, separate from
those of other old colonial centres.

Its political affiliations have strengthened rather than
diminished its exclusiveness. In 1639, it received at the
hands of Davenport and Eaton the impression of an ultra
political and religious conservatism, of ambitious commercial
enterprise, and of zeal for education. Under the heat of
adverse fortune the vision of commerce melted away, but the
belief in the destiny of New Haven as a port for traffic,
though intermittent, endured.

It seemed on the point of realization at the beginning of
this century. That hope faded; yet the city has kept a
stronger grip upon commercial life than many of its quondam
rivals along the New England coast, and it occupies to-day a
respectable rank among the national harbors.

Connecticut's laws, in 1664, could abolish the official but
not the popular conservatism. Davenport's church was still
"The famous Church of New Haven," the stronghold of
purest orthodoxy, proud of its early distinction as one of the
few New England churches framed on the apostolic model,
with a complete presbytery within itself. The course of the
Church, the real core of the town, is more significant of the
local feeling in the ancient day than the quiet development

of the secular government. It is not surprising, therefore, to find Davenport's church a stickler for pure Congregationalism long after the more radical brethren of Connecticut and Massachusetts had leaned more and more toward the Presbyterian or "Parish way." Hooker's church, at Hartford, was thus split in 1669.

The New Haven Church was once again on the conservative, orthodox side during the quarrelsome days of the Saybrook Platform (1708), and although the New Haven pastor, Pierpont, was a master-builder of that platform, his church sent no delegates to the synod and held aloof from its conclusions.

In the great awakening of 1741, the shibboleths had changed, and the Saybrook Platform now meant Orthodoxy, while the "New Lights" were Calvinist and Radical Reformers. The New Haven Church, in 1742, therefore, ranged itself for the first time under the Saybrook banner. The progressive minority rejected this action as "Contrary to the known fundamental principle and practise of said church time out of mind, which has always denied any juridical or decisive authority under Christ, vested in any particular persons or class, over any particular Congregational Church."[1]

So the first division in the religious community was proclaimed in the name, not of new truth, but of conservative traditions. The tendency of New Haven's ecclesiastical thought and custom has steadily retained its primitive character. It has been slow-moving, soon solidified, tenacious of past modes and traditions, backward in admitting change or in recognizing new movements. Society in general, both lay and clerical, has moved along slowly and ponderously in the rear rank, gaining perhaps in wide outlook and the judicious adaptation of means to ends, but possibly losing also in early fortune and in enthusiasm.

Some light has now been cast upon the causes which have

---

[1] Trumbull, II. 340.

made Yale College so conservative; yet it should not be forgotten that the institution has also reacted upon its environment as a promoter of permanence. It is not necessary to dwell upon the events of 1744, when the college made war upon Locke's essay upon "Toleration" and expelled two students for attending a Separatist meeting in a private house. The events were the fruits of a bitter and extraordinary controversy. But Yale has brought to New Haven a scholastic atmosphere unfavorable to a normal political and social development, and a population which has cared everything for the administration of the college, little or nothing for that in the City Hall. All these peculiar influences were particularly potent while the town was small, and they have increased with the city, though not proportionally.

Until a recent day, the best interests of the city have suffered because so many of its most intelligent residents were men who looked upon the affairs of the community as foreign to their world; who may have been profoundly interested in Roman politics of the time of Cæsar, or even in national politics of their own day, but who overlooked the civic structure which immediately contained and concerned them. There are numbers of people who have made New Haven their home in order to facilitate the education of their children, or in order to enjoy for themselves the privileges and sentiments of a university neighborhood. Such motives do not frequently underlie an active participation in the duties of good, energetic citizenship. Still it must not be forgotten that this relation of a life of "slippered ease" to the duties of a citizen involves but one aspect of the town's common life. Where New Haven, as a university town, has lost in one direction, it has gained a thousandfold in many others. In its political development, the Town-State is only one among many; through its identification with Yale the community has exerted an educational influence unique and far-reaching.

In the political world, also, New Haven's long unbroken,

slowly-changing party majorities have illustrated her claim
to a large share in the inherited title of Connecticut, "The
Land of Steady Habits." In 1800, as in 1770, it was the
cities and trading centres of the State that held back the more
radical country-districts. New Haven, like the major part
of New England, passed unmoved through the national
awakening of the West and South in 1808–16. The final
overthrow of Federalism was achieved by confounding it
with Congregationalism and attacking it—first, as a denomi-
nation, secondly, as a political party. The town remained,
indeed, for twenty years under Whig domination. The old
conservatism had been mostly broken down, the new conservatism had not yet arrived; but the anti-slavery sentiment,
which had been so pronounced in the era of the Revolution,
was counteracted by the multiplication of commercial relations, and found a feebler and feebler utterance after the
narcotic compromises had weakened the moral strength of the
whole country. With the beginning of railway connections,
in 1848, came the crowds of Irish and other foreign laborers,
and the political balance slowly, steadily indicated the growing preponderance of the untrained voters.

The rivalry between New Haven and Hartford means
much more than commercial competition between two urban
populations. It is the contention of regions rather than of
cities. It is traceable through the whole history of the State
back to the charter-quarrel of 1662–64, when one colony was
pitted against the other. Waymarks of the struggle that
ensued for supremacy within the colony are recognized in the
accession of New Haven to the honors of a capital town in
1701, and in the acrimonious disputes over the final settlement of Yale at New Haven in 1717;[1] afterward, common
knowledge recalls the unceasing competition between the
cities, terminating, perhaps, in the "Single-Capital" contest
of 1873. That dependence of the former New Haven Colony

[1] The two cities were also among the active competitors, in 1823, for the
possession of the future Trinity College.

upon New York, which geographical location necessitated, was further encouraged by these successive animosities. If a line be drawn diagonally across the State from the north-west corner to the mouth of the Connecticut River, the towns and cities to the west of that line are found to rest upon New York as an economic and social basis, just as those upon the east side derive their inspiration from Boston. Of the former of these tracts New Haven is the capital; of the latter, Hartford. This division of influences should be borne in mind when we read that, in the Revolution, New Haven and Fairfield Counties contained many Tories, while the eastern part of the State was almost unanimously patriotic; that a Windham County mob forced the New Haven stamp-distributor to resign in 1765; and that, one hundred years later, it was, as usual, the Hartford end of the State, the eastern counties, which held the State firmly for Nation with a big "N," and neutralized by steady and large majorities the conservative, oligarchical, pseudo-democratic tendencies of Southwestern Connecticut.

VOTERS OF NEW HAVEN CITY

Elect
{
  By Wards .. The Court of Common Council ..
  {
    33 Councilmen elect
    {
      6 Commissioners of Pleasure
      1 Clerk.
      1 Page
    }
    33 Aldermen elect ..
    {
      4 Commissioners of Finance
      6   "   "   Public Works.
      6   "   "   Police.
      6   "   "   Fire Department.
      1 Page
    }
  }
  At Large
  {
    Mayor.
    Treasurer.
    City Clerk.
    Auditor.
    Sheriff
  }

COURT OF COMMON COUNCIL conjointly

Elects
{
  Corporation Counsel
  Asst. City Clerk.
  1st Judge of the City Court.
  3 Members each for Boards of Compensation.
  Any Number of Special Constables.
  Needed Number of Weighers, Measurers,
    Surveyors, and Inspectors.
  One or more Inspectors of Gas Meters.
    "   "   "   Water "
  Sealer of Weights and Measures.
  3 Supervisors of Steam Boilers.
  Janitors. Bath-house Keepers.
}

COMMISSIONERS OF PUBLIC WORKS elect
  Supts. of Streets, Sewers, and Public Parks.
  City Engineer, and all Employees on Roads, Bridges, Sewers,
    and Parks.
COMMISSIONERS OF POLICE elect
  Chief of Police—appoints Supervisor of Vehicles.
  All Members of Police Department.
COMMISSIONERS OF THE FIRE DEPARTMENT elect
  Chief Engineer and Assistants.
  Fire Marshal   "   "
  Supt. of Fire Alarm Telegraph, and all Officers and Men of
    the Department.

THE MAYOR

Names
{
  And Court of C. C. confirms
  {
    The Coroner.
    3 Commissioners Municipal Bond Sinking Fund.
    3   "   Sewerage   "   "   "
    3 Commissioners of Public Buildings.
    3   "   "   East Rock Park.
    6 Members of Board of Public Health.
  }
  And Aldermen confirm ....
}

Nominates—to the Aldermen their Standing Committees on
{
  Lamps—chooses Clerk and Inspector.
  Buildings.
  Licenses.
  Numbering Streets.
}

Board of Public Health—elects Health Officer and Assistants.

Supervisors of Steam Boilers—elect Inspector.

Sealer of Weights and Measures may name, and Court of Common Council—appoint Assistant Sealers.

Harbor Commissioners—elect Inspector and Clerk.

Various Boards, in general, elect their own Clerks.

Chairm-Donors of East Rock Park elect, and the Mayor confirms—3 Park Commissioners.

The Mayor and the President of the Board of Councilmen nominate to the Court of
  Common Council, the

Joint Nominating Committee,
which nominates the Joint
Standing Committees on ....
{
  Annual Reports. Appropriations.
  Auditing. Bath Houses. Building Lines.
  Claims.
  Commercial and Manufacturing Interests.
  Fire Department. Nominations.
  Ordinances. Printing.
  Railroads and Bridges.
  Retrenchment, Reform, and Abuses.
  Sewers. Squares. Streets. Water
}

THE LEGISLATURE
Elects
{
  6 Harbor Commissioners.
  The Judge of the City Court—appoints
  {
    Clerk of City Court.
    Asst. Clerk of City Court.
    City Attorney.
  }
  Asst. "   "   "   "
}
City Attorney appoints, and the Judge confirms—Asst. City Attorney.

VOTERS OF NEW HAVEN TOWN, including City,

Elect, at large........
- 7 Selectmen.
- 1 Town Agent.
- Town Clerk.
- Tax Collector.
- Treasurer.
- Registrar of Vital Statistics.
- 2 Town Auditors.
- 2 Registrars of Voters.
- 3 Sealers of Weights and Measures.
- 5 Assessors.
- 5 Members of Board of Relief.
- 5 Managers of Town Deposit Fund.
- 5 Pound-keepers.
- 5 Haywards.
- 6 Grand Jurors.
- 7 Constables.
- 7 Surveyors of Highways.
- 7 Fence-viewers.
- 7 Gaugers and Inspectors.
- 9 Packers.
- 9 Weighers.
- 56 Justices of the Peace.

Voters of New Haven School District elect—9 Members of Board of Education.

Board of Education makes all School appointments.

Selectmen choose—Clerk.

Heads of Departments choose—Clerks and Assistants.

Two Years' Term for
- Mayor.
- City Clerk.
- Auditor.
- Sheriff.
- Aldermen.
- 4 Commissioners of Finance.
- Corporation Counsel.
- Sealer of Weights and Measures.
- Officers of the City Court.

Three Years' Term for
- Coroner.
- Commissioners of Public Health.
- " " " Works.
- " " Police.
- " " Fire Department.
- Board of Education.
- Supervisors of Steam Boilers.
- Harbor Commissioners.

By City Charter, the Town Tax Collector's Department has common jurisdiction over Town and City. The same person is, customarily, Town and City Treasurer.

The Mayor is President of the Boards of Aldermen and Finance, and ex-officio Chairman of the Commissions of Public Health, Works, Police, Fire Department, and of the Park Commission.

Removal of Commissioners is possible only by a two-thirds vote of the Aldermen, except that the Mayor may remove for cause any Park Commissioner chosen by the citizen donors.

The City's supply of gas and water is controlled by private companies. New Haven has, by vote, refused to deprive the Water Company of its monopoly.

CHAPTER IX.

THE PRESENT MUNICIPAL ADMINISTRATION.

"To the end it may be a government of laws, and not of men."
—Massachusetts "Body of Liberties," 1641.

The spirit of moderation which has generally been dominant in New Haven has ensured to the municipality a constitutional development that is, at least, continuous. There has been no succession of brand-new city charters of diverse patterns, such as have been bestowed upon New York.

On the contrary, the first charter has afforded a kernel to all the others, and reform has been sought by amendment rather than by substitution. Efforts to condense and simplify have stopped short of the limits that might have been attained. The praiseworthy tendency to hold firmly to the past lends a line along which future development, if healthy, must take place. Every analysis of existing forms should give due weight to this municipal growth by cell-formation.

THE SCHOOL DISTRICT.

Besides the town fabric, New Haven Township contains school-district, city, and borough organizations.[1] As a school district, the greater part of the town[2] is under the control of nine men who compose the Board of Education.

---

[1] The borough of Fair Haven East is a minor municipality whose operations are foreign to this inquiry. However, in order to complete the view of the town's official structure, it may be said that the borough elects annually, on the second Monday in May, six burgesses, three assessors, a clerk, bailiff, treasurer, collector, and a warden.

[2] New Haven School District includes all the township excepting Westville, and a small district at South End.

Members of the board serve without salary for three years, and three are chosen yearly. They are elected neither upon city nor town tickets, but a special election-day is devoted to them. Their powers are large. The board appoints a Secretary, a Superintendent of Schools, and all the teachers and assistants in all the schools. The position of the Board of Education in the school district is similar to that which the Board of Selectmen holds in the town. It manages the district's affairs, and is amenable only to the voters of the district in school-meeting assembled. In this meeting, comprising usually but a handful of people, the amount of the annual taxation for school purposes is determined upon the basis of the estimates made by the board. In the tax bills the school tax is reckoned by itself, but its collection is entrusted, with the usual formalities, to the common financial officers. The Board of Education maintains committees upon finance, schools, and school buildings, and may be said to unite administrative with legislative functions. The majority of those who have directed New Haven's educational progress has wrought with singleness of purpose for the good of the schools, and has extended over them the care that only ability, interest, and long experience could provide. Under their oversight the district has obtained remarkably efficient schools and good school buildings, without accumulating any considerable indebtedness. Although the danger that party-spirit would dictate the election of unworthy men to the board has been possible rather than probable, yet the exigencies of popular elections have occasionally supplied the board with factious and fractious members.

The Superintendent, who is the board's chief subordinate, finds his intimate relations with his superiors and with the schools sources of perplexity. If he establishes a cordial understanding between himself and the board, and exerts himself to improve the administration of the schools, the cry of "One-man-power" is raised. Promotions among the teachers are hampered by resort to political influence and by

claims for locality-representation. The latter result of our
practical politics has produced some absurd phenomena in
New Haven. In the summer of 1885, the Superintendent
and the majority of the board agreed to call a teacher from a
neighboring city to preside over one of the New Haven
grammar schools.

Politicians, small-minded men, and even reputable newspapers, raised a windy protest against " Inviting an outsider
to come and live on New Haven taxpayers." This folly might
be deemed exceptional, if it had not occurred in the same
community that, twenty years ago, favored the employment
of " New Haven laborers only " upon a sewer. Such dis-
advantages naturally attend a democratic supremacy, and
must be endured. One improvement in the existing condition of affairs seems practicable, and that is the lengthening
of terms of membership upon the Board of Education. There
is no reason why men who are qualified to serve in this capacity
should not be elected for six years instead of three.

Greater permanence in school government would be a
positive advantage. Above all things, the Superintendent
should feel assured of a steady supporting influence for as
long a time as possible.[1] His tenure of office is determined
by the board, and has of late been fixed at two years; but
in 1886 the board saw fit to elect, by a unanimous vote, a
Superintendent for one year only. This was a move backward, and plainly in opposition to the better tendencies of
our municipal life. An uncertain tenure will either divert
or paralyze administrative energy. The man who is fit to be
elected at all to a subordinate executive office, is fit to stay

---

[1] An oft-asserted point in the administration of the schools of the district
is the extent to which classical instruction should be contained in the
curriculum of the High School. The question is not a new one. The
school included a Preparatory Collegiate Department from 1839 to 1867.
The onslaught upon the school in 1866 led to the abolition of the Preparatory Department, but that course was re-introduced in September,
1877. Again, from year to year, the argument gathers force that the
community should not pay for the special education of a few.

elected.   A faithful Superintendent could work untrammeled, if he were chosen either for six years or during good behavior, subject to removal, under a long notice, by a two-thirds vote of the board.

The Town Government.

The government of the town of New Haven is the parent trunk upon which all the other local organizations have grown.   Every year the electors of New Haven choose incumbents for the time-honored offices of sealers, assessors, pound-keepers, haywards, grand jurors, constables, surveyors of highways, fence-viewers, gaugers and inspectors, packers, weighers, justices of the peace, selectmen, members of board of relief, managers of town deposit fund, registrars of voters, auditors, a town clerk, tax collector, treasurer, town agent, and registrar of vital statistics.   These officers, numbering in all 151, rule a town three-fourths of whose territory are within city limits.   Their authority extends over city and country alike unless, in the former case, the city charter has provided other channels of administration.   Apart from the officers connected with the Treasury and Tax Department, the most important town trusts are those of the selectmen and town agent.

The powers of these and the other functionaries are, in general, such as are customarily possessed by town officers. But the existence of the city intensifies the responsibilities of the selectmen, and the town agent holds what politicians consider a strategic position.   The town agent is the financial representative of the board of selectmen, and, as such, practically controls the distribution of "Outdoor Relief."   His tenure of office by popular choice is not strictly according to law, which supposes him to be elected by his colleagues upon the board.   So long as the selectmen acquiesce in the selection made by people at the polls, there will be no trouble, but, should the board ever reject the officer so selected, there would be an unpleasant collision between law and custom.

Furthermore, the town agent, who holds his office by reason of an election in Town-Meeting, is virtually, if not legally, responsible directly to the voters in Town-Meeting assembled. Such a responsibility might work no ill in a quiet country town, but a town which contains a city is in different circumstances. A Town-Meeting of two hundred voters will know how such a trust is administered; a Town-Meeting of thirteen thousand voters will never know.

It is not intended to imply that the town agency in New Haven has been mismanaged. Under existing circumstances it is almost inevitable that some duties of the office should be shirked, but, for the present, it is sufficient to assert that the principle rather than the practice is at fault. When the town agent was appointed by the selectmen as a body, and was plainly accountable to them, he was under the control of men necessarily familiar with the business of his office, and able to remove him if he should be incompetent or unsatisfactory. In case of a dispute between the majority of the board and a town agent, the latter can now assert against his colleagues the authority of a separate mandate from the people. Such an argument might be made both powerful and pernicious. There is a principle of government which must, sooner or later, win acceptance — viz.: "Subordinate administrative officers should be appointed, not elected." The town agent is, by the nature of his duties, subordinate to the selectmen, and no worthy reason demands his elevation. The town agent himself does not touch a cent of the money that is distributed. To every applicant he can give no more than an order upon the town treasury. This is better than the arrangement in some of our cities, where the town agent hands the money directly to the one who seeks relief. Hartford publishes annually a list of the names of those who have obtained money from the town agent, and the sum paid is placed opposite to each name. Such a detailed publication is so eminently proper and useful that no false sentiment should prevent the adoption of the custom by the town of New Haven in its town agent's report.

The Town-Meeting.

The ultimate fact in the town government is the annual Town-Meeting, the ancient General Court for the town, the folk-moot of all the voters resident in the Republic of New Haven. At one time it elects the town's officers; and, at another day, as a business-meeting, it hears the reports of the town's overseers, it authorizes or sanctions expenditures, it reviews the estimates of proportion, and determines the annual town-tax for seventy-five thousand people. Besides the dignity with which it is endowed by actual service, it is ennobled by the glory of antiquity and by the charm of historic associations. This most venerable institution in the community appears to-day in the guise of a gathering of a few citizens who do the work of as many thousands. The few individuals who are or have been officially interested in the government of the town meet together, talk over matters in a friendly way, decide what the rate of taxation for the coming year shall be, and adjourn. If others are present, it is generally as spectators rather than as participants. Only the few understand the subjects which are under discussion. Even if Demos should be present in greater force, he would almost inevitably obey the voice of some well-informed and influential member of the town government of his own party. But citizens of all parties and of all shades of respectability ignore the Town-Meeting and School-Meeting alike. Not one-seventieth part of the citizens of the town has attended an annual Town-Meeting; they hardly know when it is held.

The newspapers give its transactions a scant notice, which some of their subscribers probably read. The actual governing force of the town is, therefore, an oligarchy in the bosom of a slumbering democracy. But the town is well governed. The town government carries too little spoil to attract those unreliable politicians who infest the City Council. If the ruling junta should venture upon too lavish a use of the town's money, an irresistible check would appear at once.

Any twenty citizens could force the selectmen to summon the town together, and the apparent oligarchy would doubt-less go down before the awakened people. The possibility of such a folk-moot will be sufficient to avert from school dis-trict and town the danger of dishonesty, if not of unwisdom.

CONSOLIDATION.

The proposal to abolish the dual system of town and city government, and to substitute in its place a single adminis-tration for the whole territory, is now becoming familiar to every one. Several other cities in New England have the same combination of jurisdictions, and the same problem has been discussed there also.

Agitation of the subject in New Haven circles dates as far back as 1852. The abortive attempt at that period has been already noticed. The good feeling between town and city was not then disturbed, and the first sign of a rupture did not appear until June, 1865, when a Town-Meeting expressed strong resentment against recent action by the city government. A protest was placed upon the records against objectionable amendments to the city charter, then pending in the Legislature, which threatened to augment the power of the city at the undue expense of the town. In 1870, the greater part of the eastern portion of the township was sub-jected to the city government, but, eleven years later, the loss was replaced by the union with the town of the western and more important half of the town of East Haven, including the borough of Fair Haven and all the lands bordering the eastern side of New Haven harbor. The consent of the inhabitants of that district and of East Haven Town could be gained for the annexation only under the condition that the junction should be with the town, and not with the city. No little opposition has been excited, therefore, by petitions from the city to the Legislature in 1883, and again in 1884 and 1885, to secure " The consolidation of the governments of the City of New Haven, the Town of New Haven, and the Borough of Fair Haven East."

The ordinary city-voter probably deems it to be plainly absurd that he should help to support two separate governments in one community. It seems reasonable to him that one set of officers should do all the public business. In the majority of the one hundred and fifty-two offices on the town ticket the average voter has but little interest. In the party conventions the Board of Selectmen and the Board of Relief are partitioned in the ratios of four to three and three to two, usually in favor of the Democrats, without expectation of a contest. The auditorships, and the registrarships of voters are evenly divided between the parties. For the remaining town-offices, one hundred and thirty-eight in all, each political camp presents its candidates, indeed, but neither convention cares to remain in session for their nomination. Each convention delegates the selection of the host of scalers, weighers, viewers, etc., to its chairman, or to a committee, and adjourns. Then a few gentlemen meet around a table and arrange the rest of the ticket as seemeth best to them. The citizen possibly learns the names of his party's candidates upon the town-ticket by a hasty glance at the morning paper, or at the printed slip which is given him at the polls. Thus the composition of the town's government for another year is determined.

Under these circumstances there is nothing surprising in the impression that the town-government is a luxury rather than a necessity. It has been contended, therefore, that the interests of economy, and prompt, impartial administration, demand the rule of the whole township by one government—that the city-government should be the one preserved ; and that the burdens of taxation in the outlying township could be made commensurate with the privileges enjoyed. It is complained that the proceeds of town-taxes, which come chiefly from the pockets of the city, are expended mainly upon the outlying portions of the township. Over the conduct of that expenditure the city-government has no control. It is asserted that the city's money ought to be used in the improvement of the streets of the city rather than of the suburbs. Another assertion is that the care of the poor is too important a trust to be administered by the town-agent and selectmen. The independent jurisdiction of the Town-Meeting is the greatest stumbling-block, and it is claimed that, since a common power succeeds in collecting town and city taxes, a common power might also manage the imposition of taxes. Mayor Lewis declares, "The plan of laying taxes and making appropriations in Town-Meetings like ours has never, since the Dark Ages, been tried by any community of 75,000 inhabitants. Boston discarded it when she numbered but little more than 40,000, and when her taxes were but little more than half what our Town-Meeting now annually votes."

To this presentation of the case there are weighty objections and eager objectors. So long as any part of the township remains outside the city-limits, the whole town-organization is essential, and if either government is abolished, the city must be merged in the town. There are constitutional reasons why town-officers must be retained.

Article V, Section 5, of the State Constitution reads: "The Selectmen and Town-Clerk of the several towns shall decide on the qualifications of electors at such times and in such manner as may be prescribed by law."

Also Article X, Section 2: "Each town shall annually elect Selectmen, and such officers of local police as the laws may prescribe."

These obstacles are small in size, but great in authority. The town-government cannot be directly abolished. If the city-limits should be extended so that the territory of town and city should be everywhere co-extensive and coterminous, and so that the town-boundaries should become also the city-boundaries, it is evident that the one city-government would practically enjoy single sway; but it will be a long time before the city can thus grow apace. About one-quarter of the township and about one-eighteenth of its population now lie outside the city. Against every proposal to extend the city it is, and will be, urged that a large proportion of this out-lying territory is farming land, unfit for share in urban police, fire, gas, and street privileges, and unable to bear the burden of urban taxation.

There would always be a tendency on the part of the city to tax the suburban districts as heavily as possible, and rascally politicians would discover a fine quarry for jobs in new portions of the city. It is asserted that no adjustment of the city-taxation is possible which would not make the rates upon farm-lands higher than at present, without con-ferring a single benefit in return. There is already some farm-land within the city, but the border districts of the city bear, with the central portions of the same, the uniform rate of $19\frac{1}{2}$ mills. If a large outlying tract were united with the city on condition of taxation proportional to benefits, some considerable part of the present city might reasonably call out for justice. The city of Burlington, Vt., includes some agricultural territory, and the assessors, in making up the grand list, reckon the farms at a figure which prevents excessive taxation. But the population and territory of New Haven Town and City differ much in quantity, quality, and situation from those of Burlington.

The certainty of a tempered breeze upon the shorn lamb would be much less assured in New Haven, and, indeed, the feasibility of proper "tempering" would be less practicable. Only about six hundred people dwell upon the farm-districts of Burlington, and it seems improbable that the compact portion of the city will seek extension in their direction.

It will be seen that neither party pleads without a reason. The city is the taxpayer of the town, and has a right to demand economy. The town-government, on the other hand, is rooted in the fundamental law of the State, and,

while it exists as at present, it averts even the danger of
undue taxation from suburban districts. Two principles
which seem to me almost axiomatic would, if properly
heeded, settle the dispute.

1. No city should extend farther than it is built up.

2. A city needs room for growth. Remembering that a
city exists for business purposes, there can be no good reason
for even pretending to put policemen, pavements, and gas
mains in the middle of a sand-plain. When the outlying
districts are crowded with inhabitants, the people will, of
themselves, demand admission to city-privileges.

Secondly, there can be no more favorable conditions for
expansion than where a parent town is the rind covering and
surrounding the city at the core. The city can then spread
out its skirts without infringing upon the rights of another
town. Every dollar which the city-taxpayer expends for the
improvement of the outlying township helps to ensure the
growth of the city and of its traffic, and the contentment of
its inhabitants.

No city can exist without a suburban belt of partly rural
dwellers who live by means of the city, but are unable to
shoulder its burdens. If the city reaches out to include this
belt, no amount of adjustment will prevent the formation of
a new girdle outside the new boundaries. At present, the
most practicable improvement seems to me to be a consolidation of functions, rather than of jurisdictions. So far as
possible, the same man should hold the similar offices of both
town and city. The principal objection to the existing Town-
Meeting might be obviated if the care of the poor, of roads and
bridges, was entrusted to municipal boards, subject, indeed, to
the mayor, but containing elected representatives of the suburban districts. The expenditures of such departments could,
by the aid of the grand list, be apportioned between city and
suburbs. Alterations of such a nature might possibly produce
satisfactory results, always providing that the outlying township, so long as it remained rural, should not be subjected to

the City Council. The structure of the city-government is not yet so sound that a suburban population would care for shelter under it at the price of additional mills on the dollar.

THE CITY-GOVERNMENT.

There is an historic propriety, if no other, in choosing town-officers upon party-tickets, for the town is a miniature republic, a mirror of the State, a State-atom. But the city is an economic, and not a political unit. It is a business corporation, endowed for business purposes, and it bears the least intrinsic resemblance to the ancient city, which was, indeed, a State. When the true essence and meaning of the modern city shall be generally comprehended, there will be a wondrous reformation in city-administrations. A mayor will then be chosen as a railway corporation chooses its superintendent—for good character and business ability—and there will be no more attention paid to his views about the tariff, or States' rights, than to his opinions concerning predestination and original sin. But, like most of our cities, New Haven has been governed, since Jackson's day, with prime reference to political partisanship. Here and there a member of the city-government commands more than a party-fealty, and is universally recognized as deserving office by reason of ability and integrity. But, in general, the voters of the city hear and obey the party-whip in matters purely municipal, and offices are shared at each election with every reference to long purses, to popularity with the "Boys," to the claims of clique and party service. The partisan qualification is deemed as necessary in one camp as in the other.

The city is gradually advancing upon the same road over which its neighbors, New York and Brooklyn, have already traveled. Saloons are becoming the seed-beds of official enterprise, and the whiskey-vendor is a growing factor in political calculations. For some time the machine of the corrupt, selfish, and irresponsible "Boss" has been grinding effectually. The factors of the problem, both for him and for ourselves, must be clearly apprehended.

First, what may be expected of the voters?

The dominant elements furnish many obstacles to any scheme for better government that includes universal suffrage. Criticism must be based, to a certain extent, on the supposition that the popular majority can be depended upon to choose good rather than evil. But the ideal municipal structure, if it could be erected to-day in New Haven, would, unquestionably, soon be wrenched out of shape, because it must perforce rest upon some foundation of ignorance and foolish partisan prejudice. It is equally true that the interests and motives of the mass of the people are good and true, and worthy, in the long run, of confident trust. Sooner or later, honest men, without regard to party, profession, birth, or education, stand together and strike the evil down. But, until the moment of righteous indignation comes, the demagogues and selfseekers of either party are likely to muster the most voters. How shall the city live during the intervals when the public conscience is inactive?

Is it better to attempt continuous regulation by a system of checks, divided powers and responsibilities, and external interferences, or to give each sphere of government its normal freedom of action, leaving to the people the responsibility of approval and condemnation? It seems to me that the latter course is the wiser. The reasonable safeguards of public inspection and of minority representation need not be discarded, but, in general, every legislative or executive organ of government should have an undivided allegiance, simple functions, and should be within easy reach of the freemen at the polls. The verdict of the people, tardy, ill-formed, and unjust as it may be, is properly conclusive in all our legislation and administration. However disappointing the actual daily conditions and results of popular election may prove to be, it is certain that every political act, be it good or ill in itself, contributes unceasingly to the popular education, and the trend of popular education is, as yet, upward, not downward. Public opinion can be conquered by public opinion. Every allowance being made for the difficulties that will inevitably retard the realization of theory, the principal problem of our municipal life is ready for analysis.

The City Judiciary.

At the outset it appears that the city government is patterned closely upon the old English plan, and bears, with its legislative charter, executive head, bicameral council, and separate judiciary, the usual resemblance to the American type of government, whether national, provincial, or local. But here at once the observer stumbles upon a relic of ancient usage in the practical separation of the city judiciary from the electors of the locality. Constables, justices of the peace, and a sheriff are elected by the citizens, but the city courts derive existence directly from the Legislature. From the beginning the State Legislature has been a prominent agent in New Haven's history. The retention of power over the judiciary is a part of the same jealousy of civic action that caused the Legislature to hold the mayor in office at its own pleasure until 1826, and to elect probate judges until 1851. There is no longer any fear that city officers will set up monarchical forms of government and subvert the liberties of the State, but the power of the Legislature over the City Court is now exerted in order that the Republican party of the city may find more ample representation in its government. The mode of selecting judges for New Haven is this: the New Haven County delegation to the dominant party in the Legislature assembles in caucus and nominates two of the same political faith to be, respectively, judge and assistant judge of the New Haven City Court. Their choice is adopted by their party, and the nominations are duly ratified, often by a strict party vote. Inasmuch as the Legislature is usually Republican and the city of New Haven is unfailingly Democratic, these usages amount to a reservation of judicial offices from the "hungry and thirsty" local majority, and the maintenance of a certain control by the Republican country towns over the Democratic city. During the present session of the Legislature (March, 1885) this argument was put forward in answer to a Democratic plea for representation upon the City Court Bench: "The Democrats possess all the other offices in New Haven. It's only fair that the Republicans should have the City Court." Each party accepted the statement as a conclusive reason for political action.

It would be gratifying to find the subject discussed upon a higher plane, and the incumbents of the offices who had done well continued from term to term without regard to party affiliations. But, in the present condition of political morals, the existing arrangements are probably the most practicable that could be made. It goes without saying that country districts are, as a rule, more deserving of political power than are cities. The method of selecting the judiciary is everywhere a mooted question, but it seems to me that the State authority should designate every judge of a rank higher than justice of the peace. If the city judges were locally elected upon the general party ticket, the successful candidates would often be under obligations to elements in the community who are the chief source and cause of the criminal class — an unseemly position for a judge.

The civil jurisdiction of the City Court includes all causes, both at law and in equity, whereto any of the parties reside in said city, except suits affecting land outside the city. When the value involved exceeds $100, a defendant residing outside the city may appeal to higher courts, and when the value involved exceeds $500, an appeal may be taken by any of the parties. The City Court has jurisdiction of all cases of summary process within the city, and the power to issue search-warrants. Its terms begin on the first Monday of each month. The regular sessions continue through the next two days, and include also the last week-day of each month.

The criminal jurisdiction of the court maintains, within the town of New Haven, the same powers which justices of the peace usually possess ; it includes the cognizance of crimes whose penalties do not exceed a two-hundred-dollar fine, or six months' imprisonment, or both.   Appeals may be allowed except upon convictions for drunkenness, profane cursing, and Sabbath-breaking.   Daily sessions are held on week-days, and on Sundays if the city attorney requests it.   The salaries of the two judges are $1,500 and $900 respectively, but in addition there are fees for each of $5 per day for each day of the civil session, and also of $2 for every hearing upon complaint for a commitment to the Connecticut Industrial School for Girls.   The judge has the sole right of appointing a city attorney at a salary of $2,500, and an assistant city attorney at a salary of $900 is appointed by the city attorney, subject to the approval of the judge.   The judge also appoints a clerk of the court and an assistant clerk at salaries of $1,000 and $200 per annum respectively.   Both the clerk and the attorney are further provided for by fees. Therefore, the judge controls, directly or indirectly, all appointments in his court, his own assistant alone excepted, involving salaries aggregating $4,600 aside from fees.

To sum up, the city judiciary is amenable to the State Legislature, and has no legal responsibility to the people of New Haven, who are represented in it only by the sheriff and by jurymen.   The court has both civil and criminal jurisdiction, subject to appeals to the County and Superior Courts.   The two judges are selected in a party caucus, and are generally local politicians, but the character of the bench has been good notwithstanding.   The chief judge wields practically all the patronage of the court.   The salaries to different officers of the court amount to $7,000, any or all of which may be raised, but not diminished, by the City Council.[1]

---

[1] The receipts of the court in fines and costs are less than they were formerly.   In 1875, the total amount of cash received was $18,633.64, of which the city treasury obtained $10,768.60.   In 1834, the estimated income from the City Court was $5,000.

THE CITY EXECUTIVE.

The structure of the city judiciary is clearly defined and simply planned. Defects in its operation can be easily traced to the culpable officer. But the city executive possesses no such merits. As a separate department it can hardly be said to exist. The Court of Common Council is the supreme authority in the city government. Some of the most important executive branches depend upon it, and owe no responsibility to the mayor. There exists, consequently, a variety of accountabilities.

The commissioners of public works, of police, and of fire, are the choice of the aldermen alone. The boards of compensation, the various sealers, supervisors, and inspectors, result from the joint action of the City Council. The commissioners of public buildings and of public health are the creatures, officially, of the mayor plus the consenting aldermen. The coroner acknowledges a similar genesis, the Court of Common Council being substituted in the place of the aldermen. The Park Commission is produced by the most intricate process of all.

Two of them are chosen in the same manner as the commissioners of public buildings and public health. Three are first elected by citizen donors to the East Rock Park, the votes being cast in proportion to the amount contributed, on a basis of one vote for every gift of $100 in money or two acres of land. The elections must be ratified by the mayor. These three citizen commissioners form a close corporation, electing their own successors, but always subject to the approval of the mayor. Furthermore, the mayor may remove any such citizen commissioner for cause, and, in case of failure to elect a successor, he may appoint to the vacancy. Moreover, several executive officers who are elected by the whole town, such as the tax collector and the Board of Education, have unabridged authority throughout the city. Finally the city elects at large a sheriff and a mayor. Here are seven different sources of executive power, and four of them are double. Only the mayor and sheriff in the city executive are directly responsible to the people. The most vital parts of the administration feel the sway of the City Council only.

The city government is emphatically a government of commissions. This will be apparent when the actual functions of the mayoralty are examined. The mayor serves the city for two years at a salary of $3,000 per annum. The great majority of the list of powers expressly delegated to him by charter are those of a conservator of the peace. He is the chief sheriff, and reaches the height of his powers when, under great stress, he makes requisition for the militia of the city. His appointing power, as we have already seen, is limited, and is practically absolute only in respect to the citizen park commissioners, but even then only under certain conditions.

As chairman of the different boards, the mayor wields a more direct influence upon the governmental action. He can preside, with a casting vote, in the Board of Aldermen, and likewise in the joint convention of the Common Council, which can be called in case the separate boards fail to make the necessary elections. He has merely a delaying veto, the majority vote in each board being sufficient to overrule his objection. The mayor is also *ex-officio* member and chairman of the Board of Public Health, with only the casting vote. He is *ex-officio* member and chairman of the Boards of Public Works, of Fire, and of Police, but is deprived of his usual casting vote when the question concerns the selection of voting-places in the city or town, by the police commissioners, and the election or dismissal of any employee by any of the boards. The mayor is also an active member of the Park Commission.

Finally, the mayor exerts his greatest actual power in the department of finance. He is an active member and a presiding officer of the Board of Finance, which is one of the most important wheels in the city machinery. Here the mayor may make himself really felt in determining the amount of appropriations and loans, the rate of taxation, in examining accounts of officers, in allowing and counter-signing tax liens, claims, and orders.

Thus it seems that the mayor's chief duties which afford employment are his very limited appointing power, and his oversight and share of the management of the city's financial affairs. His legal inability to dissolve a tie in the commissions over a proposed election or dismissal directly removes from him responsibility for the conduct of the various departments, and constitutes a readiness to read the Riot Act under possible provocation his chief personal obligation. By virtue of the mayor's power as guardian of the public peace he is vested, through the city's ordinances, with a number of police duties of a minor sort. He may restrict the use of steam whistles, offer rewards for the arrest of criminals, give advice to subordinate officers, designate horse-car stands, and recommend licenses to vendors, but, in the majority of such functions, the assent of the aldermen is requisite. The aldermen, indeed, are empowered to override the mayor's possible refusal to allow the city clerk to license a street peddler. Thus it will be seen that New Haven has not as yet adopted the modern theory of centralising all the executive powers and obligations upon one single head. When compared with a city like Brooklyn, whose mayor is a despot, and, on the other hand, with one like San Francisco, whose mayor is largely ornamental, New Haven resembles the latter rather than the former. At any rate, it is on the San Francisco side of a middle line.

THE CITY LEGISLATURE.

The mainspring of the urban administration is not in the mayoralty. We must search for it elsewhere. Only through the consultative and legislative machinery of the City Council some of the most important executive powers are made practically operative. Omitting reference to the sheriff, a judicial rather than an executive officer, and deferring consideration of all commissions for the present, we are confronted first by the question, "How was the existing equilibrium, or lack thereof, attained?"

The present position of New Haven's Court of Common Council is the reasonable result of the municipal development of a century. History has already shown the extreme caution with which the freemen of the city have bestowed enlarged powers upon any authority not wholly their own representative. It has been observed how, at every turn, quick jealousy, both in State and city, hedged in the monarchical mayoralty. Consent of the freemen themselves, in City-Meeting assembled, was necessary to ratify actions of the mayor and Council. Not until 1854 was a remedy sought for this state of things. When the City-Meeting disappeared, the mantle of its supremacy naturally fell upon its nearest representative, the City Council, composed of delegates of the people. So, when the increase of wealth and numbers necessitated an expansion of the administration, and a new co-ordination of departments, the Council was consistently endowed with full control, and with the originating authority.

The twelve wards of the city choose sixty men, of whom thirty-six are called "Councilmen," and twenty-four, "Aldermen." These two boards together form the Court of Common Council. Of each board the presidents of the Police, Public Works, Public Health, and Fire Commissions are *ex-officio* members, with every right except that of voting. By city ordinance the aldermen meet regularly on the first Monday of every month, and the councilmen on the second Monday; but the mayor may convene them whenever he deems it expedient. · Each board elects a president, and the president of the Board of Aldermen is the vice-mayor of the city. The city clerk is the clerk of the same board. In either branch a majority is a quorum. Attendance may be made compulsory, upon warrant issued by the mayor or president to the sheriff of the county or the city, whenever such warrant is requested by the members of the board in attendance. No measure can be put to final vote in one board on the same day when it passed the other, except by unanimous consent. A proposed enactment may be referred to the suitable commissioners as though they were a standing committee, and a majority vote can pass ordinances over the mayor's veto. Elections within the council must be by ballot. Presiding officers of the council, or of its committees, are competent to compel witnesses to attend and testify. The Board of Aldermen has standing committees upon buildings, lamps, licenses, and numbering streets. There are joint standing committees of the Common Council upon appropriations, auditing, building lines, claims, the fire department, nominations, ordinances, printing, railroads and bridges, sewers, streets, squares, and water. The Common Council, by ordinance, may also appoint a committee to manage any sinking fund that may be established, and a joint committee of amusement, which performs the functions of a Board of Compensation. The charter provides that no vote, unless by unanimous consent, shall be taken in either branch upon a measure that has not been examined and reported upon by the proper committee or Board of Commissioners.

The Common Council alone controls the finances and can borrow money. It can appropriate funds, and order taxation, and the charter places some checks upon this right. Not more than six thousand dollars can be devoted yearly to the necessities of the Park, and fifteen hundred dollars is the limit put upon expenditure for any public celebration. Most important of all is the provision that no appropriation for any object shall exceed the estimate by more than one hundred dollars, unless by a vote of five-sixths of each board. Publication of the proceedings and votes can be insured by any member of the court. The principal joint committee is the Board of Finance, chosen by the Common Council from among its own members, and comprising also the mayor.

The mode of determining taxation is substantially as
follows. In November of each year the Board of Finance
prepares an estimate of the necessary expenditure of the city
for the year ensuing, of its liabilities and resources, and of the
necessary rate of taxation. The calculated expenditure must
be specific, classified under the proper heads and departments.
The report forthwith is submitted to the Common Council
and published in the newspapers. Before the first of January,
the Common Council shall have revised the estimates, levied
taxes upon the last completed grand list of the town, and
shall have specified all the items of appropriation. The
charter forbids that the total annual appropriation shall
exceed the estimated income for that year, and that any officer
shall make any payment or incur any liability in excess of
the amount appropriated by the council to any object. All
special taxes must be laid in a similar manner. Whenever
a tax has been duly laid the proper rate-bill is prepared and
signed by a committee of four aldermen, with the mayor, and
then delivered, with a warrant for the collection of the specified
tax, to the collector of the city. The charter, which generally
sins by omission rather than by commission, nowhere gives
the mayor the right to veto parts of appropriation bills, and
there is no clause limiting the possible indebtedness of the
city. The tax for city expenses alone is now about nine
dollars *per capita*, or eleven dollars on the thousand. This
rate is probably nearly double the actual cost on the thousand
upon a full valuation in either New York or Philadelphia.

LEGISLATIVE CONTROL OVER THE COMMISSIONS.

Turning now to the confirming and appointing powers of
the Common Council, we shall discover the legislative branch
trenching upon the proper prerogatives of the executive, and
granting to its own creatures the usage of the moneys which
itself has appropriated by taxation. The old style of city
government, which was modeled upon the ancient pattern of

the London municipality, accorded to the unpaid committees of the City Council the executive disposition of the same which the whole council had appropriated. In other words, " The individual members spent the money which the whole body voted." New Haven's present plan offers these three variations from the usual custom : The aldermen alone choose the Commissions of Public Works, Police, and Fire ; with the exception of the mayor, as hereinbefore stated, no member of the city government is eligible ; and it is intended that the commissions shall be non-partisan. There are six members of each commission, who serve for three years. Two commissioners for each board are annually chosen in January. The provision for securing non-partisan commissions is that each alderman shall have but one vote, and that the two persons receiving the highest equal or unequal numbers of ballots shall be declared elected. Ordinarily, this must secure a commission evenly balanced between the two parties.

Further restrictions upon membership are : 1. That no one shall be a member of more than one commission at the same time ; 2. That no member shall enter into any contract to do work for the city ; 3. That no member shall receive any employment under the commissions ; and 4. That no police commissioner shall be engaged as principal, agent, or employee in the manufacture or sale of intoxicating liquors. If a vacancy occurs, the charter provides that only a member of the same political party as the outgoing commissioner shall be eligible to succeed him. The Commission of Public Works is forbidden to begin any operation other than ordinary repairs until the task has been authorized by vote of the Common Council. Such is the genesis of these three commissions, which demand a high degree of executive ability on the part of their officers, which form the bulk of the municipal administration, and which absorb two-thirds of the total annual expenditure. The actual expenditure of these departments in 1883 and the estimated expense of the same for 1884 are thus compared :

	1883.	1884.
Public Works, . .	$109,844.71	$233,735.00
Police, ...	108,400.00	106,325.00
Fire, ...	82,275.00	80,925.00
Health,.	6,800.00	7,400.00
	$396,319.71	$428,385.00
Harbor Department, . .	250.00	200.00
Sundries, ...	218,313.00	224,880.00
Total of City, . . .	$614,882.71	$653,465.00

Without reckoning the wages paid to ordinary labor, and without reckoning fees, a little more than two hundred thousand dollars is annually paid by the city in salaries. Of this sum fourteen thousand and seven hundred dollars are paid in accordance with charter stipulations, and to officers chosen outside of the Common Council, excepting in the latter respect the corporation counsel and the assistant city clerk. The residue is disposed of directly by vote of the Common Council, or of one of the four commissions. In the item of salaries there might profitably be some retrenchment, and the charter itself creates the most expensive sinecure in the city government. The corporation counsel receives five hundred dollars a year more than the mayor obtains, but does very little to earn his wage. A better economy would direct the city to consult an ordinary lawyer and pay the fee on the few occasions when a legal opinion is needed. The city ought not to maintain a prize for the New Haven Bar Association.

Finally, the confirming power of the council together, or of the aldermen alone, is, of course, confined to those few officials who are subject to the mayor's nomination, the coroner, the three commissioners of public buildings, the six commissioners of public health, and two park commissioners. These commissions, however important in duties, are comparatively weak in authority. The park commissioners are limited to a six-thousand-dollar appropriation for the East Rock Park. The thirteen other inclosures in different parts of the city are cared for by the Board of Public Works.

The commissioners of public buildings can only submit

recommendations to the Board of Aldermen. All the aforesaid appointees combined do not control appropriations of more than fifteen thousand dollars. The restrictions upon membership in these commissions are, in general, similar to those previously described. All the commissions are unpaid, but these last-named differ from the former in that there is no endeavor to render them non-partisan.

Excluding the Park Commission, which is entirely unique in structure, all the city commissions enjoy yet another common feature. Removal of any commissioner is at the discretion of the Board of Aldermen alone. Although the mayor nominates seventeen different commissioners, the only officers in the whole city government who are in this way amenable to him are, in the first place, as it seems, a coroner, and secondly, three park commissioners, whom, in all probability, he did not nominate, and whom he may only conditionally remove. The charter-law regulating removals and tenure of office is that city officers chosen by electors shall hold office through their term, or until a successor is chosen and sworn, but that in case of resignation, death, removal, or incapacity of an officer, the Court of Common Council shall order a special election.

A subsequent section provides that all persons holding any office created by law by virtue of an election or appointment, may be removed by the body having the power to appoint them. In general, "Appointees and employees shall be removable at the pleasure of the person or body having the right to employ or appoint them."[1] But, in order to preclude the possibility of a dispute between the appointing power of the mayor and the confirming power of the aldermen, the responsibility of the five commissions was thus asserted:

"Any member of said boards shall be subject to removal by the Board of Aldermen for cause, upon charges made in writing by any member of either Board of the Court of Common Council, provided said charges are found to be sustained

---

[1] Sections 17 and 86.

by a two-thirds vote of the Board of Aldermen."[1] The numerous public servants who are, or may be, elected by the Court of Common Council, acting conjointly, play for the most part a minor *rôle* in the municipal economy.[2]

No matter what laws and theories may affirm, the body which elects and removes is the dominant authority. Therefore it is fair to say that the city executive owes directly a divided allegiance—the mayor to the people, but the commissions to the Common Council first of all. In the Common Council the Board of Aldermen obtains the lion's share, and thus practically becomes the truest centre of the municipal activity in all branches except the judicial. In other words, the law-making, tax-laying power can dictate not only *how* money shall be spent, but also *who* shall spend it. If the executive departments of the National Government were managed by commissions of six men each, elected by the Senate, or by the House of Representatives, or both, without the possibility of any interference by the President, the state of affairs would be outwardly parallel. The idea suggests such possibilities of non-performance of duty, of political engineering and scandal, of the most nebulous of Star Routes, that the explanation of the common degeneracy of cities under our forms of government seems to leap to the surface.

The commission appointed by Governor Hartranft, of Pennsylvania, to study the problems of municipal govern-

---

[1] Section 36, *ad finem*.

[2] The number of town-officers elected by ballot, including the Board of Education, reaches one hundred and sixty. The city government contains two hundred and fifty-two individuals who annually draw a stated salary, but only sixty-five of the city's officials are chosen directly by popular suffrage. Therefore four hundred and twelve persons perform the more prominent functions of municipal life in school-district, town, and city. Two hundred and twenty-five of them are elected by the people. An estimate of the entire number of men employed in any capacity, principal or subordinate, occasionally or continuously, in the local public service, places the sum at twelve hundred. About one in every fifty-eight of the people of New Haven is guarding the common interests of the municipal bodies politic, and is encamped upon the common pocket-book.

ment in that State reported in 1877 as follows: "The heads of departments appointed by the councils are merely the agents of committees, not only in the administration of trusts supposed to be committed to departments, and in the appointment of subordinate officers, but in the payment of bills and current expenses not embraced in special contracts, thus affording opportunity for, if not inviting, corrupt combinations between the two branches of the city government. This condition of things exists only in city governments, and is found neither in State nor Nation." New Haven cannot be classed with the cities that are discussed in this report. There has been no scandalous misuse of the public funds, and the commissions are not quite the same as committees of the council. There is, however, one exception to the general authority of the commissions. The street-lamps of the city have never been placed under the care of the Public Works' Department, but are under the sole supervision of an aldermanic standing committee. This committee manages the entire lamp account, and chooses the lamp inspector. No valid reason appears for the retention of the old usage in this single instance. It seems to be merely a sop thrown to the Board of Aldermen.

CONDUCT OF COMMISSIONS.

The political equilibrium maintained in the commissions supplies a check upon some kinds of possible misconduct. But the evils appertaining to the system have been pushed beneath the surface, not eradicated. The probe of examination reveals the confusion that attends an intermingling of responsibilities.

Of course King Caucus rules; the Democratic aldermen determining one-half the membership of the Public Works, Fire, and Police Commissions, the Republican members naming as absolutely the other half. The history of the Police Commission during the winter of 1886 is one of the best practical commentaries that can be offered upon the whole system. Near the beginning of the year the chief of police was removed by death.

This is the most important office within the gift of the police commissioners, both by reason of the salary and of the influence involved. It is the chief of police who, among other duties, issues licenses for billiard tables, bowling alleys, public exhibitions, and public conveyances, and who receives information from his force of all violations of city laws and ordinances. These facts, added to a realizing sense of the activity which an energetic and right-minded chief can impart to the police force in general, stimulate the liquor-selling and drinking interests of the city to take a vigorous interest in the choice of this officer. Therefore it was not surprising that when the half-dozen commissioners met for election, the three Democrats and the three Republicans were found to entertain totally diverse ideals of the coming incumbent.

The commission first assembled to fill the vacancy January 8th, 1885. The remarks of Democratic Commissioner Catlin, himself his party's nominee for the chieftainship, struck the key-note of the struggle as it seemed to him and to his friends. He said that the "Board [*sc.* of Commissioners], as constituted, consisted of three Democrats and three Republicans. The officers of the force stood about 8 to 3. Elect a Republican for chief, and the force would have a preponderance of Republicans among its head officers."[1] He could not, therefore, vote for a Republican candidate, and he hoped that the Republicans would see things as he did. Republican Commissioner Sheldon contended that politics had nothing to do with the matter.

Mr. Catlin replied that he desired fairness. "He thought that as good a man could be got on the Democratic side as on the Republican."

After this explanation of the prime motives for the bestowal

---

[1] Report in *Journal and Courier*, January 9th.

of municipal responsibilities the voting began, and resulted in a tie. There the question hung while the presiding mayor looked helplessly on. Candidates were proposed who would ensure a business-like, non-partisan, and law-supporting administration of the police force, but no agreement was reached, and there seemed to be some justification for the advertising squib in the newspapers, " Wanted—a Chief of Police for New Haven. Nobody who is fit for the place need apply." During the deadlock, the terms of two commissioners ended, and the aldermen chose their successors, but the contest remained unaltered. Meanwhile, the captain of the police force was acting chief, and perhaps, if strict ideas of Municipal-Service Reform could prevail, the captain ought to stand in line of promotion to the permanent chieftainship.

Finally, during the third week in July, the prolonged contest was ended. The commissioners were, in a sense, compelled to elect a Democratic fellow-commissioner, who was too good a man to be chosen in the first place. A few days later the Democratic aldermen met to select a commissioner to succeed the new chief. They exemplified their fitness to control the city executive by falling straightway into a violent quarrel over the claims of German Democrats to representation upon the commission. One City Father, of Teutonic extraction, was enraged because he had been told that no Dutchman could have the place, and that, if he didn't like it, he could lump it. The supporters of the non-German candidate, having the advantage of numbers, deprecated the raising of a race-issue. Upon such a plane an important executive appointment was discussed, and made.

We can see now out of what material the aldermen construct their commissions; and we can also see how the present system lacks order, directness, and free motion. The executive is hampered. The legislative branch does nothing to clear away obstacles. So far as elections like the foregoing are concerned, the idea of non-partisanship in the commissions becomes farcical.

Here is a so-called non-partisan commission which protracts a partisan deadlock through seven months. Yet, without the balance of parties in the commission, the state of affairs under the existing supremacy of the aldermen would be worse. The question reduces itself to a dilemma, illustrative of the disordered system of government: if the non-partisan boards are maintained, the administration is likely to be clogged, and there are unseemly disputes and delays; if the non-partisan feature is abandoned, and the present source of election retained, the administration is likely to fall into the hands of less competent, and possibly less honest, officers.

It must be conceded, moreover, that the determination of a so-called non-partisan board is, in very many cases, not the agreement of the board's united wisdom, but is the resultant compromise of the conflicting party interests that are represented in the board; it is apt to be a temporary makeshift, not a permanent solution. Non-partisan commissions are, in themselves, confessions that party government in cities is a failure, and that politics should be removed from municipal matters. These commissions seek to redeem the failure by balancing one party against another so evenly that neither of them can do anything without corrupting or overpowering the other. Is it thought that a dog does not chew his bone properly? Put three dogs at one end of the bone and three more at the other end; then the non-partisan commission will proceed at once to arrange matters. The method is clumsy, if not dangerous.

During the winter of 1885, a demonstration was made before the State Legislative Committee on cities and boroughs in favor of the election of non-partisan commissions on a general ticket by the voters at large, no elector being allowed to cast a ballot for more than half the membership of each commission. Some advantages appear in this plan. The commissions would directly represent the people, and the fatal entanglement with the City Council would be removed. But there are insurmountable objections. All co-ordination and dependence in the municipal executive would be destroyed, and the city would be provided with so many more mayors. "Subordinate administrative officers should be appointed, not elected."

Executive Organization.

The course of municipal development in our principal cities has been toward the consolidation of the Executive Department. New Haven, though a small city, has now in its charter the same provisions which proved disastrous to its larger neighbors, and which impelled them to recast their system of government. Their experience has emphasized the truth of this principle:

"The popular branch should tell *how* the money of the community shall be spent, but should not tell *who* shall superintend the spending." The officers of administration should be closely connected with the body of taxpayers—whose work these officers do—and not with a legislative body, which should be freed from every inducement to warp the laws for selfish purposes. System and uniform action in the administration can be secured only by the strong hand of a single superior.

The mayor, therefore, should appoint the heads of departments, and the mayor and his heads of departments should have the control of all their subordinates. The mayor is the servant and representative of the people, and he should be responsible to his employers for every branch of the municipal service, from city engineer to lamp cleaner. The people can fasten responsibility upon a mayor; it is difficult to trace it in a crowd of common councilmen. A representative body which wields executive power affords an inviting opportunity for log-rolling, disbursing, and partisan management; at least some of its members are always comparatively unknown men, who can traffic in the public welfare under the shadow of obscurity. The mayor must act in the full light of public opinion. He is a character known and read of all men; if

such an officer is allowed to pursue evil courses without hindrance, it must be because the majority of his constituency is
no better than himself.

A mayor who is directly responsible for the local administration is by no means free from check and rein. Public
opinion presses hard upon him, and " The People " to the
mayor does not mean a little knot of party-workers, as it does
to the alderman. The mayor's position makes him sensitive
to the blame or approval of a wide and large constituency,
the real people. The public opinion of the counting-house, the
press, and the pulpit is the most terrible of critics, and the
most inexorable of judges. The mere consciousness of this
tribunal is often enough to strengthen the moral backbone
of a weak man, and to elevate an average citizen into an
ideal public officer. Executive officials, from mayor to
President, are illustrations of this. Furthermore, the courts
of law are always open, and the right of impeachment should
be a recognized privilege and a vigorous possibility. The
practical freedom from the judiciary which the executive
enjoys is impolitic, and is the great defect in what may be
called " The Brooklyn Idea " of city government. A bad
mayor may do nothing which can bring him under the criminal jurisdiction of the courts. Public opinion is the hand
that threatens him, but it may have no weapon with which
to strike until the far-off election-day. Moreover, we are
such fools that we make a fetich out of a party-name and
abase ourselves before a shadow. Party-ties are so strong
that, in Brooklyn's last city election, a very small change of
votes would have defeated the admirable mayor, Low, and
elected an unknown and untried competitor.[1]

Administrative Courts.

It is just that the appointing power should also possess the
right to suspend or remove. If, however, the whole Execu-

----

[1] Written in the summer of 1885.

tive Department rests in the hand of the mayor, a bad mayor may do much to destroy the good that his predecessor created, and yet may not become liable to ordinary process of law. It seems to me that the continued success of a reformed municipal service may be more thoroughly assured by the introduction of administrative courts. These courts are well known in Europe, and there is nothing in their constitution or functions which is in any manner repugnant to our customs and institutions. Administrative courts exist for the examination and settlement of all official differences between members of the administration, and for adjudication between officers and the non-official world in disputes that affect administration solely. Complaints against public servants are brought before these courts, and a judicial inquiry is at once set on foot. Incompetent or untrustworthy officers are called to answer for their derelictions before the administrative court, and an adverse verdict is ground and sufficient motive for the culprit's dismissal.[1]

If powers like these could be conferred upon our city and county judiciaries, or, better still, upon a separate system of municipal administrative courts, with the right of appeal to the higher tribunals, and if, within proper limits, removals or interferences with the course of promotion could be based only upon the decisions of such courts, a long stride would have been taken toward a model municipal service. The proposed court, if judiciously constituted, would powerfully support a good government, or restrain a bad one. No objection could then be urged against the plan of appointments by the mayor. The tenure of office would sooner or later depend largely upon good behavior, and the idea might, at least, begin to penetrate the mind of the citizens that the

---

[1] In German cities a "Complaint-Book" (*Beschwerdebuch*) is kept under the inspection of the authorities, and any one who discovers instances of official incapacity or injustice describes in that book his grievance. The complaints are examined and, if necessary, investigated by the officers of the administrative court, and the faults, if there be any, are punished.

mayoralty also is an office which demands a good administrator, and not a politician, and which, when once well filled, should retain its occupant as long as possible.

FREQUENT ELECTIONS.

There is already a tendency in the New Haven municipality toward lengthening terms of service. In the early history of the city a public officer remained at his post until death removed him. With the rise of the Jacksonian Democracy annual changes became more frequent. The reaction has been small and slow. In 1860, some daring spirits broached the idea that a two-years' term for the mayor would not endanger the popular liberties. That suggestion finally found favor, and now all the principal commissioners serve for three years. In town and city there are now in all forty-three officers who serve for three years. Perhaps the existing tendency may be carried still further without harm. If the mayor could have at least a three-years' term, and the subordinate members of the administration a much longer term, the city would profit by the increased experience and security of its servants. Professional politicians are the gainers by frequent elections.

THE BOARD OF COUNCILMEN.

Why is it that, in city and nation alike, the Legislature incurs distrust? Why is it that in most of our cities the legislative branch contains so many men unfit for public trusts? The great majority of New Haven's councilmen undoubtedly desire to promote the city's best interests, but at the same time many of them are not men who can form an exalted idea of the city's best interests. If the Court of Common Council should lose its powers of patronage, of appointment, of political coercion, membership in it would be less inviting to the small politician, and more so to the better sort of citizen.

It is difficult to see what would be lost if the Board of Councilmen should be abolished, and if the City Council should consist of aldermen alone. There is and has been no respectable reason for the existence of the lower council, except the fact that it helped complete the analogy between the city, State, and National governments. The argument which Washington used to justify the division of the National Congress into two houses is adduced as a support for the bicameral council—viz.: the assurance of dignified and calm consideration. But undue haste in legislation may be prevented by requiring an interval between the proposal and the passage of an ordinance, and by publishing the proposition in the newspapers during that interval. It has been found, also, that if any potent interests demand hurried law-making, the mere existence of two branches in the council is a very small obstacle.

Moreover, there is no federative principle that seeks preservation in a city. Two chambers should imply two constituencies. A second chamber might explain its existence if it were chosen by a body of taxpayers. But the aldermen are as completely representative of the people and of the wards as the councilmen are. It is time that the complete distinction in essence between a corporate government and a nation should be admitted on all sides.

The fact that New Haven was once an isolated community with aspirations toward independence does not affect the consideration of the present city government and its needs. As Mr. Simon Sterne has clearly pointed out, the modern city is a corporation, charged with the administration of property, and, properly, so far as its internal operations are concerned, it has no political functions whatever. The administration of a city government should therefore be executed with ideas and methods similar to those which other corporations find advantageous. Nobody can say that the boards of aldermen and of councilmen contain very different material, either in respect to age or wisdom. The lower board is merely an additional house of refuge for the ambitious aspirant and the corner-grocery politician. No healthy corporation would retain in its service two organs when one could do all the allotted work as well.

Let the Board of Councilmen, therefore, be evolved out of existence. Then if, in addition to the aldermen from wards, there were chosen aldermen-at-large in numbers proportioned to population, perhaps one to every full ten thousand, allowance being made for minority representation, the New Haven Council would count to-day thirty-one members—a good working number for a city legislature.

The charter of the city wisely provides that the presidents of the various commissions in the city government shall be entitled to seats in either branch of the council, with every privilege except that of voting. It would be no more than an expansion of the same idea if all ex-mayors who had been elected by the people, and who had served honorably throughout their terms, should be entitled to membership in the Board of Aldermen. The honor might include the right to vote, and might cease in case of removal from the city or of election to another office. Most of the incumbents of the mayoralty attain that height after having served the city in less important trusts. That the city should lose the benefit of their ripest judgment and experience is faulty economy and poor politics. The reasons that support the retirement of ex-Presidents to the Senate for life also favor the theory that ex-mayors should continue to aid the city which has honored them. There are additional arguments in the case of the mayor. Membership in the Board of Aldermen would convey now no social distinction. It would be a continuation of public work rather than the bestowal of a public reward.

The Choice of Aldermen.

However, it seems to me that still better results could be attained by a still more radical change, by a change in the mode of election. In many quarters the opinion gains ground that ward representation is corrupting and belittling, and that aldermen ought to be elected on a general ticket by the people at large.

New Haven has completed its first century of city-life, and for only thirty-two years of that time have wards existed. In the earlier day the best men in the city were honored by the name of alderman. It is not always so now. The plea that an alderman should be able to champion the " Local interests " of a ward is a strong argument against electing aldermen by wards. What broad-minded and upright man will care to sit in the City Council, knowing that he is expected to secure as large a slice as possible of the public funds for improvements in his locality—jobs which will bring money into his ward and into the pockets of the clique that worked for his nomination? How can any but the small-minded man set himself to represent or to uphold the alleged " Interests " of a few square feet of ground?[1]

---

[1] That species of city councilman whose highest idea of achievement for the public good is to keep his band of local workers "solid," to assist the more importunate of them to jobs at repaving streets—in his own ward, if possible—and to vote taxes that better men must pay, has become an object so familiar as to be almost unnoticed.

An exceptionally fine specimen of the performance of these duties is preserved in Baltimore, a city whose municipal government is deplorably bad. During Mayor Latrobe's first administration, a certain district was represented in the City Council by a nonentity whose only claim to political preferment was his affiliation with the controlling clique. This councilman, being unable to secure a sewer, or freshly painted curbstones for his district, cast about him for some other means of vindicating his claims for public trust and his reputation of watchfulness for the needs of his locality. One day the political magnates of the neighborhood were holding sweet converse in their customary headquarters, the corner grocery. A bright idea flashed upon the intellect of the councilman. He observed that every district in the city except his own had an avenue. Such injustice should be redressed, and he solemnly summoned himself, amid the plaudits of his comrades, to the work of securing an avenue for his suffering district.

The party decided that Chuptank street, which extends across the district, should be the future avenue; but with what name should it be

The ward-workers of either party can nominate a mediocre man for aldermanic honors, confident that their neighbors will not bolt the ticket, because their man is the regular nominee, even if there is no worse reason. The rest of the city knows very little about the ward or its candidates, and can have no voice in their election, at any rate; and so the ward elects a bad alderman. If, on the other hand, the city convention which nominates a mayor should, in a similar way, nominate aldermen, there would be a better chance of securing aldermen whose mental and moral calibre would be as good as that of the mayor. If the whole city were to be the constituency of each alderman, the candidates would be more closely scrutinized by both the press and the people. The best citizens would be more likely to desire aldermanic honor if it were the gift of the whole community, and not of a comparatively insignificant group in that community.

The root of the whole matter is in the primaries. Unless

---

christened? Some member of the company, with more intelligence than the rest, waggishly and maliciously proposed that Choptank street should become Collington avenue, in honor of the renowned English admiral, Lord Collington. Seeing that the proposal was favorably received, he narrated the services and many exploits of Lord Collington, who had, forsooth, crowned a long and illustrious career by commanding the fleet which brought to Maryland its first settlers at St. Mary's. Yet this noble mariner's name was not preserved in a single street or alley of the whole city of Baltimore. The story was greedily swallowed, and the councilman was unanimously advised to rescue Admiral Collington from the oblivion into which he had undeservedly fallen. In due time a bill was offered in the Board of Councilmen changing Choptank street—in its course through that district only—to Collington avenue, and the wondrous history of the name was recited.

Playing with the names of streets is recognized as a prerogative of Baltimore councilmen, and such bills pass as if by an act of personal courtesy. There is nothing to show that bill and story were objected to in either branch of the City Council. But in the mayor's office there was some one who knew a little history.

Mayor Latrobe sent to the council a message exposing the absurdity of the Collington anecdote, and berating the honorable gentlemen for their disregard of everybody's convenience excepting their own, *but His Honor signed the bill.*

the better elements in each party assumed and control the primaries, reform-movements will always limp. To elect a good mayor and leave the City Council and the primaries in their present status is only to whitewash the same old sepulchre.' If aldermen are chosen by wards, the primaries determine who the candidates shall be. If the aldermen are chosen upon a general ticket, the primaries can elect only delegates to the nominating convention. It must be that the latter distribution of powers is incomparably the safer.

The first and last need of New Haven's government is one which it shares in common with all institutions—the need of intelligent and conscientious discussion. Children in the schools should be familiarized with the working of the different governments under which they live; but that instruction is only a small part of the requisite political education.

The press, the bar, the pulpit, and the private citizen should actively teach and preach upon the subject, and disseminate the doctrines that local taxation furnishes problems as pressing as those of the national tariff; that a high standard of morality is as essential for the City Hall as for the Church; and that the choice of clear-headed and honest men of business for municipal offices is as vital a matter as the election of Democrat or Republican to the Presidency. Then, perchance, one might obtain a little clearer vision of that better age of municipal government to which the gliding years are leading us, wherein the local machinery shall move almost unaffected by political influences and revolutions; wherein men grow gray in faithful public service without fear of removal; wherein the right of municipal suffrage is

---

' A recent writer has suggested that one way to improve primaries is to improve the surroundings of primaries. They are too often held in or near some low groggery—in rooms where the more decent citizens would dislike to go. Of course, this does not excuse the decent citizen, who ought to go, and to help secure for his party a more respectable vote. A city ordinance might require every ward or district to provide a ward-hall free to all parties, suitable for public meetings, remote from saloons—a place where every voter might be glad to go.

proportioned to the burden of taxation that is borne;[1] and wherein every organ and every officer of the municipality feels an actual responsibility not only to superior organs and officers and to the people, but, more immediately, to the courts of the community; "To the end," as the old Puritans phrased it, "it may be a government of lawes and not of men."

---

[1] Is this doctrine thought undemocratic? There can be no better Democratic authority than the following : " Municipal officers, having no power over persons, but only that of applying the proceeds of taxes, ought to be elected by those alone who contribute to such payments."—*Albert Gallatin* (1833).

APPENDICES.

A. MR. PIERSON'S ELEGY.
B. THE TOWN OF NAUGATUCK.
C. DR. MANASSEH CUTLER'S DIARY.
D. A TOWN-COURT OF ELECTIONS. NEW HAVEN, A. D. 1656.

APPENDIX A.

MR. PIERSON'S ELEGY.

Mather's delineation of Governor Eaton would almost remove the taint of extravagance from the well-known, peculiar epitaph :

> " Eaton, so fam'd, so wise, so meek, so just,
> The Phœnix of our world, here hides his dust,
> His name forget New England never must."

Eaton's ancient friend, the Rev. Abraham Pierson, of Branford, expressed his grief at the Governor's demise in an elegy of thirty-eight stanzas, closing with half a dozen Latin verses. Such pure, unaffected sorrow is manifestly ill-concealed behind the stilted Puritan phrase that the excuse for farther reference thereto must be a desire to vindicate the real merits of the muse of Michael Wigglesworth.

Mr. Pierson, after comparing Governor Eaton to a lion and a dove, ingeniously managed to describe him as possessing the combined good qualities of Moses, Noah, Abram, Isaac, David, Jacob, Joseph, Joshua, Samuel, Jonathan, Solomon, Hezekiah, Josiah, Nehemiah, Mordecai, and Job. These stanzas, culled at random, will serve as examples of the sentiment, erudition, and rhythm of the whole :

> " Joshua like strong, and of good courage too,
> A terror to the vile, they would him fear,
> But to the saints he stretched out his hand,
> Them he esteemed the precious of the land.

" In's house of judgment mercy did hee sing,
In our courts of justice hee sate as king,
His comely person few could parallell,
The pleasant stories hee was wont to tell!

" In all the changes of his life hee held
The Orthodox truth, the Heterodox hee queld.
He had a quick passage up to Heaven,
Was well, and sick, and dead in houres seven."

(The poem can be found in Mass. Hist. Soc. Coll., Vol. VII., Series IV., p. 477.)

APPENDIX B.

THE TOWN OF NAUGATUCK.

This town furnishes one of the best examples of township-evolution that our subject affords. Its development is, of course, a matter of easily-ascertained history, but the composite character of the town and the prominence of the ecclesiastical element in its formation make Naugatuck at once typical and interesting.

Milford and New Haven together are responsible for the origin of the towns of Derby and Woodbridge. In the middle of the eighteenth century the northern part of Derby was occupied by the ecclesiastical Parish of Oxford, and the similar portion of Woodbridge by the Parish of Bethany. Immediately adjoining these two parishes on the north was the town of Waterbury, which owed its original settlement mainly to the town of Farmington. The southern portion of the old town, however, derived its population largely from the New Haven towns. In 1765, the people living near the intersecting boundaries of Waterbury, Oxford and Bethany grew tired of much Sunday travel to their respective churches, and began to agitate the question of sanctuary privileges nearer home. For the story of the struggle which produced a parish and a town, I am indebted to the kindness and courtesy of Mr. Wm. Ward, of Naugatuck, of Mr. Homer F. Bassett, Librarian of the Bronson Library, at Waterbury, and especially of Hon. Calvin H. Carter, of Waterbury, who, at the request of Mr. Bassett, copied the following records of the Ecclesiastical Society of Salem from the original papers:

ECCLESIASTICAL RECORDS, VOL. XIV. 1763–1764.

Page 57. "April 22, 1765. Forty-six petitioners in Waterbury and Oxford live from four to seven miles from places of public worship, and pray for liberty to have four months' winter-preaching."

It was wintry preaching that they would get, too, no doubt; but, even for four months of that, official permission was necessary. There was one man in the neighborhood who intended to avoid the reproaches of slothfulness and fondness for creature comforts; as witnesseth:

Page 56. "May 15, 1765. Samuel Porter is opposed to so much division into small parishes, and thinks it sinful when men cannot meet their obligations. The petition is continued."

It was doubted whether Brother Porter's house would fall within the desired parish; but

Page 55. "Oct. 23, 1765. The surveyor says that Porter's house is south of the proposed line, and included in the said parish."

The result was that the objector was allowed to travel over the Sunday-snows to his heart's content; for

Page 58. "Oct. 23, 1765. A winter-parish is granted, exclusive of the part of Oxford, and of S. Porter."

This winter-parish may be regarded as the first municipal germ of Naugatuck. It was wholly in the town of Waterbury, and was known as the district or parish of "Waterbury South Farms"; or, more colloquially, as "The Farms." The winter-preaching was probably discontinued in 1766; but

Page 59. "April 21, 1767. Forty-four petitioners in Waterbury, Milford (Bethany Society), Oxford (Society), and Cheshire'
(West Cheshire), pray for a Society 6 miles by four."

The petition was continued and denied in May, 1768.

Page 60. "Sept. 25, 1768. Thirty-eight petitioners renew request for a Society, or for a five months' winter-parish."

A winter-parish was the extent of concession; and

Page 61. "Oct., 1768. They are allowed five months' winter-preaching."

A Society, and not an intermittent parish, was the goal desired. Therefore,

---

'Cheshire was then a Society in Wallingford.

Page 64. " Nov. 13, 1771. Thirty-five petitioners in Bethany, Waterbury, Cheshire, and Oxford renew the petition for a Society or a Committee."

"Committee" probably means a legislative committee of investigation, such as was afterward appointed. West Cheshire was a house divided against itself by this subject; for

Page 62. "Oct. 21, 1771. Thirty-nine remonstrants in Cheshire, West of the mountain, wish not to be included. They cannot get to Waterbury South Farms in winter, and hope hereafter to be constituted a separate Society."

This is the first suggestion of what afterward became the Society and town of Prospect. The petition of 1771 finally accomplished its object. A committee of investigation was appointed in October, 1772, which reported:

Page 66. " Nov. 27, 1772. It is difficult to cross the River from the Farms to Waterbury. The Grand List of the proposed Society amounts to £3484 11s. 0d., exclusive of the adherents to the Church of England. Possible boundary-lines are described."

In accordance with this report, the new Society was incorporated in May, 1773, and was named Salem.

Page 67. " May, 1773. Upon the memorial of Gideon Hecox of Waterbury, in the county of New Haven, and others, praying for Society-privileges. Bushnell Bostwick, Thomas Darling, and James Wadsworth were appointed a committee in October last, who have reported that it is convenient and necessary that a distinct Ecclesiastical Society be made and constituted within the following limits—viz.: ' Beginning at a rock near the road from the Town Platt in Waterbury to New Haven, distant from the Meeting-house in Waterbury two miles one half mile and sixty rods, called "'The Mile Rock," to Wallingford line—thence in said line to the Tree called the Three Brothers—thence south to the Beacon Cap—thence to the southeast corner of a farm formerly belonging to James Richard, lying on Beach Hill—thence West to the mouth of the Great Spruce Brook, the west side of the Naugatuck River—thence, keeping the Brook, Westwardly to the mouth of the Brook that comes off from Red Oak Hill—thence Northwestwardly to the place where Moss Road crosses Derby line—thence Northwardly in said Road to Enos

Gunn's dwelling-house—thence a North line so far as to inter-
sect a west line from said Mile Rock.'

"Which Report is accepted and approved. Whereupon, It is
resolved by this Assembly that the Inhabitants living within
the limits aforesaid be, and they are hereby, made and constituted a distinct Ecclesiastical Society, with all the Privileges,
Powers, and Immunities to such Societies usually belonging in
this Colony, and shall be known and called by the name of
Salem.

> " Passed in the Lower House,
> Test.   WM. WILLIAMS, *Clerk.*
> " Concurred in the Upper House,
> " GEORGE WILLIS, *Secretary.*"

The Society of Salem existed as an ecclesiastical municipality
for seventy-one years.

February 16, 1844, a petition was filed from the parish of
Salem praying for incorporation as a town. Waterbury,
Bethany, and Oxford probably offered no opposition.

The town of Naugatuck was created by legislative mandate
with substantially the same limits that had been given to Salem
Parish in 1773.

We are accustomed to think of the formation of a town upon
a church-foundation as a peculiarly Puritan practice. But as
our fathers did so do we.

The avenue to municipal existence may still lead through the
church-door.

APPENDIX C.

DR. MANASSEH CUTLER'S DIARY.

The famous Dr. Manasseh Cutler, who graduated from Yale
in 1765, has left in his diary a picture of New Haven as it
appeared to him in 1787.' The following is a condensation of
his account, Dr. Cutler's phrases being preserved so far as
possible:

" Tuesday, July 8. I took a walk through the principal
streets of the lower part of the city. It seems to have been

' Published in the New Haven *Palladium* in 1858.

nearly new-built since I left the town. The Long Wharf was the most natural, though much enlarged. The sign of a sailor's grog-shop upon this wharf is truly diverting. The design is a table, on which are placed bottles, glasses, lemons, loaf-sugar, etc. In the midst is a huge bowl full of punch. A sailor stands by the table with a piece of cordage hanging over one of his arms, clasping the bowl with both arms, in the posture of lifting with all his might. He is looking down the wharf with the air of queerness and humor; and in a label, which goes from his mouth, are these words: 'Halo! Brother Jack Tar! Come lend a hand to strap this block.' Inclosing the burying-ground, and erecting a number of publick buildings on the publick square has greatly altered it. But the most affecting change to me is the loss of Mother Yale,[1] by far the most sightly building of any that belonged to the University, and most advantageously situated. It gave an air of grandeur to the others. These (Connecticut Hall, the Chapel, and the Commons building) are all of brick, but so situated as to make very little show. The streets of New Haven are tolerably wide, and some of them ornamented with rows of trees. A line of trees is set out around the publick square, which were very small when I was at college, but are now become large, and add much to its beauty. A row across the centre has been very lately set out, in a line with the State House, two large Meeting-Houses and the Grammar-School House. Within the square and on the borders of others adjoining to it, are six steeples and cupolas on publick buildings within a very small compass of ground. These steeples, when you approach the city in whatever direction, have an agreeable effect. The houses in general are good, some of them elegant, and a great proportion of them built with brick. The streets are generally dry, but very sandy, and will probably never be paved, as it must be attended with great expense.

"The harbor is good, and the shipping very considerable, principally in the coasting and West India trade."

Dr. Cutler was much impressed—hard-hit—by the various charms of Miss Channing, of Newport, who was visiting at the house of Dr. Stiles, President of Yale College. She was mistress

---

[1] The earliest college-building.

of French, Latin, Greek, and of the whole circle of sciences; she discoursed with great judgment on "Eloquence, oratory, painting, sculpture, etc."; she had a cultured taste for the fine arts, took advantage of every incident to render herself agreeable, and no subject came amiss; she was exceedingly correct and elegant without the least symptom of affectation. Perhaps, after all, New Haven has not changed in some respects in a century!

APPENDIX D.

A TOWN COURT OF ELECTIONS.   NEW HAVEN, A. D. 1656.

Several days beforehand the drum gave warning of the approaching Court. Again at the tap of the drum, on the appointed morning, the planters issued from their homes and walked along the streets converging upon the market-place. As the hour of nine approached, John Benham ceased drumming and descended from the turret of the meeting-house, while the late-comers hurried to be present when their names were called. The names of absent brethren were marked for fines. Robert Pigg, a dweller in the suburbs, was excused for absence from a previous Court because, the morning having been wet, the drum had not been beaten around the town. After it had been ordered that William Andrews should pay ten shillings for not reporting to the Secretary his recent marriage, Presiding Magistrate Gilbert announced the annual town-election. As no paper had been supplied, affirmative votes were represented by a kernel of Indian corn, negative minds by a bean. Two deputies to the General Court of the jurisdiction were nominated and elected, and four deputies to the Monthly Plantation Court. One of the latter was Mr. John Davenport, Jr., son of the pastor. This young man, according to his custom, arose and said that though in himself he was "mean and low," yet he did not ordinarily refuse to do the town service. But now he felt that his spirit was not equal to the call for this year. However, he was soon persuaded. The display of modesty was not finished. Gilbert, who was the Deputy-Governor of the colony, gravely and ponderously informed the Court that more magistrates must be nominated. "But, as for myself, it is a great discouragement to me to be in a place above my ability, and I hope no one will think of me, as there is one here better qualified." This Parthian shot struck Mr. Wm. Jones, at whom it was aimed. He besought the freemen not to hearken to Gilbert, and benevolently told the latter that the town wished him not to be discouraged. Amid some decorous smiling the business proceeded. Seven townsmen were elected, and Mr. Gibbard was continued in the offices of Secretary and Treasurer. Vacancies in the military service were filled by the election of a Lieutenant, Ensign, and two Corporals, and Thomas Kimberley for the tenth time was chosen Town-Marshal. The more important offices were now provided for, and Mr. Evance and several others, on plea of pressing business, obtained leave to depart. A crowd of minor offices were rapidly disposed of. John Benham, the drummer, was elected Town-Crier. Two men were chosen "Collectors of Colledge Corne."[1] Two Viewers of Dry Measures, Weights, Yards, and Wands were selected, and two others were made Viewers of Liquid Measures. Fence-Viewers in each quarter were elected, and three men were designated as Canoe-Viewers. It was voted that no one should lend or use any "cannou" not bearing the Viewers' mark under pain of a twenty-shilling fine. Thos. Beamont, and Mr. Goodyear's man, Robert, citizens in the humbler walks of life, were elected Sealers of Leather, and Beamont was also made Corn-Viewer. Robert Talmage was chosen public Pound-keeper, and it was voted that after the 15th of the month swine should not be allowed to roam abroad outside of the town, and the droves of cattle should be turned into the common pasture. Last, but not least, Roger Allen was elected Horse and Cattle Brander; and the Court, upon motion of Farmer Camfield, affirmed the urgent need that "Every man bring in the ear-mark of his swine." The Court ordered that two of the townsmen should send home all children who bothered the master of the Grammar School by learning to spell English. The teacher was advised not to receive any more such pupils, and to "Bring his boys on to latting as fast as they are capeable." ·This was Mr. Pearce's opportunity, and he notified the town

---

[1] For poor students at Harvard.

through the Secretary that he was ready to instruct children in
"Wrighting and arethmatick." The Court assented to Mr.
Jones's motion that "No Boys or Youth under 18 years of age
shall be covered with their hats during the time of the
Assembly."

The business of the day was completed by the reading of a
letter from Cromwell's Government to the faithful subjects of
England in America.

"The Governor acquainted the Town and read to them a
letter from the Counsell of State in England, for providing of
Tarr and with certain goods at cheap rates sent over to pay for
the same; and desired that every man would do the best he can
to further the worke, which will be an acceptable service to the
Commonwealth of England, and a great benefit to the Country,
if it can be attayned."

NOTE.—The foregoing sketch is not a record of any actual town-meeting.
All the incidents mentioned are taken from the Records, but they did not
all occur upon the same day. The intention is to furnish a fair picture of
the transactions at a Court of Elections, two hundred and thirty years
ago.

INDEX.

D